****

Retribution

Book Five of the Falling Empires Series

By
James Rosone & Miranda Watson
****

Published in conjunction with Front Line Publishing, Inc.

Disclaimer

This is a fictional story. All characters in this book are imagined, and any opinions that they express are simply that, fictional thoughts of literary characters. Although policies mentioned in the book may be similar to reality, they are by no means a factual representation of the news. Please enjoy this work as it is, a story to escape the part of life that can sometimes weigh us down in mundaneness or busyness.

Copyright Information

ISBN: 978-1-957634-19-7
Sun City Center, Florida, USA
Library of Congress Control Number: 2022904170

Table of Contents

Chapter One
Texas Lull

February 2022
Brownwood, Texas

Sergeant First Class Matt Higgins of the 2nd Armored Brigade Combat Team had been enjoying the hell out of this posh duty in Brownwood. Not only had they avoided any major fighting the last several months, they were finally getting some downtime. Higgins had been spending all his newfound relaxation time with his new girlfriend, Carla. Since the Chinese didn't appear to be heading toward Dallas any longer, she'd stuck around and spent every one of Higgins's off days camped out in his hotel room with him.

Unfortunately, he'd had his last night off for a while. His platoon was about to go pull a couple of days' duty on the roadblocks and perimeter. He lay in bed, staring at the ceiling and contemplating whether he should force himself to get up or if he should wait another five minutes for his alarm to go off. He glanced over at the naked woman lying next to him. Seeing her sleeping next to him had a calming effect on him. He wasn't sure what it was, but he felt safe, satisfied.

Higgins sighed. He knew he needed to get up. Carla was fast asleep, and he didn't want to wake her.

Boom.

A sudden loud explosion shook the building and promptly brought Higgins to his feet. He reached for his boxers and then stepped into his boots, cinching them tight. He had his body armor on and his rifle in hand before Carla grumbled, "What the hell is going on?"

Boom, boom!

Higgins snapped his helmet in place. "Stay here until it's safe to move," he told Carla. "Then you may want to go to the next town until I can call you and tell you it's safe to come back."

Higgins left his room before she had a chance to reply. He bounded down the stairs. Most of his platoon was in the stairwell; many of them were in their underwear like him, although some had on more of their uniform. Regardless of their state of dress, everyone had their body armor on and weapons at the ready.

When Higgins reached the pool at the center of the hotel, he heard the sounds of sporadic gunfire. He turned to face his soldiers, who were all looking at him, waiting for him to give them an order.

He pointed to where sounds of gunfire had come from, and like every combat leader in every war in American history, Higgins looked to his men. "Follow me!" he shouted. "It's time to hunt!"

He charged toward the gunfire, and the rest of his platoon swiftly followed. As they turned off Main Street and onto Commerce Street, two friendly soldiers came into view. They ran behind a vehicle and shot at something, although Higgins couldn't tell what it was yet.

Higgins and his platoon had come within twenty meters of the two soldiers when a barrage of large-caliber bullets hit the vehicle they were hiding behind. One of the soldiers was ripped apart by the rounds, dead before he even knew what had hit him.

Suddenly, a Chinese Type 89 tracked armored fighting vehicle blew right past the car it had just shot up and rolled around Higgins and his men.

Taken aback by what he had just seen, Higgins paused for just a second as his mind tried to figure out how they were going to take the thing out. They had all just grabbed their rifles and run out to see what was going on. He wasn't even sure if anyone had an antitank rocket with them.

Then he heard some chattering in Chinese. A group of six PLA soldiers turned the corner to head down their street, and both groups of men found themselves facing off, less than ten meters away from each other.

The Chinese soldiers seemed temporarily stunned at the discovery of the Americans, and Higgins's men had their weapons up first. "Contact front!" a soldier shouted. In unison, they unloaded on the Chinese soldiers, decimating them before they had a chance to fire.

Maybe having half our guys in their boxers just saved us, Higgins thought. That one second of hesitation had cost the Chinese their lives.

"Check around that corner," Higgins yelled. "Does anyone have an AT4 or something that can take that vehicle out?"

"I got one, Sergeant," shouted one of the new replacements.

"Private, give the AT4 to Staff Sergeant Rippon. Then run back to the hotel and grab several more from the armory," Higgins ordered, pointing at two other soldiers to go with him.

The specialist who'd poked his head around the corner turned around and loudly announced, "We got another APC heading our direction. Looks like at least another twenty PLA soldiers with it."

Crap, thought Higgins. *How did all these vehicles and soldiers get past our perimeter and the roadblocks?*

"AT4 up! Rippon, kill that thing. I want four of you across the street in that building there. The rest of you, fan out in these other buildings along the road leading back to the hotel—make sure at least six of you are covering that road to our left. I don't want them to flank us." With their tasks assigned, the soldiers steeled themselves for a fight and took off. Everyone knew that in a few minutes, there was going to be a warzone in their little piece of heaven.

Higgins started setting up a machine-gun position facing the corner of Main Street and Commerce Street. He spotted Captain Peavler and another platoon of soldiers heading his direction and trotted over to the captain to get him up to speed and explain his current plan.

"I'll take my platoon and head to the road behind the hotel," said Captain Peavler. "If they try to encircle us, we'll be ready."

Peavler and his men headed out before Higgins had time to ask any questions, but Higgins was pretty sure the captain had already called in their SOS to the QRF unit. That unit had a platoon of Abrams tanks, a detachment of Bradleys, and two platoons of Strykers—more than enough firepower to take out whatever armor vehicles had breached their lines.

Higgins's radio crackled. "Here they come," said one of his squad leaders.

One of the M240 gunners opened fire on the approaching troops and lone APC. The armored vehicle turned its turret to return fire on the American machine-gun crew, but before they could fire, Sergeant Rippon appeared on the roof of a nearby building and unleashed his AT4. The antitank weapon penetrated the lightly armored engine compartment of the vehicle. Belching smoke, the APC ground to a halt. Seconds later, it blew up, killing several of the soldiers who had been using it as cover from the Americans. Shrapnel and debris flew outward. What few enemy soldiers remained were then mowed down by Higgins's machine-gun crews.

A few minutes later, several of his runners returned with six more AT4s. They passed them out amongst the squads and then fanned out in the city to look for any additional APCs or PLA soldiers. The civilians living in the town wisely stayed indoors, but several people snapped pictures and videos through their windows of the half-naked soldiers that had jumped out of bed to save them.

Two hours went by before they finally believed they had secured the town again. At that point, Higgins and the rest of his platoon who still weren't dressed in their uniforms went back to the hotel to get changed before heading back out.

When Higgins opened the door to his room, he saw his girlfriend, Carla, draped in the sheets.

"My hero," she said coyly. "How can I ever thank you?"

He dropped his body armor and weapon on the floor next to the bed and allowed himself a few minutes of fun before he changed into his uniform and put everything back on. He was out the door less than ten minutes after walking in, a satisfied smile on his face as he corralled his platoonmates to head back to where the captain had positioned his platoon.

When Higgins and his men arrived, their captain had them advance to one of the roadblocks to find out what all had happened and relieve the QRF force that was currently holding it down. It took Higgins's platoon twenty minutes to walk across the small town and get in place. When they reached the roadblock, one of the Abrams battle tanks was positioned in the center with a couple of Stryker vehicles on either side. A few school buses helped to block the road, and a handful of soldiers stood near some sandbag positions they'd hastily put together.

One of the men approached Higgins. "Sergeant First Class Higgins, I'm Captain Andrews," he said. "It looks like the Chinese must have snuck up on your guys here. From what we can tell, it looks like you probably had four guys on guard duty while the other eight guys in the squad were asleep. Two of your guards were killed over there." Andrews pointed to one of their lookout positions on the far side of the hill overlooking the highway. "The other two guys were taken out here," he said as he waved his hand in the direction of the two dead soldiers. "Once they got your sentries, they pretty much slit the throats of the rest of the guys who'd been sleeping before they even knew what had happened."

Andrews shook his head. "It looks like you guys got lucky, Sergeant. The ChiComs only hit you guys with a scout platoon. They probably just wanted to probe your defenses and see what kind of opposition they might face in this sector. Had it been a company-sized element, I think they might have wiped you guys out before you got yourselves organized."

Higgins shook his head. "Thank you, Captain," he responded. "Are you guys sticking around for a while?"

"For a few hours," Andrews responded. "Then we'll probably go out on a deep patrol into the borderlands to see if there are any other ChiCom units nearby." His company had enough armor and infantry support to carry out a large patrol like that. Higgins's unit had mainly been relegated to light infantry as they garrisoned this little town.

"Nicholson, Matthews, it's time for cleanup duty," Higgins ordered. A while back, he'd assigned his replacement troops to be the ones to place any dead bodies into the standard black zippered bags the military used for fallen troops. He wanted them to see firsthand what would happen if they screwed up. One or both of the guards in these positions had either fallen asleep or failed to spot the enemy soldiers sneaking up on them—in either case, thirteen soldiers from their sister platoon had paid for their mistake in blood.

An hour after the QRF company left to go out on their patrol, Higgins heard some cannons shooting and a few loud explosions off in the distance. The sounds of fighting only lasted a few minutes before they tapered off. Since Higgins didn't hear any distress calls over the radio, he assumed they must have found what they were looking for and moved on.

It's time to get this position put back together, Higgins thought. They needed to figure out what else needed to be done to make sure the roadblock stayed secured. Hopefully, in a few weeks or a month, Big Army would start another campaign to push the Chinese out of Texas once and for all.

****

Bellingham, Washington

Jake walked into his office at the Whatcom County building, feeling a renewed sense of purpose. In the months since their liberation from the UN and the local militia goon squad, Jake's fortunes had turned. He was no longer a bombmaker living a double life. Jake had found himself elevated from his position as a county civil engineer to the lead person in charge of the county's reconstruction effort.

It had taken a few months for peace to finally return to the county, but once it had, people just wanted to move on with their lives. It was Jake's job now to try and put the county back together—get roads repaired and bridges rebuilt, manage infrastructure that had been neglected. It was a tall order, but he felt blessed to have survived this last year.

The head of DHS in Washington State along with the I "Eye" Corps commander at Fort Lewis knew about Jake's contributions to the war effort. They'd kept his participation quiet and made sure no one else knew about it. One of the reasons he'd been chosen for this new prominent position was because no one questioned his loyalty to the Constitution or what he was willing to do to defend it. The fact that he had risked his life, and his family's lives, to wage an insurgency building complex IEDs spoke volumes to the people that mattered.

One of his project managers walked over to his desk. "Hey, boss. We got the building material for the I-5 bridge in Bellingham last night," he announced.

Jake smiled. "It's about time. It's the last piece we need to get the bridge completed."

Repairing the I-5 bridge over Whatcom Creek was one of Jake's top priorities. It was a major artery that connected the city with the lower portion of the state, and it would make a huge difference if the work could get completed before winter set in.

Jake's administrative assistant, Tara, flagged him down. "Jake, the superintendent for the school district wanted to let you know they should have the school system ready to start classes again in October. He wanted to thank you for helping them get those buildings repaired. He's got an army of teachers working to get the new classrooms ready for the kids."

"That's great, Tara. If you can, send him a message and tell him I'm looking forward to seeing him and his family at the BBQ this weekend," Jake replied happily.

When the UN had invaded, the CDF militia and UN forces had used several of the school buildings as training bases. This had sadly made them a target during the war, leaving many of them looking like gutted shells, reminiscent of devastated cities in World War II. Getting the schools fixed was important to Jake. Returning people to their normal routines would help to heal the community and the state as a whole.

Tara smiled at the mention of the BBQ and went back to typing on her keyboard.

Logging in to his own email, Jake perused his inbox, looking for anything of importance that needed to be actioned right now. Not seeing anything, he typed up a handful of emails to his various project managers. One was about repairs to the local post office: another was about a request for several new fire engines for one of the firehouses. The needs of the county were many. Steadily, though, they were getting them met, with resources being shipped in from other parts of the country. There were shortages in the supply chain that still needed to be worked out, but by and large, he was making progress.

As Jake hit the send button on his last email, he noticed he'd just received an email from his wife, Marcy, with the subject line "SOS." His heart beat a little faster. She rarely tried to contact him at work at all and had especially given him some space now that he was having to pull extra hours with the reconstruction efforts.

The email was one line. "Call me when you can, please. We need to talk."

Jake started to panic. *Did one of her parents go to the hospital?* he wondered.

He pulled out his cell phone and called Marcy right away. "Hello? Marcy, are you OK?" he asked as soon as she picked up.

"I don't know," she said, clearly crying.

"Oh, God, what happened?" Jake asked.

"I know I should probably have waited until you came home to tell you this, but, babe…I'm pregnant."

There were three uncomfortable seconds of silence. "I, uh, I, wow," Jake stammered. "But you were on the pill."

"I know, but it's not a hundred percent effective," she said. "I just don't know what to do. I don't want to lose another baby."

A flood of emotions rushed over him. He was simultaneously filled with the joy of being an expectant father and the grief of the previous miscarriages and the loss of his own family.

"Well, honey, if you got pregnant on the pill, I think this little baby really wanted to be here," he replied. "We are going to do everything we can to make sure that you and they are healthy. Your family is here this time, and you can take time off work if you need to. Whatever you need, it will happen."

Marcy cried some more, but the sound was different this time. "Jake, I really needed to hear that. I needed to hear your voice and know that you weren't angry about it."

"Angry? How could I ever be angry that you're carrying a little baby?" he asked.

"I don't know, but I'm glad I talked to you. Listen, I know you need to get back to work, so I'll let you go. Thank you for calling me. I love you."

"I love you too, Marcy," he replied. "You are going to make an awesome mom."

Jake hung up the phone and went back to work, a smile on his face. Rebuilding the community had suddenly taken on a whole new meaning.

Chapter Two
Battle of Texas

Corpus Christi, Texas

Lieutenant Haverty of India Company, 3rd Battalion, 6th Marines, looked at the mission order, reading each objective carefully. He looked at the supporting units and saw the 24th MEU was going to be the ones to spearhead the entire assault, which warmed his Marine heart. They'd be the tip of the spear lunged into the heart of the enemy.

A month after their initial capture of NAS Corpus Christi, their unit was now at one hundred percent strength. It had taken nearly that much time to deploy the rest of the 2nd Marine Division to the beachhead they'd established around the naval air station. After a series of battles by their Army brothers to their north, it was now time for the Marines to launch their breakout attack and start liberating the state. His Marines were lean and spoiling for a fight.

Once they retook San Antonio, it would put a sizable enemy force behind the pockets of PLA soldiers in Houston and Austin. Haverty could easily see how it would force the Chinese to either surrender or pull back. In either case, they'd finally be able to liberate Houston and Austin after more than five months of occupation.

"You have any questions?" Captain Lacey asked as he came up behind him.

Haverty looked up. "So, if I read this right, skipper, my platoon is going to be the lead unit for the battalion as we move up Interstate 37, correct?"

"That's right," Lacey responded. "Our company was chosen to lead the assault for the division, and I've chosen your platoon to be the eyes and ears for the battalion. Your objective is to advance ahead of us until either you find targets of opportunity to destroy or you're able to position yourselves so you can call in air or artillery strikes. If we're lucky, we'll be having dinner tomorrow night at Boudro's and drinks at the Bier Garten on the River Walk in San Antonio."

"What kind of air support will we have?" Haverty asked.

"We've got our attack helicopters, those new Vipers that came out, for close air support from the NAS that'll be supporting us along with a squadron of Super Hornets, but you can bet they're going to be super taxed providing air strikes. We've also got a squadron of Harriers as well. Oh, and before you complain about the lack of air support, I was told the Air Force is going to provide us with a substantial number of aircraft for this offensive."

Haverty chuckled at that last comment. "Well, I'm glad they're going to provide us some support as we look to liberate one of their largest airbases."

The two laughed together. Then Haverty asked, "So, when does the operation kick off and when do you want my platoon to move forward toward the front?"

"The H-hour is 0300 hours, so I want your platoon in position around 0200. Also, just so you're aware, half an hour before the attack starts, the Air Force is going to carry out a large bombing run on the Chinese lines. This won't be a few F-16s dropping some two-thousand-pounders—this'll be a B-52 strike. They'll be carpet bombing the Chinese lines with what I've been told will be hundreds of five-hundred-pound bombs before our tanks and armored vehicles move forward. This'll hopefully punch a quick hole for us to exploit before they can react to the gap in their lines."

Haverty nodded. "You know, I'm kind of impressed we're making a mad dash up Interstate 37. You'd think the enemy would have it either heavily patrolled or mined."

"I thought the same thing, but the intel weenies believe it's open. The PLA has been using the freeway system to move their forces around the state just like we would. Why blow a critical piece of infrastructure that's allowing you to hold on to your captured territory, right? In either case, some recon teams have checked the route. Imagery and MASINT didn't find any units or nasty surprises lying in ambush along the way or anything else that might slow us up. Brigade's had that road under round-the-clock drone surveillance for a while now."

"Speaking of drones, sir, have we heard any more word about those Chinese suicide drones?" Haverty asked. "Should we expect to see them in our sector?"

The Chinese Army had just started using small suicide drones called "Zisha drones," and word was spreading like wildfire. The Americans were calling them Z Drones. The little quadcopters were roughly twelve inches in circumference and packed about a half pound of explosives. They didn't have a huge range, but the PLA soldiers would deploy them near the front lines and then use them almost like dive bombers to hit small clusters of soldiers or armored vehicles. The Marines had first encountered them in California several months back, but now they were starting to show up in nearly every PLA unit. Fortunately, they didn't appear to be concentrating them or using them in some sort of swarm tactic yet. But the fact that small numbers of them were appearing in California, New Mexico, and Texas meant the Chinese factories were starting to crank them out.

Captain Lacey sighed. "I don't know about the drones, Haverty. The S2 didn't say anything new about them. I'd plan on encountering them, but I can't say how many or where we may see them."

"OK, sir. No worries. Just thought I'd ask," Haverty replied. "If you don't have anything else for me, I'm going to go pass the word to my platoon sergeant and my squad leaders, sir. We'll be ready bright and early tomorrow." Then he got up and headed off to go find his platoon.

****

The Marines in Haverty's platoon had been standing on top of their vehicles, marveling at the thunderous bombardment of the enemy lines they were witnessing. For close to fifteen minutes, the Chinese lines had been getting hammered by high-altitude bombers. The explosions lit the night sky up like day and shook the earth with every thudding boom. It was awe-inspiring to see but terrifying at the same time.

By the time 0245 rolled around, Lieutenant Haverty had climbed into the back of the JLTV he had made his command vehicle. Their drone operator, his RTO, the driver, and his .50-caliber gunner were all riding with him. Even after closing the door to his vehicle, the sound of artillery and tank cannons and the heavy crescendo of gunfire a few miles away were almost numbing. The attack was well underway, and Haverty knew it was just a matter of time until they were given the go-ahead to breach the lines.

"The lead vehicles are on the move," called out his driver. The Marine was using a pair of night vision goggles. All their vehicles were running with no lights or even their blackouts on.

"Copy that. Let's get this shindig started, then," Haverty replied. He got his own NVGs situated, and everyone else in the vehicle followed suit.

Moments later, their vehicle lurched forward, following the tanks that would stay with them until they got on the interstate to San Antonio. Haverty's platoon had four LAVs and five JLTVs—more than enough firepower to handle whatever they came into contact with until the rest of their company and battalion linked up with them.

It took them a little while to get to the actual front lines. Once there, Haverty saw the carnage of the most recent fight. There were a lot of torn and twisted bodies, intermixed with the burning wrecks of what had to be forty or fifty enemy vehicles. And that was just in one area. Several blown-apart tanks were interspersed with the wreckage, and so were a few Marine tanks and LAVs. This stretch of the lines had been a bloody patch of land that had required a hard fight, but the battle had created the hole they needed.

Steadily, they weaved their way through the wreckage until their little convoy could make its way toward the I-35 interchange. Thus far, the drone footage above them hadn't shown any enemy activity along the road, but that could change once the Chinese figured out what they were doing. So far, the PLA had been focused on the armored force that had punched a hole in their lines a few kilometers to their west. While the PLA was busy dealing with that threat, India Company would hopefully slide past undetected.

Ten minutes into their drive down the interstate, Haverty's drone operator called out, "Lieutenant."

Flipping his NVGs up, Haverty turned to look at the young Marine. "What do you have for me, Corporal?"

"I'm looking at the drone feed above us. It doesn't look like there's any immediate activity on the interstate right now. However, one of the recon teams about twenty kilometers ahead of us sent a short message to battalion letting them know a small convoy of troop transport trucks and two infantry fighting vehicles are headed toward us. There's no indication that they know we're on an intercept course with them."

Haverty thought about the news for a moment, realizing they might have an opportunity to ambush this unit and wipe them out if they moved now to get their position set up. He pulled out his map and tried to calculate where would be the best place to initiate the ambush.

Lieutenant Haverty turned to get his driver's attention. "Sergeant, I want you to pull off at Marker 43. There's a rest stop on the side of the road. That's where we'll set up an ambush point to hit those vehicles that are heading toward us."

The sergeant nodded, and Haverty went to work letting his squads and vehicles know what was going on and reporting back to his company CO what they were going to do.

In less than ten minutes, they had two LAVs and two JLTVs parked on either side of the road, hidden from the view of traffic. The incoming vehicles were about to get hammered by unseen crossfire from the Marines.

Two of Haverty's LAVs were outfitted with TOW launchers while the other two had 25mm chain guns. To increase the effectiveness of the crossfire, Haverty placed a TOW-2B-equipped LAV on either side of the road, paired up with the heavy gun truck. Two of the JLTVs were equipped with the Mark 19 grenade guns while the other three JLTVs had the M2 .50-cals mounted on their turrets. As the vehicles moved to their respective ambush points, the infantry spread themselves out in the grass along the sides of the highway, ready to unleash a barrage of bullets on the troop transport trucks.

It was still dark, though dawn was no more than forty minutes away. For the moment, they'd leverage the darkness to their advantage. A short while later, Haverty spotted the first set of vehicles through his NVGs. He almost chuckled at the infantry fighting vehicles as they came around the bend, since the Chinese had attached all sorts of tree branches to them to give them extra camouflage. However, his mood immediately turned more serious when he saw the long trail of heavy transport trucks following the IFVs. With the open beds on the trucks, it was easy to see that they were packed with soldiers.

Depressing the talk button on his radio, Haverty whispered, "Miller, you take the lead IFV. Tyson, you take the second vehicle. Jamison, your gun truck needs to take that third vehicle. Prepare to fire on my mark. Stand by…fire!"

Seconds later, he heard the distinctive whooshing of the TOW missiles being fired. That noise was rapidly followed by the jarring reports of the 25mm Bushmaster chain gun as it tore into the third infantry fighting vehicle.

Lieutenant Haverty watched the two guided antitank missiles cover the distance between them and the enemy. In seconds, they slammed into the armored vehicles and the IFVs blew up in a ball of flames, illuminating the darkness.

Several strings of red tracers flew toward the third armored vehicle, and soon it was clear that the rounds were effectively punching holes through the front. The driver of that vehicle swung them off the road to try and escape the heavy-caliber bullets, and he must have hit the smoke screen button because a series of smoke grenades were released all around the IFV. Haverty's LAV kept his gun trained on the enemy vehicle. After a few more rounds had hit it, the Chinese vehicle suddenly exploded.

Meanwhile, the eight troop trucks further down the road had stopped and their human cargo of infantry soldiers had dismounted and were seeking cover. The JLTVs and the LAVs moved out of their covered positions so they could get a better angle on the Chinese soldiers as they tried to scatter. The American vehicles opened fire with their Mk 19s and .50-caliber machine guns, cutting down dozens of enemy soldiers before they could make it off the road into one of the side ditches. The Mk 19 gunners rained down 30mm fragmentation grenades into the ditches while the machine gunners did their best to cut down any soldiers they saw scrambling for something to hide behind.

The ambush lasted maybe sixty seconds before the dismounted Marines advanced with the cover of their vehicles. It took them another five minutes to clear the site and make sure they had killed all of the enemy soldiers. Once they were sure no one had survived the attack, they loaded back up in their vehicles and continued their blitz to San Antonio.

****

Soon after the JLTV was back on the move, the corporal who was monitoring the drones above them waved to get Haverty's attention. "Sir, I've got a shared feed from one of the Reaper drones. They've spotted an enemy armor column heading toward us, about forty klicks away."

"Can you see how many vehicles we're looking at and what type?" Haverty asked.

A minute went by as the corporal talked to the drone operator through a chat box. Then he looked up. "It appears to be a brigade-sized element—mostly main battle tanks intermixed with infantry support vehicles. The other drone operator said they're probably moving down to block our breakout along the front lines."

Nodding, Haverty reached for his map and found an off-ramp a few kilometers ahead of them. Getting the driver's attention, he ordered, "I want you to get off here. Move us to this location about a kilometer away from the highway." After the driver saw where Haverty was pointing to on the map, he nodded and gave him a thumbs-up.

The morning sun had risen, and Haverty knew they needed to get off the road and find a place to hide before they were detected. He spent a few minutes on the radio with battalion to let them know what they'd found, and then he switched over to get in touch with their forward air controller.

"Storm Two, this is Rogue One," he said to the FAC. "I'm requesting a priority air strike. Break.

"I have a brigade-sized element of tanks inbound to my location. My grid is TX 5426 8752. Enemy is moving southeast on Interstate 37. Enemy grid is TX 5754 8631. Request antitank-equipped fast movers if possible. How copy?"

A few seconds went by before the battalion's FAC replied, "Rogue One, Storm Two. That's a good copy. Have your location as grid TX 5426 8752 and the enemy location is grid TX 5754 8631, moving southeast on Interstate 37, rate of march approximately forty-five kilometers per hour. How copy?"

Nodding to himself, Haverty depressed the talk button. "That's a good copy, Storm Two. What do you have in the area that can help us?"

"Stand by," came the quick reply.

Haverty waited for a few minutes to see what type of air strike would be inbound. Until the enemy tanks had been cleared, they needed to do their best to stay out of sight. Their mission relied on speed and stealth—something they couldn't accomplish if they ran into a brigade of enemy tanks.

"Rogue One, I've got six Hornets inbound to your location in ten mikes. Can you get eyes on the target to assist in BDA?" Battle damage assessment was crucial to let the pilots and the FAC know whether their attack had been successful.

"Storm Two, that's a good copy. We'll get some eyes on the interstate. Are there additional aircraft inbound?" Haverty asked. He didn't think there was any way six Hornets would slow down the incoming Chinese group.

"Yes. The Air Force just confirmed eight A-29 Super Tucanos armed with Mavericks will be on station in fifteen mikes. I'm working on getting us a larger strike package from the fleet, but that may take a bit of time. I'll update you if I can get additional aircraft from the Air Force. Out."

Haverty nodded. "Well, that's not too bad, guys," he announced. "Six Hornets, ten mikes out. Scouts out, up on the hills overlooking the interstate so we can give a BDA when the smoke clears. In the meantime, priorities of work, get a perimeter established and be prepared for an anti-armor fight. Make ready and stay ready, gents. I think we may be here for a little while until the brown shoes pound these guys into the dirt or they pass our position. In either case, we're not about to try and take on that large of a force."

With nothing more to be said for the moment, the Marines went to work on getting themselves ready for the pending air strike. If they got spotted, they'd have to move out fast.

Shortly after the Marines got some defensive positions set up, Lieutenant Haverty heard jet engines in the sky above. He scrambled up to his scout team that was on top of one of the hills, where they could easily see the interstate less than a kilometer away. When he reached the crest, one of the sergeants handed him his field glasses.

"Take a look, LT. The Hornets just made a pass over the column. Probably checking out what they need to hit."

The noise of the jet engines overwhelmed his senses. A lone Super Hornet banked hard and climbed high into the sky. Haverty looked off in the distance to where the enemy convoy had been steadily moving toward them. He kept his eyes focused on the convoy while his ears listened to the jet engines changing in pitch as they maneuvered to attack the tanks below.

"Whoa. Look at that," one of the Marines called out. Two objects from the ground flew up toward the fighters. Then half a dozen AA guns opened fire, sending strings of tracer rounds into the sky.

Haverty lowered the field glasses so he could see the bigger picture. Close to a dozen small objects fell toward the convoy of tanks, igniting a series of explosions that rippled through their lines. Then as one of the Super Hornets lit its afterburners and tried to get away, it suddenly blew up. The next group of Hornets swooped in, popping flares as they flew. They were swiftly greeted with a barrage of ground fire. More missiles streaked up for the Hornets. Two of the American warplanes broke off their attack, spitting out more flares as fast as their defensive systems could release them. One more Hornet was hit, but this time, the pilot was able to eject. The remaining Hornets broke off their attack as they called in for help in dealing with the enemy SAMs.

While the American planes moved away, Haverty's sergeant got on the radio with the forward air controller, giving them the battle damage assessment of the strike and letting them know two of their fighters had been shot down. The FAC let them know the Air Force planes were heading into the box to begin their own attack run.

Meanwhile, the enemy column continued to get closer to them. The noise of the heavy diesel engines of the tanks filled the air, and the ground shook a bit as the metal beasts approached.

"You hear that?" asked one of the privates.

"Yeah, it sounds like propellers," his sergeant replied. The mechanical buzzing noise was consistent with World War II–style prop planes instead of the jets they expected.

Turning to look behind him, Haverty saw a line of eight A-29 Super Tucanos. They hadn't been engaged by the Chinese SAMs yet; they had just come into range and were flying just above the ground.

Before any of them could make a derogatory comment about the old-fashioned ground attack planes, bright flashes and plumes of smoke raced from the pylons under their wings as they unleashed twenty-four Maverick air-to-ground missiles at the armored column. Then the planes dove for cover in the surrounding hills and retreated to rearm.

They watched the missiles fly over their heads, scoring hit after hit against the enemy tanks. "Wow. I'll be damned," his sergeant remarked.

"Hot damn, Sergeant. I think the Marines should get a few of those bad boys," said one of the privates excitedly. "They just smoked like an entire company of tanks in a single pass."

Lieutenant Haverty snickered at the comment. "I was just about to joke about the Air Force going backwards to find an A-10 replacement, but that was pretty impressive." He paused for a second. "Send the BDA in to the FAC and tell them we need more air support like that or this unit's going to collide with our company and the battalion within an hour. Our guys aren't that far behind us at this point."

The sergeant nodded and relayed the information.

"Sir, what do we do now?" asked the new replacement Marine. "Do we stay here or find a way around this enemy force and keep heading toward San Antonio?"

Haverty looked at the young private as he thought about his response. "Right now, we do our best to stay out of sight and keep calling in air strikes on this enemy force. If we're still here in about thirty minutes, I think the battalion or brigade artillery units will be in range, so we'll probably get stuck calling in rounds for them."

Seeing the confused look on the private's face, Haverty shrugged. "Marine, sometimes things just go to hell, and you have to Semper Gumby if you want to survive. That's what we're doing right now."

The low grumbling sound of heavy diesel engines and the creaking and cracking of tank tracks on pavement continued to grow as the armored beasts crawled on toward them.

"Those tanks are getting pretty close, sir," called out his sergeant, shooting Haverty a nervous look.

Lieutenant Haverty was starting to feel pretty uncomfortable in their current position himself. Although they were off the main highway, they weren't that far from the large enemy force that was moving to engage their battalion and brigade further down the road. Still, their platoon was positioned perfectly to keep calling in air strikes—so they couldn't just run away from the fight, either.

"I know," Haverty responded. "If you see vehicles or patrols heading toward us, I need you to let me know. In the meantime, I'm going to find Gunny and see what kind of E&E route he's found for us in case this place gets too hot." Then Haverty grabbed his M27 rifle and headed back to their cluster of vehicles doing its best to hide in the tree line.

Seeing his platoon sergeant, Haverty walked up to him. "Gunny, you have an evac route for us that could still put us back on track to complete our mission?" Haverty called out as he walked up to Gunny Lucas and a couple of other Marines who had an area map spread out on the hood of a JLTV.

Lucas looked up at him. "I think so," he responded. "If the PLA finds us, we'll beat feet out of here to this spot." He pointed to a country road that led them further away from the interstate. "From here, we can either follow this state road all the way to San Antonio or link back up with the interstate along any of these three points, about sixty kilometers northwest of here." He spat a stream of tobacco juice on the ground.

Haverty studied the map. The more he looked at the escape route, the more he liked it. He began to wonder if they should just bug out right then. They could always circle around and above this enemy force.

Lieutenant Haverty nodded. "I like it, Gunny. I'm going to check with the CO and battalion and see if they'd like us to go ahead and move now. For all we know, this is just the tip of what could be a division or more headed our way."

"Yeah. That's a good idea, LT," Gunny Lucas replied. "You're probably right. I can't see the PLA sending only this unit to try and plug the hole in their lines. They know we're hitting them with our entire division given the world of hurt we unleashed on them this morning."

The next five minutes went by rapidly. The battalion CO agreed with Haverty's assessment. He wanted them back on the road to see if they could figure out what was behind this force. In the meantime, they'd rely on some of the drones in the local area to assist them in calling in more air strikes and BDA assessments.

Thirty minutes later, the platoon raced through the Texas countryside, seeking to get around the enemy force that was heading toward their division. Throughout their mad dash, Haverty heard wave after wave of warplanes being sent in to hammer the enemy armor. There was a relentless shockwave of thunderous booms, and Haverty could feel the ground quaking even while they were racing down the road. It was surreal.

Then, as they rounded a bend in the road ahead of them, Haverty saw the lead JLTV violently swerve off the road. He hoped they were careening toward a field. The JLTV that had been immediately behind that lead vehicle suddenly blew up in a spectacular fireball. The LAV that was thirty meters behind him rounded the corner and immediately started firing its Bushmaster chain gun.

"What the hell is going on?" Haverty shouted over the radio. As he spoke, he spotted a small town a couple of kilometers in front of them, connected to a nature preserve. At the edge of that town was at least a company-sized element of Chinese main battle tanks and some tracked infantry fighting vehicles.

Damn! he thought. *We've run right into an enemy unit.*

The vehicles in his platoon popped some smoke grenades and did their best to find some cover. There were a few buildings off the country road that were probably a part of a large family farm—unfortunately, they were the only available shelter at the moment.

One of his sergeants, who was in charge of one of their LAVs, responded over the radio. "I'm engaging those tanks with our TOWs."

Bang, bang, bang.

The 25-mike guns fired armor-piercing rounds at the enemy vehicles. Haverty's men did their best to score a few lucky hits or cause some chaos and confusion in the enemy ranks.

Haverty grabbed his radio. "Break contact!" he shouted over the platoon net. "Everyone, fall back down the same road we just used. We'll look to find another way around this area."

His driver was in the process of turning them around when Haverty's vehicle shook violently from a nearby explosion that peppered their vehicle with shrapnel. One of the LAVs that had just fired its TOW missile had been blown apart. It was a burning wreck of flame and debris.

"Get us the hell out of here!" he shouted to his driver, who gunned the engine to get them around the burning vehicle.

The turret gunner above him turned the gun to face behind them and started banging away at something. More explosions rocked the area as they raced to get out of the line of fire.

"Those are mortars, sir!" shouted the turret gunner.

His mind filled with a torrent of obscenities. By the time Haverty's vehicle had made it out of the line of sight of the Chinese tanks, half of his platoon's vehicles had been blown up.

"Pull the vehicle over!" he yelled at his driver, then grabbed the radio and told everyone else to pull over. "I want a head count before we leave. Make sure we don't leave any wounded behind." He hated leaving their dead, but he wasn't about to get the rest of the platoon killed trying to recover their bodies, either.

The remaining vehicles came to a stop while the squad leaders did a quick check to see who all remained. One of the Marines pulled his drone pack out of his JLTV and got one of them spun up and in the air. He then zipped it back up the road they had retreated down to the site of the ambush, searching the wreckage and the area around it for signs of survivors.

What he found was four burning wrecks and no one left alive. The Chinese appeared to be gearing up to come after them. The Marine turned the drone around and brought it right back to their position. He relayed what he'd seen to Haverty and Gunny Lucas, who concluded they needed to get the hell out of the area before that unit got them locked down in a battle they couldn't win or retreat from.

The remains of their beat-up platoon limped back to the road as they sought another way around the enemy force. The next few hours were both scary and frustrating. The further east they moved to find a spot to slip past the enemy, the more Chinese units they came into contact with. By the time it was dark, Haverty's platoon had spent the better part of eight hours driving all over the countryside and they'd burned through nearly all their fuel.

Then they received a recall order from battalion to do their best to make their way back to Corpus Christi. Apparently, the Chinese commander had realized the threat the Marines would pose in their rear area, and rather than lose a major logistical hub, they'd abandoned their positions around Houston and Austin, consolidating their line around San Antonio.

Chapter Three
Frustrations Brewing

Washington, D.C.
White House

"Is there anything we can do to stop them?" NSA Robert Grey asked, his glasses low on his nose as he looked up over their rims.

CIA Director Marcus Ryerson shook his head in frustration. "I don't see how."

"What are our options?" Grey pressed, unhappy with the response.

"We're doing everything we can, Mr. Grey," General Markus replied. "Some things are just outside our control. I've lost tens of thousands of soldiers, airmen, and Marines these last three weeks in Texas. The Chinese are fighting like fanatical maniacs; they dig in when any sane man would withdraw."

The general was frustrated by the lack of progress on many of the fronts, but more than anything, he was frustrated with the losses they were continuing to sustain, which were very high. They were also losing equipment and aircraft at a prodigious rate—equipment they couldn't readily replace.

"What's the assessment of Houston so far?" asked President Sachs. "How bad is the city?"

Vanderbilt, a colonel from the Army Corps of Engineers who had just returned from Houston eight hours ago, spoke up. "When the Chinese first captured the city several months ago, they began dismantling our petroleum refineries, oil and natural gas import and export terminals and other pipeline equipment. At the same time, hundreds of their engineers started to dismantle much of Houston's electrical grid. They removed transformers, routers, and switching stations from around the city and the local area; they took down the electrical lines and even ripped out many of the fiber-optic wires from the ground."

While Colonel Vanderbilt was explaining this, he displayed several slides on a PowerPoint that showed what he was talking about. General Markus couldn't help but feel that the sight was incredible. Images of dismantled petroleum facilities and electrical poles suddenly absent of any wiring almost seemed unreal.

Could that really be Houston? he wondered in awe.

"What are they doing with the equipment?" asked President Sachs. "I mean, if they wanted to destroy it, they would have just blown it up, but this was done in a very methodical manner. So clearly, destroying it was not their intent."

"Our best guess right now is they took everything apart so it could be shipped back to China," Colonel Vanderbilt answered. "This equipment is incredibly valuable and complex to make."

"I can buy that explanation," said NSA Grey. "It makes sense. But why are they systematically destroying Houston's infrastructure? I mean, they're stripping the city down to bare bones."

"Sir, a month or two ago, it became clear the Chinese weren't going to be able to hold Houston for much longer. When that became apparent, their engineers started destroying the water treatment facilities, power plants, and even the city's water mains and sewers, knowing it would leave the city in complete and utter rubble. They're leaving us with an extraordinary humanitarian crisis we'll have to divert resources to, when we could really use those resources elsewhere." He paused for a second before adding, "I'm afraid they've so thoroughly destroyed the infrastructure across much of Houston that I don't believe it's livable. It's going to take a lot of effort to restore parts of the city so the residents can even return."

For a moment, everyone sat there in stunned silence. They had all expected destruction in the occupied zones, but no one had anticipated this. When they'd liberated Santa Fe and Albuquerque, they hadn't encountered this level of destruction.

This is a whole new playbook, thought General Markus.

"Do you think we're going to see this kind of destruction in more of the major cities, or do you think this was a one-off because they wanted our petroleum equipment?" asked Grey. He shot the President a concerned look.

Colonel Vanderbilt lifted his chin up. "I suspect we'll see this kind of damage in some of the more strategic cities but not all of them. The level of effort required to do what they did to Houston is something I've never seen before. It's actually far more destructive than if they had just bombed everything. At least in the rubble, we'd be able to recover components and parts that could still work. In this case, they've simply removed everything. It'll take years to rebuild what's been destroyed—"

"What about the people?" the President interrupted. "Surely there were some survivors, people who got caught behind the lines. How many are there? How are they surviving given the destruction of the water, sewer and power services?"

General Pruitt, the Army Chief of Staff, answered this question. "The Chinese enforced a pretty tight curfew on the city, Mr. President. No one was allowed outside after dark. If you got caught, they shot you—no trial or arrest. But toward the end, they started shooting anyone they saw. People did their best to stay hidden when a Chinese patrol was nearby. Many of the residents that were armed continued to carry out guerrilla attacks against them; however, for every PLA soldier that was killed, they killed five civilians. By the time our forces had liberated Houston, things had become pretty medieval, sir. They'd run out of regular food supplies months ago. The civilians had been killing birds, pigeons, cats, dogs, anything you can think of for food. We even heard stories of cannibalism. Practically anyone we found alive was just skin and bones, sir."

"My God. How could they have done this to our people?" Robert Grey asked in a voice barely above a whisper.

"It's payback for us destroying the Three Gorges Dam," Admiral Smith said under his breath.

"What?" Sachs inquired indignantly.

All eyes turned to Admiral Smith, whose face promptly turned red. "Sir, when we destroyed that dam, we wiped out a huge swath of their own electrical grid. It's been estimated that more than ten million people were killed in the ensuing flood, and more than eighty million people lost their homes. I think what the Chinese did to Houston is some sort of revenge."

"Maybe," Sachs responded hotly. "But we made it clear to them what would happen if they attacked us. And they didn't just attack—they used nuclear bombs on us! Four of them! They still haven't stopped the practice of kidnapping our women or executing our citizens in the occupied zones, even after we began bombing their major cities. How many of our people have been killed in the occupied zones because we can't liberate them fast enough? Too many. We need to find a way to convince the Chinese that this war has to end. They have to stop."

General Markus was exasperated. "We're already bombing their major cities, Mr. President," he countered. "Heck, we've already practically demolished six of them. We're attacking the enemy lines so hard right now we're grinding both our armies into the dirt. I don't know what more you think we can do to get them to capitulate, sir—not without placing some seriously drastic and, frankly, evil options on the table."

Sachs paused for a moment before responding. "We're not going nuclear. That'll cause more harm than good. So let's remove that from consideration. Besides, I think there are far better ways to bring them to heel than by using nukes. We went after the dam because it provided them with a tremendous amount of hydroelectricity. The secondary effect we got was the flooding and damage it caused to several critical manufacturing cities. How can we further turn the lights off in China? How can we further wreck *their* infrastructure and grind their country to a halt?"

While General Markus was the Chairman of the Joint Chiefs, he had previously been the head of the US Air Force. Given his history, his first thought was logistics. "We go after their ability to feed their people and the energy resources needed to keep their country running," he responded.

"And how do we do that?" asked the President. "How is what we're currently doing different than what you're proposing?"

"Right now, we have twelve B-2s and our lone B-21 carrying out the bombing campaigns in China. We need to shift their focus," Markus explained. "Instead of bombing a city each day, we go after their food stores. We go after rail tunnels, bridges, pipelines, ports, and storage facilities. We hit everything that's critical to the survival of the regime."

Sachs held a hand up. "That's fine. You can shift the focus of the B-2s. But I want our lone B-21 to continue its strategic bombing campaign. Make sure you're rotating its target cities so it's hitting locations all around the country, but keep it up."

General Markus nodded.

"Also, when will the new B-21s start coming off the assembly line?" asked the President.

"We have four of them entering service in a couple of weeks," Markus replied. "The crews are fully trained, and they'll be ready for combat before the end of the month." The general smiled at his own good news.

Sachs nodded his approval. "OK. When those four enter service, here's how I want them used. Two of them are to focus their raids on Beijing—I want that capital turned to rubble for what they've done to our nation. The other three are to carry out random raids across the country. I want one bomber to hit a city, then the next day it should be pounded by the second bomber and on the third day, the third bomber should take down even more targets. Then they can move to the next city. That way, the residents of that province get a feel for what their country is doing to ours. I want them to pressure their government and clamor for an end to this godforsaken war."

"Respectfully, strategic bombing isn't enough, sir," interjected CIA Director Ryerson. "We need to crack through their electronic firewall and show their people the truth about what started this war. They need to know what their leaders are doing and that this entire war has been predicated on a lie. If we can sow division among their own people, like they've attempted to do with us, then I think we can collapse the regime."

General Pruitt nodded. "I agree, Mr. President. We have to make this a multidimensional war. If the Air Force can go after their food stores and the CIA and NSA can crack through their electronic firewall, we may be able to break the leaders' hold on the country. If we can make that happen, it'll end this war a hell of a lot faster than trying to slug it out with them like we are now."

The President blew some air out through pursed lips. "All right," he said. "I guess we need to figure a way to burn the Great Firewall of China to the ground."

****

Detroit, Michigan

Vice President Powers toured the ruins of the Ford Motor plant with the company's CEO, Todd Ripper. As he stepped over some of the rubble, Powers was amazed at the level of destruction surrounding him. It had been months since US forces had retaken Detroit, yet huge swaths of the city's industrial heart still lay in ruins.

"When do you start construction of the new plant?" Powers asked.

"Next Monday," Ripper answered with a smile. "Once we've cleared all the rubble away from the structure, we're going to rebuild the plant from the ground up. Only this time, the plant will be designed to allow us to retool the factory from one model of vehicle to another as consumer preferences change and demand for each model fluctuates."

"Really? How will that work?" asked the Vice President, his interest piqued.

"So right now, when we want to build, say, trucks, we manufacture them in one plant while we fabricate Mustangs in another plant," Ripper began. "In the past, each plant had been configured to build a certain model of vehicle. While that worked in the past, it's not efficient now. Consumer preferences change. The old plant structure didn't allow us to be flexible and adjust. For example, when we stopped producing our small vehicles, we couldn't just swap out the tools to have them produce trucks. The plant wasn't designed to build trucks, so we ended up closing the whole plant to retool it. That costs money and time and there's nothing to say the demand for trucks may not change in the interim period."

"So I take it you found a way around that?"

"We did," Ripper responded with a nod. "We're essentially building a modular plant that'll allow us to shift from one production line to another by simply swapping out a couple of modules within the plant."

Todd motioned for one of his people to come forward. The woman handed him a tablet they had preloaded for this very discussion. "If I can, Mr. Vice President, I'll show you exactly how this works," he said, motioning for them to walk over to the hood of a nearby truck.

The two stood there with the tablet on the hood and watched a short video that showed Powers exactly what the CEO was talking about. Tools, equipment, and molds were all changed out almost seamlessly.

When the video ended, Ripper explained, "While the destruction of our plants here in Detroit has hurt our business and the city, it's actually going to allow us to build a better, more efficient production facility. This new plant will help us produce more vehicles at a cheaper price than our old facilities."

"That's great, Todd," Powers said with a smile. "How long will it take to get the facility up and running, and about how many people will this new megafactory you're building employ?"

"We'll be building this new factory complex in four phases. Each phase will be built simultaneously and employ a total of eight thousand construction workers. It'll take about eighteen months to build. Once constructed, the entire factory will employ some eighteen thousand autoworkers. The community and support functions for the factory will create roughly one hundred and ten thousand additional jobs."

Powers beamed with excitement. Despite the war raging in the southern half of the country, President Sachs was adamant about getting the industrial Midwest rebuilt. The country needed jobs, it needed an industrial base to rebuild its depleted military, and the country needed hope and healing. Rebuilding what had been lost and putting people back to work would accomplish all that.

"The President is going to be pleased, Todd. Is there anything we can do to help?"

"No. That's OK, Mr. Vice President. The government's been helping us with everything we've requested up to this point. You guys just focus on defeating the Chinese and restoring our country and we'll handle rebuilding our factories," Ripper replied with a smile.

The two talked a bit longer before they headed back to the airport. Powers was flying to Toledo, Ohio, next to meet with another group of industry leaders and CEOs to talk about the reconstruction efforts in Ohio. He'd spend the night there before traveling to Pennsylvania and New York. Once he completed a five-day tour through the Midwest and Northeast, he'd be able to report back to the President on the status of the reconstruction efforts a lot better than some briefer who hadn't been on the ground to see things firsthand.

Chapter Four
Weapons Check

March 2022
Newport News, Virginia

Vice Admiral Ingalls stood on the bridge of the USS *Warhammer* as the engineers from DARPA and a few contracting companies worked through the few remaining wrinkles that still needed to be ironed out of the system. Several months ago, they had gone through a weeklong sea trial, which had allowed the engineers to identify any problems. After several months of twenty-four-hour work crews running seven days a week, they believed they had most of them resolved. This new sea trial would allow them to check a few more of those items off that list and see if any new issues popped up. They were now two days into the test.

As Ingalls sipped some coffee on the bridge with the lead engineer for the project, he watched as an F-35 came in on final approach on the portside runway. The aircraft wobbled a bit from a cross breeze but straightened itself promptly. The warplane moved steadily closer to the floating runway, adjusting itself from time to time as the ship rolled a bit with the waves. Finally, the plane touched down on the flight deck and caught the second arrestor wire. The plane reduced its engines and then taxied toward the rear parking ramp, making room for the next plane to land.

Ingalls turned to the starboard side of the ship to watch one of the EA-18 Growlers come in. Like the F-35, it made a flawless landing. For the next ten minutes, the group watched as one aircraft after another landed, filling the ship up with its airwing. The flight ops group would continue to run through their list of system checks to certify the ship's flight operations.

Satisfied that the air operation side of the new Arsenal ship appeared to be functioning well, Ingalls took a moment to look out the front windows of the bridge. He saw the main gun turret and the forward section of the ship covered in VLS pods. Past them, a storm was brewing.

Good. This'll be a good test of the ship to have to handle some rough seas, he thought.

Mr. Bullard, one of the lead project managers, walked up to Ingalls. "Admiral, we've successfully worked out the computer bugs on the weapon systems," he announced.

Mr. Lake smiled. "I'm glad the programmers got those kinks ironed out so quickly. I was afraid they'd be the ones to hang us up."

Ingalls grinned too. "It's often the more mundane things like a short in an electrical station or a problem with the HVAC system that ends up causing the delays in fielding a new warship. For the most part, none of these weapon systems we've added to this ship are technically new. In one form or another, they've been in development for more than thirty years. We're just finally able to miniaturize the power source needed to make them work on a warship. That said, if the ship is essentially combat-ready but still requiring some work, I'm going to let the CNO and the SecDef know we'll be ready for combat operations on the first of November. Is there anything that would prevent the ship from fighting by then?"

Mr. Lake looked like he had just bitten into a lemon. "I, um, I know the weapons work," he stammered. "We've gone through dozens of tests with them. I'm still concerned with the multitude of other functions on the ship that still need to be worked out. As you said, there are other mechanical and electrical functions that still need to be run through." He shook his head before he looked back at Ingalls. "I really wish we had a few more months. I feel like the ship is one major problem away from being dead in the water. I'd hate for something to happen just as she's getting ready to go into battle."

Ingalls nodded. "I understand the sentiment, but we don't have a few months. This war has to end, and that means we have to rush a lot of things through completion. Can this ship still fight while we keep a crew of contractors on board to work on some of the miscellaneous issues that come up?"

Mr. Lake paused. "We can," he said with a nod. "Look, I'm not saying we'd need this, but I'd bring a few tugs with us, just in case. Also, I'd like to have a troop ship nearby where we can have more of the contractors sleep. We can bring more of them with us if we have space for them. We can continue to close up the inside of the ship while it's underway and fix any additional electrical or computer problems so long as you can keep a ship nearby for our workers to sleep on when they're not working."

Ingalls smiled at the novel idea. "Excellent. Then that's exactly what we'll do," he responded. "We'll use helicopters to bring your workers over for their shifts and back when they're done." He stretched his back. "See? I knew we'd find a work-around to get this ship underway."

Ingalls felt better about the situation. All the focus thus far had been on getting the weapons systems fully functional. However, they had hundreds of corridors and rooms that still needed to have their wall or ceiling panels attached. Everywhere he walked in the ship, he could see exposed wires and miles of piping and other parts of the HVAC system. All of that still needed to be sealed up. The permanent lighting needed to be attached, the floors put in, the bedding and bunks installed for the rooms, and nearly everything else that made this floating city support the men and women who'd be fighting it soon enough.

This is a modern man-of-war, Ingalls thought. It was the largest battleship ever built. *When we engage the Chinese, I just hope the damn paint is dry.*

****

Washington, D.C.
Pentagon

The Chief of Naval Operations, Admiral Chester Smith, read the latest updates on the growing fleet near Norfolk. The United Kingdom had sent the HMS *Queen Mary* along with most of its surface warfare fleet. Two of their submarines had joined the US in the Pacific and had already had an impact, sinking some of the enemy merchant marines crossing the vast ocean.

What concerned Admiral Smith the most at this point was getting his warships supplied with the munitions they needed for the coming operation to liberate Panama and seize the canal. The Army had been hard at work drawing up their plans for an airborne assault using paratroopers while the SEALs would capture the actual locks to make sure the Chinese didn't blow them. Smith's challenge was finding enough Tomahawk cruise missiles to outfit his destroyers and cruisers—they still hadn't fully equipped the *Warhammer* or *Spartan* yet.

Smith reached over for his coffee and lifted the hot liquid to his lips. He turned his chair to look out the window and just stared outside for a moment, letting his mind wander. He heard a knock at the door and turned around to see Mike Howell, the Secretary of Defense.

Smiling, Smith stood up as he welcomed him to his office. "Mr. Secretary, it's good to see you. Did we have a meeting this morning or did you have something specific you wanted to talk about?" Smith tried not to betray his annoyance, but he hated unannounced visits like this; he did not enjoy being caught off guard.

Secretary Howell didn't immediately answer the question. Instead, he made his way over to the overstuffed leather couches that sat at the opposite side of the admiral's office and motioned for Smith to join him. As the two of them sat down, an aide came in and brought a pitcher of water and some glasses.

Mike Howell was one of those rare individuals who routinely floated in and out of the government. He'd served six years as a Marine infantry officer before going on to earn a PhD from MIT, spending another six years in academia before he was offered a senior position at DARPA. Then he'd worked at Microsoft for a stint before moving to the Pentagon during the Obama years as the Head of Research and Development. When Secretary McElroy had been killed at the outset of the war, it had been hard to find a replacement. However, the Senate had finally held a vote and confirmed Howell, so he'd no longer be acting secretary.

The Secretary of Defense took a sip of water and looked at his senior naval officer with his steely gaze. "Admiral, I wanted to talk with you about our ordnance inventory problem," he said.

Great—the one area I'm totally hosed in, thought Admiral Smith. *This ought to be fun...*

Trying to portray a positive attitude. Smith asked, "What part would you like to talk about?"

Howell smiled and leaned in. "We obviously have a production problem with the Tomahawks and the SM series of missiles. We've burned through most of our stocks of these missiles in the last nine months, and two of our critical production facilities were sadly trapped behind enemy lines. What are your thoughts on how we can handle this?"

Admiral Smith blew some air out of his lips as if releasing an imaginary smoke ring. "The best idea I've come up with is to strip all the ships that are currently in port for repairs of their SMs and Tomahawks to get the ships in the Task Force as close to one hundred percent as possible. However, I don't think we'll be expending a lot of these missiles in the coming Panama campaign—that's mostly going to be a ground war. Our fight will start once we've reentered the Pacific and we start to interdict the Chinese Navy convoys and attack their ground forces in California and Mexico."

"You're right. I'm glad we agree on that, Admiral," said Howell. "I honestly wasn't sure what you were going to say when I asked that question. I think everyone is fretting about the Panama campaign when they need to be looking at what's coming after it. When our naval force breaks out in the Pacific, we aren't going to have our West Coast facilities to rely on. I mean, we'll have Washington State, but that's in the North Pacific. Our main battles will take place in the Central Pacific, especially around Hawaii, which has largely been cut off."

"I agree. Our biggest battles will take place well after Panama," Admiral Smith concurred. "If I could, I have a question for you about that," he said.

"Sure. What's your question?" Howell asked, sipping his water.

"What's our end state, sir?" Smith pressed. "I mean, let's assume we get the Chinese ground force cut off from the Mainland—what do we do next if they refuse to surrender? We're in no shape to carry this fight to China."

Lifting an eyebrow at the question, Howell inquired, "Even with these new Arsenal ships? You don't think we could take the fight to them?"

"Perhaps the Arsenal ships could, but they also need support ships," Smith countered. "That's where we'll run into problems. It's going to take us months to hunt down the remaining Chinese subs. In the meantime, they'll continue to pose a threat to our own supply and surface ships. Besides, what're we going to do? Sail up and down their coast taking potshots at their cities and harbors?"

Secretary Howell snorted. "No, I suppose you're right about taking the fight to the Chinese," he admitted. "I think the President's new air campaign has a strong chance of forcing them to the negotiating table. The bigger challenge is how do we repatriate our citizens they've kidnapped and taken back to China?"

Smith swore under his breath. "That still pisses me off, pardon my French. What those animals have been doing, kidnapping our women like that and carting them off to be given away as brides to their soldiers…well, it makes me want to nuke their entire country," Smith growled. He had a brother who had been trapped in California, and he feared his nieces might have become victims themselves.

"I can assure you, the President won't end this war until they're returned," said Howell adamantly. "He'd sooner bomb every one of their cities than leave them trapped in China."

"If we have to bring back every ship from mothballs and sail the USS *Constitution* herself, we will be ready, sir," asserted Smith.

Howell nodded. With nothing more to be said, he got up and headed to his next meeting.

Chapter Five
Operation Tropic Thunder

April 2022
Fort Davis, Panama

The C-17 descended to twenty-seven thousand feet as it prepared to disgorge its human cargo. Back in the cavernous bay, two SEAL platoons stood ready to jump into history. The operators had just hooked themselves up to the aircraft's oxygen system as the plane got ready to depressurize so the first platoon could jump.

The crew chiefs finished attaching themselves to the onboard oxygen system, signaling the SEALs in the bay that they were about to begin the process of depressurizing the aircraft. When everyone gave a thumbs-up, the internal lights flicked from blue to red. Next, the air inside the cabin was vented, allowing them to acclimate to the pressure at twenty-seven thousand feet. Then the ramp slowly lowered until it was level with the floor of the cargo bay.

The crew chief gave them a signal that they were ready for them to start lining up. At this point, the first platoon that would be jumping disconnected themselves from the plane's oxygen system and hooked up to the portable drop tanks they'd be jumping with. Sixteen operators lined up on the ramp, eight on each side. The second platoon would make their jump ten minutes after the first. This would place each platoon of SEALs on opposite sides of the Gatun Locks and Gatun Dam, their primary target to secure.

SO1 Chuck Black, "Blackjack," stood near the edge waiting for the order to jump off the rear ramp. He looked to his left. His friend Chubby was ready as well. This would be their first high-altitude, high-opening jump of the war. Once they jumped, they'd descend for nearly thirty minutes as they crossed some twenty-eight miles to their objective, hopefully undetected.

The crew chief suddenly nodded, giving them the signal to jump. Without further thought, Blackjack took a couple of steps forward and leapt into the dark void. His body fell for a couple of seconds before he deployed his chute and grabbed for his guide handles. He briefly looked behind him to make sure the others had exited the aircraft and their parachutes had deployed. Seeing that everyone had made it, Blackjack knew it was now just a matter of time until they landed in Panama. Every few minutes, he'd check his compass and GPS unit to make sure he was leading the platoon in the right direction.

Steadily, they got closer to land. As they neared ground, Blackjack knew they were nearly to the drop zone. At approximately 0245 hours, four members of the Marine 2nd Reconnaissance Battalion who'd been on the ground for almost a week would activate an IR strobe light, letting them know precisely where the DZ was. The recon Marines had scouted the area out for the SEALs and would provide them with the lay of the land once they were on the ground.

With no more than five minutes left in their descent, Blackjack saw the IR strobe light come on through his night vision goggles. He pulled on his guide wire, angling his chute. The others stacked up slightly higher and behind him; they'd follow his lead toward the IR signal.

When he was no more than thirty feet above the ground, Blackjack detached his drop bag with his ruck and other equipment to dangle below him. Seconds later, he pulled hard on the guidewires of his chute to control his landing. He'd captured the air at just the right angle—his landing was practically as light as a feather. He took a couple of quick steps forward, then detached himself from his chute and went to work on rolling it into a tight ball.

Meanwhile, the fifteen other operators of his platoon landed and did the same thing. Once they all had their chutes collected up along with their rucks and weapons, the Recon Marines guided them into the jungle. They had a place ready for the SEALs to bury their spent chutes so they'd be out of sight.

Next, the Marines led them to a small encampment they had set up a few kilometers away. When they reached the base camp, they'd do a quick radio check and make sure their sister platoon had made it to their encampment without a hitch as well. Once all the platoons reported in, SOCOM would send a message to Big Army that it was time to get the Rangers in the air and let the 82nd Airborne know they were on deck.

As they trudged through the rainforest, Blackjack couldn't help but smile. This was the kind of thing he and his fellow adrenaline junkies lived for. The operation to seize the critical canals linking the Atlantic Ocean with the Pacific was officially underway.

****

Tampa, Florida
MacDill, Air Force Base
SOCOM HQ

General Royal breathed a sigh of relief. He'd just received official word that all eight platoons of SEAL Team Two had made it in. Infiltration was the riskiest part of the operation. Now they had to get the SEALs moved into position before the really difficult part started—the actual seizing of the canal locks and dams without destroying them.

Turning to find his operations officer, General Royal asked, "Are the Rangers ready?"

Major General Ned Dekker nodded. "They are. The 82nd's 3rd Brigade Combat Team just arrived in Havana. They'll be prepared when the go order is given."

Royal nodded.

"Should we go ahead and get the Unit in the air?" asked Dekker.

General Royal glanced at his watch. "I think we should give the SEALs another four hours. Once they report that they've made it to their staging areas, that's when we should spin up the Unit and get them airborne. In the meantime, has anything changed with General Song?"

"Negative. He's still at his villa," said Dekker. "If he keeps to his schedule, he'll be making a speech at the port and then another one at a local high school in the city. Around 1900 hours, he's supposed to be hosting a dinner at his villa with the mayor and some other local city officials. Our recommendation is still to grab him at the villa around 2300 hours, and the locks at 2330 hours."

"We have to hope like hell the Air Force can suppress those enemy SAMs so our transports can deliver the Rangers. Those SEALs won't last long if we don't get them more help rapidly once they kick things off," General Royal commented nervously.

"They will. The Recon Marines have had a week to find the radar and launcher sites," said General Dekker reassuringly. "They'll make sure the Air Force knows where they are when the time comes."

"I sure hope you're right," countered Royal. "We have less than twenty-fours before the fight to retake the canal begins."
****

Gatun Locks, Panama

Brushing aside the vines that were blocking his way, Blackjack moved stealthily through the undergrowth leading to the southern side of the Gatun Locks. When he reached the edge of the dense jungle, he stopped and waited for the rest of his team to join him.

Lieutenant Tebo saddled up next to him. He pulled out his detailed map of the lock chambers. On it were markings of the most likely places where the Chinese might have placed charges.

Talking just above a whisper so only their throat mics would pick up the noise, Blackjack instructed, "Chubby, get the drone ready. Start scanning the lock chambers, especially the locations that the lieutenant identified."

Chubby pulled off his backpack and unzipped it, revealing a sleek jet-black quadcopter drone that had been specially designed for SOCOM. Not only did it have an extended-life battery pack, but the drone itself was also stealthy. Its quadcopter blades were practically silent, allowing it to sneak up on a position without being detected. Chubby attached the highly sensitive optical suite to the drone and then fastened on the battery pack. Once that was completed, he turned on the tablet and made sure the two devices were connected.

Chubby handed the tablet to the lieutenant and Blackjack before he put his VR glasses on. Using the handheld controller, he turned the drone on and got it airborne. Once it was up, Chubby moved it toward the first of the three locking chambers.

The locks were on the Atlantic side, where they connected ships with Lake Gatun, an artificial lake created to make a deep enough shipping channel that massive freighters could pass through it as they journeyed from one ocean to the next. If either end of the lock system was destroyed, it would empty the high water table in the artificial lake, making it virtually impossible for large ships to transit the canal for months if not years to come, until the lake's previous water level was restored. It was imperative that the locks be captured intact.

Chubby carefully maneuvered the drone toward the gate doors of each chamber. Blackjack turned to the other three operators on his team. "Hawk, get your rifle set up and ready to cover me, Turtle, and Beatle."

Hawk nodded as he pulled his Mk 11 Mod 0 sniper rifle off his back. He extended the bipod on the rifle and pulled out two magazines of ammo. One was marked in red tape, the other in blue. He slapped the blue-taped magazine, which contained his subsonic rounds, in place. They would genuinely be silent when he fired them through a suppressor.

They all waited anxiously to see if Chubby spotted any charges. Blackjack looked at the tablet the lieutenant was holding; the drone had just reached the first chamber on the lock. Fortunately, there were no ships passing through since the Chinese had just closed it off to shipping traffic.

When the drone reached the first moveable gate leading to the next section, Blackjack thrust his finger at the tablet screen. "There," he hissed. A small set of charges had been attached to both of the gate doors. The drone then rose above the gate and moved to the next chamber, and sure enough, they found charges placed on that end as well.

Blackjack made sure Turtle and Beatle knew the locations of the explosives. They nodded. Once everyone was clear about where all the charges were, Blackjack and his two other SEALs took their body armor off along with their rifles and helmets. For this mission, they were only going to use their silenced pistols, a knife, and the essential equipment they needed to defuse the charges.

Fortunately, there was a lot of cloud cover blocking the moon and the stars that evening, making the night extremely dark. The PLA also kept the place intentionally dark, apparently wanting to make it difficult to observe the locks or see where their guards were located.

The three operators advanced silently from their covered positions toward the locks. The lieutenant watched from his spotting scope—if he spotted a guard near them or one appeared to be looking in their direction, he would call it through his throat mic so they could drop to the ground or find cover. Between the LT and his scope, the drone flying above them and Hawk with his sniper rifle, they had the place pretty well covered.

When Blackjack reached his chamber, he crept over to the gate and found the metal ladder that led into it. He holstered his pistol and descended until he was next to the explosives that were attached to the gate. Examining the charge, he found the remote-control unit firmly attached to the top of the charge. As he looked at the r/c unit, Blackjack noted the soft, blinking red light which told him the charge was active and ready to be blown—it also meant the person who could detonate the explosives was probably close by.

Tracing his fingers around the r/c unit, Blackjack eventually came across the wire that connected it with the blasting cap that would be tucked inside the charge. He followed the wire until he found the spot where it was connected to the explosives. Reaching down into his front pocket, he pulled out a small pair of wire cutters. Using his left hand, he held a portion of the wire just above the blasting cap and moved his right hand with the cutters to it. A second later, he had snipped the wire, rendering the explosives inert. Not wanting anyone to see that the wire had been cut, he tucked it to the side of the r/c unit, using a piece of gum he'd been chewing to hold it in place.

With the first set of charges disabled, he swiftly shifted to disabling the three other charges. Before he left, Blackjack pulled a small black box out of his cargo pants and stealthily moved toward a small building nearby. Checking to make sure that no one was in the building and all was clear, he fastened the small device to the underside of the roof, near the rain gutter. To an unassuming observer, it would look like it was part of the drain, but in reality, it was a remotely activated radio frequency jammer. In the event the Chinese had placed other explosives they hadn't found, this little device would hopefully jam any attempts to remotely detonate them.

With less than twenty minutes before dawn, the operators had disarmed all the charges on the chamber gates and made a hasty retreat to the edge of the jungle, where the rest of their team was waiting for them. With their primary objective completed, they donned their body armor and other equipment and faded away into the thick vegetation. Once back at base camp, they'd settle in and get a few hours of sleep before they prepared for the big event.

****

Piscinita, Colombia
Gustavo Rojas International Airport

Colonel Patrick "Paddy" Maine looked at his group of Delta operators. They were tough-looking men, ready for battle. This mission was going to be unlike any they had previously attempted—they were going to fly right into the heart of Chinese territory and snatch the commanding general right from under his soldiers.

Paddy looked at the map of the target again, then turned back to Deuce. "Go over your part of the plan again," Paddy ordered.

Leaning over the map, Deuce responded, "My team is going to breach the home, clear it, and secure the package. We'll then exfil to this point here, load the package on the helicopter, and hopefully get the hell out there."

Nodding, Paddy turned to his assault team. "Mickey, go over your team's actions."

"When the helicopters land, my team will neutralize the guards at the entrance to the island. We'll also neutralize the guards here, here, and here," Mickey said, pointing to several areas on the map with a red circle on them, where they anticipated finding Chinese guards.

Satisfied with the answers, Paddy looked at them. "This has to be a quick hit. We have to get in and out of the area *fast*. Once word gets out that he's been grabbed, the entire country is going to go into lockdown and the PLA is going to lose its ever-loving mind looking for him. The SEALs are also going to make their move to secure the locks twenty minutes after we touch down. The first Ranger units will start to arrive at 0100 hours, with the 82nd Airborne hitting their objectives by 0600 hours. It's imperative that we remove the general from the equation."

The group talked for a bit more before they broke to grab their gear and get ready to head out. Their rides were leaving in thirty minutes.

****

When the operators entered the hangar near the end of the airport, they really had no idea what to expect. They'd been told Air Force Special Operations had moved an experimental helicopter of theirs to the small island just for this mission. When they opened the door, more than a few of them let out a soft whistle. What they saw was not just one mythical unicorn staring back at them, but two.

"Holy crap. I don't think I've ever seen something like that before," said one of the guys.

The pilot, an Air Force major, walked up to them, beaming with pride at his aircraft. "That, my friends, is the future of Special Operations aviation," he said, waving his arm toward the two flying beasts.

"What the hell is it?" asked one of the operators.

"This is the V-100 tiltrotor, and it's what's going to allow us to sneak in undetected on the Chinese." For the last two days, the military had been hiding them in the hangar to keep them away from prying eyes and make sure there was no way the Chinese could find out about them before the mission. This would be the V-100's first combat mission.

Deuce chimed in. "It looks like those fly helicopters they had in the movie *Avatar*."

Smiling at the reference, the pilot replied, "That's because they are. By enclosing the rotor blades in a metal shroud like you see here, they become practically silent. We're not totally stealthy on radar, but they'll never hear us coming, which in our world is far more important."

"OK, enough gawking," shouted Paddy. "Everyone, get in the helicopters. We have a mission to complete!"

The gaggle of soldiers scrambled to get themselves on the two experimental helicopters and ready to go. Ten minutes after the operators boarded the tiltrotors, they were in the air and heading toward Panama.

The pair of V-100s flew just a few feet above the water at a rate of three hundred and forty miles per hour. When they reached the coast of Panama, they continued to hug the ground, flying just above the trees, almost touching the valleys and small ridges. The pilots did their best to keep the helicopters hidden in the ground clutter—the last thing they wanted to do was show up on a Chinese SAM's radar scope.

Forty minutes into their flight over Panama, they emerged on the other end of the country, over the Pacific Ocean. The pilots kept the V-100s low over the water as they steered toward the Ocean Reef Islands—two ritzy isles filled with luxury homes, condos, and a private marina.

As they neared the targeted home, the pilots maneuvered to give a couple of small patrol boats a wider berth. The entire artificial island and the city were lit up like a Christmas tree, so it was easy for the pilots to find the empty lot near the target home, which was waiting for a wealthy individual to purchase it so they could build their dream home. The tiltrotors bled off speed at a prodigious rate, until the V-100s were in a slow hover over the lot.

Deuce had his foot on the ground about the same time the tiltrotor touched down. He sprinted full out toward the side gate on the property wall that led into the compound, the rest of his team in hot pursuit behind him as they raced to get through the first obstacle between them and the package.

While they were running to breach the perimeter wall, the second team of operators was already in the process of neutralizing the perimeter guards, the guards on the roof of the house and the guards in the patrol boat just opposite the compound they were breaching. Another team of operators was in a full sprint down the road to reach the guardhouse at the entrance to the island; they needed take out the guards and lock down the gate to prevent any reinforcements from storming ashore.

Up ahead of him, Deuce saw Spider reach the side gate into the compound. He pulled out a small aerosol can and proceeded to spray the locking mechanism with liquid nitrogen. Then he placed a towel over the lock before he hit the frozen device as hard as he could with his breaching hammer. The metal made a very quiet crunching noise as the gate busted inwards. The only real sound was the creaking from the gate's hinges.

When the door broke inwards, Deuce and the rest of the team raced past Spider, their guns raised as they rushed into the rear of the compound. There were several spitting noises as the operators killed the guards with their suppressed SCAR 16s. It didn't take them long to clear the patio and the pool area of the compound before they made their way into the building.

Deuce and Larry moved swiftly through the lower level without finding anyone. Once they located the stairs leading to the second floor, they bounded up them two at a time until they came to the landing at the top. Deuce split right while Larry moved left, and the two of them cleared each room they came across until they made it to the master suite.

Deuce waited until Larry was ready to enter the room before he reached down, gently turned the handle, and pushed the door open slowly. Entering the room, Deuce moved to the left side of the bed while Larry moved to the right. A man and a woman appeared to be snuggled under the covers.

Deuce and Larry each held a hand up, letting their rifles hang by their single-point slings. They both reached into their pockets, pulling out a syringe. They undid the caps on the needles, leaned down and jabbed the substance into the thighs of the man and the woman while holding their other hand over their mouths to mute any screams. Seconds later, both of the sleepers slumped back down, out cold.

Deuce pulled a small biometric scanner out and placed General Song's finger on it. A second later, the machine gave a green signal, and a picture of the general in uniform showed up on the screen.

Deuce nodded. "It's a match," he announced. "It's him. Leave her zip-tied on the bed and let's get him out to the chopper."

They radioed the rest of the team that they had the package and were heading out. It was time for everyone to collapse back on the V-100s and get the hell out of there. A few minutes later, the operators were back in the empty lot and climbing aboard the two tiltrotor aircraft that would ferry them back to the Panamanian jungle and a waiting fuel truck.

The pilots moved them further out to sea, away from the lights of the harbor and the entire area. They then cut back toward the blacked-out shore as they traveled at treetop levels toward a predetermined field. They landed, did a hot refueling and then got back in the air, headed to the small Colombian island a hundred miles off the coast of Panama.

Deuce looked at his watch. He thought to himself that every normal man must be tempted at times to spit upon his hands, hoist the black flag and begin slitting throats. A wry smile spread on his lips.

He pointed out the window. Suddenly, the lights of Panama City disappeared, and the entire country was plunged into darkness. Though the interior of the V-100 was lit only by the slight glow from the instruments in the cockpit, he could see smiles on the faces of his men.

****

"That's the signal," said the lieutenant over the radio. "Everyone *move*!"

As Blackjack emerged from the edge of the jungle, rifle raised to his shoulder, their sniper, Hawk, was already picking guards off. Blackjack dashed toward the building where most of the local guards were housed. Suddenly, the door to the building opened, and a solitary soldier emerged. Blackjack squeezed the trigger three times, hitting the man with two bullets to his chest and one to his head. As his head snapped back, he fell backwards into the building he had just exited.

A second later, another soldier emerged with his rifle at his hip and fired a burst of automatic fire at them, the bright muzzle flashes fully illuminating him in the otherwise dark building. Blackjack fired another three rounds from his own rifle, killing the man instantly. The guard's body slumped to the floor with that of his other comrade.

At this point, Blackjack switched the selector to full auto and unloaded the rest of his magazine into the walls leading up to the door in anticipation of one or more new attackers emerging. Then he dropped to a knee, replaced the spent magazine with a fresh one and continued to advance on the building. When he reached the doorway, Blackjack grabbed for one of his fragmentation grenades, pulled the pin and threw it into the building.

When the grenade blew up, Blackjack rushed into the building, followed by Turtle and Beatle. The three operators proceeded to clear the guardhouse, eliminating the rest of the guards before they even had a chance to react. Many of the men were barely dressed, clearly having been woken out of their sleep by the sudden attack.

The SEALs raced through the entire area of the locks and the nearby hydroelectric dam to secure it and eliminate the Chinese soldiers standing guard. With their initial objectives met, they now had to hold the position until a Ranger company parachuted in and was able to assist them until the 82nd Airborne arrived later in the morning.

****

Panama International Airport

Staff Sergeant Silverman, 1st Battalion, 504th Infantry Regiment, jumped out the open door of the aircraft and waited for his chute to open. Seconds later, he felt the familiar jerk as his parachute filled with air, slowing his descent. Looking down, Silverman saw the ground swiftly approaching. When he reached roughly fifty feet, he disconnected his drop bag to allow it to dangle below him. Seconds later, he bent his knees and prepared to tuck and roll as his drop bag touched down.

Once on the ground and his chute disconnected, Silverman ran for his drop bag and retrieved his ruck. He threw the ruck over his shoulder, grabbed his M4 rifle and started looking for the rest of his squad. Seeing that several of them were rallying up on the lieutenant, Silverman ran toward him. He spotted a couple soldiers in his team and yelled out for them to follow him.

It took Silverman close to five minutes on the ground to get everyone in his squad assembled and ready to move. In the meantime, the crescendo of gunfire further away near the city continued to grow in intensity as the paratroopers came into contact with more of the defenders.

"Listen up, First Platoon!" shouted their lieutenant. "We're going to advance down to Farfan Beach and the boats that'll take us across to the other side. Keep it wired tight, gents! When we board the boats, we won't have long to try and get across the channel. Once across, we're going to relieve a Ranger unit hunkered down on Cerro Ancón. It's a hilltop that overlooks the Pan-American Highway and the Port of Balboa. Squad leaders, maintain your squad integrity and let's do this thing."

The platoon moved toward the beach, where a number of civilian boats would hopefully be ready to ferry them across. A handful of Rangers had been commandeering dozens of private speedboats from the harbor and had placed them on the shores of Farfan Beach ahead of the paratroopers' arrival. This way they'd be able to ferry themselves across the channel without having to risk getting shot up trying to cross the massive bridge that connected the two sides of Panama.

While Silverman and the other soldiers sifted through the jungle, he could hear the jet engines overhead as American F-15s and F-16s did their best to provide close air support to the Rangers and SEALs who were engaging the PLA units around the city. Silverman looked to his left and saw that the company trying to protect that side of the airport was having a tough go of it—they were fighting a huge cluster of PLA tanks.

I'm glad we didn't get sent in that direction, Silverman thought. He would much rather be fighting in the woods or an urban environment than have to deal with confronting a tank unit with little in the way of armor support. For the time being, the only thing the paratroopers had jumped in with was a few dozen JLTVs and TOW-equipped Stryker vehicles.

As they emerged from the jungle and found themselves on the beach, Specialist Leary called out, "Would you look at that!"

"I'll be damned. OK, Second Squad, on me!" shouted Silverman to his twelve guys. He raced toward a large speedboat that had his name on it. It had two large engines on the back and looked like it could easily carry twenty people if it had to.

A platoon of engineers raced toward the boats with them—for better or worse, they'd been tagged to drive the boats. They'd deliver Silverman and his unit and then come back for the next company of paratroopers waiting to cross. Until everyone was across the channel and they had secured both sides of the bridge, this was going to be their primary way of getting back and forth across the channel.

Once everyone had gotten loaded onto the speedboat, the engineer revved the engines in reverse a bit as he backed them off the beach. Then he angled the boat as he sought to give the engines some more room before he gunned it.

Bang, bang, bang.

A Chinese armored vehicle that was maybe eight hundred yards away down near the Port of Balboa shot at the motley crew of speedboats that was racing the paratroopers across the channel.

Silverman couldn't help but think this whole scene was almost comical, like something on the old World War II movie *Operation Petticoat.* But this wasn't Hollywood, and these were real bullets. Against that APC's cannon, they were not on the top of the food chain.

Red tracers zipped past the boats, splashing up water. Some of them hit nearby. The untrained speedboat drivers starting zigging and zagging all over the place to avoid getting hit. One of the strings of tracers connected with one of the boats and blew it apart in a bright flash of flame and debris.

Then, as rapidly as the shooting had started, it ended. The flotilla of speedboats zipped out of the vehicles' line of sight. When they reached the marina, the soldiers jumped off the speedboats. Silverman was thankful to be alive and back on dry ground. The boats turned around swiftly. They would make the high-speed journey back to pick up the next load of paratroopers.

"Second Squad on me!" shouted Staff Sergeant Silverman as he hoofed it through the Balboa Yacht Club. As the sounds of battle raged all around them, the squad ran after their leader, a man who had been with them since the beginning—Silverman had been promoted to staff sergeant and taken over command of the squad five months ago.

Gunfire echoed off every building, making it hard to know exactly where it was coming from. Silverman heard loud booms, vehicles blowing up, and tanks firing rounds into buildings. It was pure chaos and confusion. The Chinese soldiers scrambled to stop the paratroopers from filtering into the city and linking up with the pockets of Army Rangers who were still holding on to various strongholds and blocking positions.

"Shooter on the roof!" yelled one of Silverman's soldiers.

Up on the roof of the Latin-American Parliament building, Silverman spotted a handful of soldiers setting something up. One of his soldiers fired on the people on the roof, which caused everyone else in the squad to open up.

Several figures fell from the top of the building and thudded on the ground. Their bodies bounced once or twice, ending in grotesque and awkward positions.

Zip, zip, zip.

Strings of bullets landed all around Silverman's squad as they dove for cover. Chunks of tree bark, clumps of grass and dirt flew into his face from near misses.

"Where is that shooting coming from?" Silverman yelled.

"It's coming from the roof we just shot up!" one of his soldiers shouted back.

"203!" yelled one of his grenadiers, who popped out from behind a covered position and fired his grenade gun. The round sailed at a slight arc as it flew up toward the roof and impacted just short of it. A few of the soldiers around him cursed at the near miss.

"Dude, you suck, I got it!" yelled another soldier as he fired his M4. He got off three single shots before whoever was manning that enemy machine gun stopped shooting.

With the machine-gun crew neutralized, Silverman jumped back to his feet and ran up the road to the next major intersection. Their platoon needed to reach those Rangers, and he couldn't let his squad get bogged down by every shadow along the way. They had to keep moving.

When they reached the massive interchange connecting the Pan-American Highway with Cinta Costera Road, Silverman's squad came face-to-face with not one but two Chinese ZTZ96 main battle tanks.

Silverman held a hand up and signaled for his guys to scatter; they all dove behind parked cars and other objects. So far, the tanks had their turrets turned up and were firing on the Rangers positioned on a nearby hilltop.

Then a couple of Chinese infantry fighting vehicles stopped near the tanks and disgorged their infantry, who all advanced toward the Rangers' positions, oblivious to the American paratroopers just a few hundred meters to their rear.

Turning to look behind him, Silverman saw the rest of the platoon racing to catch up to him. He scrambled to grab their attention and direct them to get under cover and to stay down.

A minute later, the platoon sergeant and the lieutenant came running up to him.

"What do you have, Staff Sergeant?" asked the lieutenant, who was a little out of breath from the run.

"Take a look," Silverman beckoned as he pointed to the vehicles just around the corner.

"Damn, good call, Silverman," said the platoon sergeant. "They would have smoked the whole platoon if we had come around that corner. Let's get some of our rocket teams up here to take them out. Then we can hit that Chinese infantry from the rear."

The LT wisely nodded in agreement and ordered it so.

Three SMAW teams ran forward and got themselves ready. One by one, they prepared themselves for what was about to come next. They'd have to act quickly and neutralize the enemy vehicles before the gunners realized they were in trouble.

Silverman looked at the soldiers who about to pull the trigger and gave them all a thumbs-up. Then he turned to his squad and told them to get ready.

The first soldier popped around the corner and fired, then the second, then the third. As each soldier fired, his partner got the launcher ready with the next rocket. In less than thirty seconds, all six enemy vehicles were burning hulks.

Once hit, the tanks cooked off their internal rounds, causing all sorts of secondary explosions. One blew up so forcefully it took the entire turret with it while the other just vented flame through the top hatches, incinerating everyone in the vehicle.

"Now!" yelled Silverman as he rounded the corner, his rifle raised to his shoulder.

His squad advanced with him. Moving past the burning vehicles, Silverman ran across the highway and raced for the other side. He saw movement near a house and fired. A lone figure fell to the ground. Then another appeared where the man had just been and fired a couple of shots at them.

Bullets whizzed past Silverman's head. It only spurred him to run faster while trying to do his best to aim at the shooter. He squeezed the trigger several times; his rounds hit the building. A couple of the bullets shattered the window before one of his shots connected with the soldier.

More gunfire erupted from the tree line about a hundred meters to his right, and Silverman realized it was coming from the Chinese infantry whose vehicles they had just blown up. The enemy soldiers fired at the

Americans as they ran across the highway, hitting a few of them but mostly missing that first group. However, the volume of fire stopped the rest of the platoon from crossing the highway, at least for the time being.

"Silverman, those soldiers in the tree line—kill them all! And the rest of the platoon, cross the highway," their platoon leader ordered over his radio headset.

Silverman depressed the talk button to reply. "Roger that. Kill them all. Lay down some suppressive fire on their positions while we maneuver to hit them."

"Copy that. Remove them from my AO, Staff Sergeant!"

Silverman turned to the soldiers that had made it across the highway with him, and quickly told them what they needed to do. They broke down into two groups; one would fire on the enemy positions along with the rest of their platoon from across the street, and the other group would go with Silverman to flank the enemy position and try to overwhelm them from the side.

A few minutes later, Silverman was weaving through the houses of this upper-class neighborhood as he sought to get above and slightly behind the enemy soldiers in the tree line. When he reached the edge of the exclusive community, he turned to Specialist Leary and two other guys with him.

"I want you to start lobbing grenades at those bastards down below," he directed. "When you've thrown three each, we're going to charge down that hill, screaming like possessed men until we get inside their lines. Then it's just going to be a free-for-all until we kill 'em all. You guys think you can handle that?"

Leary shook his head but smiled anyway. "You're crazy as hell, Staff Sergeant, but if anyone can pull this off, it's you."

The others laughed, which broke the tension a bit. Ever since the battle in the Allegheny Forest six months ago, Silverman had been tagged as the squad's good luck charm. Not only that, but he'd been a one-man wrecking machine in combat, a regular John Rambo if ever there was one. He'd been awarded three Silver Stars and three Purple Hearts in eight months, and it was true that he had never once tried to get reassigned a safer duty when the opportunity had been offered. Instead, he had gotten promoted and taken charge of their squad when their previous squad leader had been killed by a landmine in Canada—Silverman had been standing next to the man when it had blown up, but all that had happened to him was that a few pieces of shrapnel had lodged in his right leg, which the platoon's medic had been able to cut out and stitch up. Ever since then, the platoon had stuck to him like white on rice, perhaps believing that he somehow had powers to protect them. Not a single soldier in their squad had been killed in the five months he'd been in charge.

"OK, guys. Then on the count of three, we start lobbing grenades and then we charge."

Silverman counted down, just loud enough for them to hear. Then he pulled the pin on the first grenade and let it sail. He grabbed a second and then a third grenade, throwing them right into the enemy positions in the trees and underbrush below.

Depressing the talk button on the platoon radio, he called out, "Cease fire! We're going in!"

The shooting by the rest of the platoon tapered off just as the grenades started exploding amongst the enemy soldiers. Then Silverman let out a loud, guttural rebel yell as he ran down the hill and right into the woods toward the Chinese positions.

He ran fearlessly, like a superhuman creature that was impervious to anything that might kill him. A few seconds into his charge through the woods, Silverman came across a cluster of Chinese soldiers who were trying to shake off the effects of the grenades that had just gone off near them. Some were tending to their wounded; others were jumping back on the machine guns they had been using to pin down the rest of Silverman's platoon on the other side of the highway.

They were utterly caught off guard when Silverman emerged from the underbrush, screaming like a wild animal and firing his weapon. He hit the first man he saw with several bullets to the face. The soldier who had been tending to one of his wounded comrades collapsed in a heap.

Staff Sergeant Silverman swung his rifle toward two soldiers who were manning one of the enemy machine guns and fired a couple of three-round bursts into their chests. Then he instinctively dropped, taking a knee as a string of bullets flew right over his head where he had just been. He pivoted slightly on his rear leg and fired several rounds into the man who had nearly killed him, hitting the guy in the neck, face, and head.

As he spun around to his left, Silverman practically fell to the ground, trying to get his body out of the line of fire again. He emptied the rest of his magazine into three enemy soldiers who were charging right at him, screaming as they tried to react to his sudden body movements. Two of the soldiers clutched at one wound or another as they went down, but one of the men just kept coming despite Silverman pumping four rounds into the soldier's chest, pounding his body armor.

Before Silverman could react, the man leapt into the air, throwing himself at Silverman. Anticipating the impact, Silverman repositioned his right rear foot, bracing himself and lowering his left shoulder. The man's body crashed into Silverman, who leveraged the enemy soldier's forward momentum to lift the man up and over his body and slam him back into the ground.

Silverman clutched at the brass-knuckled trench knife he kept strapped to his right shin. With his fist clenched and the blade down, he pounced on the enemy soldier he had just body slammed to the ground, landing a solid punch to the man's face. He felt the soldier's cheekbone crack and buckle from the force of his hit. Blood gushed out of the fresh wound, and Silverman noticed that at least a couple of teeth had been knocked out. Not giving his attacker a moment to recover from the blow, Silverman plunged the blade of the trench knife right into the side of the man's throat so deeply it emerged from the other side. He ripped the razor-sharp blade out at an angle, which left the man's head dangling by his spinal cord. They made eye contact for a brief moment; the man blinked in disbelief and then died.

Silverman turned to find the next threat, only to receive a spinning roundhouse kick to the face. The force of the blow sent him hurtling backward over the man he'd just killed.

As Silverman was temporarily stunned from the violent blow to the head, the Chinese soldier pounced on him and tried to drive his knife into his chest, screaming obscenities in his face. The man's face and eyes were a mixture of fear and rage.

While he instinctively fought the incoming attack, Silverman slowly regained more of his senses. The metallic taste in his mouth reminded him that he was bleeding from the hit. Silverman sniffed hard and drew as much of the bloody mixture into his mouth as he could before he spat the red mucous into the man's face. Simultaneously, he drove his left knee into the man's groin as hard as he could. For the briefest of moments, the Chinese soldier lost his position on Silverman.

With his right hand now free, Silverman hit the enemy soldier in the side of the head with the brass knuckles. He heard something crack and then the Chinese soldier moaned and dropped to the ground.

Silverman looked around. Specialist Leary and the others had jumped into the melee at this point as the fight became a brawl. That particular clash ended when Silverman grabbed his Sig Sauer and fired three shots into the man who was about to drive a knife into Specialist Leary's chest. He then turned the Sig on two other Chinese soldiers and ended the fight.

Sitting upright on the ground, Silverman spat some blood from his mouth. Then he closed one nostril at a time as he sought to blow the blood and gunk out each of them. Next, he stood up and grabbed his M4 out from under the body of a dead Chinese soldier. With the rifle in hand, he went to replace the spent magazine when suddenly, one of the dying Chinese soldiers released a grenade in their midst.

Without thinking or hesitating, Silverman grabbed the enemy soldier whose skull he had just cracked open and rolled him on top of the grenade. Then he jumped on top of the soldier's corpse.

Crump.

Both their bodies were lifted slightly off the ground as the concussion from the blast raised them up. Pieces of shrapnel sliced right through both the Chinese soldier's and his body armor, hitting Silverman, peppering both his legs and his left arm with tiny bits of hot metal.

Silverman lay motionless on the dead enemy soldier for a moment, until he felt the roar of pain in his left arm and both of his legs. He rolled off the enemy soldier and moaned softly to himself, not sure if he still had his limbs or if they had been blown off.

"Holy crap, Staff Sergeant! You just saved our lives," Specialist Leary said as he ran over to check on him.

Silverman moaned again before he yelped out, "I think it tore my legs up pretty good." Shock began to set in. He felt like his legs were on fire, and there was nothing he could do but take it.

"How bad am I?" he asked in a hoarse, pain-filled voice.

Leary dropped down next to him and grabbed for the first aid pack on his IBA. "You still have your legs and arms, Staff Sergeant, so that's good," he said reassuringly, "but I think you're going to need a bit more stitching up than the platoon medic can give you."

Grunting at the reply, Silverman laid his head back on the ground as his comrades started applying some bandages to his wounds.

A few minutes later, the rest of their platoon had made it across the highway and up to their positions. When the lieutenant and his platoon sergeant saw the mess of bodies all around Staff Sergeant Silverman, they clearly didn't know what to say. The area was covered in dead, and somehow, someway, Silverman had once again found a way to survive.

The platoon's medic dropped his medical pack next to him and worked on getting him patched up. He shook his head. "Um, this is going to take more care than I can provide, Staff Sergeant. It looks like you're finally going to have to go to the rear, with the gear."

The next thing Silverman knew, the medic had slapped him with one of those new battlefield painkillers, and suddenly he didn't have a care in the world. He felt like he had just drunk an entire bottle of red wine and he was floating on a cloud.

Turning to Specialist Leary, the lieutenant asked, "What the hell happened?"

The three soldiers that had been with Silverman during his marauding rampage through the jungle recounted what had happened. Meanwhile, the rest of the platoon finished clearing the area and linked up with the Rangers.

Thirty minutes later, Staff Sergeant Silverman found himself lying on the side of the highway along with half a dozen other wounded soldiers, waiting to be picked up and driven back to the airport, where the brigade's combat support hospital unit had set up shop.

****

From *Fox News Online*:

> In a daring move, US Special Forces and Airborne units descended on Panama in the early-morning hours. Pentagon sources, speaking on conditions of anonymity, reported, "The success of the attack can largely be attributed to the US Army Delta Force, who succeeded in capturing the Chinese commanding general just prior to the attack, and SEAL Team Two, which successfully took the canal locks before they could be blown."

Shortly after the capture of the Panama Canal locks, the 1st Battalion, 75th Ranger Regiment conducted an airborne assault of Panama City and the surrounding area. Several hours later, the 82nd Airborne captured the Panama International Airport and began to battle the Chinese forces in and around the city.

By the end of the first day of the battle, the British Royal Marines of 3 Commando Brigade landed at several points along the Panamanian coast and began to move inland, attacking the Chinese forces at multiple points. The Royal Marines are reported to have met stiff enemy resistance around the city of Santiago, along the Pan-American Highway, some hundred and fifty kilometers north of the capital.

After gaining control of the airports around Panama City and the canal, the US and British Air Forces attacked Chinese naval vessels in the area, and the first sets of US and British destroyers and frigates began to transit through the canal.

The White House said in a statement: "The battle for Panama is over, but the battle for the Pacific is about to begin."

Chapter Six
Great Firewall of China

Hong Kong, China
Central Government Complex

As James Chan stood on the upper deck of the ferry, the cool air blew through his thinning hair. Feeling the elbows and shoulders packed tightly against his body, James couldn't help but feel like he was just another cog in some giant machine. Every morning, he got on the same ferry and saw the same people, all headed to the same place—Hong Kong Island.

The ferry was a bit more packed than usual this morning. Perhaps it was last night's broadcast from Beijing. People were on edge.

This damn war is ruining this country, he thought. He wondered if it would ruin everything they'd worked toward there in Hong Kong.

Despite the ominous broadcast last night, no one dared to openly complain about the changing situation in Hong Kong or across much of China—not after the most recent crackdown. The mood of the people was decisively different, though. They were more hostile to those non-native citizens of the Hong Kong Special Autonomous Region than they used to be.

In the HKSAR, the protests against the war and against the conscriptions had been brewing for months over the summer. In the fall, Beijing had finally lost its patience with the special autonomous region. They had sent troops in to put down the growing insurrection, which had only further fueled animosity against the central government.

James felt bad about the entire situation. It had grown out of his control. He had to act, to bring order. His part in the crackdown had cost him dearly, but it had also solidified his position with the Director.

The ferry whistle blew, shaking him from his thoughts. The ship docked. Moments later, the front ramp lowered, and the stampede of morning commuters began to exit the ferry.

When the people in front of James shifted, he made sure to hold on to his briefcase a bit tighter as his body was pushed along with the throng of people surging toward the exit. Once off the ferry, James made his way toward the footpath that led toward his place of employment.

Along the way, he made his standard morning stop at a local bakery to grab a caramel macchiato and a croissant before continuing on his way. Just prior to leaving the café, he poured the contents of his coffee cup into his thermos, just like he always did. This was all part of his morning routine—a routine he did his best never to stray from while he continued to blend into his surroundings.

A wolf hiding within the flock...

Moving along the footpath along the water, James saw the food trucks starting to line up as each owner tried to get the best position for the eventual lunch and dinner crowds. The surrounding area was a mecca of commercial and government buildings, housing tens of thousands of people. The crowds who came to eat would be hungry.

James, for his part, usually packed a lunch. His morning stop at the bakery was his one daily indulgence. A crowd gathered, and he waited along with them for the traffic light to indicate that it was safe for pedestrians to cross. When the green man appeared, a surge of people raced across the street.

Once the horde finished crossing, groups broke away from the main pack. Some folks headed toward the Hyatt Grand Regency Hotel while many others made their way to one of the numerous large office buildings along Victoria Harbor. James's destination was someplace entirely different. While many of the people in Hong Kong worked in the financial, insurance, shipping, technology, or textile industries, James worked in the Central Government Complex, right next to the PLA military headquarters building—the two places most citizens of this quasi city-state did their best to avoid.

As he made his way to the side entrance of the building, James saw a military helicopter land on the helipad nearby. A lone figure got out and handed some sort of bag to another person, who ran inside the building with it.

A courier of some sort, James thought.

When he approached the side entrance, the guards manning the gate recognized him at once. James smiled and nodded as they held the door open for him. When he entered the building, he placed his briefcase on the table so it could be inspected as he pulled out his national identity card.

"Good Morning, Mr. Chan. I hope the weekend was enjoyable," one of the guards said with a nervous smile.

James grinned at the weak attempt at small talk and nodded. "It was, but as always, the weekends are too short and the weeks too long."

"Agreed," the guard responded. "If you can, please place your hand on the verification pad." The guard motioned for him to begin the usual biometric checks that were a part of James's daily routine before being allowed into the VIP elevator bank, which was hidden from the rest of the occupants who worked in this massive edifice.

A light turned on, and a moment later, his palm print and fingerprints were compared against the data on his national identity card and in the database of individuals assigned to work in the building. In less than three seconds, the light turned green and the machine beeped. The display showed a picture of his face and his full name: Director James Chan, Ministry of State Security.

The guard handed him back his identity card, then ran his coffee thermos and briefcase through the scanner before returning them to him on the other end.

Once he was through security, James made his way to the elevator bank and rode until he reached the top floor of the building, where all the senior executives and bigwigs worked. He made his way toward his office, enjoying the view from the floor-to-ceiling windows on this floor. From here, he could easily observe the hustle and bustle of the city.

James opened a door, which led him to the corridor in front of his office. As soon as he did, his assistant, Ignatius, stood up from behind his desk to hold the door open for him.

"Good morning, Director," he said with a slight bow. Then he immediately moved to business. "We received a security alert from Beijing ten minutes ago. I thought you would like to see it first thing before your eight o'clock meeting." Ignatius handed him a folder marked with the highest classification possible. At that level, it would have to have been hand-delivered.

Lifting an eyebrow at the sensitive folder, James took it from his assistant. "I'd like to be left alone for the next ten minutes while I read through it," he said.

Ignatius nodded and exited the room.

James sat down in his leather chair and pulled out the report:

TO: Director James Chan
FROM: Minister of State Security

Director Chan,

One of our British assets has learned of an attempt to place a malicious code onto the Hong Kong server farm. Should this malware make it into place, it could create vulnerabilities within the government's firewall and our ability to control information on the internet. This would impact the control of information on the government's internal intranet systems as well.

Our source within British intelligence has learned that this attempt will take place within the next three days at the Hong Kong Central Government Complex. While our source does not know the name of the mole in our midst, we have identified the perpetrator as someone from within the Administrative Government. You need to identify this saboteur. Find the mole within the Administrative Government and make a public example of them.

Director Chan, it is imperative that you use whatever resources are necessary to identify and neutralize this threat to the People's Republic of China. If you require additional resources or agents, please make these requests known as soon as possible.

James thought about the message for a minute, trying to figure out who this source was inside British intelligence. He wondered when they'd learned of the threat, and more importantly, who they suspected to be involved within his district.

Turning to his secured video phone, James placed a highly unusual and unannounced call to the Minister's office in Beijing. He needed more information before he made his next move, and he needed to see the man's face as he asked these questions.

The device buzzed a couple of times before the familiar face of the most feared man in China next to the President himself appeared.

"Director Chan," said the Minister. "I take it you received my message?" The voice on the other end sounded distant, yet fully in control. His facial expressions gave away nothing.

Maintaining his own poker face, James readily responded, "Yes, Minister. This is an alarming discovery, but one I am not surprised to hear about."

The Minister lifted an eyebrow at the admission. "Then you already had a concern about this before my letter?"

James nodded. "I did. But if you could help me understand a bit more about our British asset, it might help me narrow down who our saboteur is."

The Minister's face became a blank stoic void again. "I cannot share who our asset is," he quickly countered. "But I can tell you they are highly placed. They informed me that Chief Executive Lau has several private companies that provide services within the Central Government Complex building. Is that part true?"

James smiled. He knew where this line of questioning was leading. "Yes, sir," he replied confidently. "He leverages two janitorial services that clean the building. One works during the operational hours of the building, and a second during the nonoperational hours. He also uses a contracting service for the cafeterias and the waste disposal of the building's daily trash."

The Minister snorted in disgust. "And I suppose the owners of these contracting services all have some sort of family relationship as well?" he pressed.

James nodded. "They do. They are owned by either his siblings, his cousins, or his uncle."

"And you've seen no need to bring this to my attention, or to his?"

Despite the implied accusation, James didn't miss a beat. "I know of them, and I've allowed them to continue intentionally."

A slight smirk spread across the Minister's face. "I see. I suspect you have a reason for this."

"Chief Executive Lau has opened the district up to a potential insider threat by leveraging contractors as opposed to vetted and monitored government employees. However, he's not doing anything different than a native-born person of Hong Kong would do. Everything here is incestuous. It's all about leveraging family in every aspect of business. Mr. Lau is using his position as Chief Executive to enrich his family and improve his power base within the district. By allowing this to continue, I've been able to place my own moles within his network of family-run businesses."

"And you've found useful information that we can use against him should we need it?" asked the Minister. "Is that what you're saying?"

James shook his head. "Worse. I've found a few individuals within his family's businesses working for several foreign intelligence agencies."

Slapping his hand on his desk, the Minister blurted out angrily, "And you are allowing them to continue? Why have you not busted these rings, and why have you kept this information from me?" His boss leaned forward in his chair, making his face appear much larger on the video screen. James had seen that look before, and it didn't bode well for him if he didn't come up with something immediately.

"Minister, please, if I can. I have left these spies in place for a reason. My own assets, who are working alongside them, have been feeding them false information for months. My assets are also helping me uncover additional people in this spy ring. I haven't brought this information to you yet because I'm still ferreting out exactly who is involved in each of these contracting companies. More importantly, I've been trying to determine if Mr. Lau is directly involved, or if he's unaware of what is going on in his family's businesses. A wrongful accusation against such a powerful figure in Hong Kong could upset the tenuous balance we maintain in the district."

His boss visibly relaxed a bit. "So you believe the individual who's going to attempt to disable our firewall works for one of these family-run businesses?" he probed.

James nodded. "I do. And now that you've told me more about the threat, I believe I know which company."

The Minister's left eyebrow rose before a smile that seemed almost sinister spread across his face. "When do you plan on taking our saboteur into custody, then?" he inquired.

James paused for a moment to contemplate his response. He knew he needed to give a realistic answer, but he also needed to make sure that when the time was right, he'd roll up the entire cell and liquidate them swiftly so nothing could lead back to him.

"I need to meet with one of my assets today, but I believe I can catch the person in the act by tomorrow, the day after at the latest," James finally answered. "Then we'll move in to take down the rest of the cell."

The Minister sat back in his chair. "Good," he responded. "I would like to report to the President that this individual has been captured. I will make sure he knows you personally uncovered this plot. When this war is over, James, I will reward with you a much bigger posting than Hong Kong for your loyalty." With that, the call was disconnected.

James practically fell back into his chair when the connection ended. His heart was racing. Beads of sweat formed on his temples. He reached for a bottle of water and chugged half of it down in one gulp. He needed to calm his nerves and lower his blood pressure. However, he also knew he needed to hurry if he was to make sure his own cover wasn't blown.

Swiveling his chair around, James leaned down to access the safe that was bolted to his floor. He pulled a key out, placed it in the safe and turned it. This lit up a small pad, where he placed his thumb. He heard a soft hissing noise before the safe popped open.

Inside, James had a couple of different passports, along with a few bricks of euros, British pounds, and US dollars. He also had four different burner phones and two smartphones—the tools of the trade.

He examined the burner phones and then grabbed the one he wanted, scrolling through the saved numbers until he found the one he was looking for. He sent a quick text with a coded message, telling his asset he had to meet today, ending it with the emergency code word.

A loud knock at the door jarred him, and he put the phone down as he turned around to see his assistant standing in the doorway.

"Is everything OK, sir?" Ignatius asked. He had a nervous look on his face, and he was clearly suspicious at the sight of the open safe. The man meant well, but sometimes James felt he was a bit nosy. *Then again, look who he works for*, he thought.

"Yes, it's fine, Ignatius," James said reassuringly. "I just had an interesting call with the Minister. I need you to tell Tsang to come see me. Tell him it's urgent." James turned around to look at the safe. He grabbed for one of his other burner phones and typed out a couple of quick messages on it as well.

Then the first burner phone buzzed. Glancing down, James saw that his first message had been received and that his asset could meet at Site W for lunch. James sent a swift response, letting him know the meeting had to be pushed to dinner. He couldn't meet in four hours—it'd take him at least three hours of wandering through the city to shake any possible trails he might pick up as he left the building. Plus, he still had other balls he needed to get in motion before they met.

****

Thirty minutes later, his head of counterintelligence, Mr. Tsang, made his way into his office. As the two men sat down at the small table next to his desk, James relayed the pertinent information from his call this morning with the Minister.

"I need you to work your sources today and firm up any connections we may have that lead back to Mr. Lau or clear him. I believe we're going to need to make our arrest tomorrow, and once we do, we need to be able to grab the entire cell. Do we have enough information yet to connect Mr. Lau to this foreign intelligence ring?"

Mr. Tsang shook his head. "Not in the court of public opinion," he replied. "Mr. Lau and his family are institutions in Hong Kong politics. Removing him or a close relative is going to cause problems. One of my sources said his cousin may have been recruited by Australian intelligence, but I'm still trying to verify that with our sources in Australia. We could probably lay most of the blame on a distant relative, but going after Mr. Lau will cause problems if it isn't rock solid."

James sighed. He needed to pin what was going to happen next on someone. *But who?* he wondered nervously.

"Hmm...OK...I agree with your assessment," he said. "That's essentially what I told the Minister as well. But if these saboteurs are going to make their move tomorrow or the day after, we don't have much time to ferret out these other leads. We'll have to snatch everyone else up, or they'll go to ground and we may never find them again." James cracked his knuckles. "I need you to do your best and be ready to grab them when I tell you. In the meantime, have your people start connecting all the dots that'll tie Mr. Lau in with all of this or clear him."

Mr. Tsang nodded and went to work.

Next, he spoke with a couple of his IT guys, who would surreptitiously place several concealed cameras in the server room. If this malware was going to get introduced into the system, that was where it'd be done, and he wanted a set of eyes watching it when it happened.

****

Around 2 p.m., James grabbed one of his burner phones and some petty cash from his safe. He shoved a new hat, some fake glasses, a change of pants and extra shoes into a bag. Leaving his office, James walked to the stairwell and headed down a couple of floors before he made his way over to a janitor closet, out of the line of sight of the CCTV cameras. Once inside, he donned his new outfit.

With his appearance changed, James made his way to one of the side elevators and used his special access code to take him to the sub-basement level of the building. Then he traveled down a long corridor that connected his building with the subway system nearby. James opened a couple of hidden door panels and then slipped into the throng of people traveling the underground transportation system of the city.

As he stood in line waiting for the next train to arrive, his eyes suddenly focused on one of the TV monitors, which was playing a creatively edited battlefield video from somewhere in America. The Ministry of Information in Beijing had been producing these videos—they almost seemed choreographed to James, but they were meant to assure the people that China was winning and to inspire the young men of the country to join the armed forces. James noticed that they had added a segment to explain the incentive program of awarding American wives to those who served in the war effort and returned home at the end of the war. With more than thirty million men without a wife, the idea was very alluring.

Of course, the videos made no mention of the mounting casualties, the stunning defeat of Chinese forces in Colorado, or more recently, the loss of the Panama Canal. All they focused on was China's continued support of the UN peacekeeping mission to liberate America from the tyrannical dictator Jonathan Sachs.

With no access to news outside of what the government allowed people to see, the rest of the commuting public had no way of knowing that the UN peacekeeping mission had collapsed. The news made no mention of how the UN had been manipulated into removing Jonathan Sachs, and it certainly didn't mention that China was now fighting this war alone. James realized that if the people knew the truth—knew what the government was doing with the Q Program—they'd revolt.

When the train arrived, James hopped on and began his three-hour countersurveillance route. He jumped over to a couple of different lines, then took several different taxis before he ended by walking a couple of miles through some of the densely packed sidewalks and alleyways of the city. Eventually, he wound up at the bar and noodle shop that was the agreed upon Site W.

Ten minutes after he placed his order, his food was placed in front of him. When the server put his spoon down, he also placed a small piece of paper next to it. James opened the folded note and found a message telling him to use the bathroom in the back.

Grabbing the note, James crumpled it up and placed it next to the candle on the bar. The paper burned up moments later, leaving no trace of the message. James waited a few minutes, just long enough to eat some of his food before he got up and headed to the washroom.

When James entered the bathroom, he saw a man standing against the wall, relieving himself into one of the urinals. James approached the urinal next to him and did the same.

In a hushed tone, the man next to him said, "You said you had something urgent that we needed to talk about."

Not taking his eyes off the newspaper article attached to the wall in front of him, James softly replied, "Yes. They're on to us. You need to make your move by tomorrow, or the day after at the latest. I won't be able to hold off the raids on your cell for much longer."

A moment of silence passed between the two men before the man inquired, "Do you have the thumb drive with you?"

Moving a micro USB drive into his left hand, James replied, "Yes. Everything is there. But you have to have it ready by tomorrow."

A short pause ensued as the man briefly glanced down at his hand and the USB. "That might not be enough time, but we'll do our best."

"Make sure you're out of sight once this goes down," James insisted. "Once we have your guy in custody, we're going to nab the rest of your cell. We have to make this look legitimate."

While James was talking, his asset took the small USB drive from his hand and placed it in his pocket. The man walked over to the sink and proceeded to wash his hands before he looked into the mirror at James. "This had better work," he asserted. "A lot of good people are going to die for this."

"A lot *more* are going to die if this war continues."

****

"Do you trust him?" asked Fong's handler, a man known to him only as H.

Fong didn't answer right away. He hadn't thought about it. His mind had been focused on getting the program ready for tomorrow. Eventually, he responded, "He hasn't lied to us yet."

"That doesn't mean he won't pinch us if it means saving his own ass."

"True. But if he wanted to take us down, he would have. He wouldn't have warned us, and he sure as hell wouldn't have given us this," Fong replied, holding up the thumb drive.

"Is the information on there legit?" H asked, still skeptical.

Their IT savant, Benedict, had been going over the lines of code in the program for several hours at this point. He turned away from his computer screen just long enough to say, "It's legit. It's pretty incredible. They've really put a lot of IP redundancies in place to make sure nothing actually gets in or out of their closed internet ecosystem."

H turned his attention to the engineer. "Are you going to be able to punch enough holes in it that we'll be able to start propagating the *real* news of what's going on outside of China?"

"I think so," Benedict replied. "Right now, I'm preparing the videos of the major battles, the casualty numbers, names of Chinese POWs, and all the information we have about the genocides and kidnappings taking place in North America and here in China. This'll get propagated to tens of thousands of chat boards and popular sites throughout the country, making sure everyone that has a smartphone or internet access sees it."

"I'd settle for opening up the internet so the people can readily search for news and the truth about what's really going on with this war," Fong countered.

"Something about this still doesn't sit right with me," H insisted.

"What is it, boss?" asked Fong.

"I know you trust your source, but I'm not sold on him. The last-minute meeting today, the insistence on launching the operation tomorrow, the warning that a dragnet is coming…no, I don't like it." He cracked his knuckles. "Once the USB is ready for delivery, have several other copies made and distributed to our other sources. If this is a sting operation, I want to make sure we have several backup plans in place."

It took until around 2 a.m. before Benedict had finished making the necessary changes to the code from Fong's source. H again insisted that other copies be made. "I'll work to make sure the other cleaning crews have these, ready to be inserted into the first available USB terminals

they can find," he explained. "If our cell is about to get burned, then I'm going to make sure we go out with a bang."
****

Beijing, China

General Wu Guanhua looked at the small gold coin in his hand, and his thumb ran across the inscription. He'd been summoned—for what he didn't know, but as he looked out the window, he saw that the vehicle was already pulling up to the gate leading to the private villa.

Though he never expressed his opinion aloud, General Wu always enjoyed these private dinners that Peng An hosted whenever he called a meeting of the Society. Sadly, they hadn't held a meeting since the start of the war. The few members Wu knew were like him—incredibly busy trying to make sure China didn't lose the fight it had picked.

Tonight's summoning felt different. Wu wasn't sure how or why just yet, but he was certain that whatever was going to be discussed tonight was something that would change all of their lives.

His driver pulled the vehicle around the circle driveway and stopped under the covered courtyard entrance. An attendant dressed in a three-piece suit and white gloves stepped forward and opened Wu's door for him. Then Wu was ushered through the outer courtyard to the main entrance of the home.

As soon as he stepped through the door, Wu saw his friend Peng An standing there waiting for him. The two bowed and greeted each other. Wu and Peng had been friends now for more than thirty years. Peng's family were bankers, money changers, and Wu's family were military officers within the PLA. Through the decades, both of their families had benefited greatly from the arrangements they'd made together—the purchasing of a specific weapon system here, the investment in the right company at the right time there. It was all a well-orchestrated power grab.

Wu and Peng were both also members of the Thule Society, although Wu knew Peng to be a much higher-level member of the secretive organization than he was.

"General, I am glad you were able to meet," Peng said as he motioned for them to head toward the well-appointed quiet room he'd created.

"It's been more than a year since we last met," Wu responded. "I'm sure we have much to discuss."

Peng smiled at the comment. "Indeed, we do."

The two made their way through the luxurious house to the study in the rear. Once there, they walked over to shelves, where Peng pulled a couple of different books partially out and then stood back. Moments later, there was a slight hissing noise as the bookshelf slid inward, revealing a hidden hallway.

General Wu had been down here once before, many years ago. Most of the time, they'd just discuss what they needed to in the study. Apparently, that wouldn't suffice today.

The two of them made their way down the hallway to a set of stairs. At the bottom was a room adorned with overstuffed leather chairs, maps, and several ornate wooden end tables made of teak. There was also a self-service bar for those who wanted a stiff drink.

Upon entering the room, Wu lifted an eyebrow when he saw two other men there: General Ma Xingrui, one of Wu's subordinates and the head of the PLA Rocket Forces, and Zhou Gang, the head of the Bank of China. Seeing that the two most powerful military men in the country were present as well as the two most influential financial men in China, Wu immediately knew what this meeting was about.

The others already had a drink in hand, so Wu made his way over to the wet bar and fixed himself a bourbon. Then he walked over to one of the leather chairs and took a seat.

Peng cleared his throat. "Please produce your coin and place it on the table in front of you," he directed.

Moments later, Wu, Ma, and Zhou each placed an identical gold coin on the table.

Smiling, Peng said, "There, now you each know the other is a member of the Society, in case you didn't already. I called this urgent meeting because we have important business that needs to be discussed. Time is of the essence, and decisions need to be made."

There was an awkward moment of silence as they all sized each other up. Then Peng An asked, "How many of you know who Roberto Lamy is?"

General Wu and the two other men nodded solemnly but said nothing.

"Good. Then this will make sense. As you may know, the Americans captured him many months ago. He's the main reason why the UN peacekeeping mission collapsed. Unfortunately, he's also divulged the Society's involvement. Once the Americans knew it was the Thule Society that had engineered everything from the beginning, that we were the ones pulling the strings, they've been systematically hunting down our members—"

Leaning forward and interrupting Peng, Zhou insisted, "Roberto doesn't even know who everyone in the organization *is*. He can't provide them with all of our names." Zhou lifted his drink to his lips and took a swig of the dark liquid.

Peng shook his head dismissively. "That's not entirely true. Roberto led them to Erik Jahn. The Norwegian government detained him, placing him under house arrest while they tried to figure out what to do with him. Before they processed Erik through their justice system, the Americans captured him. Since then, the Americans have been debriefing him for months. I don't know if he is being tortured for information or if he's cut some sort of deal—but what I *do* know is that members of the Society have been regularly disappearing."

"How many people are we talking about, Peng?" inquired General Wu.

"Gentlemen, I think you're missing the bigger picture here. It's not the number of people who are missing. It's the fact that the Americans know about the Society, and they are systematically dismantling it. Worse, they may be using our associates' membership to blackmail them to do what they want, when they want. This is a profoundly serious situation," Peng explained with greater urgency.

General Ma leaned forward in his chair. "Peng, while this is serious, we have bigger problems than members of the Society going missing. If we don't figure out how to bring this war with America to a close, *none* of this will matter, at least not to General Wu and me. President Chen is losing patience with our strategy. He will look to make a change if we're not able to deliver him some victories soon."

Wu grunted at the prognosis but didn't challenge Ma. He knew the writing was on the wall, and he wasn't going to stay in power much longer if he wasn't able to turn the war around.

Peng furrowed his brow. He turned to look at Wu as if asking if Ma was telling him the truth. Wu nodded softly but didn't say anything.

Shaking his head in frustration, Peng finally blurted out, "Then Chen needs to be replaced."

Zhou was the first to speak. "You can't be serious, Peng," he asserted. "He's too protected, and I doubt the Society would back that play. He was specifically appointed to his position to lead China into the future."

Peng snorted dismissively at the comment. "Yes, he was," he admitted. "But he was specifically chosen to lead China into becoming the dominant power in Asia. Do you still believe that's possible, given how the war has turned out up to this point?"

Zhou shrank back a little deeper in his chair.

Seizing the moment, Peng added, "Exactly, Zhou. The Americans just captured the Panama Canal. Even now, their naval force, led by their two new Arsenal ships, is sailing up the California coast. In less than a week, our forces in North America will be cut off from our supply lines. Our Navy will have to retreat, abandoning our forces thousands of miles from home. Am I right?" Peng looked at Wu for support.

Under any other circumstance, General Wu would never disclose nor acknowledge such classified information. However, these were members of the Society—men he could truly trust.

Wu sighed. "Peng is correct, Zhou. I'm afraid there isn't anything we can do to stop their Navy," he admitted. "We're going to marshal our remaining naval forces in the South China Sea, but we don't have a weapon system that can defeat this new Arsenal ship they've built."

General Ma added, "Short of using nuclear mines or torpedoes, our Navy isn't going to be able to defeat them. And if we do resort to nuclear mines or torpedoes, you can bet the Americans will retaliate with further nuclear weapons of their own. While I'd like to say we could weather their strikes, in reality, we can't. The country is already experiencing continual brownouts. We barely have enough electricity to keep our factories going. We're running out of fuel, we're running out of raw materials, and we're running out of food, Zhou. The situation is much worse than most people realize."

The banker looked at the two military men in shock. He clearly couldn't believe things had become so bleak.

Sitting forward in his chair again, Zhou asked, "What are we supposed to do Peng? I suppose you have a plan?"

Smiling, Peng nodded.

****

Hong Kong

"Are we set?" asked James nervously.

"Yes," answered Bruce, one of the network security guys. "We've disconnected that row of servers from the intranet and internet. If the janitor attempts to insert the malware via a USB device, it'll be quarantined at once."

"What if the janitor tries to use a USB port on any of the thousands of computers in the building?" James asked, wanting to make sure nothing had been overlooked.

Bruce shook his head. "It won't matter. They've all been disabled. Even if they did find a way into the network, the malware would still have to travel through that server." He pointed at the screen. "In either case, it'll be quarantined before it'll be able to do any damage."

James could see that Bruce seemed very confident. He hoped the man was right.

****

More than three hours later, James still sat in the security room, watching multiple screens of cleaning crews. He began to wonder if these saboteurs were going to act today or not.

Just as James thought for sure it wasn't going to happen, the janitor that regularly cleaned the server farm finally entered the room and everyone perked up. Four of James's best security agents joined him in observing the multiple camera angles of the janitor. They watched scrupulously as he began his cleaning routine. Normally, the man would run his broom up and down each row of servers, gathering up all the dust bunnies that had formed since his last visit. Next, he'd prepare a fresh bucket of water and disinfectant and mop the floors. Finally, the man would swap out the trash bag, and then he'd leave the server farm.

Nearby, a couple of network administrators continued working in the room as if he wasn't there. James was certain that in their minds, he was a ghost, unworthy of their attention.

Janitors make the best sources, James thought, almost chuckling. They operated in plain sight, yet they were invisible to everyone around them.

****

Chow Yick-hay always admired the spectacular view from the Chief Executive's office. Victoria Harbor was absolutely stunning from here.

But I'm not here for the view, he reminded himself. He went back to cleaning.

He walked around the desk. The trash can was half-full. As he reached down to grab the can so he could change it out, he grabbed for the small USB device he had hidden in a compartment in his watch, disconnecting the keyboard from the USB connection and then attaching his own microdevice on the end of it before reconnecting the device to the computer. The entire process took a couple of seconds.

Chow then grabbed the half-full trash bag in his hand and brought it over to his cleaning trolley. The Chief Executive still sat on the couch, reading his newspaper—oblivious to the Trojan horse that had just been left in his office.

"Are you nearly done?" Mr. Lau asked. "I have work I need to get back to." He impatiently scanned the headlines of this periodical that was one of the few authorized newspapers in China.

Lowering his head out of respect, Chow mumbled something to himself and collected up his cleaning supplies, leaving the room.

Once out of the office, he did his best to blend in with everyone as he made his way over to the elevator and eventually the exit, leaving the building. Now it was a race against time, time to get as far away from here as possible.

****

Just when James didn't think the janitor was going to insert the USB device, they watched him fiddle with something on his watch.

"Wow. Did you see that? Talk about hidden compartments," said one of the agents watching the screen in admiration.

James had to admit, that was a pretty slick move, having a false crystal on a watch to hide something in. With a sleight of hand, the janitor had produced the device from the hidden compartment on his watch and effortlessly inserted it into one of the USB ports on the back of the server as he used a dust rag to grab at a dust bunny behind the server rack.

The entire thing had happened so fast, they had nearly missed it. Had they not placed so many different cameras to cover the area, they might have. The man was good, and highly trained. He knew how to do this sort of thing without being caught.

"Should we arrest him?" asked one of his security agents.

James shook his head. "No, not yet. Have our agent place the tracking device on him. I want a full surveillance team on this guy from the moment he leaves this building. We're going to follow him back to wherever he goes from here and see who else he leads us to. In the meantime, I want that device removed and analyzed. Let's see what they just tried to do, shall we?"

The others nodded and went to work on making it so.

****

For the next hour, James's surveillance teams followed the janitor after he left the building a full three hours ahead of the end of his shift. This was clearly the man they were looking for. The guy knew they'd be after him and he was doing his best to leave the scene of the crime. What he didn't know was that, on his way out the door, one of his security guards had sprayed him with a liquid that would show up under a certain UV light setting they could change their surveillance cameras to detect. This effectively let them follow anyone they wanted through a crowded city without fear of losing them, so long as the individual stayed in sight of one of the millions of CCTV cameras that covered practically every inch of the city.

Now they'd sit back and wait to see who else the janitor led them to, and then they'd move in.

****

Mr. Lau logged back in to his computer terminal once he had finished his morning tea and caught up on the latest headlines. He had waited another twenty minutes after the janitor had left before he'd made his way back to his desk to resume his daily duties.

As the Chief Executive for Hong Kong, he was a busy man. The city, while not completely autonomous from the Mainland, did enjoy a level of freedom and autonomy not found in the other provinces. Then again, like Shanghai, Hong Kong brought an enormous amount of wealth to China.

Once Lau was logged in to his computer, he finished typing up his report on the most recent round of protests. People had taken to the streets nearly every day for the last two weeks, frustrated with the lack of information being shared by the government about the war in North America. Sure, they were being fed choreographed messages by the Ministry of Information, but many of them had loved ones fighting in the military and they had no idea if they were still alive or dead. Many thousands of people would just suddenly stop receiving letters from their loved ones in the Army.

The report Lau was about to send was one he'd been working on for several days. In it, he made several recommendations to address the problem and return good order and discipline to the city. Namely, he was advocating for the Army to release the casualty figures. People had a right to know if their loved ones had been killed or captured. Lau was confident that if he could obtain this concession from the Central Committee, his popularity within the city would go up.

It was shortly after three p.m. when he finished the last touches on his report. Once that was completed, he typed up a short email message and attached the report to it. With nothing more to do, he hit send and it was dispatched to his superiors in Beijing.

What Chief Executive Lau didn't know was that when he'd logged in to his computer terminal, the malware on the USB device attached to his keyboard had already gone to work. When he attached his email and sent it out, that email traveled from the server in Hong Kong to another server on the Mainland. From there, it was sent to several more servers before it landed in the inbox of the recipients he had sent it to. Like a sick person traveling through an airport, each time the email landed on a new server, it infected that server.

As each server became infected, the malware spread like an unknown patient zero who didn't yet know they were sick. Within a day, the malware would be in every server across the country, and the government would be powerless to do anything about it—that was, once it was activated and they discovered what had happened.

****

Later that evening, James placed his call to his boss. He'd just received the final report from one of his surveillance teams. They had taken the last person into custody. In all, they had captured a spy ring of eighteen janitors across both cleaning companies. Tomorrow, they would make their arrests of the other known spies in the contracting companies. These arrests would cement James's position within the MSS and assure him of a much higher-level position.

The video call connected on the third ring.

"Director Chan, I hope you're calling me to tell me you have neutralized this threat to our country?" his boss asked.

James lifted his chin up a bit as he replied, "I am. We caught one of the individuals in the act of sabotaging one of our servers. We followed him throughout the rest of his day and he eventually led us to several coconspirators. In all, we apprehended eighteen spies working among the two janitorial contracting companies."

The man's demeanor changed dramatically. "This is excellent news. Have you found any other spies in these contracting companies?"

James nodded. "Yes. We have identified another nineteen, spread across three other vendors. We're continuing to monitor them to see if they lead us to any additional people or a wider network of spies," James announced, laying out his grand plan.

"Excellent news, Chan. Just make sure you don't allow these spies to carry out whatever mission it is they're trying to do," said the Director sternly. "What about Mr. Lau? Is he involved? Does he know what is going on?"

James shrugged slightly. "I'm not sure. We have no direct link that says he knows what they're doing. But he may have been intentionally left out of the loop. I'd like to continue my investigation into his brother, cousins and uncle to determine if they're also involved in this or if their firms were just being used for this purpose without their knowledge."

His boss nodded. "OK, Chan. Continue your investigation, but I want some sort of results by the end of the month. We need to make sure the people of Hong Kong know we are the ones in charge and not them. Our granting of autonomy to run as a semi-independent state is largely dependent on their being compliant with our laws, and not undermining our government."

With nothing more to be said, the call ended. For the time being, James Chan continued to believe his cover was safe and that he had properly identified and apprehended his patsies.

Chapter Seven
Project Cyberstorm

Camp Peary, Virginia

When the brief finished, Major General Lancaster looked at Leah Riesling and Tony Wildes, feeling both awe at what they had come up with and a bit of skepticism about its success.

"Do you really believe this could end the war?" he asked.

Tony jumped at the question before Leah had a chance. "Yes. Our source in China says the average person has no idea what's going on outside the country. The information about what's going on with the war is so tightly controlled, the government hasn't even been releasing the casualty figures. The aerial bombardments of their cities is also having an impact on the people's psyche. Prior to the war, the average Chinese citizen had a positive opinion of America. They had friends and family that lived here. Even under the tight controls of information, they were still able to find out what was going on outside their borders. Now, the government has so thoroughly clamped down on the flow of information that the average person is completely in the dark."

Leah added, "It's more than just being kept in the dark—their government has been feeding them disinformation about the start of this war and its continuation since the beginning. Right now, the average Chinese person still believes this is a UN-led mission and that their army is fighting alongside American patriots trying to liberate their country. They've been systematically lied to from the very beginning. When the truth gets out, when they learn what's really happening, it'll shatter their support and trust of the central government."

The room was silent as they digested what they'd heard. Then Lancaster announced, "Then I think it's time we brief this to the President and get his permission to initiate this operation."

****

Washington, D.C.
White House
Situation Room

"So you're telling me all we have to do is send a coded message and their entire firewall will collapse?" asked the President skeptically.

"It's more than that, Mr. President," insisted Deputy Director Wildes. "We designed the Cyberstorm malware to propagate the testimony of Roberto Lamy to every bulletin board, chat room and news agency across China. It'll also post all the casualty numbers the PLA has been hiding from them. It'll show the videos of the mass executions their Army has been doing and the abduction of our women and where they're being held in China. Once this goes live, it's going to blow up their entire country and government."

The NSA had been relishing the chance to unleash the Cyberstorm malware on China. After all that had happened to their organization during the war, they were itching for some payback to be fully unleashed on America's adversaries.

"If the NSA moves forward with this, you say it'll blow up their government, their country. Isn't it possible that the government would just shut down the internet?" asked Robert Grey. "Or wipe the infected servers clean of this malware?"

"Yes and no," Wildes responded. "They could shut down the country's internet. The challenge in doing so is that, like the rest of the world, they've become dependent on it. They use the internet for banking, email, order fulfillments and other important functions just as we do. If they turned the internet off, they'd effectively be turning China off.

"As to wiping the servers clean, they can try, but they won't be successful. We designed this malware in such a way that it would be virtually impossible to wipe out. The challenge in destroying the malware is it self-replicates. In the five days since it was released, it's been able to propagate itself to nearly every server in the country. It's on almost every smartphone, laptop, tablet, smartwatch, smart fridge, microwave and desktop computer in China. Hell, Mr. President—if you ask Alexa, she'll tell you the Party is full of malarkey. Any device that can send or receive email has likely become infected with it."

The President leaned forward. "If we do this and it does implode their government, what happens next? How do we end this war?"

Mike Howell, the Secretary of Defense, boldly said, "We negotiate with the senior PLA commander in North America. We get him to agree to an end to the war, and we work to get his soldiers returned to China."

"I think the bigger question we haven't asked is if this brings down the regime, who's going to replace them?" said Secretary Kagel. "How will we get our citizens repatriated to America? What happens to the rest of the country?"

The President nodded. "That's something else we need to consider before we unleash this thing," he replied. "Do we have to activate this plan now, or can we wait a little while longer to figure some of these questions out?"

"It doesn't need to be released now," Wildes responded. "The longer it sits dormant, the more it continues to propagate. That said, the longer it sits dormant, the better chance there is of the Chinese stumbling across it before it's able to activate. If that happens, they might be able to start wiping it out before we're able to initiate it."

President Sachs sighed audibly. He sat back in his chair as he thought about what Wildes had just said. They weren't ready to release this thing yet, but holding off too long could jeopardize the one thing that might end the war.

Sitting back up and leaning forward, the President turned to Kagel. "I want a plan drawn up for what to do if the regime falls. We need to figure out what'll happen with Taiwan and other places. I suspect if the regime falls, it'll fracture into smaller regional countries—which is fine, but we need to make sure it doesn't become another Balkans or Afghanistan of warring factions. I also want to know what the Indians are going to do. If they aren't going to open another front soon, then I want them to tell us now. They've been stringing us along for six months and I'm done with waiting. The tides have turned; they can join us and be on the winning side, or they can sit out. But I want an answer."

"Yes, Mr. President," Kagel said, scribbling a few notes in her notebook.

Sachs turned to his military leaders. "Mike, I want you guys to cut off the Chinese ground forces from the Mainland—strangle them until they capitulate. We've put everything into those new Arsenal ships. I want them put to use now that we've retaken the Panama Canal. I also want you guys to step up your operations on retaking Texas and the rest of the southern border. We have to stop this butchery of our people. My fear is that the PLA Army will only become more genocidal than they already are if their homeland falls apart."

The next hour was spent going over what specifically needed to happen before the NSA unleashed the Cyberstorm attack on China. Once that genie was out of the bottle, there would be no going back.

Chapter Eight
King for a Queen

Camp Peary, Virginia

Lieutenant Colonel Seth Mitchell sat in the discussion room, looking at the map of the United States on the wall. His eyes then wandered over to the map of the world. Little yellow flagged pins had been stuck into the countries where Erik Jahn had said the Thule Society either had a member in control of the government or effectively controlled the nation from behind the scenes. There was also a red-flagged pin assigned to each country that had participated in the UN peacekeeping mission that had attacked the US. There were many countries with both yellow and red flags pinned to them.

Ashley walked into the room, bringing a couple cups of fresh coffee and a sugary pastry with her. She smiled when she saw Seth.

"I brought you some brain juice," she said as she sat down in the chair next to him.

Seth smiled. "Awesome. I was needing a break."

He grabbed the coffee and took a sip of the piping hot java juice. Then he eyed her pastry. "You know those things are terrible for you, right?"

Ashley blushed. "Of course they are, but a girl's gotta have some indulgences," she replied in defense.

Seth snickered. "I'd normally be on that pastry like a fat kid on a Snickers bar, but I've been trying to stick to this diet my wife has me on."

"When's the last time you saw your wife?" asked Ashley.

He paused to think about that for a moment. "June," he answered. "I had a four-day pass. I flew down to Tampa to spend some time at home in my own bed and just be lazy with the family."

"Well, I'm sure you can splurge and have a Danish if you want," Ashley said with a smirk. She pushed the cinnamon apple Danish toward him.

"This is how it starts…I cheat once, then it's all downhill from there. I think I'll pass," he replied mischievously.

Ashley let out a guttural laugh. "Well, I wouldn't want you to cheat," she said with a wink. "But back to business. I'm troubled by something—maybe you can help me out."

Seth went back to business mode. "Sure. What do you have?"

"Why is Erik telling us all this?" she said as she waved at the map with all the little yellow flags on it. On the wall next to it were pictures and dossiers of everyone in those countries that Erik said was part of this Thule Society.

Leaning forward in his chair, Seth said, "It's simple. He wants us to take them out for him."

Her left eyebrow rose. "Really? Is that all?"

Seth shrugged. "Does it matter why he's doing it?" he pressed. "His information has checked out thus far. While I'd like to know the why, it doesn't matter right now. The fact that he's helping us unravel this global conspiracy does."

"You know that drug kingpin El Chapo that was busted a few years ago, right? You know how they got him, don't you?" Ashley asked.

"I had my head buried in some other work at the time," Seth said, shaking his head. "I wasn't following the case."

"OK. But you know who he is, right?"

"Of course."

"Well, they caught the guy because they caught his IT guy," Ashley explained. "The IT guy flipped, and he was able to provide the FBI and DEA with all the information we needed to arrest and convict him."

"OK. What's your point?" Seth asked.

"I feel like Erik is the IT guy. He's giving up information on these guys to save his own ass. But there has to be more to it."

Seth smiled and shook his head. "Not quite, Ashley. You have it backwards. Erik is El Chapo. He's selling out the organization so he can skate free with his money and freedom intact."

Ashley opened her mouth to say something, then stopped as if she was letting what Seth said sink in for a moment. Then she became visibly angry. "If you know this, then why are we letting him get away with it?" she grilled him. "And what do you mean by ratting out the organization so he can keep his money and walk?"

Seth held a hand up. "We've known for a little while what he's been doing, Ashley. We're letting it happen because the powers that be have a higher purpose for Erik."

Ashley paused. "You mean he's being recruited by the CIA to be a source for them once all this is said and done?" she inquired.

Seth shrugged. "Does it matter, Ashley?" he countered. "Right now, our country is in the fight of its life. We have to figure out how to defeat the Chinese and put our country back together. When all this is said and done, we're going to need some well-connected friends to help us put the world back together, not tear it further apart."

"Huh. Well, how do you suppose he's going to help us with China?" Ashley asked.

"That is the big question. I suppose we'll find out in twenty minutes when he gets here. General Lancaster and Leah Riesling from the NSA are going to question him on that very topic."

****

Major General Lancaster walked into the conference room that had turned into the task force's unofficial war room of sorts. The walls were adorned with maps, dossiers, and other pieces of information pertinent to their mission of hunting down the persons responsible for the rigging of the US election.

The others in the room all stood when Lancaster entered, and he motioned for them to take their seats. Lancaster sat down at the head of the table. On one side of him sat his JSOC commander, Paddy, and his Agency reps, Lieutenant Colonel Seth Mitchell and Admiral Chester Smith. On the other side of the table were his two NSA reps along with his DoD rep and their guest of honor, Erik Jahn, who looked surprisingly upbeat.

"OK, people. We've done a good job of vetting Erik's information and identifying the coconspirators involved in this entire UN debacle and invasion of our country," Lancaster began. "Now we have to figure out how we can weaponize the information we have to destabilize and topple the Chinese government."

Lancaster turned to look at Erik. "Mr. Jahn, I appreciate what you've done up to this point—helping us identify and track down these people has been an important part of your restitution in all of this. That said, I have another big ask. If you can help us with this, I have been told all charges against you will be dropped. Furthermore, you'll have the option of returning to your old life in Norway or be given a new identity and be allowed to disappear inside America. In either case, you'll be given back a portion of your wealth, but obviously not all of it."

Erik looked a little pained. Someone who had worked hard enough in life to have gotten where Erik had wouldn't want to lose it all, General Lancaster thought.

Erik Jahn looked around the table. "What can I do for you, General?" he asked.

Lancaster stood and walked over to the map. He pointed to China. "I need to know from your perspective. How would you topple China?"

Erik sat back in his chair. He looked up at the ceiling for a moment and then back at the map. Then he suddenly sat up straight, as if a lightbulb had been turned on.

"I would try to pit their military against their political leaders—get them to fracture the government from within," he suggested.

"And how would you do this?" asked Lancaster.

"Money. I'd buy them off."

"Not everyone can be bought, Erik," interjected Leah Riesling from the NSA. "Some folks are loyal to their unit, their state or their country."

"Point taken," Erik replied with a nod. "But you don't need their entire military to turn on their government. I've followed the news about what's going on in Texas and California. The Chinese have a several-million-man army that's about to be trapped here—abandoned by their government. I'd try to see if these commanders could be bought. If you offered to allow them to head back to China and pay their Army's salary, they could liberate a region or two of China and call it their own country. Especially if you offered them military support until they got themselves organized."

"That's a proposal we've been circulating at the Joint Staff as well," added the DoD rep from the Pentagon. "It could work."

Turning to look at Erik, Lancaster followed up. "You said Peng An is a senior member of the Thule Society. Is it possible to use Peng to instigate this takedown?"

Erik looked up at the ceiling for a moment. "It's possible," he replied. "You aren't going to like this, but I'd have to talk to Peng about it."

Seeing that Erik wanted to say something more, Lancaster said, "I'd like everyone to leave the room. I need to talk with Mr. Jahn here alone."

As everyone was getting up, Erik lifted his right hand. "If you don't mind, General, I'd like Josh here to stay," he said, pointing to Seth. "I trust him."

Lancaster grunted. "If he stays, so does Smith, OK?"

Erik nodded. The room cleared and it was just the four of them.

"I saw you pause when you said you needed to talk to Peng," remarked General Lancaster. "I cleared the room, so it's just us. What was the hesitation?"

Erik smiled. "I didn't know who had been apprised of the deal I've reached with you, your President, and your CIA."

"Fair enough. It's just us—me, our two CIA guys, and you. So let's talk."

"When this war is over, I'm going to be able to assume control of the Society a lot more easily, which means I'll have a better pulse on what's going on in the world than any intelligence agency. That said, I think I can end your war with China if I can talk with Peng."

"How so?" Lancaster pressed.

Sighing, Erik looked at Lancaster. "You aren't going to like this, but this is how it'll have to work. I can probably convince Peng An to side with us, but only if you—meaning America—and I, the soon-to-be new leader of our group, assure Peng that he can replace Chen Baohua as the new leader of China. The man's always had his eyes set on the ultimate prize, but he was never going to be in a position to rise up to be President—not after Chen made himself leader for life."

Lancaster scoffed at the idea. He turned and looked at the map as he mumbled a few words to himself. Shaking his head, he turned back to look at Erik. "I don't think that would work. Peng doesn't have the trust or backing of the military. He may be one of the key money guys in China, but all that means is he can be the piggy bank. He couldn't be the leader. We need someone that has pull and respect within the military."

Lancaster paused for a second before adding, "It might be easier if we looked at a strategy that broke China up."

"You mean break them into regional powers?" asked Erik. "I don't know that that would work. China has a long and rich history that ties them together. I don't know that you can divide them up like that."

"What do you know of General Wu Guanhua?" asked Smith.

Erik's eyebrows rose. "The head of the PLA?"

Smith nodded.

"He's a member of the Society," Erik confirmed. "If I can talk with Peng, he might be able to convince Wu of the need for a change at the top. This is all pretty risky, though. If Peng is turned in, he'll be killed. He's our senior member of the Society in China."

Lancaster sighed out of frustration. He looked at Erik. "Take the next couple of days and think about this problem. Work with Smith and 'Josh' here, and let's reconvene in a couple of days with ideas about how we can make this work."

Chapter Nine
Battle for New Mexico

April 2022
EMRTC Facility

"I can't wait to get off this damn mountain," complained Crispy as he lay on his back, finishing off part of an MRE.

Janus flicked a bug off his hand. "You know what's underneath this place, right?" he asked cryptically.

Crispy and Punisher, their team lead, looked at him quizzically.

"What do you mean 'what's under this place'?" asked Punisher. He stretched his back, causing a few vertebrae to pop and crack.

Janus waved his hand around in a circle. "This entire place is a secret weapons lab and storage facility," he explained.

"What? No way. If that were the case, the Chinese would have a lot more defenses set up around here," Crispy replied nonchalantly, whisking his hand through the air as if he were literally waving away the statement.

Classic Janus—always trying to prove he knows more about every topic, thought Crispy.

Janus shook his head disapprovingly. "No. You don't get it, man," he insisted. "This place is called the Energetic Materials Research and Testing Center—that's a code word for secret weapons lab. You forget, my family's from these parts. My uncle used to work here many years ago, before he retired and moved to Colorado. He said they used to test all sorts of weapons: railguns, direct energy weapons, special bullets, munitions and things like that. It's all done underneath the mountain here. Inside this place are more than forty different storage facilities and weapon testing ranges. It's all being done out of sight, out of mind."

"Really? So, you're trying to say this is some new Area 51 test facility that no one's heard of except you?" Punisher chided. "Come on, Janus. You're going to scare Crispy here. You know he's afraid of things that go bump in the dark and little green men." He chuckled good-naturedly.

"Look at the roads down there," Janus insisted, pointing. "They all head to the mountain, and then they end under a pile of rubble. Whoever was manning this place buried everything before they left. I don't even think the Chinese know what was here."

Punisher shrugged. "Maybe you're right. Or maybe you're just trying to help us kill some time with stories your uncle told you as a kid. In either case, we have four more days on this damn mountain before we change out with the next team. Right now, we need to keep an eye on the interstate and what the PLA is doing. Big Army is going to gear up for another offensive shortly, and we're their eyes and ears out here."

Janus grunted, but the guys all went back to their tasks. They had another hour until they finished their current shifts and swapped duties. Until then, Spider and Bang-Bang would stay up at the observational post around the top of the mountain, using the spotting scope, drones, and some other electronic equipment to monitor the area. When the hour was up, Punisher and Janus would take over at the OP while Crispy monitored the radios and the other two got some food and shut-eye.

****

Punisher lay on his back, reading a spy novel on his Kindle Paperwhite. Suddenly, he heard the double click on the radio, letting him know the guys on the OP had found something of importance. Since they were so close to the enemy, they were trying to minimize their radio transmissions as much as possible. Punisher put his Kindle away, then replied with a single click, letting them know he'd heard their message and was on his way.

Crawling up to the OP, Punisher wiggled his way past a couple of the rollable solar cells at the edge of the hide. The DARPA-designed solar panels allowed them to keep their electronic equipment charged up, which greatly reduced the need to lug around extra batteries and enabled them to leave their equipment up and running continuously.

Punisher lifted the rear lip of the hide and crawled into the little enclave; it had become home during these long and often grueling intelligence-gathering missions. When they'd set up the OP, they had used one of SOCOM's newly designed camouflage netting systems. Not only was it IR inhibiting, it also helped to reduce or eliminate their thermal signatures at night.

Talking just above a whisper, Punisher said, "This had better be good. I was in the middle of reading my favorite David Baldacci novel."

Spider pointed to something. "We've got heavy movement along the interstate," he replied. "It looks like they are bringing some heavy armor toward the front lines. We're also seeing a lot of troop trucks and artillery units. Looks like they might be planning a spoiling attack—or just getting ready for whatever Big Army's about to do."

Punisher nodded. "What about SAMs or AA guns?" he asked. "Those are what the Air Force is concerned about."

"Yup, saw a lot of them as well," Spider said with a nod. "It looks like the Chinese just moved eight new tracked AA gun trucks and a couple of SAM units into the city."

Punisher bit the edge of his lip. "Where are the new SAM trucks located, and how many are in the area now?" he asked.

Spider reached for his map and his notepad, then pointed to a few spots. "Two new SAMs are at the mouth of the valley—the other two split up. One is sitting a few thousand meters below us at the base of the mountain, and the other opposite us on the other side of the valley. They still have two of their SAMs set up near that little airport further south of us and then sixteen of those Type-90 Oerlikon 35mm guns have been placed on the ridges either side of the town."

Punisher sighed in frustration. It was clear the PLA was building this place up with a lot of anti-aircraft guns—that meant they were gearing up for something. They needed to report what they were seeing and stand by to see if the Air Force wanted some help taking these targets down.

"But none of these are HQ-9s, right?" he clarified.

"Hold that thought, guys," Bang-Bang announced. "I see another convoy moving along the interstate." He didn't take his eyes away from the long-range spotting scope as he spoke.

Punisher moved toward him. "What do you see?" he asked. "Just call 'em out, and we'll write it down."

"We've got two HQ-9 trucks along with two radar trucks," Bang-Bang began. "Next, I see ten of those MLRS-type artillery trucks. I can't make out the exact type, but they look to be the ones that launch those 122mm Katusha rockets. There's also a long line of ammo trucks for the rocket artillery following behind them." Bang-Bang paused for a moment before turning to look at Punisher. "I think we're going to see a lot more of these convoys today. Maybe we should send up the drone and have it head down the interstate and see what else may be headed our way. We should also get the Air Force to hit some of these vehicles before they have a chance to set up those new SAM systems."

Punisher nodded. "I agree. Pass me the radio, and I'll get it going."

A moment later, he was holding the hand receiver. Before calling everything in, Punisher took a moment to write down what they'd seen so far, where they were all located, and what the priority targets should be. They were still more than seventy miles behind enemy lines, so it would take some time for air support to get on station. Punisher wanted to be sure that once they showed up, they hit the right targets.

"Hammer Six, this is Halo Two. How copy?"

Punisher sat there waiting for the reply, hoping it wouldn't take too long. The Chinese were getting a lot better at their signals intercept game, dropping ordnance on recon teams operating nearby when they got too chatty on their comms.

The radio crackled a second before he heard the familiar beep of the SINCGARS radio.

"Halo Two, Hammer Six. Send. Over."

"Halo Two requesting immediate air strike. Break. Identified two HQ-9 transporters and radar trucks. Break. Identified two battalions' worth of Type 99s. Break. One battalion worth of MLRS artillery trucks. Break. Two battalions' worth of motorized infantry support."

Punisher continued to relay the details of his SITREP to Hammer Six for the next thirty seconds. Looking at his map one last time, he said, "How copy? Over." A few seconds went by before he heard a reply.

"That's a good copy. Crank up your BattleNet and stand by for contact with air units."

BattleNet was a new app feature DARPA had come up with as a means of identifying enemy units to be prosecuted by attack aviation without forcing the ground units to stay on the radios any longer than needed or paint targets with a laser designator, requiring them to remain in the vicinity of the target. BattleNet was a Special Forces version of JSTARS but with a much closer "boots on the ground" flavor. Despite the radio's frequency-hopping capability, the Chinese were getting much better at both jamming the spectrum the SINCGARS radios operated on and using the spikes across the spectrum to narrow down where the transmissions were coming from—BattleNet was a new way for them to avoid this problem entirely.

Before he could say anything, Punisher noticed that Spider had their Toughbook opened to the BattleNet app; an overview of the battlespace was already displayed. He used the mouse to click on certain areas of the map and wrote a short note of what was where. It took him a few minutes to get it all done, but once he had it, he sent it off to the JSOC Southwest, their Special Forces parent command that was coordinating all the Special Operations Forces activities along the front lines, and deep behind them.

For the next ten minutes, Spider and the operator on the other end communicated through a chat box, identifying the priority of targets and where they were all located. It was going to take the Air Force time to get a mission spun up and aircraft loaded out, so they had some time to make sure they got it right.

In the meantime, Punisher had crawled back to their hide and had Janus and Crispy start breaking down the site and preparing to execute their E&E plan. Once the bombs started falling, the ChiComs would know they had trespassers in their AO.

A short time passed and then Bang-Bang suddenly asked, "Boss, do you want the bad news, or the really bad news?"

Punisher crawled back to Bang-Bang and looked through the spotting scope. He lowered his head and clenched his fist.

"Damn," he muttered through clenched teeth.

It only took him a few seconds to realize that the PLA had been busy—the HQ-9 systems were nearly operational. The missiles themselves had been raised and the radar trucks appeared to be in position as well. However, what really caused his stomach to churn was what he saw forming up around the radar trucks. The Chinese had rounded up whatever remaining civilians were left in the town and placed them around the radar trucks. Punisher moved the scope to look at some of the other SAMs that had arrived a few hours ago—more civilians were being held next to them as well.

"What do you want us to do about this?" Bang-Bang repeated, a pained look on his face.

Punisher lowered his head for a moment. He knew there nothing they *could* do. Those vehicles had to be taken out, even if it meant killing the civilians. He looked up at his friend and exhaled slowly.

"Right. We still have to take those vehicles out," he said, angry at his own words as they came out of his mouth.

Punisher was pissed that they were going to have to kill civilians. More and more, the Chinese were using civilians either as human shields or as hostages, killing them publicly unless the American militia groups in the area surrendered or gave up. Citizens were caught between a rock and a hard place with nowhere to run or hide.

Spider broke through the somber mood and silence. "We got our first aircraft on station," he announced, just loud enough for them to hear. "Four F-35s, loaded for ground attack. They're going to prosecute the HQ-9s and the radars with a mixture of JDAMs and AGM-88s. Second sortie is a mixed flight of F-15E and A-10s for the Type 99s and the APCs."

For the next few minutes, they conferred with the pilots, letting them know the situation on the ground. The initial set of AGM-88s were going to go after the radars; then they'd hit the HQ-9s nearly simultaneously and head home. With the most dangerous SAMs neutralized, the other aircraft would then carry out their attack runs on the remaining units and start going after the Chinese tanks and infantry moving toward the front lines.

"Here comes the pain," Spider announced.

Punisher turned his attention to the HQ-9s just in time to witness several massive explosions. Chunks of dirt and several million dollars of now worthless Chinese equipment flew into the air from the force of the blast. For a moment, Punisher smiled—until he saw what else was falling from the sky. The mangled bodies of the civilians who had been forced into being human shields drifted about like torn rag dolls.

Seconds later, the next JDAM hit, blowing apart the last HQ-9 missile pod. With the main threats eliminated, the follow-on sortie of American fighters then went after the defenseless support trucks with their remaining ordnance before heading back to the American lines to rearm and prepare for their next mission.

"Halo Two, Overwatch. How copy?"

Punisher was surprised to hear from the Global Hawk flying above them. He depressed the talk button on the radio.

"Overwatch, Halo Two. Send it."

"Your position is compromised. We're showing a company-sized element of PLA soldiers moving toward your position from the Southeast. How copy?"

Crap! "That's a good copy," Punisher replied. "Do they know where we are, or are they bird-dogging for us?"

A couple seconds of silence passed. "They're spreading out in a line and preparing to advance toward you. They don't appear to have a bead on your position. Estimate you have about thirty mikes until they spot you."

Damn it.

"Good copy. Keep us advised on enemy positions. Moving to secondary location. Out."

Punisher turned to look at his guys. "Guess who's coming to dinner, boys? We gotta boogie! Secondary pos now."

The others had heard Overwatch, so they had already begun breaking down the hide and collecting up their electronic equipment. As soon as they had repacked their rucks and other bags, they jetted over to the secondary position, just below the top of the mountain.

When Punisher arrived, Janus and Crispy were already prepped and had their mechanical BigDog loaded up as well. Bang-Bang finished loading up some of their surveillance gear into the robot to lighten his own load. Having this new tool was useful in that it allowed them to carry more gear on a mission like this, but it was also challenging to keep it powered, and it wasn't always stealthy behind enemy lines. Their team had been tasked with trying to test the BigDog on this mission since they'd largely be in a reconnaissance role.

Once the entire place was packed and sanitized, Punisher led them off the ridge and toward their alternate location. Punisher's helmet emitted a small beep, letting him know his BattleNet was about to transmit a message.

"Halo Two, Halo One. How copy?" It was the other half of their ODA team, positioned on an adjacent ridge.

"Halo One, Lima Charlie. Send it," Punisher replied as he continued his stalk down the backside of the ridge.

"Position has been compromised. We're on our way to join you at the tertiary pos. Break. A PLA patrol stumbled onto our OP. We dealt with it but can't confirm that they didn't send a message for help. Break. I'm asking Hammer to place the QRF on standby and work to get us an evac. How copy?"

Damn it, thought Punisher. If the Chinese had found the captain's team, then they'd be able to find them at this location.

He depressed the talk button as he continued to move. "Good copy, Halo One. Good call. On the move. Out."

For the next twenty minutes, the two ODA teams continued to move toward their tertiary location. Meanwhile, Punisher heard a series of explosion behind them, on the opposite side of the ridge they had just left. The loud thumping of heavy-caliber anti-aircraft guns joined the ruckus—the air strikes they had called in earlier were beginning to pound the enemy armor and APCs as they headed toward the front lines.

As he advanced through the underbrush and the pine tree woods of the area, Punisher heard a tree branch crack. He instinctively raised his right fist and the team froze, slowly lowering themselves and raising their weapons.

Punisher paused midstride and listened. Explosions and AA gunfire continued off in the distance, but he was certain he had heard something nearby. Straining his senses, he tilted his head to the side to feel the air around them. Then he made out a voice speaking Chinese.

Depressing his throat mic, he whispered, "Enemy front. Back the way we came. We're going to slip past them in the draw we passed thirty meters back."

Punisher turned slowly and began to move back the way they had just come. He passed Crispy, who had his rifle up, ready to lay down covering fire. As Punisher passed Crispy, he softly squeezed his shoulder, and his teammate instantly followed him to Janus, who was next in line. When they reached Janus, he turned and followed the two of them until they reached Bang-Bang. Then all hell broke loose.

Bang-Bang had just joined them when BigDog got snagged on some underbrush. The machine couldn't untangle itself like a human would have, so it used its mechanical power to pull itself free of the entanglement, which caused some of the underbrush to uproot and sent rocks sliding down the slope.

Bang-Bang looked at the machine and hissed, "Bad robot!"

Crack, crack, ratatat, ratatat.

"Contact rear!" Spider opened fire on the nearby Chinese soldiers with his Mk 48 machine gun, sending dozens of 7.62mm rounds at their attackers. The flexible feed chute system strapped on his back had five hundred rounds of ammo he could throw at the attackers to cover their retreat.

As Spider shifted his position, Bang-Bang suddenly let out a grunt and collapsed. He'd been hit in the back by a string of rounds from an enemy machine gunner.

Punisher turned around and dropped to a knee behind a fallen tree and returned fire with his M27 rifle on full auto, screaming to his teammates, "Get on line!"

Crispy grabbed Bang-Bang by the back of his plate carrier and pulled him behind some cover so he could look at his wounds and try to get him patched up, but he realized almost instantly that his comrade was dead. Crispy pulled Bang-Bang's body behind him to lodge himself between a large felled tree and a boulder and was sighting one PLA soldier after another with his M1A EBR sniper weapon system.

Crack! Crack!

Janus pulled the pin on an M67 fragmentation grenade and hurled it at the attackers, immediately following it with a second. "Frag out!"

Then Janus pulled his SCAR Mk 16 rifle up and started tearing into the enemy patrol. The shooting lasted for maybe sixty seconds before Punisher yelled, "Cease fire!"

When the shooting stopped, the entire area was silent. The area between the Special Forces and the PLA Soldiers was completely torn apart. Chunks had been torn out of trees and the underbrush was blown apart. The smells of cordite and sulfur filled the air. Some of the grass was smoldering, and smoke trailed in the air above underbrush that had caught fire from the grenade explosions. And just like any other battle Punisher had been a part of, the smell of death wafted in the air.

"Janus, on me," Punisher called out, then advanced with his rifle at the ready.

The two of them bounded forward while Spider stayed behind to lay down suppressive fire again should they need it.

When Punisher and Janus made it to where the Chinese soldiers had been, they found a mess of bodies that were torn and ripped apart. They counted ten enemy soldiers, spread out in a line. None of them had survived the barrage of bullets and grenades they had rained down on them.

Drawing their suppressed Sig M17s, Punisher and Janus did the grim work of ensuring each enemy soldier was actually dead. Then they made their way back to the rest of their team. Crispy was sitting down next Bang-Bang's body. The engagement had lasted less than sixty seconds, but it had cost them one of their own.

Punisher shook his head in frustration that the BigDog that had given their position away. Punisher told the others to see if they could get their friend's body attached to the mechanical robot and let it carry him out. They'd double up and redistribute kit if they had to, but they were going to bring his body back with them.

Punisher radioed the captain, letting him know what had happened and about Bang-Bang. He also asked that he get the evac moving along because the entire area would have heard them shooting. Very soon the enemy would figure out where they were and start maneuvering on them. The hunt was on, and time wasn't on their side.

****

Albuquerque, New Mexico
Kirtland Air Force Base

"Hurry up and get in formation!" shouted their lieutenant as the platoon began to fall in.

Staff Sergeant Riker, of the 1st Battalion, 506th Infantry Regiment, took his place as the squad leader once he made sure his guys were all present and ready. The captain of Charlie Company had called a company formation ten minutes ago, so everyone was scrambling to find their soldiers and fall in.

The CO walked up to the head of the formation and called them all to attention. Then he put them at ease before he briefed them on what was going on.

"Listen up, fellas," he began. "Since our battalion is on QRF duty, the battalion CG handed us a hot priority mission. We just received an emergency tasking that's going to take us nearly seventy miles behind enemy lines. Apparently, an ODA team has run into some trouble. We've been tasked to go bail them out.

"I want everyone to grab your gear and head out to the helos. We're mounting up now and will be in the air within the next ten minutes. The ODA has already had a gunfight with one Chinese patrol, so it's likely this'll be a hot extraction. Be ready for it. Platoon leaders—take charge of your platoons, and let's get it done!"

In unison, the men all yelled the battalion motto: "Currahee!"

With the orders given, everyone ran back to the hangar they'd been staging in to grab their rucks and any last-minute items they might need.

Before they could walk out to the choppers, one of Riker's squadmates stopped him. "Staff Sergeant, do we really need to bring two days of MREs?" he asked. "Wouldn't it be better to just bring more ammo?"

Sergeant Riker smiled at the question and turned to look at the soldier. "We have BigDog to carry the ammo, not you. But, yes, we need to be ready for anything. This should just be a quick turn and burn, but we won't know that until we get in the area. Maybe the snake-eaters will be able to climb on the bird without a problem, but if they're in a fight, you can bet we'll be in one as well. Remember, troop: if it can go wrong, it will, and at the worst possible time."

"What, Staff Sergeant?" asked the soldier with a puzzled look.

Riker laughed, then yelled over the sound of the rotors. "Murphy's Law—you'll get used to it. He always gets a vote!"

The soldier's head bobbed up and down as he took in the information. The platoon was still getting accustomed to the idea of having a semi-autonomous mechanical robot tagging along with them. Not all the companies or platoons had them, but theirs did. It was a bit of an experiment with the heliborne units to see how well they could integrate them into the platoons' operations.

"Come on, mount up!" shouted their lieutenant from the back of the Ch-47 Chinook.

Riker's drone operator had the Boston Dynamics robot follow him onto the helicopter. The whole thing was still taking some getting used to. He'd seen a lot of things in his time in the Army, but a mechanical mule was a new one. He couldn't help but wonder what would happen one day if the AI computer that controlled BigDog ever gained awareness and decided to turn on his human masters.

Skynet always seems to find a way, thought Riker with a chuckle.

With the platoon piled into the back of the helicopter, the beast took to the air, along with three more Chinooks and two Blackhawks. Four Apaches were going to come along as their close air support, should they need it.

Once the air armada was up, they flew west for a little while. This took them much further away from the actual front lines, south of Albuquerque. Their flight path had a lot more rugged terrain and would give the pilots a better shot at slipping through the lines to reach their objective. For the most part, these outer rings of the front lines didn't really have any serious combat units.

After fifty minutes of racing at near ground level through valleys and scattered open spaces, the helicopters neared the location where the Special Forces soldiers were located. Suddenly, the ramp gunner swiveled his M2 .50 machine gun to the right, and the helicopter gained altitude and banked hard. Looking out the rear ramp, Riker suddenly had a terrible feeling. The snake-eaters had taken refuge on a small hilltop, and it looked like two large enemy forces had encircled them.

The Chinooks carrying the 101st Air Assault troopers changed direction to move away from the enemy soldiers as the Apaches dove in to engage them. While the Apaches laid down a barrage of antimateriel rockets, one of the Blackhawks swooped down to the hill; Riker realized they were attempting to recover the team without having to drop in additional troops to secure the area.

When the Blackhawk went into a hover, a string of tracer rounds reached right out for it. From Riker's view, it looked like bullets were flying every which way around the helicopter until, suddenly, the entire thing blew up. Debris and fire rained down on the Special Forces soldiers below as they scattered.

A couple of MANPADS rose to chase away the Apaches. The attack helicopters spat out flares to lure them away. Two of the helicopters broke formation and took up a higher orbit. Their chin guns fired down into the area from which the MANPADS had originated while the other two Apaches circled around for another attack run with their rockets.

A single missile streaked through the air from somewhere further away. One of the Apaches banked hard for the ground, completing a roll as it dove to evade the SAM that had come out of nowhere.

A second SAM swooped in and nailed the other Apache, blasting it apart into a flaming wreckage of parts that swirled to the ground below.

One of the crew chiefs yelled to Riker to be heard over the chaos. "We're moving further away while the Air Forces deal with this new threat!" Riker just nodded; the lieutenant looked a little green.

The Chinooks retreated a little further away with their remaining Apaches and lone Blackhawk. Minutes later, a series of black mushroom clouds rose into the sky. Then a fast mover flew through the valley near the Special Forces soldiers and released what looked like a cluster bomb. Hundreds of little explosions rippled through the forested area below where the Chinese soldiers had just been.

The Chinook carrying Riker's platoon abruptly changed course again. This time, they were headed for the hilltop where the SF soldiers were. Red and green tracers raced past the helicopter as the pilot deftly moved them from side to side and changed their altitude, racing to relieve the guys on the ground.

Staff Sergeant Riker said a quick prayer that they would make it to the ground; he felt the helicopter's nose pull up just in time for them to land hard in a small clearing that the snake-eaters had created for them with some det cord. As soon as they touched down, Riker was up and out of his seat, racing out the back of the helicopter into an uncertain situation.

When his platoon had emptied out of the Chinook, the pilot gave the engines more power and did his best to escape the area. The door and tail gunners fired away at the enemy soldiers, who were doing their best to shoot them down.

"Second Squad, on me!" Riker shouted. He ran toward an SF soldier who was using a machine gun with one of those flexible feed chute systems strapped onto his back. Riker had never seen one of those setups in person before. It was impressive to witness the incredible amount of suppressive fire a lone operator could lay down for them and their helicopter.

"Where do you want us?" hollered Riker. Bullets started cracking all around.

"Get your men lined up along this area here and hold those bastards from advancing any further!" shouted the snake-eater.

"Bravo team, take the right flank. Set up a base of fire there," Riker yelled, pointing to a group of trees that could provide some cover. Riker then took his Alpha team and anchored them on another part of the line. As his guys got into their positions, the level of gunfire from the American lines increased as they brought their rifles and machine guns to bear.

While Riker's squad was holding down this side of the line, the rest of the platoon had spread out on the other side of the perimeter. In the center near the top of the hill, his newly arrived medics began treating three of the Special Forces soldiers for various injuries.

Another Chinook began its descent. The enemy tried to shoot at the incoming helicopter, but the Apaches circling above rained down more gunfire and rockets on them.

Explosions rocked the ground below Riker. It was pure chaos and madness. When the Chinook landed, the next platoon of soldiers and their mechanical BigDog rushed off and the wounded Special Forces soldiers were thrown on before the helicopter took off again.

One of the Special Forces soldiers came up to Riker as he was moving along his line, checking on his guys. "Staff Sergeant, start conserving ammo. Apparently, the Chinese got some fast movers of their own, so the helicopters are gonna bug out until the Air Force can clear the skies."

"Copy that," Riker replied as he looked at the dirt and blood caked on the man's uniform.

This just went from bad to worse, Riker thought as the next Chinook flared its nose to land. *Then again, if it doesn't suck, we don't do it.*

The remaining helicopters were going to drop the troops they were carrying and then run for safety. They didn't want to risk getting shot down while full of soldiers. Fortunately, the volume of enemy fire lightened up considerably as the Apaches continued to circle overhead. Every now and then, they'd hammer an area with a couple of rockets or fire their chin guns down on a cluster of enemy soldiers they spotted moving toward the Americans.

Five minutes later, the last two Chinooks and the lone Blackhawk had unloaded their human cargo. They immediately took off and began their mad dash to safety.

As he watched at the last helicopters leaving the valley, Riker saw a missile streak toward one of them, blowing it right out of the sky. He heard the roar of a jet engine as a Chinese fighter flew after the remaining helicopters. Then the very Chinese plane that was chasing after their remaining helicopters was blown apart as an American fighter zipped past their hilltop.

Damn. How long are we going to be stuck on this hilltop? Riker wondered. They had flown in as a QRF to retrieve these guys, not get stranded with them.

Riker sighed. He knew he'd better get his men ready, so he walked up and down his squad, passing along the new information and ordering them to dig in. If they were going to be here for more than a few hours, then he wanted some fighting positions.

God only knows how many enemy soldiers are still in the area, he thought.

****

Hill 592

Punisher walked up to their ODA team leader. "So now what?" he asked.

Captain Swiss, aka "Blade," sighed and shook his head. "We settle in and wait for another ride," he replied.

Snorting at the response, Punisher waved at the burning wreckage of a Blackhawk. "Well, that was supposed to be our ride out. Now we have about one hundred and twenty regular Army soldiers with us instead." He swore and kicked the ground.

Blade laughed softly. "I don't disagree, Punisher. But look at the bright side—we aren't about to be overrun anymore."

Before they could say anything else, the man in charge of the air assault unit that was now trapped with them joined their discussion. "Captain Swiss, I'm Captain Gervais from Charlie Company, 1st Battalion, 506th Infantry Regiment. This is First Sergeant Ladd. I was told you guys needed rescuing," Gervais said with a smirk on his face.

Blade chuckled. "I think we're all going to need some rescuing now," he responded. "But, yes, thanks for the assist. I wasn't sure we could hold this position for much longer when you guys showed up." He pointed to his senior NCO. "This is Punisher," Blade continued. "If he tells your guys to do something, listen to him."

Gervais nodded. "So what do we do now?" he asked. "Do we stay up here on this position, or do you want us to try and fight our way out of here to another location?"

Punisher shook his head. "I wouldn't recommend it, sir. We should hunker down here. One of our surveillance drones spotted a column of enemy vehicles moving toward us from the Southeast. They're going to set up some sort of blocking position to make sure we can't move off this hilltop. We also spotted another element, at least company-sized, heading toward us from the Northeast. Our best bet now is to fortify our positions here and continue to rely on the Air Force to hammer these guys into the dirt while headquarters organizes another unit to come fetch us."

"Wow. When you guys stir up a hornet's nest, you go all out, don't you?" Gervais said, popping his knuckles.

Punisher snickered. "Well, it's what we're here to do. We hadn't intended on getting bogged down like that. A couple of our guys got hit during a couple of skirmishes. It slowed us down, but we weren't about to leave a man behind. So, here we are—surrounded. Our own little Bastogne."

Captain Gervais smiled at the reference. "Then I guess it's good you have the Screaming Eagles here."

"Just get your guys ready, Captain," Punisher directed. "When the enemy gets themselves organized, they'll attack again. I'm going to work on getting some air support stacked up for the rest of the evening, but chances are we'll be spending the night here."

With their marching orders given, Captain Gervais headed off to inform his platoon leaders and make sure everyone was ready for what would be coming next.

****

With only an hour of sunlight left, Staff Sergeant Riker positioned his last claymore against the side of a tree. He inserted the blasting cap into the mine and tightened it down. Next, he grabbed some leaves and underbrush and covered the mine. As he got back to his knees, Riker made sure he didn't see any enemy soldiers nearby as he unwrapped the firing wire and moved it back toward their lines. He carefully wrapped some of it around a nearby sapling so that if someone tripped on the cord, it wouldn't unseat or move the mine.

Sergeant Riker had spent the last two hours placing nearly a dozen of these bad boys in different positions around his platoon's side of the line. When the enemy did eventually assault their position, the claymores would wipe most of their attacking force out.

Steadily moving back to his fighting position, Riker placed the firing wire down and grabbed the firing device. Once he performed a quick test to ensure everything was working, he placed the clicker down next to the others. In all, there were six of them in his fighting hole and another six in their platoon sergeant's hole.

"All set, Staff Sergeant?" asked Captain Gervais, who had taken a knee next to his position.

Riker looked up at the captain. "About as ready as we're going to be," he replied. "Any word on whether we're getting out of here tonight or waiting until tomorrow?"

"I don't know," Gervais replied, shrugging. "I think Brigade is thinking of making a stand here. My last call with battalion said they were looking at a landing zone a couple of kilometers away, where they can bring in the rest of the battalion."

"What do the Greenie Beanies think?" asked Riker.

"You know those guys—they like to fight. I think they stirred up a hornet's nest and figure if they can tie the Chinese down here, it only weakens their position at the front."

"Yeah, with us as the bait," Riker retorted, crossing his arms. "Ammo's going to be a problem if we have to stay here too long."

"Yeah, that's what Top said," Gervais responded with a nod. "We should have a supply run soon. A couple of Blackhawks are bringing us additional water, ammo, and some other items when they pick up our wounded." Gervais stood, put his hands on his hips and stretched his back. "But I need to get moving," he said. "Stay safe, Staff Sergeant. Let the rest of the guys know we aren't alone. We do have help on the way."

****

Night eventually set in, bringing with it the uncertainty of what would come next.

"Captain, you need to see this." Janus motioned for Gervais to look at the drone feed.

"What do we have?"

"Movement."

"Come on, Janus. Another bowel movement?" teased Spider.

Blade laughed. "Don't mind Spider," he said to Janus. "He's just jealous of your toy."

Janus shook his head. "A dozen new trucks just showed up over here," he explained in an annoyed tone, pointing to a spot on his map before showing them what the drone was seeing.

Even with the drone in night vision mode, it was providing them fairly detailed images of what was unfolding around them. For the last several hours, truckloads of PLA infantry had been arriving, filtering into positions around the hilltop where the Americans had dug in.

"They know we're trapped," Blade commented. "They're gearing up for another attack."

"I think we should start calling in some of that air support we've been promised," said Punisher. "If we can hit them before they get their attack going, maybe we can keep it from even starting." They all knew he'd spent the last several hours getting various air units spun up on their situation, stacking up units they'd need.

Captain Gervais nodded. "Call it in, Punisher. Let's get some fighters lined up. Janus, can you see if Overwatch can tell us what's going on in Socorro? It'd be good to know if those PLA reinforcements are still heading toward the front lines or if they're being redirected to deal with us."

"Roger that, sir," Punisher replied. "I'll get on it."

****

First Sergeant Ladd scrambled over to Staff Sergeant Riker's position. He tapped him on the shoulder and whispered, "Riker, tell your squad to be ready for contact. We've got inbound fast movers. They're going to light up those guys down below us."

Before Riker could say anything or ask any questions, Top had already scrambled off to pass the word to the other squads along his lines.

Riker got out of his fighting hole and started telling the guys what was up. He was at the end of his part of the line when the night sky above them suddenly lit up with half a dozen illumination rounds.

Without hesitation, Riker dove into the closest fighting hole with two of his soldiers. The incoming rockets screamed overhead.

Boom, boom, boom!

Rockets landed all around their lines and the rest of the hilltop, ripping trees and underbrush apart. Hot pieces of metal and chunks of trees flew in every direction, cutting down whatever they came into contact with.

The ground beneath them shook so violently from the impacts that Riker thought the fillings in his teeth were going to come loose. The intense rocket attack continued for maybe five or six minutes; then it ended just as quickly as it had started.

Cries for medics began to echo across the hilltop. The wounded screamed out for help, although some just cried or moaned for their mothers, girlfriends or wives. Riker winced. Those were the hardest cries to hear because they came from the men who were severely injured and most likely going to die.

"You guys OK?" Riker asked the other men who'd ridden out the bombardment with him.

They nodded.

Sergeant Riker popped out of the fighting hole and immediately moved down the line, making sure the rest of the squad was all right. Aside from one of his guys having a few cuts, his squad seemed to have gotten lucky.

Just as Riker's ears had stopped ringing, the loud rush of jet engines overwhelmed his senses. The darkness was broken by the brilliance of five-hundred-pound bombs exploding a few thousand meters in front of their lines.

Shortly after the first blasts rocked the area around the American positions, a new and terrifying sound erupted—the whistling of artillery rounds. Judging by the pitch of the incoming shrieks, Riker estimated they were about to be hammered with 152mm rounds.

Riker jumped back into his own fighting position just as the rounds started to hit. Many of them were ground impacts—his body bounced off the bottom of his fighting position, only to slam back down when gravity took back over. Then came the airburst rounds, raining shrapnel down on their heads, the top-down attack slicing through soft flesh. Their fighting positions offered them no protection from this type of attack.

Meanwhile, more illumination rounds appeared above their position, casting an eerie light as the magnesium rounds drifted down from little parachutes. Riker could smell smoke. He knew fires had spread on the hilltop as the artillery and rocket rounds had caused some of the dry timber to catch.

Curled up in the bottom of his fighting position, Riker grabbed his knees and tried to make himself as small a target as possible. He screamed uncontrollably from the sheer terror of it all, and he realized he'd lost control of his bladder.

Then he heard one of the most horrifying sounds of his life, the whistles of Chinese officers urging their men forward. Riker knew that the shrill screeching meant a human wave was charging toward him with bayonets fixed.

Knowing he had to take charge of his emotions and the situation, Staff Sergeant Riker did the toughest thing he could do—he stood up in his fighting position and proceeded to shoot at the enemy. He quickly realized they were still a little way off, out of immediate rifle range but closing in fast.

Riker's training immediately took over. With the overhead enemy bombardment finished, he got out of his fighting hole and moved down his line. He grabbed his squad members by their helmets or body armor. "Stand up! Get ready to shoot at the enemy!" he bellowed.

Since he was already up, he continued down the rest of their line, encouraging the rest of his platoon and getting them ready.

The whistles and the screams of the enemy soldiers grew louder. Bullets zipped around Staff Sergeant Riker, somehow thudding into anything but his flesh as he moved along the line.

Riker brought his rifle to his shoulder and fired several times at a cluster of enemy soldiers as he scrambled back to his fighting hole. He knew he needed to be ready to light off the claymores if it came to that.

The roar of gunfire from the Chinese and the American lines increased to a point where it was nearly continuous, and the individual pops were indistinguishable from each other. The yelling and screaming of soldiers on both sides as they desperately sought to kill each other added to the growing crescendo.

When the enemy reached about two hundred meters from the American lines, it was as if the finger of God reached out of the sky above them and lit up the ground all around the enemy soldiers. The red line of tracer rounds, which looked like solid red lasers, strafed up and down the enemy lines, intermixed with smaller explosions from the 40mm Bofors cannon and the 105mm howitzer from the AC-130 gunship circling somewhere above them. Hot brass casings rained down everywhere as the aircraft passed overhead.

Riker involuntarily closed his eyes for just a moment. When he opened them, the entire scene had changed. Where seconds earlier, the ground in front of him had been packed with enemy soldiers screaming as they charged toward him, there was now only a mass of torn and shredded bodies. It seemed like any survivors were wounded and screaming for help.

With its work there done, the AC-130 moved its attention to another part of their hilltop, using its godlike power to resume its close air support mission.
****

"Keep 'em coming, Punisher!" called out Janus. "The Chinese look to be moving another wave of troops to the southern portion of the lines." He didn't take his eyes off the shared drone feed from their Overwatch unit.

How many more soldiers can they keep throwing at us? Punisher wondered. *This is a pure slaughter.*

He looked at his notebook to see what kind of aircraft they had on deck next. "The Air Force is sending another gunship to replace the one on station. He's bingo on fuel and ammo," he announced.

While Captain Swiss, aka "Blade," was talking on the radio, Captain Gervais, the CO from the 101st scrambled over to their position. He waited a second for Blade to finish talking on the radio before he spoke.

"We need to try and get some CASEVAC helicopters in here," Gervais urged. "We've got a ton of wounded that need to be flown out or they're not going to make it."

Blade grimaced at the news. "What's your casualty count as of right now, Captain?" he asked.

Gervais glanced at a piece of paper in his hand. "Twenty-eight KIA, another forty-nine wounded," he responded.

Blade shook his head and blew some air forcefully out of his lips. "Copy that, Captain. I'll do what I can to get us some help. I was told your battalion is finally on the way. They were originally going to set up shop nearby, but since the enemy pretty much wiped out the trees on our hilltop, they're going to bring in another company's worth of soldiers to reinforce us. Then they'll drop the rest of your battalion about five kilometers to our west and try to pincer move the enemy and relieve the pressure on us."

"Just get me those damn helicopters to get my wounded out of here—not in two or three hours, but right now!" Captain Gervais exploded. "I'm not going to lose more of my guys because headquarters can't figure out when and where they want to drop the rest of our battalion." He stormed off as the clatter of gunfire starting to pick up again.

Punisher grunted. The rest of the 1st Battalion, 506th Infantry Regiment was supposed to have arrived four hours ago, then it was two hours ago. Now they were saying they'd be arriving in an hour. The higher-ups didn't want to send in CASEVAC helicopters without a proper escort, and they couldn't get an escort because those helicopters were tied up with the airlift of the battalion, which kept getting pushed back. The situation seemed to be devolving.

****

It was 0230 hours when the next set of illumination rounds ignited above them, just in time for the arriving helicopters. Two Chinooks landed in the clearing on the hilltop and immediately offloaded two platoons' worth of soldiers. As the reinforcements got off the birds, the medics and anyone else that could help rushed the wounded on board.

Artillery rounds began to land sporadically around their makeshift LZ. One of the Chinooks got airborne and zoomed away, trying to avoid the incoming fire. The second Chinook turned to run away and got nailed by one of the artillery rounds. The ensuing explosion ripped the helicopter apart, firing debris raining down on the soldiers below.

Tracer rounds started to fly in as the next pair of helicopters landed. The enemy gunners were trying to hit them before they could offload their human cargo and supplies. Again, as the soldiers exited, runners and medics moved more wounded soldiers onto them, hoping and praying their wounded brothers would be able to make it back to a higher-level field hospital.

"You Staff Sergeant Riker?" asked a gruff voice behind him.

Turning to see who was asking, Riker saw a sergeant first class and thirty or so soldiers scattered behind him. *Reinforcements have arrived*, he thought with a smile.

"Yes, Sergeant First Class. I am," Riker replied. "I've got a huge hole in my lines over there, and at that position there," he said, pointing to the problem areas.

During the last several hours of the battle, Riker's platoon sergeant had been injured and was out of action. Their lieutenant had been killed an hour later during one of the artillery bombardments. Riker had suddenly found himself in charge of the platoon, again.

"Copy that, Sergeant. I heard you're the guy in charge here, so I'll follow your lead until I get a lay of the land. What can you tell me so far?" the man asked as he directed a couple of his squad leaders to where Riker had pointed.

"How about you tell me what you know, and I'll fill in the blanks?"

"I'm going to like you, Riker," the man said with a chuckle. "Direct and to the point. I'm Gilman, by the way." The two briefly shook hands. "I don't know much other than to say we heard you guys had gone in to rescue an ODA and somehow got trapped on the hilltop."

Riker chuckled. "Yep, now you're all caught up. We've been stuck on this hilltop since 1100 hours yesterday. They've hit us with five direct assaults. Each time we've been able to break it up with gunship and close air support, but the artillery bombardments have been hammering us."

"You ain't joking on that artillery. The Chinook we flew in on took a direct hit as it was leaving. I assume you have claymores set up in front of our positions?" Gilman queried.

"We've got twelve of them. I have six clickers here with me and the other six are on the far side of our line over there," Riker answered, pointing to the other position with the claymore detonators.

"Sounds 'bout right. I'm going to have some of my guys filter out there and get some more set up. I have a feeling the worst fighting is still ahead."

Lifting an eyebrow at the comment, Riker said, "Really? What do you know that we don't?"

"Not a lot, but we saw a lot of tracer fire on our way in. We also saw a lot of burning fires all around the place from the air strikes. Some of those fires were from armored vehicles and trucks. God only knows how many more enemy soldiers are still out there."

"They should have gotten us out of here yesterday when we had a chance. Someone decided they wanted to make this their Little Bighorn moment," Riker said as he pulled an energy bar out of his pocket.

"It doesn't matter," Gilman replied, shrugging. "The rest of the battalion is finally here, so I'm sure this fight will be over soon enough."

****

Albuquerque, New Mexico
Kirtland Air Force Base
101st Air Assault Division HQ

Major General Sims looked at the drone footage from Overwatch and grimaced at what he was seeing. Instead of disengaging from his soldiers, the Chinese appeared to be moving heaven and earth to wipe them out. They'd already reinforced the company of soldiers hunkered down on Hill 592 with the ODA. Now it looked like the Chinese were sending even more soldiers to attack them.

"I know this doesn't bring any solace, Sims, but your troopers have drawn off at least a full brigade of soldiers that were headed to the front lines," General Tyndall said. "My division is going to punch a hole right through them in a couple of hours." He too studied the digital map.

Turning to look at the 4th Infantry Division commander, Sims knew he was right, but he felt terrible that his guys were being used like the cheese in a mousetrap. It didn't sit well with him.

"I have to get another battalion in there ASAP. Those guys aren't going to hold out against many more assaults like the one we just saw," Sims replied angrily.

Walking up to join them, an Air Force colonel added, "If you'd like, General, I can try to see if I can get a B-52 strike to hit this area here." He pointed at a position a few kilometers from his battalion. "Then you can drop another battalion in. It's not too far away from the rest of your units. They could link up with them."

Sims shook his head. "No. Keep those units on task to support Tyndall's offensive. I'll send another pathfinder unit to find us a couple of good LZs we can set another battalion down in."

The Air Force colonel nodded, then walked away, leaving the two Army generals to talk.

"You know, when we break through their lines, it's going to push the Chinese to the bottom half of the state. We'll finally be able to cut off their forces in Texas from the rest of their Army on the West Coast," Tyndall explained.

"I know. I'm just annoyed that my division is being used as bait. I know it's working, but damn if we're not taking a lot of casualties. That Chinese commander should have just collapsed their front lines and fallen back to Las Cruces."

"Yeah, but look at it this way—your guys have them so bogged down that when my division attacks in a couple of hours, we'll not only be able to slice through their weakened lines, we can use your forces to block their lines of retreat. If we can remove two enemy divisions from the equation, it'll put us one step closer to winning this war," offered Tyndall.

Sims sighed. He knew his friend was right. They were so close to pushing the Chinese out of the state and cutting off their forces in Texas. Turning to look at Tyndall, he said, "Let's just hope the Brits and Poles are going to be able to pull off their part of this operation."

****

Hill 592

Looking down the hill from his fighting position, Staff Sergeant Riker noticed the first slivers of light starting to push through the darkness of the previous day. He'd survived to see another sunrise. Now whether he would survive long enough to see a sunset was the next big question.

The Chinese had only attacked them sporadically with artillery since they'd been reinforced, and they'd only sent some probing attacks with platoons instead of the human waves. The Air Force had been carrying out air strikes all night.

Maybe the fly boys finally got some of that enemy artillery off our backs...

As the sun continued to climb in the sky, it revealed the true horror of what had taken place throughout the night. The ground all around and below their positions was covered in bodies, parts of bodies and shattered tree trunks. What they saw was something out of a horror show.

With the daylight, Riker started making the rounds along his platoon's position, checking on his soldiers, making sure they were still doing OK and checking on their fighting positions. Many of the positions had been damaged during the artillery attacks and would need to be shored up. God only knew if the Chinese would try and throw another attack at them or not.

Most his soldiers were pretty shaken up from the night battle and the sight of what they had inflicted on the enemy. Even still, they had work to do. He needed to have them use the time they had to fill their bellies with MREs and get their positions ready for what might or might not come next. Most importantly, he needed to keep them focused. They needed to stay sharp.

Twenty minutes later, the roar of jet engines picked up. This was followed by several thundering booms and explosions off in the distance. Then they heard a lot of shooting in the distance. It sounded like the rest of their battalion either was being attacked or was attacking the enemy. Intermixed with the sounds of battle off in the distance, they heard the familiar sound of a buzz saw ripping through the air—the telltale sign of an AC-130 or A-10 strafing an enemy position.

The rest of the morning for the soldiers on hilltop 592 went by rather uneventfully. The PLA didn't launch any further attacks against them. The worst part of the morning was when their company commander told Riker his squad needed to go down to check on the enemy casualties. They needed to make sure they were dead and, if any wounded needed attention, then to call out for a medic.

Half the soldiers in his squad puked their guts out within the first few minutes of moving through the enemy lines. The dismembered bodies, the pieces of legs and arms, bowels torn open and the stench of it all was overwhelming. One of Riker's soldiers couldn't take it anymore. The man started screaming at the sky with tears running down his cheeks. He dropped his weapon to the ground and just collapsed into a crying heap.

At this point, Riker didn't care what the captain said; he wasn't going to have his soldiers keep doing this duty. None of them were going to keep their sanity if they did this for much longer. One of the replacement units that hadn't seen combat could do this, but he was done with it. He ordered his squad back to the hilltop and told the captain what had happened. Luckily, Captain Gervais understood, and they opted to skip checking on the enemy. If some of them were playing possum or needed help, well, they were on their own.

By midday, a helicopter arrived with additional soldiers on it. It also brought their division commander, who wanted to see hill 592 for himself. What he saw brought tears to his eyes. He spent several hours talking with the men about what he had endured the previous day and throughout the night, consoling a few of them and praising them for their heroism during the battle. He told them the 4th Infantry Division had broken through the Chinese lines. Their lead elements should link up with them in the next couple of hours. He also told them that thousands upon thousands of PLA soldiers were surrendering. The relentless air strikes and the slaughter of several battalions' worth of infantry in the previous day's battle had finally broken them.

With the enemy force now shattered, General Sims told them he was going to pull their company off the front lines and send them back for some R&R. They needed to recalibrate and get brought back up to strength if they were going to be of any use to him in the coming battles. They had the Chinese on the ropes; now they just needed to keep hitting them with blow after blow until they knocked them out. As Sims headed for his helicopter, he passed Staff Sergeant Riker and a few of his soldiers and stopped and assessed the young men. He extended his hand to Riker, who looked at it for a moment before he shook it.

"Good work, soldier." Sims said solemnly.

Riker looked hard into the division commander's eyes before he replied through gritted teeth, "Currahee."

Chapter Ten
India/China Conflict

New Delhi, India
Secretariat Building

Prime Minister Bhamre looked at the report in front of him; he only needed to sign it to initiate offensive military operations against the People's Republic of China.

For the past day, his advisors had been going over the details of the invasion. It was a complex operation his planners had been developing for the past six months. Now it was time to make the decision to either move forward or stand the army down.

"What are your initial thoughts?" asked Defense Minister Sitharaman as she refilled her cup of tea. She'd spent days and weeks making the case for war and answering his questions and was growing tired with his indecisiveness.

"I'm still concerned about Pakistan. How can we be sure they will not take advantage of the situation and attack us?" Bhamre asked. This was a question he'd gone around and around with his advisors on: what would Pakistan do?

"They'll attack us is what they'll do," blurted Deputy National Security Advisor Khandare.

Staring daggers at the man, Sitharaman waved his comment off with a flick of her wrist as she leaned in and looked the Prime Minister in the eyes. "The Americans have made it abundantly clear to the Pakistanis that any nuclear attack on India would result in an overwhelming nuclear response by them. The Americans have already carried out several nuclear attacks against the Chinese, so there is no question as to whether the Americans will launch more missiles. They will—"

"President Sachs has also told the Pakistanis that if they stay out of the conflict, the Americans will provide them with fifty billion dollars USD in aid," interrupted Dr. Gandhi, the head of the Research and Analysis Wing. "Say what you want about Pakistan, they want to survive this conflict and they can see just as everyone else can that the Chinese are losing this war. They will take the money and stay neutral."

"I'm sorry, Mr. Prime Minister. This is a war of choice, not necessity. This is going to cost the lives of tens of thousands of our people, and for what?" Khandare countered. "As Dr. Gandhi has rightly stated, the Chinese are losing this war. India has nothing to gain by invading China. We're better off sitting this one out and letting it run its course."

"And that position, Khandare, cost the lives of more than thirty million Chinese civilians," shot back Sitharaman angrily. "You said the Americans wouldn't dare attack the Three Gorges Dam, yet that is exactly what they did. You've been consistently wrong on every issue during this war. You've seen the videos and pictures of what the Chinese are doing to the American cities as they withdraw. It's a genocide, and the people of India have a chance to help put an end to it by opening a second front against China. We cannot sit idly by and do nothing while millions of people are killed. We have a moral obligation to get involved."

Raising his hand to stop the infighting, Prime Minister Bhamre said, "Khandare, I don't like the idea of war any more than you do. We've stayed out of this war the last year, but the Defense Minister is right. Millions of people are being killed, and millions more will be killed if we do not intervene. I have my reservations about this operation, especially about starting a war in the winter. I don't want to go to war. But I also don't want millions more people to die on either side. If our entry into this conflict can help to speed up its demise, then I believe we should fight."

The PM then turned to Minister Sitharaman, asking, "How fast will we be able to get a new government in Tibet established?"

"With the help of the Dalai Lama, I believe we should be able to get a functioning government in place within the first few months of the war. It's going to take some time to push the Chinese Army out of the province and arm the populace, especially during the winter months. But this is an operation our army is more than suited to handle. Our battle plan does not call for us to drive deep into Chinese territory, just liberate Tibet and the western half of China," she replied confidently.

Jumping back into the conversation, Dr. Gandhi added, "I also believe some of the PLA commanders can and will switch sides. There is a growing discontent within the military ranks, particularly among the senior military leaders. The war in America is costing them dearly. The units in western China are being stripped of their tier one equipment, to be shipped to North America. Many of them are becoming disillusioned with the war and the high casualties and the string of defeats after defeats. The Americans have cut their army in North America in half. It's only a matter of time until their army in Texas is forced to surrender."

Sitting back in his chair, Bhamre thought about what his spy chief had said. Finally, he nodded in agreement. Picking up the pen next to his teacup, he signed the order authorizing military operations against the People's Republic of China. The time for India to sit on the sidelines had ended.

****

From *Amar Ujala Today News*:

> In the dark of night, the Armed Forces of India invaded the People's Republic of China. The Prime Minister's office provided the following comment: "The people of India have a moral obligation to help bring an end to the war between the People's Republic of China and the United States. The Chinese government needs to be stopped. The genocide they are committing in North America needs to end."
>
> Other sources within the government say the decision to take the country to war was not unanimous. Several factions within the government argued for India to continue to remain neutral, arguing that this was a war of choice and not necessity.
>
> Stay tuned as we continue to bring you news and updates from the front lines.

From *BBC Online*:

> The swift attack by the Indian Army appears to have caught the Chinese by complete surprise. Indian paratroopers landed deep behind enemy lines, capturing several airfields, critical bridges and rail lines.
>
> Beijing denounced the surprise attack by India, calling it an act of cowardice. The Chinese President said in a statement, "The PRC will win this fight against India and send their army scampering across the border with their tails tucked beneath their legs."

****

Washington, D.C.
White House

"It's about damn time the Indians joined the war," President Sachs said as he signaled for a refill of his coffee.

The steward topped off his mug and then offered a refill to the others in the Oval Office.

"I agree. But the war is in the early stages," replied NSA Grey. "We'll have to see how it goes." He was clearly trying to undersell expectations in the hopes of overdelivering later.

"Mike, what's your take on the how well the Indian offensive is going?" asked the President as he pivoted to his Secretary of Defense.

Mike Howell shifted in his seat a bit. "It could be going better," he admitted. "They surprised the Chinese and caught them flat-footed initially, but they didn't seize the initiative like they should have. Their Air Force should be pulverizing the Chinese, but they've focused their initial efforts on providing close air support instead of neutralizing the enemy's Air Force first."

The President nodded as he listened. "I suppose you have an idea of how we can help?" he asked.

"I do," Howell answered. "I'd recommend we send some Special Forces units to assist and advise. Once we get some boots on the ground, I'd like to see if we could use some of our B-2s to assist them."

Sachs lifted his chin as he thought about the idea. "Don't you think we should keep our stealth bombers on their current missions? If we take them away to assist the Indians, won't that negatively affect our current operations?"

Mike sighed, more to himself than as a response to the question. "Yes and no, Mr. President," he replied. "We've been carrying out strategic bombing missions across China for six months. It's having an effect in some areas of their economy, but it hasn't forced them into surrender like it did Germany. I don't think we should abandon the mission, as it is hurting their military, but we could certainly shift four of our bombers to Diego Garcia or even to India proper. We could use them to specifically go after the Chinese Air Force across Tibet and the western provinces. That would help the Indians achieve a much faster victory. They only have a limited amount of time left to get their forces into Tibet before the winter weather makes it nearly impossible to move via the roads."

Lifting an eyebrow, the President pressed him, "Speaking of the weather—how do the Indians plan on keeping their army supplied and fighting?"

"One of their biggest coups of the new war was seizing Nyingchi. The bulk of their paratroopers landed at the airport and captured it. They held out long enough for their ground force to relieve them and consolidate the position. The capture of this city cuts off the major supply artery for the PLA to their western provinces and Tibet. If the Indians can keep the Chinese Air Force off their backs, they should be able to make use of the airport to keep their forces supplied," Mike replied as he produced a map of the area he was talking about.

After spending a few minutes looking at the map and where the Indian and Chinese forces were, NSA Grey suggested, "Would it help if we sent a Group or Wing of C-5 Galaxys to augment their airlift capability?"

"Yeah. What about that, General Markus?" asked the President. "Would that hurt our efforts here or could we spare them to help the Indians?"

"I think we could shift those forces around without it severely impacting us," Markus replied. "If we're going to do that, I'd also like to shift a squadron of F-15Es to go with them. I'm not comfortable with our pilots being solely dependent on the Indian Air Force for fighter cover and support."

"If we send a fighter squadron, we'll need to send a squadron of refuelers as well," added Secretary Howell. "I'd also recommend sending a couple of AWACS and a JSTAR for support. We should also send additional aircraft and support units if we intend on sending some C-5s. And since it's an Air Force heavy deployment, let's get AFSOC involved and chop the 24th Special Tactics Squadron to the mission."

The President stood but held his hand out for them to stay seated. When he needed to make an important decision like this, he usually paced the room for a moment before he came to his final conclusion. He liked to run through the various ideas and scenarios in his head before he committed.

"While I don't want to take units away from our current efforts here in the US, I think the more we can help the Indians in their war against the Chinese, the more it'll help us in the long run. Let's move those additional resources with the C-5s. If we need to send some ground units to help, keep it small. I like the idea of sending the 24th in; I'd rather send some Special Forces units than regular ground troops—at least until we finish recapturing Texas and California. Speaking of which, let's shift our discussion to Texas. What's going on there?"

General Markus motioned for his military aide to set up the map board near the mantel between the two couches, then moved to stand next to it, pointing to several demarcation lines where US and Chinese Forces were.

"III Corps along with the XVIII Airborne Corps is moving to finish encircling the Chinese Army group we trapped in Texas. With the capture of the Panama Canal, the 82nd Airborne is going to conduct a combat jump here." General Markus pointed on the map. "When they capture Chihuahua, we'll effectively cut them completely off from their supply lines in Mexico and their forces on the west coast. The 4th Infantry Division along with the 101st Air Assault captured Janos in northern Mexico and El Paso. Now that we have them contained, it's just a matter of time until either they surrender or we wipe them out."

Robert Grey asked, "Have we spoken to whoever the PLA commander is in Texas and tried to see if he'll surrender yet?"

Shaking his head, General Markus replied, "We've tried to speak to him on a couple of occasions, but nothing so far. Either he doesn't want to talk, or he's not being allowed to. I think that'll change in the next week or so as we tighten the noose."

"What about civilians still in occupied Texas? Do we have any idea of how many people are still trapped?" Grey asked as a follow-up.

"We're estimating a few million at most. A lot of the civilians fled ahead of the Chinese Army. The ones that chose to stay are dead from either the mass killings or starvation at this point. We honestly have no idea how many people may have been killed in Texas yet, but I suspect the number will be pretty high," General Markus replied glumly.

"OK. What about California? How are things shaping up there?" inquired the President, seeking to move the briefing along.

"I Corps is gearing up for a major push from Oregon down into California. Now that we've cut their forces off in California from their supply lines, it's only a matter of time until they start to run out of war stocks—munition, fuel, and other supplies. We're moving the Arsenal ships toward San Diego. As we move along the coast of Mexico, we're attacking any ports or supply depots we come across. Soon, we'll be able to use the railguns to start raining projectiles down on the Chinese forces in and around the coastal cities of Mexico and California—"

"What about Hawaii?" interrupted the President. "If we've broken through the Chinese Navy between California and Hawaii, are we getting supplies sent to the island?"

"Yes, Mr. President. We're starting to send food and other critical items to Hawaii from our ports in Washington State and Alaska. They're in pretty bad shape out there, but we'll do the best we can for the people still there," the SecDef said.

"OK, good. Let's do whatever we can to help the people of Hawaii. I do have a question about Echelon. Are things still ready to proceed in China with Operation Cyberstorm?"

"We'd need to talk to the NSA for the specifics, but, yes, they're ready to initiate it as soon as you give the order," Mike replied. He waited a moment, apparently waiting to see which way the President might be leaning. They'd held off on activating the program now for more than a month. The longer they waited, the more likely it was that someone would eventually discover the malware.

Leaning forward in his chair, the President looked his SecDef in the eyes. "I have some deep concerns about this. First, suppose we do take down the firewall and all the information we want gets disseminated across the country. How do we know it'll have any effect on the people? They've been so conditioned and brainwashed up to this point, they may not even believe what we show them or what they see on the global internet."

"I agree, Mr. President. It's a gamble. We have to try and convince parts of the military to either rebel against the central government or seize an opportunity to take over and then broker an end to this war," Mike replied.

Sighing, President Sachs looked down at the floor for a moment as he thought about it. He'd been holding off on activating Cyberstorm until they could firm up more resistance support within the country.

Finally, he turned back to Mike. "OK. No more sitting on this. Let's get it activated and hope for the best. Let's see how much chaos we can create with the Chinese once we take down their Great Firewall."

Chapter Eleven
Operation Cyberstorm

Hong Kong Island
Central Government Complex

Chief Executive Lau was nervous. He knew he needed to act, but he hated the unknown. His entire family, his legacy, depended on what would happen in the coming days and weeks.

Shrugging his nervousness off, Lau placed the Maxwell leather briefcase on his desk. Opening it, he placed some documents inside.

Looking at the picture frame on the desk, he saw the smiles of his wife and two daughters. *God, I hope this works...* He grabbed the frame and placed it in his briefcase as well.

Leaving his office, he walked toward the VIP elevator bank that would take him to the garage and his vehicle. Just as the elevator was about to close, a hand slid in between the doors, tripping the sensor and reopening them.

Looking up to see who had just joined him, Administrator Lau saw it was James Chan.

Reaching inside his suit jacket, James pulled a smartphone out and then typed something on it. He then turned to look at him.

"Lau, I've placed the video and audio recording of this elevator in a loop. We don't have long, so be quick. Are things on your end ready?" James asked hurriedly.

"Yes. Everyone on my end is ready. Is the military on board with us?" Lau asked, hoping James had been able to hold up his end of the bargain.

"I'm on my way to meet with the general now. They'll be ready."

Lau nodded, then let out an audible sigh of relief. This entire plan relied upon the garrison and local commanders being on board. If they didn't back them, this entire plan would collapse.

"What about the others? Outside of Hong Kong? Are they going to be a problem?"

"I'm still working on that. Some of them are with us, some are still a little shaky. I'll know more after my meeting with the general. Were you able to move the money to the account I gave you?" James asked urgently.

Three days ago, he'd asked for another tranche of money. The buying off of key generals and military commanders was becoming expensive.

"Yes, the money has been moved. I added an extra hundred million in case they ask for more at the last minute," Lau replied.

"Excellent. Good luck."

Just then, the elevator dinged as it reached the parking garage. The doors opened and the two men exited, heading their separate ways.

****

Macao
Mandarin Oriental Hotel

Entering the loading dock of the exclusive hotel, James Chan moved past the hotel workers like he owned the joint. Passing through the loading bays and the internal warehouse in the rear, he made his way toward the employee-only elevator bank that would lead him to the presidential suite.

Once on the elevator, he pressed the button that would take him to meet with the final piece to this grand puzzle. When the elevator reached the top floor, he made his way down the hallway toward a couple of black-suited security guards at the end.

The guards gave him a hard look. They were about to search him when he produced his credentials, quickly bringing these guard dogs to heel. One of them lifted his hand to his mouth and spoke softly into a microphone near the cuff of his sleeve. A moment later, the door opened, and James was led inside.

Upon entering the spacious living room, James saw General Zeng Shaoshan, dressed in an expensive suit. Apparently, he was doing his best to appear like a wealthy businessman and not the general in charge of the Chinese Southern Command. The general stood and walked toward him. The two bowed slightly and then Zeng gestured for James to take a seat. They'd met a number of times over the years and knew each other socially, so this wasn't the first time they had interacted. He could tell that the general was uneasy.

Taking his cue, James asked in a voice barely above a whisper, "Zeng, would we be able to speak in private?"

Nodding ever so slightly, Zeng turned to his security detail. "Leave the room," he ordered. "I don't want anyone disturbing us, understood?"

The guards obediently left the suite and stood guard outside the room to make sure no one entered the floor without their approval.

When the room was clear, James pulled a small device out of his suit jacket and placed it on the table near them. With the device turned on, it created a small electronic void around them, blacking out any ability for someone to eavesdrop on their conversation.

Turning to look at James, Zeng announced, "This is a risky move we're making, Chan. How certain are you that this scheme will work?"

Not missing a beat, the spymaster replied, "Please call me James. This plan will work. Right now, your command is the only missing link to the puzzle."

Turning to look at James, Zeng asked, "After generations of carefully choreographed news, how can you be so certain that the people will even believe what they are seeing and not assume it to be propaganda? Because once this goes live, the Ministry of Industry and Information Technology is going to come out swinging. So will the President."

"True. But the people will have the ability to see for themselves. They will be able to search the internet freely. Many of them for the first time. But that is not what will make this work. What will make this effective is commanders like yourself stepping forward to take charge of things and put an end to this terrible war and this Orwellian government," James said passionately.

Pausing for a moment before he said anything, Zeng finally explained, "James, not all of my officers may be open to this kind of change. You and I were both educated in the West. We lived in the West, so we know what kind of country China can become. Not everyone in my command has that shared experience or will see it that way."

Crinkling his eyebrows at the news, James asked, "So what are you saying, General? This won't be successful?"

James suddenly felt a bit of panic growing in his stomach. This *had* to work.

Shaking his head no, Zeng went on to explain, "I'm not saying it won't succeed. I'm just trying to set the expectation with you that this isn't going to be easy. I've moved around division and brigade commanders who are loyal to me—men that see the world and China as

I do and what it can become. But that's not to say we won't have others in our midst who will try and stop us. This is going to be a bloody fight once it starts. Not only will I have to try and hold my command and the brigades and divisions within it together, I'll have to contend with the police and the militia units as well."

Leaning in closer to the general, James replied, "I've been told that once this effort starts, we might get some support from the Americans and even the Australians."

Lifting an eyebrow at that, Zeng said, "If you could somehow get the Americans not to bomb my forces during this little coup d'état, that would greatly help. Better yet, if they could focus their efforts on going after the CMC structure in Beijing, that would be better."

"I can certainly ask," said James, shrugging. "I don't have a direct link to them, of course, but I can ask for help. I'm sure they will offer what they can. They want to end this war as badly as we do." James cleared his throat. "If you don't mind me asking, General, how do you plan on taking control of the area?" he inquired. They hadn't really talked over a lot of specifics, but James felt it was time that maybe they did.

Zeng reached for the decanter of expensive liquor and poured a healthy amount into his crystal glass. He lifted it to his lips and took a couple of long, deep gulps before he turned to look at James.

"Normally I'd have to cut off communications with Beijing and the Central Military Commission. That would take them out of the loop of issuing orders to my command or my divisions. However, it appears this computer virus is going to do that for us. So instead, I'm going to switch our radio communications network over to a new encryption key. It'll buy us a few days before they crack it or someone inside our ranks gives it to them. When that happens, we'll just change to another one.

"Next, we'll close off access to the airports and airfields in the Southern Command to all outside commercial and military air travel. We'll issue a no-fly order to all civilian and military traffic. I'll probably have to shoot a few planes down to make sure everyone gets the message and listens to me. Next, we'll seal off the roads, rails and bridges leading into the region. We'll start to lock down all of the provinces and districts. I'll issue an ultimatum to the police—either side with me and my forces, or we'll execute them.

"Then my forces will consolidate power in the cities and the rural areas, getting the police and local militia units on our side. The ones that want to stay loyal to Beijing will probably fight us, but hopefully that won't be a lot of them." Pausing for a moment, Zeng then added, "To be honest, James, after the first couple of hours of us initiating this little coup d'état, all of these plans are largely going to go out the window. No plan survives first contact. None. We'll do the best we can to maintain control of the region, but our success will largely be determined by how many regular everyday citizens will support us over the central government in Beijing."

Grunting at the honest assessment, James reached over for the alcohol himself. He filled his glass up and drained it in a couple of deep gulps, the liquid courage burning its way down his throat and into his belly. He almost immediately felt the buzz from it and his confidence grew.

"Then let's hope this works, General."

Zeng smiled at the spymaster. He turned to look out the window at the majesty of the city around them—the shining lights and the buzz of activity. This was one of the few places in China that wasn't dealing with a chronic power shortage. It hadn't been bombed either. There were parts of his command that had been devastated by the American bombings, like the Three Gorges Dam region, but not here. Not the Pearl of Asia—at least not yet.

As James refilled his glass of the brown gold, Zeng informed him, "You know, this morning I got orders from the CMC in Beijing. They want me to shift close to half of my military force to the west, to deal with India and reinforce our units in Tibet."

Feeling the increasing effects of the alcohol, James asked, "Would it make a difference?"

"It would reduce the number of forces I command here, which could be a serious problem for our plan. How soon are we looking at before this operation of ours is set to start?"

James gave Zeng a crooked smile as he replied, "Tomorrow."

Nearly choking on his beverage, Zeng shot him a nervous look. "You didn't give me much time to get things ready, did you?"

"You're right, Zeng. I didn't leave you a lot of a time, and for that I'm sorry. While you've spent your life in the military, I've spent mine lurking in the shadows as a spy. I know from experience that the more lead time I give you or anyone else, the greater the chances that it'll be discovered or potentially thwarted." James paused for a second before adding, "You and I both know China is never going to rise to be the great power we can be if our people are mindless robots. We need leaders like you and me who can unleash our people's creative greatness. As it stands right now, the world already reviles us for what we've been doing with the Q Program. The sooner we can distance ourselves from that horrible agenda and the men who started it, the better," James concluded. He placed his glass of alcohol down, realizing he'd probably had too much at this point, and reached for his water instead.

"I know. And you are right. Then let's get down to the last part we need to discuss. Is the money ready?" asked Zeng. James knew if he was going to pull this off, he'd need to be able to ensure his men would still be paid. The ones that might cause problems either needed to be bought off or dealt with separately.

James nodded and pulled out his smartphone. "I can wire it to you now. There's enough money to cover the salaries of you and your men for nine months. That should be long enough for us to get a new government set up and get things sorted."

Reaching inside his own suit jacket, Zeng pulled out a small notebook and handed him a piece of paper with some numbers written on it. "This is the account."

In the next few minutes, James Chan would have effectively bought himself an army to use and control for the next nine months.

"When this is over, General Zeng, you will be remembered as the man who saved China," James said as he concluded the financial transfer.

Zeng snorted. "That, or I'll be remembered as the man who destroyed it."

James shook his head. "No. That distinction will fall to me, General."

****

Following Day
Hong Kong

James looked at his watch, nervously waiting for the appointed time. In the next few minutes, the malware would be activated. He made sure he was sitting in his office, knowing that, as soon as this thing went live, he'd get a call from the Minister. He needed to be here, ready and waiting, when that happened.

Looking at his email, he hit refresh. Then he pulled up the internet, waiting for the browser to load the news homepage. Then he saw it: a headline saying, "Government Finally Releases Casualty Numbers." Another headline appeared: "UN Peacekeeping Mission, a Farce, Collapses." The headlines continued to propagate and spread.

Clicking back to his email, James saw a dozen new messages had just arrived. Then, nearly a hundred additional emails flooded into his inbox, most of them with the same news headlines he had just seen online.

Twenty minutes went by with no contact from Beijing. Then a half hour. Just as he was about to get up and use the bathroom, his secured video phone buzzed. It was the Minister, right on cue.

Answering the call, he said, "Good morning, Minister—"

"Chan, the firewall has been breached! What is going on? I thought you had averted this crisis. What do you have to say for yourself?"

Stumbling for some words, all part of his act, James finally replied. "Did the attacks originate in Hong Kong? I would have been alerted by our IT department if they had. It must be coming from somewhere else, sir."

"I need you to find out whatever you can on your end, Chan. You may be right. This attack may have come from another location, but remember, our warning said it was going to happen in your district, so you need to make sure it didn't. I want a full report by lunch!"

With that, the call ended, and James sat back in his chair and smiled. Pandora's box had been opened. Now it was time see how the people would react with the blindfold pulled from their eyes.

****

Guangzhou, China
Southern Theatre Command

Four hours after the cyberattack, General Zeng Shaoshan was on a video call with General Wu Guanhua, the commander of the PLA.

"General Zeng, what is the status of your forces? Has this cyberattack caused any problems within your units or among your commanders?" Wu asked nervously.

The rumors had spread almost as quickly as the cyberattack. There were reports of a division commander in Tibet surrendering his forces to the Indians; and two division commanders were apparently leading revolts, one in Beijing, and one in Shanghai.

"General Wu, my forces stand ready. I've spoken with each of my division and brigade commanders. They are with us," Zeng replied confidently to alleviate any suspicion.

"Zeng, I want you to mobilize your forces. Restrict them to base and have them ready to move into the cities to support the police if needed. The Ministry of Information and the MSS are working to stop this cyberattack from spreading. But between you and me, I don't think they can," Wu confided.

Lifting an eyebrow at the comment, Zeng pressed, "I haven't received word of widespread rioting. Just some minor problems. What makes you think they won't be able to stop the cyberattack from spreading?"

Shaking his head in disgust, Wu explained, "Because the Americans infected every government server in China. From what I've been told, we're going to have to take the entire system down until the servers can be replaced."

"If we have to take down all the email servers and nodes, how are we going to communicate?" Zeng blurted out in surprise. "Will this affect our phone lines as well?"

"I don't know, Zeng. That's why I was telling you to have all your units confined to their bases. This way, if our communications go down, it'll be easier to manage your units and maintain control of the situation and the cities."

Before General Wu could say anything further, their video call started to show some static. Then it cut out entirely.

Looking at the blank screen, Zeng smiled. James's plan just might work—disable the government's ability to communicate and they just might be able to pry some of the provinces away from the central government.

Sensing that now was the time to take charge and get his part of this operation going, Zeng called out to his aide, ordering him to send an urgent message to his division and brigade commanders. They were to place all their units on alert and have them confined to base and await further orders from him. He told his aide to make sure the commanders knew they were to listen only to him, and no one else—not until they could reestablish official contact with Beijing.

****

From Taiwan's *Liberty Times Online*:

> The Great Firewall of China has fallen, and the people of Mainland China are at long last digitally free.
>
> President Chen issued a statement decrying this brazen cyberattack by the Americans as an assault on the average Chinese citizen and said, "The People's Republic of China will respond with their own cyberattacks." It is not clear how those attacks would differ from the current attacks they are waging in their ongoing war with the United States.
>
> The American President, Jonathan Sachs, made a plea to the people of Mainland China to revolt against their government and force an end to the bloodshed in North America, saying, "Too many people on both sides have died. It is time to end this war and allow our nations to begin the process of healing."

****

From Singapore's *Straits Times Online*:

> There are reports of rioting taking place across many of the major cities in Mainland China. The people are pleading for the government to end the war in America, many of them claiming that the government lied to them about the UN mission to remove President Sachs.
>
> One woman said she finally learned of the fate of her husband, from whom she had not heard in more than eight months, when she was able to read the casualty list posted online. Around the time she last heard from her husband, she said, the military had stopped paying his salary but wouldn't confirm if he was alive or dead or explain why they had stopped paying his wages.
>
> Millions of families are suddenly finding out that their sons, brothers, or husbands died many months ago in North

America. Some families are demanding answers from the government, which continues to remain silent.

****

From Japan's *Yomiuri Online*:

> The United States Navy has officially cut off Chinese ground and air forces in North America from their supply lines to Mainland China. US naval forces are now sailing toward the South China Sea, looking to land a decisive blow against the remaining Chinese naval forces.
>
> There are unconfirmed reports out of the Prime Minister's office that Japan, which has remained neutral during this war, may join the United Kingdom, Poland, Romania, and Australia in the fight against China. While there has been no official statement by the Prime Minister's office, Minister of Defense Hayashi has canceled all military leave and ordered the defense forces to their highest levels of readiness.

****

Beijing, China

President Chen Baohua was trying to contain the rage building within, but it was becoming increasingly difficult. The last two days had been marked by one blow against his regime after another.

"Why haven't you found who perpetrated this yet?" Chen demanded. "There has to be an electronic trail leading to the origin of this malware."

Lifting his chin up, Geng Yun, the head of the Ministry of State Security, replied, "We have narrowed it down to the region where it originated, but not who sent it. Not yet." Geng had already executed more than a hundred people within the Ministry of Industry and Information Technology over that agency's inability to disable the malware plaguing their servers.

Lifting an eyebrow at the omission, Chen pressed, "And where did it originate?"

"The first reported observance of the virus was discovered on a server in Shenzhen, Guangdong. From there, it spread to the rest of the country."

The President nodded. "OK. If we can trace it back to the first server that was infected, then we should be able to trace it back to the person who sent it. When will you have that information?"

"Soon," Geng replied. "I think it may have originated from Hong Kong."

"I thought Director Chan stopped that plot. Are you saying he didn't?" asked the President.

"I'm not sure. Our source in British intelligence said the attack would originate out of Hong Kong. I know Chan had disabled their servers for a period of time while they kept several potential spies under surveillance. It's possible the malware still found a way out of Hong Kong onto our servers."

Interrupting the back-and-forth, Foreign Minister Jiang blurted out, "Mr. President, at this point, it doesn't matter where the attack originated. It's happened. We have protests spreading across the country as a result, and we now have the Japanese and the South Koreans joining the Americans."

Giving Jiang a dirty look, the President chided him for speaking out of turn. Geng for his part looked relieved not to be talking about his organization's failure to find the saboteur.

"What about the Japanese? Are they really going to pose a threat to us?" Chen asked his PLA commander.

General Wu tried to remain as emotionless as possible as he responded. "It depends on what the Japanese want to do. We have thousands of short-range ballistic missiles we could use against Japanese forces and their cities if we need to. Right now, I think the Japanese are all talk. When push comes to shove, they won't fight. The South Koreans...well, they're brawlers. They'll try to stir up some trouble across the Yellow Sea, but they don't have the military power to project much beyond their borders."

Chen nodded at the good news, then moved on to the domestic front. "General Wu, what can we do about the governor in Xinjiang? How do we regain control of the region?"

Wu sighed. "Right now, we can't," he replied. "Unless the military commander is able to regain control of the governor's office and the various cities, we're not going to be able to reclaim control of the region until I can send reinforcements. At best, that's several months away."

"How about you, Minister Geng? Is there anything your office can do to help restore order?"

"I've ordered my regional director to neutralize the governor and anyone who's supporting him. I'll know in a couple of days if they've been successful or what more may need to be done," the spy chief said, seeking to provide some good news during this meeting.

Just then, a messenger walked in and handed a note to the President, who read it quickly. He then slapped his hand on the table and screamed a couple of obscenities.

Alarmed by the sudden outburst, Jiang asked, "What is it, Mr. President?"

Seething with anger, President Chen replied, "It would appear one of General Wu's military commanders has decided to go rogue."

Chen stared daggers at Wu as if he was involved in whatever had happened.

Crinkling his brow at the statement, Wu asked, "What do you mean? What's happened, Mr. President?"

Pushing the paper across the table to Wu, the President waited a moment for him to read its contents.

"What do you have to say for yourself, General?" the President asked, his voice dripping with sarcasm.

Reading the report, Wu shook his head in disbelief. "I will have him relieved immediately," he replied. "We'll round up his family and have an example made of him for any other military officers who believe they can betray you and China."

"Excellent," Chen replied, smiling. "I want it done quickly—before any other generals get the same idea."

The rest of the meeting was spent trying to figure out how they were going to regain control of the narrative of things happening within China and what to do about the war in North America.

****

General Wu walked into the command bunker of the August 14th Building, oblivious to everything going on around him. He waved off a few subordinates who tried to hand him the latest reports from North

America. Right now, all he wanted to do was seclude himself in his office and think. He needed to figure out what to do next.

This wasn't supposed to happen like this, he thought. He and General Ma were supposed to assume control of things, not have his regional commanders go rogue on them. *This is going to complicate things. I need to talk to Peng...*

****

Several hours after returning to his fiefdom, General Wu was able to get a hold of General Zeng Shaoshan, his southern military commander. They'd established a video teleconference—probably one of the last ones Wu would be able to hold. The government was going to shut down the internet and intranet for a week while the technicians attempted to purge the servers of the malware infecting them.

Looking at his southern commander, Wu didn't see a man looking tired or nervous. He saw a man who looked like he was in control. Sighing, Wu realized he wasn't going to be able to talk his friend down from this plan. However, if he couldn't convince him to change course, he wanted to do what he could to understand why he would make these choices.

"General Zeng, I'd like to say it's good to speak with you, but I've received some troubling news from your district," Wu said softly.

Looking back at him through the video call, Zeng replied confidently, "General Wu, you have been a good friend and a good mentor, and I am sorry that I have brought you shame and trouble." Zeng paused for a second as he looked like he was searching for what to say next.

"President Chen is a dictator," he continued. "He's answerable to no one, not even the Communist Party. His lust for power and his greed has ruined our country and it's going to destroy our people. I'm doing what needs to be done, General. I'm saving China. I'm saving our heritage, our culture, and our people from certain destruction if we stay under the control of President Chen."

Shaking his head, Wu countered, "You are not saving China, Zeng. You are destroying it. Our strength is our unity. The Americans can't defeat us if we stay united. Can't you see you're playing into their hands? No. You must return your forces to our control and step down as their commander."

Zeng laughed at the proposition, his gaze turning hard as his eyes narrowed. "I don't think you understand, Wu. My command is with me. My men agree with me. Our eyes have been opened to the horrors President Chen has perpetrated on not just the world but the citizens of our own country. No, the people of China are with me, as are my men. It is *you*, General Wu, who should join me."

"General Zeng, I am imploring you—do not divide China. Whatever our differences are, we can work through them once we have defeated the Americans. We need to stay united—"

"You don't get it, General Wu. It is not *I* who has divided China. President Chen has everyone so paranoid about being turned over to the secret police and sent to a work camp that we can't even have honest conversations in our country. America is not the enemy of China. President Chen is." Zeng stopped talking for a moment as he looked at something off camera before returning his gaze to Wu.

"Wu, I consider you a close friend, my mentor. I am warning you as a colleague—do not try to reassert control of the south. I've closed the airports and railways into my command. I've ordered my men to secure our borders. I don't want to have to fight your men, but I will if we have to. Please think about my offer to join me. Together, Wu, we can unite China and bring our country into a new era of peace and stability."

The call ended, terminated by General Zeng before Wu had a chance to counter him or say anything further.

Shaking his head in disgust, General Wu looked over at Minister Geng, who had been sitting along the wall, outside of the camera's view.

Walking up to Wu, Geng put his hand on his shoulder. "You tried, General. He wouldn't see reason. Now it's time for you to take charge and put this rebellion down before it has a chance to spread."

Nodding, Wu let out a long, deep sigh. "Agreed. I'm going to issue a one-week amnesty period for his soldiers and officers to leave Zeng's command before we label them traitors and enemies of the state. It'll take me at least that long to redeploy forces down to deal with him."

Geng nodded and the two of them got up. They were going to head back to the presidential palace and brief President Chen on what had transpired during the meeting. They had to gain control of the situation before this rebellion had a chance to spread and take root.

Chapter Twelve
A New Era

Pearl Harbor, Hawaii

Standing on the flying bridge of America's newest warship, the USS *Warhammer,* Vice Admiral Ingalls couldn't help but feel a little jealous. He'd spent the last several years of his life making this ship become a reality. Now it was going to be commanded by another admiral and taken into battle without him.

Walking up behind him, Rear Admiral Aikens joined him at the rail. They watched the last remaining supplies being brought aboard. "It was a beautiful ceremony," Aikens remarked. "You built a hell of a ship, sir."

"It was," Ingalls replied, not taking his eyes off the deck crew as they guided another load from a shore crane onto the ship. "Although, I wish we could have had a couple more weeks or another month to work out a few more of her bugs."

"I'm sure the engineers said the same thing during World War II, when they were cranking out carriers and other warships at lightning speed," Aikens countered.

"Bringing the contractors with us the last month made a difference, though, I think."

"It sure as hell did," said Aikens with a nod. "That was a brilliant move, having them work on the ship and sleep on a transport ship when not working."

"So, when do you leave?" Ingalls asked.

"Officially, we leave tomorrow morning," Aikens responded. "Unofficially, we'll be shoving off in the wee hours of the morning while everyone is still asleep."

Some seagulls flew by, squawking as they went. A cool breeze floated across the ship, bringing with it the fresh smell of the ocean.

"Do you know if you're heading north or south?" Ingalls asked, curious to know where the first major battle with these new weapons would take place.

"We're going to sail into the belly of the beast—right into the South China Sea. Our orders are to tear up the Chinese Navy and Air Force bases within a hundred-mile radius from the sea and move up along the coast of the country, essentially destroying every single target of military or industrial value until they surrender. Total war," Aikens said a little quieter so only the two of them could hear.

"Ballsy, I'll give you that. She'll hold up, though. There isn't a weapon system they'll be able to throw at you that this ship can't handle, Aikens. She's the toughest warship ever to sail. Don't worry about that. Just bring her home in one piece. I'm staking my career and reputation on this being the future of naval warfare," Ingalls added.

If these ships worked as advertised, the Navy would move to phase out all of its supercarriers and replace them with Arsenal ships. A standard supercarrier costs the Navy around $1 billion USD to maintain yearly. The Arsenal ships, by comparison, would cost less than $200 million. They also only required a crew of sixteen hundred sailors, compared to five thousand on a standard carrier. Add in the fact that a single Arsenal ship packed as much combat power as an entire strike group, and it was a no-brainer to move in this direction—if they worked.

Extending his hand, Aikens said, "Deal. When we get back from this voyage, I'll buy you a beer and tell you all about it. This is going to work, Admiral. You've trained a hell of a crew, and the handful of contractors coming with us are topnotch. I'm confident the weapon systems will work, and we'll defeat the Chinese." Aikens paused for a moment before adding, "I hate to kick you off the ship, sir, but we've got to get everyone out of here that isn't sailing with us."

Ingalls laughed and nodded, and the two walked back into the bridge. They made their way through a few other sections of the ship before Aikens walked with him over to the gangway that would lead Ingalls back to shore. It was bittersweet leaving the ship he'd spent nearly four years building, but he felt good about what he had accomplished.

****

From *The Guardian Online*:

> Riots continue to spread across China as the government shuts down the country's internet service. In Beijing, the government had been rocked by five days of protests. The military was eventually called in and violently put down the protest.

There are also unconfirmed reports coming from the Xinjiang Uygur Autonomous Region in western China that Governor Shohrat Quanguo has cut off all communications with Beijing and declared the region an independent nation.

The government of Kyrgyzstan has closed its border with China, fearing a mass of refugees as people look to escape what could become a violent clash between internal forces still loyal to Beijing and those vying for independence.

From Singapore's *Straits Times Online*:

General Zeng Shaoshan, the head of the PLA Southern Military Command, announced that he has taken control of the following provinces in southern China: Hubei, Zhejiang, Yunnan, Guizhou, Hunan, Jiangxi, Fujian, Guangxi, Guangdong, and Hainan. This region has declared itself the Democratic Republic of Southern China.

President Chen issued an ultimatum to the renegade general, giving his command one week to either submit to the authority of Beijing or be labeled traitors and enemies of the state.

People took to the streets of Hong Kong and Macao, celebrating the declaration of independence from Beijing. A groundswell of support for General Zeng has quickly swept through southern China as people long for peace, and a new beginning.

Within hours of declaring his region's independence, General Zeng ordered the internet servers in southern China turned back on. He also removed the Great Firewall of China, allowing the people to freely search the internet. By the end of the first day, there were over nine million new Twitter users as people flocked to the social media site for the first time.

General Zeng said, "I call on the people of Southern China to unite with me as we seek international recognition from the United Nations and the rest of the world. I ask that you support me and my soldiers as we break away from the dictator Chen Baohua and end this bloody war with America."

Chapter Thirteen
War Crimes

July 2022
San Angelo, Texas

"We're approaching the outskirts of the city," yelled Sergeant First Class Matt Higgins to the soldiers in his Stryker vehicle. "Everyone stay frosty. Heads on a swivel."

Moving down the four-lane highway, Higgins saw the two JLTVs following the highway to the right. They were heading into the heart of the city, looking for a fight. Trailing behind the two vehicles acting as scouts were a pair of M1A2 Abrams battle tanks and the rest of the battalion.

When the lead element of the convoy reached the overpass on US-67/Main Street, all hell broke loose. A pair of Kornet antitank guided missiles streaked out toward their tanks. Then a slew of advanced RPG-30s joined the fray, heading right for the rest of the armored vehicles in the convoy.

"Contact left. Apartment buildings!" shouted Higgins as he continued scanning for targets.

Pop...boom!

One of the tank's antimissile systems destroyed one of the incoming missiles, but the other missile slammed into the side of the tank, exploding into the side armor. The tanks ground to a halt as it started to spew black smoke. Moments later, the crew started bailing out of the tank.

The one tank that survived the initial wave of antitank missiles turned its main turret toward the buildings, its gunner scanning for where the missile had come from.

As this was happening, several heavy-caliber machine guns opened up on the convoy from both sides of the highway. The lead tank fired its main gun into the building where one of the machine-gun crews was located.

Bullets hit the Stryker Higgins was in, causing him to duck. Several of his soldiers returned fire, shooting at a handful of different positions.

"RPGs to our left!" shouted another of his soldiers.

Higgins turned to the opposite side of the Stryker just in time to see an RPG streak toward the Stryker behind them. It slammed into the side of the vehicle and exploded. Something else inside the vehicle blew up, causing a massive explosion. One of the soldiers standing up in the rear of the vehicle was thrown into the air, both his legs missing from his body.

Leaning down to yell at the vehicle commander, Higgins shouted, "Get us off this freaking road! We need to dismount, but not right here!"

The driver gunned the engine and the vehicle lurched forward. They drove off the highway and through a fence separating the frontage road from the highway, headed right toward a cluster of homes. All they wanted to do at this point was get out of the kill box they'd driven into.

An explosion erupted near them, slapping the vehicle with shrapnel. One of his soldiers yelled out in pain as he fell back into the vehicle. Bullets and RPGs were flying every which way around them.

When the driver got them off the main road, he stopped a block away from the highway they'd just been on. The vehicle commander dropped the ramp and started manning the Ma Deuce to cover them. Seconds after the ramp was down, the soldiers exited the vehicle as fast as they could. Moments after they did, an RPG flew out and hit their vehicle. The explosion blew the left front wheel apart, disabling their ride. The vehicle commander ducked from the blast of the RPG and then fired a slew of .50-caliber rounds at the house the RPG had been fired from. The large-caliber slugs ripped apart the house, and hopefully the enemy soldier using the weapon.

"Contact at our ten o'clock!" yelled out one of his soldiers as he started firing his rifle.

Lifting his own rifle to his shoulder, Higgins saw three figures attempting to hop into a black SUV. He pulled the trigger, hitting one of them, and then continued to fire into the vehicle. Several other soldiers in his squad did the same, but the vehicle sped away before they could disable it.

"On me!" shouted Higgins as he ran forward.

Enough of this crap. We're going to flush these bastards out.

Running toward the housing development, Higgins spotted two soldiers firing at the convoy still on highway. He depressed the trigger, sending a handful of rounds at them. One of the soldiers got hit. His partner turned the machine gun around and started shooting Higgins and his men.

"I'm hit!" screamed one of his guys as he tumbled to the ground. The soldier scrambled to find something to hide behind, bullets ricocheting off the ground around him as he tried to get out of the way.

Stopping in front of an abandoned car, Higgins took closer aim at the lone machine gunner shooting at his guys. Squeezing the trigger, he saw his bullets hit the guy, who clutched at his throat and fell over.

"Let's move!" Higgins yelled as he ran past the vehicle he had just been shooting from, wanting to make it down the block and get behind the enemy soldiers still shooting at their convoy. Running up behind him was one of his squad leaders, bringing with him ten more soldiers. With three squads of soldiers now, Higgins had them fan out and move through the back and front yards of the houses along the highway. They needed to clear this pocket of resistance so the rest of their battalion could get into the city without getting all shot up.

Ten minutes later, Higgins's platoon and the rest of his company cleared the ambush site. They dragged the bodies of twenty-eight enemy soldiers into the street so the CID and counterintelligence guys could try to ID them. When they looked at the first couple of dead enemy soldiers, they discovered something new and unexpected. These weren't Chinese soldiers—they were European. More importantly, the group that had ambushed them appeared to be private military contractors.

What Higgins and his buddies wanted to know was who did they belong to? And why would PMCs be fighting them here in Texas? The men of the 1st Armored Division hadn't come across any PMCs in their sectors before, so this was a new and scary development considering how effectively these guys had fought. In the short time it had taken these private military contractors to launch their attack, they had killed eighteen soldiers and wounded thirty-four. They'd also destroyed three Abrams battle tanks and half a dozen Stryker vehicles. By any standard, that was an incredibly effective ambush.

As Higgins's platoon worked on cleaning up the ambush site, the rest of their battalion continued to push through the rest of the city. Aside from this ambush, the rest of the city was liberated with little to no enemy contact. The only other resistance they encountered was around the Air Force base of San Angelo.

"Here comes the last CASEVAC helicopter," called out the lieutenant as he stepped out of the JLTV.

Walking up to their new butter bar, Higgins commented, "Sir, we should get everyone ready to roll and go catch up with the rest of the company."

Turning to look at him, the LT had a look of confusion on his face as he asked, "Shouldn't we bury them?" He waved his hand at the bodies of the PMCs. The CID and CI guys had just finished taking their biometrics and pictures.

Higgins shook his head. "Bury them? Not our problem, sir. Let the CID folks figure out what they want to do. We've secured the site, gotten the wounded out and kept the area clear for CID. The rest of the company may need our help. We should get ourselves ready to go help them." Higgins had been doing his best to guide the new lieutenant, their third since the start of the war.

This dude ain't gonna make it, he thought.

The lieutenant nodded. "You're right, Sergeant. Thank you. Gather up the men and let's get ready to leave."

Higgins started getting everyone loaded up into the Stryker vehicles they had left. He looked longingly at his own vehicle, but the front part of it was utterly destroyed. He wasn't going to be riding in that truck anytime soon. Fortunately, he'd gotten his ruck out of it, which was all he cared about. His few worldly belongings were in that ruck.

Piling into the remaining vehicles, the platoon of soldiers headed further into the city to catch up with the other platoons. Fortunately, all their vehicles were equipped with a blue force tracker, which made it a hell of a lot easier to see where the friendly units were.

"Look at this, Sergeant," one of his soldiers said.

Higgins got up and stood on his seat to see what the soldier was pointing at. "What the hell…?" was all he managed to say.

One of his soldiers threw up while a couple more cursed loudly.

"What the hell is going on?" yelled another as he looked to Higgins for an answer.

"Who would have done something like this?" replied another soldier angrily.

"These are some sick bastards," one of his sergeants said.

Their Stryker vehicle was driving past Angelo State University, and what they saw was horrific. Nearly every tree had a dozen or more people hanging from its branches. Many of them were naked; all of them were dead. It wasn't just a few trees, either. It was hundreds of them, plus lampposts and just about any other object you could hang a person from.

Seeing two soldiers talking to a group of civilians on the side of the road in front of a run-down house, Higgins told the driver to stop nearby. When the Stryker parked, Higgins got out and told his soldiers to spread out and stay alert. He wasn't convinced all the PMCs had left the area just yet. One could still hear a random shot or two every now and then.

Walking up to the two soldiers and the civilians, Higgins saw it was a buck sergeant and a specialist from Fourth Platoon talking with them.

Taking charge of the situation, Higgins announced, "Excuse me, I'm Sergeant First Class Matt Higgins. Can any of you please tell me what the hell happened here?"

A woman who was near tears exclaimed, "They murdered everyone. Anyone they could get their hands on. They just murdered them." She broke down into hysterical sobbing as she pointed at all the people hanging from the trees.

Turning to find one of his squad leaders, Higgins shouted, "Sergeant Rice, have your squad start cutting those people down from the trees. We're not going to leave them hanging like that. Oh, before you start doing that, though—I want someone with a camera to take photos of all this. We've clearly stumbled onto a war crime, and I want it documented.

"Specialist Hams, get on the radio and find the captain. Tell him he needs to come to my position. Get the LT over here too."

Turning to look back at the woman who was still crying, Higgins asked the man who was trying to console her, "Can you tell us what happened?"

Nodding, the man wiped some tears from his own cheeks and took a deep breath. "I'm Terry. This is my wife, Amy," he said as he offered his hand. Higgins shook it. "Five days ago, the Chinese soldiers left the city," the man continued. "They didn't say anything to us or tell us why. They just up and left. We thought we were being liberated or maybe one of the local militia units had finally forced them to leave. Then a group of several hundred Russian mercenaries arrived."

Higgins held up a hand up to stop the man. "Whoa. How do you know they were Russian mercenaries?"

Terry snorted at the question. "Because I worked for Triple Canopy in Iraq in the 2000s," he replied. "I know private military contractors when I see 'em. These guys also spoke Russian. My guess is they're probably Wagner Group."

Higgins lifted his head up at the realization. *It all makes sense now. That explains why these guys hit us so hard...*

"OK. Please continue, Terry," Higgins said as the lieutenant walked up to them. Higgins put his finger to his lips so the LT wouldn't interrupt the man as he spoke. The poor guy was practically skin and bones, as was his wife.

"When I saw this was probably a Russian PMC group, I knew nothing good was going to happen. I grabbed my wife and some of our friends we'd banded together with, and we hid. We just tried to stay out of their way and hide until either they left or you guys arrived." He paused for a moment. "Do you have a cigarette? Some water or food we can have? We haven't eaten in days."

Blushing, Higgins realized he hadn't even offered the man anything. He felt like an idiot.

"Get these people some chow! Grab some MREs, and let's leave them one of our jerry cans of water," Higgins ordered.

One of the privates brought the man a case of MREs. Another soldier gave them a five-gallon jerry can of water.

"I'm sorry about that, Terry. If you'll tell us where the rest of your people are hiding, I'll send some soldiers to tell them it's safe to come out. We'll get you guys some more food and water. We'll get our medics to take a look at your folks as well if you want."

The man nodded and whispered something to his wife, who stood. "I'll lead some of your soldiers back to where the rest of our group is hiding," she said.

"Uh, sorry about that, Sergeant. Food's been pretty scarce around here," Terry said. "Ah, as I was saying, we did our best to hide and stay out of their way. They started going house to house, grabbing anyone and everyone they could, taking them over to the Junell Center and locking 'em inside. Then they started bringing some of 'em out in small groups and hanging 'em." Terry hung his head low and started crying. "There wasn't anything we could do to stop them. All I could do was observe and try to keep our little group from being discovered.

"They were hanging people for days. Then the shooting started. Yesterday—before you guys came here. They started going house to house around the city, finding people and just shooting them. There was no rhyme or reason. They were just killing for the sake of killing. It was awful."

Higgins stepped toward the man. "This wasn't your fault, Terry. You did the right thing by protecting your wife and the group with you. These guys are professionals. There wasn't anything you could do. If you'd tried, they'd have merc'd you too."

The man nodded, but that didn't stop him from crying. He wiped away some tears before he added, "You have to hunt these people down and kill 'em all, Sergeant. Don't take any prisoners. Just find 'em and kill 'em all."

Moments later, a couple more Stryker vehicles showed up along with a couple of JLTVs. Higgins's captain walked up to them, a horrified look on his face as he saw the hundreds of bodies hanging from the trees. Higgins relayed what they had stumbled upon and introduced the captain to Terry.

Just as the captain was starting to ask questions, a gaggle of maybe two dozen civilians walked toward the group of soldiers with one of Higgins's squad and Terry's wife. The people looked terribly emaciated, reminding him of the pictures of the Jewish prisoners at the Nazi concentration camps. The people were just skin and bones, their clothes hanging on their bodies, practically falling off them.

Despite their hunger and what they had endured, the civilians were eager to thank the soldiers for liberating them. They hugged them, kissed them, and cried with them. The medics started checking up on them as they passed out food and water.

A couple of the soldiers rigged something up so they could cook up some coffee for the civilians. An hour later, the entire area was crawling with Army CID investigators and military police as they started processing the war crimes site. Their battalion commander wanted this place well documented. Higgins's men suddenly found themselves going door to door around the nearby houses and the surrounding area, checking to see if anyone was living in them or if there were any bodies. If they found a house full of dead bodies, they were to place a red X on the outside of the house so the investigators would know to come check the house out and take photographs.

What had happened in San Angelo was horrific. And as Higgins's battalion made this grisly discovery, the other battalions in the division were making similar discoveries in nearby towns and cities they were liberating—horrific scenes of atrocities and emaciated Americans.
****

Colorado Springs, Colorado
US Northern Command HQ

General Tibbets had just finished reviewing the videos and pictures of what the 1st Armored Division had discovered in West Texas. It was terrible, reminding him of what he had seen as a young lieutenant when in Bosnia, and then later Kosovo.

"The President is going to want options during our call later today," Brigadier General Estrada announced as he placed a set of photos on the table.

"I agree. The question is, what do we tell him? The Russians, like the Europeans, ended their military operations when the UN forces surrendered. We haven't had an engagement with a single Russian unit in months since the war ended. I mean it's not like we can just bomb one of their cities," Tibbets replied. It was just the two of them talking in his office. Soon though, they'd need to have something to offer the President.

"It's clear these are Russian mercenaries. There isn't any doubt about where they're from or who they're working for. Even the intel we've gotten from Task Force Avenger said the Wagner Group had been contracted to work in Texas. I don't see how this would be any different than if a country was harboring a terrorist group and we bombed them," Estrada explained.

"Yeah, I suppose you're right," Tibbets responded. "I guess that's a good way to phrase it. So if that's the case, then we need to figure out how we'd strike back at the Russians for harboring this group. We also need to keep in mind the blowback from such a strike. While the Russians didn't use any nuclear weapons during our short war, that doesn't mean they wouldn't if we bombed Moscow a second time, especially now that there's an armistice in place."

"True. Maybe we don't recommend a kinetic response. See if the Treasury Department can go after some of their financial assets, then.

Maybe that'd be a better way of responding. It wouldn't cost anyone their life."

Tibbets agreed. They'd recommend the President work with the Treasury Department to go after the Russians financially.

Shifting topics, Tibbets asked, "How soon until Task Force 70 is in range of launching their first attack?"

"Two more days. Then they'll be in range of their Tomahawks."

"Good. The rioting and civil unrest in China is really starting to grow. I'd like to try and move that along," Tibbets said. "I'd really like to get our forces in position to help General Zeng and his forces hold on to their territory. Between southern China and their western provinces revolting, this just might be the thing we need to end the war."

The cyberattack on China was succeeding beyond their wildest dreams. Within days of Cyberstorm, Beijing had ordered the entire country's internet and the government's intranet taken offline. That loss of control emboldened some military commanders and governors to assert their own control over their regions. The human intelligence reports filtering out of China said the country was starting to fall into chaos and anarchy.

Chapter Fourteen
California Dreaming

Bishop, California
Eastern Sierra Regional Airport

The plane ride from D.C. to Denver had been rather uneventful. From there, Gunnery Sergeant Mack had boarded a C-130 with sixty other Marines from 3rd Battalion to head back to California.

Sitting on the cargo seat, Mack smiled at the thought of finally getting back to his unit. He missed his guys. Technically, he wasn't supposed to be here. The doctors at Walter Reed had said he couldn't be cleared for duty. But Mack wasn't about to allow some rear-echelon doctor torpedo his chances to get back to his platoon and his Marines. He'd coaxed a gorgeous young nurse to accidentally switch his medical records with another Marine's and had the doctor sign off on him returning to duty.

It went against the rules, and Mack was certain he'd get in trouble if caught, but once he was out of the hospital and on his way back to the front, he figured he was in the clear. He owed that nurse a beer when this war was over.

Looking at the other Marines on the plane with him, Mack suddenly became aware that he was probably the highest-ranking guy. They all looked to be fresh cherries, straight from boot camp. They looked at him like the veteran he was, ready to do whatever he told them.

The aircraft buffeted a bit from the turbulence. Nothing serious, but it caused a few of the green Marines to hold on to their gear a bit tighter. For many if not all of them, this was their first ride in a cargo plane. Eventually, the aircraft started to descend. Ten minutes later, they touched down on the runway and the plane's engines changed pitch dramatically as it went through its process of slowing down. Once they were moving at a slower pace, the aircraft turned onto the taxiway and headed toward the hangars. When they reached the parking ramp, the Air Force crew chief started the process of lowering the rear ramp for everyone to get off.

Standing up and stretching his back, Mack felt the cool air from outside as it rushed into the cargo bay. The Marines inside started exiting the plane. A staff sergeant was at the bottom of the ramp, telling them where to go. He was leading them to a hangar, probably to in-process them to the brigade and then figure out where they were going to be filtered in.

When Mack finally got off the aircraft, he saw an officer walking toward him. Snapping off a smart salute, he immediately recognized Captain Ray Ambrose, his company CO.

Smiling, Ambrose slapped him on the shoulder. "It's damn good to see you, Mack. I didn't think you were going to make it when we put you on the CASEVAC."

"It's good to see you too, Skipper," Mack replied. "I honestly didn't think I was going to make it either. Apparently, the bullet settled just under my skull—no brain damage, though. It never actually went into my brain," he explained nonchalantly.

"I think you should do a product review of those new helmets. Show the guys your scar and how that thing saved your life," Ambrose replied as they laughed together.

He led them past the hangar with the new Marines gaggled inside. They made their way over to a JLTV parked nearby.

"I was coming down here to pick up some new replacements for the company when I saw your name on the manifest, and I knew I needed to come here personally and see you. When you left Denver, did they give you a new assignment?" Ambrose asked curiously.

Shaking his head, Mack replied, "No, sir. I told them I was a platoon sergeant from 3/1, returning to duty from being wounded. They didn't say anything about new orders and told me to hop on the plane with the new replacements heading here. Why, what's up? You don't have a place for me in the company?"

Stopping briefly in front of the truck, Ambrose turned to look at Mack. "Actually, no—we don't, come to think of it. However, I still have a first sergeant position open. I can get with the battalion commander and get you promoted if you want to take it. Otherwise, you're going to have to go to battalion or brigade and get a new assignment."

The two walked for a moment more without saying anything. Finally, when they reached the vehicle, Mack looked up at him. "As long as you don't saddle me with being the admin boy for the company, I'd be happy to be your first sergeant."

The two laughed for a moment before Ambrose said he'd make it happen. They got in the vehicle and drove away to head to battalion headquarters and speak with the sergeant major and the battalion commander.

Driving through the small town of Bishop, Mack couldn't believe how many Marines he saw here. It was like the entire division had set up shop in the town. Eventually, they pulled into the parking lot of the local high school.

Mack lifted an eyebrow and Ambrose chuckled. "The regiment took it over a few months ago. It's our headquarters building for the time being."

The two got out and made their way in, heading right for the battalion commander's office. When the two of them walked in, the sergeant major stood up and walked around his desk to greet Mack. The two of them caught up for a few minutes until the battalion commander was able to see them. Then the three of them walked into his office to talk.

The battalion commander was also glad to see Mack had returned to them. He'd recommended Mack for a second Navy Cross medal to go along with his third Purple Heart. He was a well-liked staff NCO and exceptional combat leader. His presence was sorely missed in the battalion. After a few minutes of talking, Captain Ambrose made the case for Mack to take over as his first sergeant—a position many of the battalions were short on. The war was taking its toll on the senior enlisted in the battalion just as bad as it was on the younger Marines coming from training.

Finally, the battalion commander relented when the sergeant major vouched for battlefield promoting Mack. This would be his second promotion in a year. Reaching into his drawer, the CO pulled a pair of first sergeant insignia out and tossed them on the table in front of Mack.

"OK, I'll heed the advice of the sergeant major and your company commander," said the battalion commander. "Congratulations, First Sergeant Mack. Don't make me regret this, OK?" He slapped Mack on the shoulder. "Get your company ready," he said. "In case you forgot while you were on vacation, there's a bit of a war on."

Mack chuckled.

"The battalion's now back to one hundred percent," the commander continued. "That means we'll be rotating back to the front. Word has it we're going to make another push against the Chinese. II MEF has finally formed up in Northern California, and I MEF has been given the dubious objective of cutting a clean line across the state so we can trap part of the Chinese Army group. The mission is simple, gents: locate, close with and destroy."

The group spent a few more minutes going over some company and battalion business—stuff Mack wasn't used to having to deal with, but things he'd have to learn now that he was taking over as the first sergeant. With the pertinent stuff taken care of, Captain Ambrose led him back to the company area.

The next couple of hours were spent catching up with some of his friends from the unit and learning who the new NCOs and some of the Marines were. He also met the various lieutenants, squad leaders and platoon sergeants. Once the pleasantries had been exchanged, Mack spent the rest of the day getting a feel for how the company was doing and what areas might need improvement. They had a couple more days in cantonment before they'd be unleashed on the PLA and head to the front to gear up for the next major push.

****

Three days later, the senior NCOs and officers were sitting in the briefing room as the battalion commander went over the mission. The battalion was going to heliborne over the mountains to the small town of Ivanhoe, northeast of Visalia. This would place them roughly seventy kilometers southeast of Fresno.

The Chinese 116th Mechanized Infantry Division and the 77th Motorized Infantry Brigade were stationed in Fresno and the surrounding area. The Marines wanted to dislodge them and force them to either retreat further north or abandon the positions and retreat south. In either case, they were going to be deep behind enemy lines until the rest of their regiment could circle around the Sequoia National Park and relieve them.

"When we set down, we're going to occupy this area here," the lieutenant colonel said as he pointed to a large open field surrounded by more farmland, giving them some good distance between themselves and the few towns and cities nearby.

"I need each company to move swiftly to secure your areas so we can get a base of operations established. We have roughly sixty minutes to get our perimeters set before Alpha battery from 1st Battalion, 11th Marines, starts to arrive. Three hours later, we need to secure objective Kilo, so Bravo battery can be airlifted in as well. These two batteries are going to be our only source of fire support until the rest of the regiment breaks through the PLA 3rd Armored Brigade and the 202nd Mechanized Infantry Brigade around Bakersfield.

"Once we have our firebases established, it'll be incumbent upon us to hold our positions until the rest of the regiment and eventually the division breaks through and links up with us. From there, it'll be a slugfest to punch a hole through the valley all the way to Atascadero and Morro Bay. At this point, we'll have cut their army in half," the colonel said. After nearly a year of fighting, they were finally nearing the end. They just needed to push a little longer.

****

Standing on the parking ramp, First Sergeant Mack saw the company was ready. Everyone had their gear packed and had extra ammo, food, and water with them. They weren't expecting this to be a contested landing, so each Marine was bringing with him as much extra gear as possible. It was going to take the pilots sixty minutes each way to deliver supplies and reinforcements, so they were trying to make each trip count.

Finally, the crew chiefs signaled they were ready for everyone to load up. Mack's headquarters crew was going to ride in the CH-47 Chinook. The company was split between Chinooks and Ospreys. The CH-53s were sling-loading the howitzers that would be coming with them, with their crews and initial ammo inside the massive utility helicopters.

The Marines in front of him moved forward, separating into two chalks, one loading up on each side of the aircraft. The center of the helicopter was full of supplies that had been brought on earlier.

Once everyone was on board, the blades turned faster, changing in pitch as the pilots built up speed until the flying contraptions lifted off the ground. Turning to look out the rear of the aircraft, Mack saw the other helicopters lifting off as well. The Ospreys took the air slightly ahead of them. The faster tiltrotor aircraft would race ahead of them, delivering the first wave of heliborne Marines to the objective. Mack's group of Chinooks carrying their immediate supplies would fly in next, followed by the artillery batteries. It was a choreographed chain of events. Moving an entire battalion of Marines in one swoop was a logistical challenge all its own. It was a move that would hopefully catch the Chinese by surprise and cause them to make a fatal mistake.

Flying through the valleys and troughs of the Sequoia National Park was beautiful—but that beauty had nearly killed Mack a handful of months ago, when his unit had fought off a brutal human wave attack on their base.

An hour into their flight, they emerged from the national park into an unfolding valley—the bread basket of California. A strange thing to get used to was the lack of vehicle traffic on the roads and highways below. There wasn't a vehicle moving anywhere—not even a tractor working the fields. In fact, most of the farm fields had gone feral, unplanted during the growing season.

One of the crew chiefs signaled to Mack. They were coming up on the LZ. Circling around the landing zone, Mack was able to see the initial perimeter the advance teams had set up. Small patrols of Marines expanded outwards, toward the nearby towns and small farmhouses. Then the Chinook landed, kicking up dirt, dust, and debris from the rotor wash, blinding them to their surroundings.

Mack and his group of Marines ran off the back of the helicopter and started dumping their gear. Then they ran back into the helicopter to grab another load, emptying the Chinook as quickly as they could. Just before the helicopters took off, their two BigDog quadpedal pack mules walked off. Moments later, the helicopter lifted off and turned to head back to where it had come from.

As the dust settled, Mack surveyed his new surroundings. He spotted a small cluster of trees along one of the perimeters and pointed. "I want our headquarters set up over there. Let's move!"

Watching the two mechanical pack mules move was still something he was getting used to. In all his years in the Corps, he never imagined he'd be going into battle with a robot. But seeing the damn thing packed down with more than five hundred pounds of gear, he couldn't imagine going into battle without them. They could carry a lot of extra ammo, food, and other heavy gear through rough terrain, leaving his Marines lighter and more maneuverable if they came into contact with the enemy. It was an awesome addition to the Corps.

While Mack was handling the HQ function of the company, Captain Ambrose went to work getting his platoons situated the way he wanted them along the perimeter. With Mack running things for him,

Ambrose was able to focus on the fighting aspect of his command knowing he had a solid, competent staff NCO in charge of everything else. The two worked well together and it showed.

Mack led his small headquarters detachment to where he wanted things set up. He wanted the place up and running quick so they could get their coms, scout drones, and aid station ready before the Chinese showed up.

Once the gear was settled in the copse of trees, several Marines went to work clearing out underbrush so they could set up their gear. They started unpacking the radios from the large Pelican case while a couple of the Commo guys put together the antennas that would extend their range. A of the Marines got a small tent and two tables set up to place the radios and the computer monitor for the drone feeds.

As the commo and Ops guys got everything set up, some of the other guys unpacked some of their portable solar panels, getting them hooked up to one of the heavy-duty battery storage units the BigDog had carried for them. This was the equipment that would keep their computers, radios, and portable drones up and running twenty-four hours a day.

With the headquarters element operational, Mack started making his rounds along the perimeter. He gathered the platoon sergeants in a school circle and gave them some instructions; soon they were barking orders and guiding the fireteams on where to build fighting positions and where to place the machine guns. In less than three hours, the Marines had established a perimeter, gotten their headquarters up and running, and scouted close to ten kilometers, pushing drones out and above them, extending the bubble around company battlespace in every direction. They were ready to receive the next unit.

****

Turning to look toward the mountains, Mack heard the rhythmic thumping of helicopter blades and saw a string of choppers sling-loading the howitzer battery that was going to set up shop inside their perimeter. Mack's company had been designated to provide security for the gun bunnies until the rest of the regiment showed up. The other two companies in their battalion would be the combat units while the units guarding the artillery would act as a ready reserve or QRF should they be needed.

It took close to twenty minutes for the Marines to get the guns unslung from beneath the helicopters and their initial supply of artillery rounds and powder offloaded. When they had completed those tasks, the artillerymen got the guns moved around and into position, clearing away any debris that would prevent them from traversing the guns from one direction to another. By midafternoon, the battalion had both of their firebases fully operational and blocking forces set up along the Golden State Highway between Fresno and Bakersfield.

****

As Captain Ambrose and Mack walked into the HQ tent, Mack overheard their drone operator say he had spotted something. The two of them moved toward the young Marine to investigate.

Mack looked at the video screen on the computer next to him. The Marine was typing something into a chat box on the side of a video feed.

The company XO, a senior lieutenant, commented, "Looks like they're sending a welcoming party."

Grunting at the comment, Mack said, "Yes, sir. Best let battalion know." Their battalion HQ had set up with India company and the other gun battery.

The lieutenant nodded at the suggestion and moved over to the bank of radios, reaching for the one that would connect him with battalion HQ.

Mack yelled out for one of the artillerymen to come over and see what was headed their way. They would need to get their guns ready to provide some fire support missions, and soon.

Steadily, the column of Chinese tanks and armored vehicles made their way down the Golden State Highway from Fresno to Visalia. Soon, the enemy would run into the temporary roadblock one of the other companies had set up.

A couple of Marines from the artillery unit walked over to them and looked at what the drone was showing them. They pulled out a map to identify where they were in relation to the roadblock, and where the artillery battery would lay down some fire. Mack suggested that the fire directional control group just set up shop in their HQ so they could leverage the drone feed for real-time artillery adjustments. The sergeant looked at Mack with a smile that said he should have thought of that himself.

A few minutes went by as the FDC guys came over and set their own computers up, getting the initial plots for the battery going. Now it was just a waiting game until the enemy came in range of them.

The drone operator turned to Mack. "First Sergeant, do you want me to get our own drones up higher and running high-angle slant tracks along our perimeter to see out further?"

Mack nodded, glad the corporal was thinking ahead. The enemy would send probing units toward them soon. The corporal could place a couple of their scout drones high above portions of their perimeter to keep an eye out for trouble before it got close to them.

Looking at his watch, Mack saw they had been on the ground now for nearly four hours. He was kind of surprised it had taken the Chinese this long to send a force down to deal with them. During the commanders' call the day before, they had anticipated the Chinese sending a scout unit to investigate their landing right away and an attack force within the first two hours. The fact that the enemy was reacting this slowly might bode well for the Marines.

"Lieutenant Williams, I've got access to Overwatch. You want me to pipe them into the main screen?" asked one of the operations sergeants.

Overwatch was the call sign for the Global Hawk UAVs, which were flying much higher than the Reaper UAV they were currently piped into.

The lieutenant looked to Mack as if asking what he should do. Mack smiled and nodded, letting him know without saying anything that they should switch over to the bigger drone feed. It had a much better situational awareness capability. The bigger the picture they could see, the more informed they would be about the enemy's intentions.

Seconds later, their thirty-inch screen was filled with several images. One larger image displayed the column of enemy vehicles, while another smaller image showed a different vantage point of the column and a third image showed the column from a rear-facing view. On the right side of the screen was a chat box that allowed them to communicate directly with the UAV operator out of Creech Air Force Base.

Walking up to Captain Ambrose, Mack said quietly, "We should try and see if we can't get some aircraft stacked up to go after that column. They've got at least a dozen tanks with 'em. Those'll be tough for the weapons platoon to take out."

Ambrose smiled and nodded. "Sergeant, see if Guardian has any heavy antitank missiles available to plus up the SMAWs and AT-4 in the weapons platoon."

Reaching for a notepad on the table, Ambrose found the call signs and frequencies he was looking for. He switched frequencies on the radio for their close air support or CAS unit and started calling in what they were seeing. Thirty seconds later, he had three pairs of F/A-18s en route to their location. The Hornets were roughly thirty minutes away, so for the time being, they'd have to rely on their own capabilities.

****

The Reaper UAV pilot, call sign Guardian, responded in the chat box that he had four Hellfire missiles available. He asked which targets they'd like hit. Captain Ambrose directed them to focus on taking out the tanks. The other vehicles they could handle on their own if they had to.

Looking at the screen, they saw four objects fly briefly through the air before they impacted against the tanks. The convoy immediately broke up as the vehicles hunted for cover. Many of the soldiers inside the armored personnel carriers started bailing out of the vehicles, and so did the ones in the trucks. No one was going to take a chance on getting blown up if more missiles rained down on them.

When the convoy stopped, the artillery officer ordered their guns to start firing. Moments later, the six 155mm howitzers fired, sending their first salvo toward the enemy. Seconds later, the second battery of guns a kilometer away joined them and fired off a volley of their own. Twenty seconds after the first volley, they sent a second.

In the time it took the first set of rounds to land amongst the enemy soldiers, the Marines had three more on the way. Now it was just a matter of keeping the pace up for a couple of minutes to make sure they pulverized the Chinese unit. If they could nail them now, before they got organized, they might not even have to deal with them until after the rest of their regiment arrived.

After the gun bunnies had fired off six rounds, for a grand total of seventy-two rounds between the two batteries, they checked fire and waited for the dust and dirt to settle.

"Loki element, Overwatch. How copy?"

Lifting an eyebrow, Mack reached for the handset. "Overwatch, Loki Nine. Send it."

Captain Ambrose walked over and so did the Ops sergeant, listening to what might come next.

"Loki Nine, we have two PLA elements moving toward you. One is coming from McFarland to your south, the other is moving toward your positions from Centerville to your north. Be advised, both groups appear to be battalion-sized elements. They look to be a mix of infantry fighting vehicles and APCs. How copy?"

Everyone turned to the monitor that had the UAV feed patched in. They didn't see the footage. "Check to see if there's another drone feed we're missing. Those angles don't appear to be showing these newest units," Ambrose said to the Ops sergeant.

The sergeant did a quick check and sure enough, there was another feed they weren't patched into, which had a much broader view of the battlespace. It wasn't zoomed in on any particular area. If they looked close enough, though, they could see the columns of enemy vehicles moving to encircle them.

"Overwatch, that's a good copy. Thanks for the heads up. We'll retask CAS to interdict. Out." First Sergeant Mack turned to the captain. "Sir, I think we should split our CAS mission up to hit those two elements before they get close to us."

The gunnery sergeant in charge of the FDC section jumped in before the captain could respond. "Actually, First Sergeant, we should focus the CAS mission on the unit to the south. We'd have to reposition the guns if we want to fire at them. We can hit that unit to the north in our current position."

"That's a good call," Mack replied. "We'll switch the CAS mission to the south. Gunny, get your guns pounding that unit to the north. Top, make sure the guys are ready for an attack from that direction."

With the orders given, Mack grabbed his rifle and trotted off toward the northern part of their perimeter to let the guys know an enemy force was less than ten kilometers away. He also grabbed a couple Marines from the heavy weapons platoon and told them to bring a couple of their Javelins with them. If there was going to be enemy armor, he wanted it taken out quickly before their heavy weapons had a chance to mess up their lines.

The next ten minutes saw a lot of artillery fire and the screaming sound of jet engines. Then one of the platoons to their north made contact with the first Chinese elements. The gunfire grew in intensity. The gun bunnies moved their howitzers practically vertical as they sought to provide fire support to the units a few kilometers away.

"Contact! Fifteen hundred meters!" called out one of the spotters on the line.

Mack scrambled over to where he was. "What do you see, Corporal?"

The young man turned. "Looks like an infantry fighting vehicle. It stopped on that large farm over there." The young Marine pointed.

Lifting his own field glasses to his eyes, Mack spotted the vehicle. Its turret was looking right at them but not firing just yet. Looking around the vehicle, Mack saw a lot of soldiers filtering into the industrial-sized farm and the terrain nearby, taking up positions.

Why aren't they firing on us?

"Can you get a shot on that guy?"

"I—um, yes, I can fire the Javelin at him," replied the corporal hesitantly, "but he'll just duck behind one of those barns or silos. I'm not confident the missile will hit it even in its top-down attack mode. He could pop his IR smoke and move. It'd be best to wait for a slightly better shot."

While Mack and his guys were trying to figure out what to do, they heard a whistling noise grow until it thudded behind them.

Boom, boom, boom.

Enemy artillery rounds started landing amongst the artillery battery behind them, throwing up huge chunks of dirt, debris, and bodies. One of the rounds hit the propellent cans, causing a massive secondary explosion. Dozens of Marines were thrown sideways and flat across the ground from the concussion of the blast.

Looking at the carnage to their rear, Mack saw three of the six guns were permanently out of commission. Another lay on its side while two of them appeared to be in working order. What was left of the crews started to work the two remaining guns. A fire direction Marine was shouting out gun corrections as he relayed information from the AN/TPQ-37 Firefinder radar, re-aiming them to start a counterbattery mission.

While they were doing that, Marines cried out for help. The ones that could move scrambled to assist their wounded buddies while the corpsmen ran forward to render what aid they could.

"They're moving, Top!" one of the Marines nearby yelled out to get Mack's attention.

Sure enough, the Chinese soldiers were bounding forward. They were moving in good order, one group rushing while the other stayed ready to provide cover. Then they'd swap positions and repeat the process. It was almost mesmerizing to watch a battalion-level movement like that, but these soldiers racing toward him were bent on killing Mack and his men.

"Hold steady, Marines! Wait until they cross within five hundred meters and then only the machine guns open up. The rest of you wait until they cross three hundred meters. Watch your rates of fire and maintain your sectors of fire!" Mack yelled so everyone on the line could hear him. He then turned to the corporal. "It may not be the best shot, Corporal, but take it anyway. I want to let him know we see him. I think that IFV may be calling in that artillery on us. If nothing else, his main gun will start to tear into our lines once their infantry get a bit closer to us. Just do the best you can, all right?"

The corporal nodded as he got the antitank missile ready to fire.

Jumping into the position next to him, Captain Ambrose said, "Thanks for getting the line organized, Top. I think they could probably use your help back there working on getting the wounded taken care of and a CASEVAC. We'll handle things up here."

Almost forgetting his position as first sergeant, Mack nodded and took off to the center of their positions, where the wounded Marines were. He saw one of the Marines with a radio, calling in a nine-line to their helicopter support group. They'd hopefully organize some sort of CASEVAC from Bishop.

There had to be close to forty wounded Marines, most of them in a pretty bad way from the artillery strike. Mack knew they needed to get most of these Marines moved out of here before the Chinese decided to send a few more rounds in to finish the job.

Seeing a guy with a leg injury, Mack knelt and helped the wounded man apply a bandage. Then he aided the guy up to his feet, pulling his arm over his shoulders and carrying him over to the headquarters section. It was far enough away from the remaining artillery guns and hopefully out of the way enough that whoever was spotting those rounds wouldn't find them.

When he got the first man moved to the casualty collection point, he went back to grab another. Mack started yelling to the corpsmen and other Marines rendering aid to get the wounded moved to the collection point he'd established. They had to get them relocated out of there before more rounds started to hit.

Mack had just helped his third wounded Marine when they heard the shriek of incoming artillery. Several rounds hit the remaining two guns, pulverizing their positions. Then the Chinese walked a few rounds in on their northern flank, where he had just been earlier.

Moving toward one of his Marines working the radios, he called out, "When are those CASEVACs getting here?"

The Marine turned to look at him, a bit frazzled from everything going on around him. "The first bird is ten mikes out. I've got two more coming ten mikes after that. Then there's a fourth one coming thirty mikes later."

Mack gave the Marine a thumbs-up and passed along the information to the corpsmen as they worked on the wounded. Everywhere Mack looked, there were injured Marines. He did his best to move along the lines, checking on each guy and helping to place dressings on wounds, tighten tourniquets, or just offer some words of encouragement. In the case of one Marine who wasn't going to make it, Mack sat there with him, holding his hand as he told the young man it'd be all right—he had done well, and Mac was proud of him. The man slipped away moments later, and Mack closed his eyes.

Then the roar of gunfire really started to pick up. Mack turned to look at their northern line. The fighting along the perimeter was in full swing. All the riflemen were joining the fray now, sending as much hot lead at the enemy as possible.

Small explosions erupted amidst the Marine lines—mortars and RPGs. Mack knew more guys would be injured and in need of help. He grabbed one of the corpsmen and told him to grab some ammo. If they were going to run over there, then they'd bring as much ammo as possible.

Mack grabbed four fifty-round belts of ammo and placed them over his corpsman. He then grabbed four belts himself, along with a patrol pack filled with thirty or so magazines. The two of them took off at a quick run, laden down with extra supplies.

As they neared the lines, bullets zipped past them, hitting dirt and underbrush around them. Mack felt at least one round zip through part of his trousers, missing his leg by fractions of an inch.

The corpsman dumped the extra belts of ammo next to one of the M240G gunners, who gave him a quick nod of thanks. The assistant machine gunner grabbed one of the belts and connected it to the current belt in the gun.

The Navy man then made his way to the wounded Marines, doing his best to treat them and get them back into the fight.

Mack moved down the line, dropping off a new belt of ammo to the machine gunners or giving a rifleman a handful of fresh magazines. When he turned to look at the charging horde, he moved his rifle to his shoulder. He took aim at one of the attackers and fired two rounds, hitting the guy squarely in the chest. The Chinese soldier went down, then scrambled to find some cover. Amazingly, the man lifted his rifle back to his shoulder and started shooting at Mack's Marines. In that moment, Mack realized that the guy was wearing body armor.

Damn, these aren't untrained draftees or militiamen, then...

Aiming back at the soldier, bullets still whipping around him, thudding into underbrush and dirt near him, Mack squeezed the trigger and saw his round slam into the Chinese soldier's face. His body went limp and he was no longer a threat to his Marines.

"Ammo! I need ammo!" yelled out a Marine.

Mack turned to see a lone Marine in a fighting position, his two buddies next to him either dead or wounded.

Jumping out of his own position, Mack ran to him. He scrambled into the slight depression and tossed the Marine a fresh magazine from his patrol pack. The two of them started firing at a cluster of enemy soldiers charging toward them. They hit four of the six attackers, causing the remaining two to seek cover.

"I'll keep them pinned down. Grab some mags from my patrol pack," Mack ordered as he tossed him the bag.

The Marine pulled some mags out and began to refill his ammo pouches. While the young man was restocking, Mack did his best to place well-aimed shots at the remaining two guys shooting at them. The enemy soldiers were probably forty or fifty meters from them. Mack reached for one of his grenades and pulled the pin, throwing it at the Chinese soldiers for all his worth.

"Frag out!" he yelled as he grabbed for his rifle again.

He watched the grenade fly and land right between the two PLA soldiers, exploding fractions of a second later. One of the enemy soldiers screamed out in pain as he writhed on the ground. His buddy yelled something at Mack as he started firing his rifle on full auto.

Mack grabbed the Marine next to him and pulled him down as a string of rounds tore through the air above them. A few seconds later, the shooting stopped as the guy ran out of ammo. Mack turned to find the man and saw him reloading. He aimed just below the enemy soldier's neck and fired a couple of shots. The guy fell backwards as he grabbed at the wound.

"Thanks, Top. I think he would have gotten me," the young Marine said as he finished slapping a fresh magazine in his rifle. "I'm all loaded up."

Mack nodded as he grabbed his patrol pack again. "Hey—if you run low again, make sure to check their ammo pouches," he said, inclining his head toward the fallen Marines in the fighting hole. "These guys have half their magazines still fully loaded. Someone may not be around to help you out like I just did."

Not waiting for the Marine to say anything, Mack moved down the line. He felt bad about leaving the young man alone with his two dead buddies, but he needed to make sure the other guys weren't running short on ammo.

The fighting along the line started to wane after a few more minutes. They had succeeded in stopping this attack for the time being. While there was a bit of a lull, Mack made sure he got ammo distributed to the guys along the line and worked with the corpsmen on getting the wounded brought back to the casualty collection point.

At this point, the CASEVAC helicopters started arriving. The first Osprey set down and when its rear ramp lowered, a squad of Marines got off, bringing with them more ammo and supplies. The corpsmen then ran forward with a dozen wounded Marines, bringing the most critical guys with them for this first set of helicopters.

The new squad of arrivals ran toward the aid station. When Mack made it over to them, he realized they weren't additional Marines. It was the brigade surgeon and a dozen additional corpsmen.

Walking up to him, a Navy lieutenant commander said, "We got word your unit had taken a lot of casualties. The battalion commander ordered me to bring our medical unit forward to your position." He paused for a moment before adding, "Top, I'm not sure we'll be able to get a lot of these guys flown out right away. There's some bad weather that's going to close up the mountain route for the rest of the day and evening."

Shaking his head in frustration, Mack replied, "I'm glad you came, then, Doc. Hopefully we can get some of our most urgent surgical guys out on the next couple of helicopters. We got hit with some artillery. Probably in response to our own gun bunnies. They hit us pretty good, as you can see." Mack waved his hand around the aid station.

The first Osprey managed to take twelve of their most critical guys out. The next was landing in a couple of minutes, and they'd get the next twelve most critical guys. The Navy lieutenant commander, along with the rest of his medical staff, went to work on some of the more injured guys.

When the next Osprey landed, ten more medical staff got off, bringing with them more supplies. Four of them lugged off two Pelican cases of medical goods and brought them over to the aid station.

For the next ten minutes, the medical staff worked on stabilizing the remaining wounded so they would be ready for the last helicopter. They had a Chinook coming, but it would be the last angel of mercy to take their wounded out because of the weather. It would also be bringing the rest of the battalion's medical supplies and staff.

Captain Ambrose walked up and talked with Mack for a moment before he talked to the battalion surgeon. For whatever reason, his little firebase was now becoming the battalion aid station.

Motioning for Mack to walk with him away from the others, Ambrose leaned in. "I don't think we have a single artillery gun that can work. What are your thoughts about our new situation?"

Mack thought about that for a moment. "I say we verify we don't have any operational guns. If we truly don't, then let's use the BigDogs to move whatever ammo and propellent we have left here over to India company. That way the other gun battery will have our supplies. As for the remaining red legs, let's integrate them into the perimeter. We took a few losses during that last attack. We could use the manpower on the line."

Ambrose nodded, then headed off in search of the battery commander for the artillery guns to find out if they had any working howitzers.

While all this was taking place, the gun battery with India company was still banging away a kilometer down the road, sending rounds downrange at the enemy—probably running some counterbattery fire on the enemy howitzers that had just messed up their sister battery.

Two hours later, the Chinese had moved more units into the area. Nearly all the companies in the battalion were now in contact with the enemy. The artillery battery they had left was firing a lot of rounds at the enemy as well, swiftly burning through their stock of ammo.

Word had it the rest of the regiment had broken through the PLA forces around Bakersfield and were now moving up the highway toward their position. The lead element, a tank platoon, was probably no more than twenty kilometers away, steadily moving toward them.

Standing in the headquarters tent, Mack was going over a list of their remaining supplies with his supply clerk. They had run through more than fifty percent of their ammo. He'd had the supply NCO call ahead to the regiment to let them know they were red status on ammo. They would normally have had some flown in from Bishop, but dense fog had settled in over the mountains, hemming them in. For the time being, they'd have to fight with what they had. Mack made sure the CO knew they were low on ammo. He passed the word down to everyone else: hold your fire unless you have a solid shot on someone. No more firing for the sake of firing or to keep the enemy's heads down; they needed to make their shots count.

Standing in the headquarters tent, one of the Ops sergeants announced, "They're moving toward the line again."

Mack walked toward the sergeant and saw that several of the groups of PLA soldiers they had been monitoring were advancing toward them. They had been watching the enemy with some of their little scout drones along the perimeter. They used the drones to make sure the enemy wasn't trying to sneak up on them from another point. When they made sure the other sides were clear, they started pulling a couple of squads from the other platoons to go shore up the perimeter that was about to get hammered.

Captain Ambrose looked at Mack. "Top, I can tell you want in on that action. Why don't you go help Lieutenant Williams and Third

Platoon? They'll need the help. I'm working to see if we can't get another CAS mission to hit those guys. I don't like all those units stacking up on us like that."

"Aye, sir," Mack replied with a smile. "Before I leave—my guess would be the Chinese see our position and realize if they can shift or dislodge us, the rest of the battalion line will fold. We're anchoring the right flank. If they turn us, they turn the battalion. They know the rest of the regiment is on its way, so if they want to stop us, they have to stop us here."

Ambrose nodded at the logic. Mack had been watching the maps and enemy movements longer than he had, and Ambrose knew Mack was a bit of a savant when it came to these types of things. During the war, he'd been right more times than he was wrong about the enemy's intentions, and Ambrose had come to trust his judgment.

"You're probably right. All the more reason I need my best down there. Hop to it, Top. I'll get us some CAS and see if the mortar platoon over in Lima company can help us out."

With that, Mack headed out with a couple of the corpsmen to the perimeter line. He got to the line just as the first wave of Chinese soldiers approached. Close to a dozen armored personnel carriers and infantry fighting vehicles moved with the enemy infantry, their heavy machine guns and cannons throwing a fusillade of lead at the Marines.

Explosions rippled all along the American lines as the Marines fired back. Several of the SMAW crews fired their rockets at the armored vehicles, hitting a few of them. Some missed and the crews worked to reload and fire another volley.

Red and green tracer fire zipped back and forth between the two lines as soldiers and Marines on both sides started taking hits. The cries for corpsmen rang out as Marines got hit by some of the machine-gun bullets or zinged by pieces of hot shrapnel.

Mack scrambled into one of the fighting positions with two other Marines. They were firing away with their M240 machine gun at a cluster of enemy soldiers trying to use an APC as a shield. When they'd been in the fighting hole for barely a minute, the whistling sound of artillery came crashing in on them as the ground around them erupted, chunks of dirt, grass, and underbrush rocketing into the air like a geyser with each impact.

As debris rained down on them, the enemy soldiers continued to charge, hurling themselves right at them, yelling and screaming louder and louder. The officers' whistles blew loud and constantly as they pushed their soldiers forward.

It was a surreal scene unfolding before them, but Mack knew he needed to snap himself out of it. He brought his rifle to his shoulder and methodically fired one shot after another at the charging horde.

Where did all these soldiers come from? I don't remember seeing this many on the drone feed was all that kept running through his mind.

With all the shooting and explosions going on around him, he hadn't even heard the sound of a tank engine. Suddenly, in the periphery of his vision, an Abrams main battle tank somewhere on their left flank, a kilometer or so away from them, fired his main gun. The tank's round flew flat and true and slammed into one of the charging infantry fighting vehicles. The armored track blew apart, throwing hot shrapnel and flames in every direction. Mack turned to look at the charging tank just in time to see several antitank guided missiles reach out for it. Two of the missiles were destroyed by the tank's antimissile system, but two others slammed into the battle tank. The Abrams ground to a halt as an explosion took place inside, the commander and loader's hatches exploding upwards into the sky as a jet of flame and pressure escaped the confined compartment.

Turning to look at the wave of humanity racing toward him, Mack heard the assistant gunner grunt as he took a couple of rounds to the chest. He looked at the Marine as he fell backwards, two large holes in his body armor. The man was dead before he knew what had happened. His partner, the gunner, kept firing away, not letting the sudden absence of his partner deter him from his mission.

Moving to take the dead Marine's place, Mack attached the next belt to the machine gun and got the extra barrel ready to be swapped out. A second later, the gun ran out of ammo and Mack started the process of swapping out the barrel. He slapped the quick release and, using the glove, he yanked the barrel out and placed the spare one in its place. The gunner quickly latched it into place as Mack handed him a fresh belt of ammo. The Marine charged the weapon and resumed shooting. Mack attached another belt to the one he was chewing through and then grabbed his own rifle and continued shooting.

The ground in front of their positions was practically covered in dead and dying soldiers, but the enemy just kept coming. More artillery rounds started to land among the Marines' positions while mortars landed amongst the Chinese.

"They're getting pretty close, Top!" yelled the gunner.

Mack grabbed a couple of grenades from his IBA and placed them in front of him. He reached for one, pulling the pin and hurled it into a crowd of enemy soldiers. He then reached for the second grenade and likewise threw it right toward the next group of PLA soldiers.

Crumpf, crumpf.

Just as Mack legitimately thought they were going to get overrun, an F/A-18 Hornet flew low and fast across the enemy position in front of them. The pilot released a pair of cluster bombs that enveloped a huge swath of the charging horde. The enemy soldiers were suddenly inundated with little bomblets exploding all around them, shredding their bodies with the tiny pieces of shrapnel thrown in all directions. A second Hornet flew over and released another stick of cluster bombs a little further back on the third and fourth lines of enemy infantry. The attacks had devastated the enemy lines as they began to falter. Then a new noise appeared on the battlefield.

Damn…it's those freaking suicide drones!

"Take out those drones!" Mack yelled as loud as he could. He raised his rifle to his shoulder and flicked his selector switch from semiauto to burst and started firing at the drones racing toward them.

Pop, pop, pop.

Mack hit one. It exploded. He moved his rifle to fire at another one.

Bang, bang, bang.

His Marines had nailed a few of the little Kamikaze drones, but many more had made their way through the gunfire, slamming into the Marines' positions.

"There's more of them coming!" another Marine yelled out.

Why did they wait so long to hit us with them?

Mack fired the rest of his magazine at one of the little buggers, but he missed. The suicide drone flew past their lines, and this time, a wave of them went after the rear area, their aid station and headquarters tent.

The drones flew in so fast, once the operator found something he thought was worth blowing up, he'd aim the drone right for it and run at it with all the speed and battery power it had left. The drone would be detonated either just before impact or right after it hit. The little bastards were hard to defend against and caused a lot of damage when they blew up.

Dropping his spent magazine, Mack put a fresh one in place and slapped the bolt, sending a fresh round into the chamber. He glanced back to the rear and saw the damage the second wave of suicide drones had caused. It angered him to no end that they didn't have a better tool than their rifles for taking those drones down.

A new noise arose. Looking beyond their perimeter, Mack saw half a dozen LAVs heading toward them, intermixed with a couple of JLTVs. He smiled, realizing the cavalry had finally arrived. Looking back toward the Chinese positions, he saw most of the attackers had settled into various fighting positions, exchanging shots with his Marines.

As the newly arrived armored vehicles from the regiment got closer to Mack's position, the remaining Chinese soldiers started pulling back. They knew they couldn't break through their lines now—not with a dozen armored vehicles and at least another forty fresh Marines showing up.

With the fighting largely dying down, Mack stood up and started moving along the line, checking on the wounded and doing his best to help organize the newly arrived reinforcements into the gaps in their lines. The wounded were finally being taken to the aid station, where they could hopefully receive the treatment they needed.

A lieutenant walked up to Mack from one of the vehicles. "Sorry we're late, Top. It was a hell of a fight down in Bakersfield."

Mack looked at the LAV. It had more than a few dings on its armor and had clearly taken a lot of hits from some small arms. He shrugged as he walked over to the young lieutenant. "You made it, and we held out. That's about all we can ask for."

The lieutenant looked behind Mack, his eyes widening a bit as he saw the ground covered in bodies—dead, dying and torn-apart Chinese soldiers. Then he saw the streams of wounded Marines being helped by their comrades back to the aid station.

"It looks like you guys barely made it, Top," he proffered.

"We live to fight another day. One more day closer to victory," Mack replied as he walked past the lieutenant to go check on his headquarters section and the rest of the company.

The fight to take California back was in full swing. It was now a race to cut off and trap as many of the Chinese formations as possible before they could get themselves reorganized and consolidated again.

Chapter Fifteen
South China Sea

Luzon Straits

Rear Admiral Aikens looked at the latest readout of the enemy disposition. When the Chinese had lost a third of their surface warfare fleet in the battles between California and Hawaii, they'd pulled all of their naval forces back to the South China Sea, moving their ships into the protective bubble of artificial reefs they'd turned into military bases to make their last stand.

These bases in the middle of the South China Sea posed a problem for Task Force 70. Aikens's task force had two major objectives: one, destroy the remaining Chinese naval ships in the Pacific, and two, attack the PLA ground forces in and around the Hong Kong area to support the growing insurrection taking place in the PLA Southern Command. He was then to sail up toward the Shanghai area and support another insurrection taking place in that area as well.

From all the intelligence he had seen thus far, there appeared to be two very successful coup d'états taking root in the Guangdong and Shanghai provinces. The higher-ups at the Pentagon had told him his number one mission, aside from clearing the Chinese Navy out, was to support those indigenous forces trying to separate themselves from the central government. Fracturing China was the surest way to end this bloody war.

A week ago, several SEAL platoons had carried out some in-depth reconnaissance of the island bases. Aside from the runways and the aircraft stationed on them, the Chinese had moved dozens upon dozens of antiship missile platforms to the islands. The missiles were well protected and posed a challenge for Aikens's fleet. Granted, the warship he was sailing on had been specifically designed to deal with this kind of threat, but it was still an untested system.

****

Sitting at the wardroom table, Aikens looked up at the ship's captain, along with several other commanders in charge of the ship's air operations, defensive weapons systems, and other division chiefs from around the ship. He had the captain of the *Spartan* and his senior division chiefs in the meeting as well. Today, they'd decide how and when to launch their attack.

Seeing that everyone was waiting for him to say something, Aikens announced, "This is it, gentlemen. The country has sacrificed much to give us the opportunity to bring these two ships to this very spot. They've given us the tools to defeat the Chinese. So how do we use them effectively and clear these islands?"

The division chief whose crew would run the railguns, Commander Dobs, spoke up first. "Admiral, if I may—I propose we hit Woody Island with a volley of conventional cruise missiles, just like the Chinese expect. While they're focused on tracking the cruise missiles, we use our main guns and go after those antiship batteries. Once we get an idea of how effective they are, we can use them against the rest of the structures on the island."

A couple others nodded in agreement. Technically, none of them knew for certain if these railguns were really going to work. Sure, they'd put them through some tests and they'd hit some test targets, but this would be the first time they would be used in combat, against a real target.

"Air Ops—any suggestions?" asked Aikens, wanting to make sure he got their thoughts.

Leaning in, the Commander, Air Group weighed in. "We're a long way outside our operational window. We'd have to use the Stingrays to get us there and back if you wanted my fliers to participate. Even with the midair refueling, it's a long flight. I think we should probably give the railguns a chance. I mean, the rounds may not even hit from this range, so there's that to consider." Aikens suspected that the fliers on the ship feared that the railguns, with their massive range and hitting power, might well put them out of business.

Chafing at the comment about his railguns, Commander Dobs replied, "They'll hit. All we have to do is adjust the arc on the guns. We'll essentially be lobbing these projectiles."

Snickering at the comment, Captain Webster, the ship's captain, added, "That's a hell of a lob, Commander. Some three hundred and sixty miles. That's more than double the range we tested."

Undeterred, Commander Dobs explained, "That's true, Cap'n. But the physics doesn't change. When the projectile is fired at Mach 10, it'll have the speed necessary to fly the distance so long as we arc it right.

Since we've got exact locations for those missile batteries, the computers will determine the elevation needed to hit 'em."

Admiral Aikens cleared his throat to get everyone's attention. "OK. Let's assume we launch some cruise missiles at these sites," he said. "What type of defensive systems are the Chinese most likely to throw at them? How likely is it that they'll get knocked down?"

The fleet's intelligence officer, a Navy commander, answered. "Our most recent intelligence of Woody Island indicates they have a multilayered defensive system. The first layer is the outer one. Several years ago, the Russians sold the Chinese twelve batteries of the S-400 Triumph model surface-to-air missile systems. They've since gone on to build another twelve batteries organically. These were the systems that gave us a hard time in Texas and California early on in the war. Intelligence says they have a single battery consisting of forty-six missiles. The missile pods could be reloaded once fired, but that'll take close to an hour.

"The second layer of air defense consists of a battery of HQ-16B, which are basically like the Russian Buk system. The Chinese variant, however, has a range of seventy kilometers. The final inner layer is the land-mounted Type 1130 or HQ-6B. This is an eleven-barrel 30mm close-in weapon system or CIWS that can fire an astonishing eleven thousand rounds per minute. According to our intelligence, it's able to intercept incoming antiship missiles up to a speed of Mach 4 with a ninety-six percent success rate."

A few of the officers and NCOs in the room let out a soft whistle. They hadn't heard about this new iteration of the Chinese CIWS, but it sounded like they might have advanced a little ahead of even the US Navy in that regard.

Grunting at the information, Admiral Aikens replied, "So what you're telling us is if we try and take either their air defense or antiship missile platforms out with missiles, we're going to go through a lot of them until one eventually gets through?"

The Navy commander nodded. "Yes, Admiral. We would. But we've also got a large magazine of missiles on this ship, so I don't see that being a problem either."

Chiming in again, Commander Dobs added, "This is all the more reason to allow us to hit them with the railguns. Worst case, Admiral, we miss, or the system isn't effective at hitting them from this distance. Then at least we'll have tried, and more importantly, we'll have learned some valuable information. But my money says we'll be able to systematically take these defenses out."

Turning in his chair to look at the map on the wall, Admiral Aikens thought about it. Looking back at the two competing camps, he finally said, "OK. Then let's send a token force of, say, ten Tomahawks at Woody Island. Once we know the PLA is actively engaging them, then I want our railguns employed. Let's hope Dobs and his boys can shoot."

****

Standing behind the Weapons Control and newly designated rating Nuclear Electromagnetic Field Operator, Commander Dobs watched the chief petty officer input the targeting coordinates into the computer. The video image of the railgun turret showed the massive guns elevating as they adjusted their position. Once the data was entered, the firing sequence showed a set of green lights.

Power ready.

EM field, stable, ready.

Rails, positive and negative, ready.

Projectile ready.

Railgun charged and ready in all respects.

Weapon ready to fire.

The petty officer waited for the order. Dobs smiled. "Let's make history," he announced. "Fire."

The small crowd of people around them watched and waited. The petty officer reached over and depressed the firing button. Looking at the railgun on the monitor, they saw the outer part of the barrel light up briefly. Then a loud sonic boom shook the ship as the first sixteen-inch projectile flew out of the barrel at Mach 10. The petty officer depressed the firing button on the second run, and it fired. Its projectile raced after the first one.

The autoloader icon went from red to green, letting them know the first barrel was ready to fire again. Then the second barrel indicated it was ready to fire.

"Keep firing. Let's fire another six rounds. That should take out the targeting radars on the island and their communication systems," Dobs said, feeling more and more confident that this would work.

It took them less than two minutes to finish their fire mission. Now they had to wait to see if the rounds had found their marks. While they were waiting, Dobs looked at the power cell for the guns and saw they had used about sixteen percent of their battery—roughly two percent per shot. That was a bit more than it probably should have used, but it appeared the batteries were recharging relatively quickly.

"Commander Dobs, we're getting a video feed from the *South Dakota*, Orca," called out one of the lieutenants a few consoles away.

The lieutenant put the video feed from the submarine on the big board. The sub had pushed one of its Orca II drone submarines to within two hundred yards of shore. Its slimline mast was barely visible above the surface. Since the war had stretched and depleted the Navy's submarine force, it was quickly becoming standard practice to get underway with two of these drone subs, adding firepower and capability to an individual submarine while minimizing risk to manned subs. Admiral Aikens had overruled the captain of the sub, telling him it was of vital importance that they know for certain if the railgun worked, but let him steer the Orca close to shore, allowing the sub to remain in deeper waters with its second Orca circling one thousand yards around the *South Dakota*, listening for any Chinese subs that lurked beneath the waves.

Looking at the screen, Dobs made out the location of the radar station controlling the surface-to-air missile batteries and the antiship missile systems. The area around the small building looked normal, with a few guards standing around looking bored.

Suddenly, the entire building blew apart. Chunks of concrete, metal rebar, sand and debris flew out in all directions. The radar station that had been there moments ago was completely gone. Before everyone could hoot and holler with excitement, the second projectile slammed into the next building and obliterated it as well. The overpressure from the impact of the projectiles was so forceful, it cracked the screen on the Orca's mast camera. For the next couple of minutes, they observed eight of the targets they had aimed for blow apart in spectacular fashion.

Admiral Aikens stood next to Commander Dobs and slapped him on the shoulder. "Well done, Commander. Well done. This ship just made history. This is the day the railgun changed naval warfare for the US Navy and the world."

"Thank you, Admiral," Dobs replied with a smile. "It's team effort, sir. I have some of the smartest, sharpest CPOs and junior officers the Navy has to offer working on this gun system."

With this success and confirmation, Admiral Aikens ordered both the *Warhammer* and the *Spartan* to fire away with their railguns at the known and suspected Chinese weapon systems on the island. Once those had been taken out, the Marines would move in to capture the artificial islands and remove them as a threat.

****

Five hours later, Admiral Aikens made the decision to split his force up. The *Spartan*, along with the two aircraft carriers that accompanied them, would lead a separate task force with their Marine contingent to finish clearing the Parcel and Spratly Islands in the South China Sea.

Aikens would take the rest of his force and sail toward Hong Kong. He didn't like the idea of splitting his force up like this, but the Secretary of Defense had been adamant. Aikens ordered *Warhammer* to flank speed; they needed to get in range of Hong Kong to provide whatever support the CIA and Special Operations Forces units on the ground assisting the rebels needed.

The Chinese government was nearing collapse. The Pentagon wanted to see what more they could do to push it over the edge.

Chapter Sixteen
Picking Sides

San Diego, California
PLA North American HQ

It was dark outside. Clouds had rolled in, obscuring the moon and the stars above. With no natural light, the flight line of the former naval air station was exceptionally dark. General Han didn't mind it being dark. It felt better this way. No light, no distractions. Just him and his thoughts.

How could things have gone so wrong for us? Where did I mess things up? What could I have done differently?

Han had been struggling with how the war had turned out. First it was the defeat in Colorado—that had been the first major sign of trouble. Then there were the continued attacks on his forces in Texas, which had pushed his Army into the southwest part of the state. It was bad enough having those forces essentially surrounded. At least there had been some hope that his Army in California could break them out, but when the Americans had recaptured Panama, that was when Han had known the war was lost. Their dream of turning the American Southwest and West Coast into a Chinese protectorate was dead.

Now it was about figuring out what to do next. His forces in Texas couldn't hold out much longer. Neither could his forces trapped in northern California. The Americans were steadily isolating his troops into smaller and smaller pockets and slowly choking the life from the PLA in the continental United States.

Shaking his head in frustration, Han knew he needed to come up with something soon. Beijing had been adamant about him not surrendering. Then again, what authority did Beijing have anymore? They'd abandoned him and his army. General Wu had ordered his forces to fight on, but with what? They weren't getting any additional reinforcements or supplies. Hell, President Chen and General Wu were barely holding on to power as it was. The country was falling into chaos, and his army was trapped here in North America, unable to do anything about the riots rocking their homeland.

Heading back to his command building, General Han Lei walked in and saw his guards go to attention. He saluted and continued deeper into the building, making his way over to the briefing room that also functioned as his map room. He walked in and began looking at the disposition of his forces and those arrayed against him.

Reading over the war stocks he had on hand and the burn rates of some of the units, he realized they were going to be in trouble. His units had enough supplies to get them through a few more months of heavy fighting, but that was about it.

One of his officers walked up to him, breaking his train of thought. "Sir, we just got this from General Boa. He said it's urgent that he speak with you."

The officer handed him the message and then walked back to the bank of computers and radios set up on the far side of the room.

Han looked at the letter. His commander in Texas was informing him that unless help was on the way soon, he was going to have to surrender his force.

Han sighed. He needed to make a decision, and he was going to have to do it soon.

"Captain, someone find me General Shin. Tell him I need to speak with him immediately."

****

It was 2200 hours when General Shin walked into the briefing room with Han waiting inside. Getting up, Han told Shin to follow him. They walked out of the building and along the runway, away from prying eyes and ears.

Speaking softly so his voice didn't carry, Han asked, "Shin, do you know the situation of our forces?"

A moment of silence ensued before Shin replied. "I do. They could be better, but we'll make do with what we have."

Han crossed his arms. "Have you heard what's going on back home?" he probed.

Shin stopped walking as he turned to look at Han. "Those duplicitous Americans have sown chaos and panic back home. Their NSA found a way to take down the firewall, spreading disinformation and propaganda against the government and the war. I even heard General Zeng Shaoshan from Southern Command has betrayed us, trying to form his own country."

"Yes. I've heard the same things, Shin," said Han with a nod. "Let me ask you a question—but before I do, I want you to know there is no right or wrong answer. I just want to know what you think I should do."

Shin nodded but didn't say anything as he waited to hear what Han had to say.

"I have two options facing me and our army. We can stay here and fight for as long as possible against the Americans. Without reinforcements or supplies, you and I both know we will only last a couple more months. The other option is we can try to work out an arrangement with the Americans to leave this place and bring our army home to help President Chen put down this rebellion and restore order."

Han paused for a moment, struggling to admit this last part and also unsure of what his deputy would say or do. Eventually he stuck his chin out, saying, "If we go home, Shin, we abandon all we have fought and died for here in America. We will have failed. But in doing so, we may be able to save our homeland in the process. What do you think we should do?"

Shin stood there for a moment, not saying anything. Then he gradually resumed walking along the blacked-out runway. The two walked for a few minutes, neither saying anything. The silence was becoming uncomfortable for Han, almost unnerving.

Han found his right hand slipping down to his sidearm, his fingers unbuttoning and making sure he could easily get to it should his deputy believe he was being a defeatist and suddenly try to replace him.

Finally, Shin stopped and turned to face Han, a string of tears having fallen down his face during their short walk. "General Han, the shame of defeat is more than I think I can bear. However, the shame of not coming to the aid of my country and our people I fear would be even greater. I do not know if the Americans would agree to such an idea. Not after all we have done to their country and their people. But if such a deal could be worked out, I believe it should be pursued."

Han breathed a sigh of relief. The two talked for a little while longer as they made their way back to the headquarters building. They had a lot to discuss.

****

Near Bolton, Vermont
Camel's Hump State Park

It was cold. A few snowflakes were starting to fall. The crowd looked up at President Sachs, waiting to hear him speak. Anthony Compo's mother and father sat in the first row, looking at him: the mother with tears streaming down her face, a tissue in her hand, the father with pride in his eyes but also sorrow and sadness at the loss of a child.

President Jonathan Sachs looked down at his notes one last time before he spoke. "My fellow Americans, today we honor the life of Anthony Compo and two of his friends, George Lake and Timothy Rakus. These three young men, college students, made the ultimate sacrifice a little more than a year ago in this very park. When our country was being invaded by a foreign army, Tony and his friends decided they were going to do something about it. Having grown up in the area and hunted on this very land, they took it upon themselves to attack a UN troop convoy.

"Service to one's country and sacrifice is something that runs deep in the Compo family. Ian, Tony's brother, was a petty officer on the USS *Vicksburg*, and their father is a retired master chief, having served twenty-six years in the Navy. When the *Vicksburg* was sunk during the battle of the North Atlantic, Tony knew he had to do something. He couldn't sit idly by as his state and community were occupied. In the end, Tony and his friends paid the ultimate price as they sought to defend their community and our great nation.

"Therefore, it is with great pride that today we change the name of Camel's Hump State Park to the Compo State Park in memory of the sacrifices the Compo family has made for our great nation."

A moment later, some people stepped forward along with the Compo family as they cut a ribbon marking the name change of the park and the opening of a new memorial to the citizens of Vermont who had died during the invasion and subsequent occupation by the UN force.

When the ceremony was complete, Sachs was able to spend a few minutes with the family before he had to get going. He had already enjoyed a lovely breakfast with the Compo family, getting to know them and hear the parents talk about Ian and Tony before the ceremony. Now, he was on his way to another ceremony in Augusta, Maine.

****

Three hours later, Air Force One had just touched down at the Brunswick Executive Airport when one of the President's military aides walked into the room. They were just about to collect their belongings and get off the plane. The group still had a short drive up to Augusta for their next meet-and-greet ceremony.

"Excuse me, Mr. President," the aide said as he approached him.

Judging by the look on the man's face, Sachs knew it was important. He told the others to go ahead down to the motorcade; he'd be along in a few minutes.

As they were leaving, Sachs asked, "What is it, Major?"

"Sir, I have General Markus on hold for you. He says it's urgent."

The President nodded. "I'd like to take the call in my office," he responded. When Sachs had made his way over to the private room, he saw the light on the phone flashing, letting him know he had a call on hold.

Picking up the receiver as he sat down, Sachs held his breath, hoping he wasn't about to hear something terrible.

"Mr. President, I have some interesting news. We received a message from General Han Lei an hour ago. He's the Chinese military commander in charge of all PLA forces in North America," Markus explained.

"OK, General. I'll bite. Is he willing to surrender? Because last I heard, they were going to fight to the last soldier if I remember."

There was a short pause, then Markus explained, "Not entirely, sir. They've given us a unique proposal—one I think is worth hearing out. Do you have time for us to explain it right now?"

Looking at his watch, Sachs saw they were going to be late if he didn't get a move on. "General Markus, unless this is time-sensitive, I can't discuss it right now. Why don't I have Robert stay behind so you can get him caught up to speed on whatever it is, and we can discuss it during the flight back to D.C. this evening?"

With that settled, Sachs headed out to the waiting motorcade.

****

Driving along the interstate, Sachs looked to his right and saw something that caught his eye. He ordered the motorcade to pull over for a moment so he could look at it. When the vehicles had stopped, he opened the door and got out, his Secret Service detail quickly forming a protective perimeter around him.

Standing on the side of the road, Sachs looked at a Leopard tank and several infantry fighting vehicles scattered in a farm field near a small farm and county road. The vehicles were charred remains of an earlier battle, but it was so odd to see. He still hadn't gotten used to the idea that battles were taking place on US soil.

The President shook his head and climbed back into the vehicle, his protective detail following suit, and they headed into Augusta.

When the President's vehicle turned on to Union Street, they saw the street lined with well-wishers. Hundreds of people had braved the cold to come out and wave American flags and welcome him to their town. There was also the presence of soldiers on the streets. Most of the civil defense force militia units had either been captured or given up, but there was still the occasional problem.

When the motorcade stopped in front of the Kennebec Valley YMCA right next to the police station, the President climbed out of the vehicle, eager to get inside and out of the cold. Many of the people who had lined the street waving American flags were also filtering into the gym of the YMCA. The place was packed, with throngs of people standing outside, knowing they wouldn't be able to get in but still wanting to be a part of the event. A couple of large TV monitors and some speakers had been set up to allow those outside to hear what was going on.

Making his way into the building, Sachs was led to a small room near the main gym to meet privately with the two families he was there to honor. He spent some time talking with both widows and their kids. They spoke briefly about their husbands and their lives. The President did his best to comfort them, knowing there was little he could do other than just be there for them and listen. He knelt to look at a couple of the kids and told them their dad was a hero—that they should be proud of their father and what he had done for them. The kids seemed to appreciate it, but mostly they just wished their dad were still here with them.

Eventually, Sachs made his way into the large gym and toward the podium. Looking at the crowd of people standing before him, he smiled. He felt their energy, their excitement that two of their local heroes were being recognized by the President, and the country.

"Thank you all for coming here today as we honor two local heroes," Sachs began. "On the first day of the war, when the UN Forces captured Augusta, Chief Wilkes and Chief Jacobs were faced with a terrible decision. They were given an ultimatum: either cooperate with the UN and turn over the background checks of all personally owned firearms in the city of Augusta and the state of Maine, or face imprisonment. Without hesitation, Chief Wilkes defied their order. During his detainment, he never lost hope. He worked with other prisoners to organize a prison break. While he died during the escape, the people he helped to release ultimately waged a successful insurgency in the state and local area that eventually resulted in the UN force abandoning Maine.

"The day after Chief Wilkes was taken into custody, Chief Jacobs became an influential militia leader in Maine. He helped organize people into small units and tied down UN forces that would otherwise have been fighting our forces in other parts of the country. Chief Jacobs was sadly killed leading an attack on a UN convoy in New Hampshire. Jacobs had been a key part of the militia movement in the Northeast and it's men like him that ultimately helped to defeat the UN force.

"Today, we honor both of their sacrifices by posthumously awarding them the Presidential Medal of Freedom. I also want the people of Augusta and Maine to know that we are here for you. America recognizes the sacrifices your citizens made in your stand against the UN. The federal government is making the reconstruction of Maine a key priority. I also want to announce that the Department of Defense will be placing orders for dozens of naval ships to be built at the Portsmouth Naval Shipyard, bringing thousands of highly skilled jobs. We will also be reactivating the Naval Air Station Brunswick. It will become a joint naval and Air Force base. I want the people of Maine to know that your government has not forgotten you, or your sacrifices during this war."

The President talked for a bit longer about the people of Maine and the two men he was here to honor. When his speech was done, he spent close to an hour shaking people's hands and spending time with the citizens of Maine that had come to hear him speak.

On his way back to the Brunswick airport, he couldn't help but think about how big of a reconstruction effort lay ahead of the country. So much of the nation's infrastructure had been destroyed during the war. It would take them years to rebuild.

When the President boarded the plane, he took a seat in the briefing room. They had a lot to discuss and little time to waste.
****

Turning to look at the President as the plane lifted off, National Security Advisor Robert Grey said, "Mr. President, while you were gone, I spent the last several hours going over General Han's message with the Chairman and the rest of the joint chiefs. We're ready to brief you on the proposal and offer you our thoughts."

"OK. Let's hear it," said Sachs. "What are the Chinese offering?"

"As you know, the rioting and protests continue to spread across China. General Zeng Shaoshan, the commander of their Southern Command, has rebelled against the central government. He's seized control of Guangdong, Guangxi, Hainan, Fujian, Jiangxi, and Hunan provinces and declared them to be the Democratic Republic of Southern China. The western province of Xinjiang has declared themselves East Turkestan, and the Indians have helped the Tibetans successfully establish a new government in Lhasa," Grey explained, bringing him up to speed on what had been transpiring inside China.

"General Han is a loyal supporter of Chen, Mr. President. He knows what's going on back home, and right now, he's powerless to do anything about it. While President Chen and the head of the PLA are encouraging him to continue fighting, General Han reached out to us with a proposal."

Everyone paused talking for a moment as the plane made a steep climb for a couple of minutes before leveling out.

"So what are you saying, Rob?" asked the President. "This General Han wants to end the war and return home to China to restore order?"

"Exactly," replied Grey with a nod. "He wants to bring the fighting here to an end and be allowed to withdraw to China."

The President snorted and shook his head, practically dismissing the idea out of hand. "Why would we possibly agree to this? The rebellion we've spent the better part of a year trying to foment in China has finally taken root. We have a senior PLA commander declaring himself ruler of a huge swath of China, and we have more than two million Chinese soldiers trapped on American soil. We have China by the balls. Why would we loosen our grip or let them slip away—after all they've done to our country and our people?"

The President was seething at this point. Letting the Chinese Army slip away to fight another day was not something he was inclined to consider.

A voice from the video teleconference chimed in. "If I could, Mr. President," Secretary of State Kagel announced, "I've received word through the Swiss government from General Zeng. He said to inform you that he has secured the camps the American women were being held in. He's in the process of having them all relocated to Hong Kong and would like to work out an arrangement to have them flown to a safe third country from which they can be repatriated."

The President leaned forward in his seat. "This is amazing," he replied. "Wow. I-I don't even know what to say. Please send word to him that we appreciate that. Tell him America would like to make peace with his forces and ensure our groups don't end up fighting. Also tell him that we would like to assist him in securing his country and resisting the central government in Beijing."

The group talked for a minute more before Grey brought them back to the original topic of discussion. "Mr. President, we still have General Han to deal with."

General Markus added, "Mr. President, if I could—I think we should consider his offer."

President Sachs was confused. "General, of all people, I would think you'd be against this idea. If we allow General Han's forces to return to China, they'll likely be used to attack General Zeng's army. If they succeed, President Chen will regain control of the country. It could lead to a several-years-long civil war."

"I agree, Mr. President. It could lead to a civil war, and it is likely that General Han's forces would be used against Zeng's. But please look at it from the other perspective. If Han is willing to leave North America voluntarily, that means the war for us is largely over. It means the killing in our country can stop."

"Yes, but it might mean we lose the opportunity to break up China," President Sachs responded quickly.

"That is a possibility, Mr. President. But we can still provide Zeng's forces with assistance," countered General Markus.

"Aren't your forces in position now to capture or destroy much of Han's forces?"

Markus nodded. "They are, Mr. President, but even in capturing and destroying them, we're going to lose tens of thousands more soldiers. They still have large numbers of soldiers concentrated in Texas and California and pockets of soldiers in New Mexico, Arizona, and Mexico itself. It's going to take us at least another three to six months to finish them off, and in the meantime, we're going to take heavy casualties. If we can come to an agreement with General Han and Beijing, we can put an end to the fighting now."

The President wasn't happy at all with the proposal. Sure, he wanted to end the fighting. He also wanted to see if General Zeng's fledgling democracy could take root. If President Chen succeeded in regaining control of the country, he'd just rebuild and try his globalist plans again.

Looking at the men and women around him, Sachs said he wanted to take a day and think about it. He directed his staff to figure out how this would happen if he agreed to it, and how they could support Zeng and his new democratic government.

****

South China Sea

"Are you sure you want to do this, Admiral?" asked Admiral Aikens's deputy commander.

Aikens grunted. "Do I want to? Hell no. But I need to," he replied. "We need to know if we can work with this man."

Looking at the small contingent of Marines that would be traveling with him, he saw they were ready. "OK, Captain. Let's get your men aboard and head to our meeting," Aikens announced. The Marine captain would be accompanying him with two squads of Marines—it wasn't much in the way of a security detachment, but he felt better having them along just the same.

Climbing aboard the two V-22 Ospreys, they quickly lifted off the rear deck of the Warhammer and headed to Hong Kong international airport.

The flight wasn't too long. The Task Force had moved to within a hundred miles of shore once a tentative cease-fire agreement had been reached between the US and the forces under General Zeng. Once the truce had held for more than twenty-four hours, Admiral Aikens had been directed to meet with Zeng and carry out an initial assessment of the man before Secretary of State Kagel would fly out to meet him.

Looking out the side windows, Aikens saw fishing boats moving about on the water below. He spotted several of the smaller islands that encompassed this area and then Lantau Island, where the airport was located. The pilot began the process of transitioning the aircraft from an airplane to a rotor wing aircraft as they prepared to descend and land. They made a short pass of the area, identifying the location where the Chinese wanted them to set down.

Steadily, the Osprey slowed until it touched down on the ground and began shutting down its engines.

The rear ramp lowered, revealing an unexpected reception. Several of the Marines got off the aircraft and were immediately put at ease, unsure of what to say or do. A band started playing some song they hadn't heard before, but it sounded friendly. There was also an honor guard that snapped to attention when Admiral Aikens stepped off in his dress whites.

Walking toward them were a couple of Chinese officials in business suits and a couple of generals. When they reached Admiral Aikens, the civilians bowed slightly while the generals saluted. Aikens snapped off a sharp salute and then shook the hands of the civilians.

"Thank you for agreeing to meet with us, Admiral Aikens," a tall general said as he walked up to him, extending his hand. "I am General Zeng Shaoshan, Commander of the Democratic Republic of Southern China. This is Chief Executive Lau. He is in charge of Hong Kong and, for the time being, my civilian counterpart. This here is Mr. James Chan, our head of intelligence. He was previously the Director for the Ministry of State Security for Hong Kong and the architect behind our coup d'état. If you and your men will please come with me, I have a comfortable place where we can talk in private."

Aikens was a bit taken aback by the reception, but he was quick to adapt. He accepted and told the Marine captain to leave a squad there with the helicopters and for the others to accompany him.

They walked for a few minutes toward an executive hangar and terminal section on the side of the airport. When they reached the terminal, they were led inside to a conference room of sorts. The Marines were asked to stay outside, while the two civilians and General Zeng ushered Aikens and the Marine captain in with them.

Aikens turned briefly to the captain, telling him he'd need to pull a pen and paper out to take notes. Prior to leaving the ship, they had inserted a small spy camera in place of one of his uniform buttons. They were going to record the entire meeting for later analysis.

When the party of five had taken their seats, a Chinese aide came in and poured them all tea and left some cookies on the table in case anyone wanted something to nibble on. He also left a couple pitchers of water and then left the room.

Not missing a beat, the man who had been introduced as the spy chief spoke first.

"Admiral, we thank you for speaking with us and agreeing to a cease-fire. We have a couple of key agenda items we'd like to discuss with you," the man named James said in perfectly accented British English.

Zeng added, "I believe James has gotten ahead of himself—but, yes, we do have a couple of key items we would like to discuss with you. First, what are your orders for this meeting?"

The Chinese general shot his spy chief a glance that said he had spoken out of turn.

Aikens smiled at the obvious interplay happening between the two. He cleared his throat. "I am here to assess whether the United States can work with you," he said. "If you are serious about this coup d'état and your desire to move toward democracy, we want to know what your intentions are with Beijing."

General Zeng leaned forward. "We are at *war* with Beijing," he replied pointedly. "For the time being, my forces are holding the territory we've claimed as our own. I am fairly confident I'll be able to hold our gains as my command is still largely intact. My forces were not sent to North America and were only just now being mobilized to head west to deal with the Chinese when we initiated our coup."

Then Mr. Lau spoke. "Our intention is to move toward becoming a democracy. For the time being, we are staying under military rule until General Zeng can ensure our security and a peace with Beijing."

"What about Taiwan? Are they going to regain their freedom and independence?" asked Aikens.

Mr. Lau shrugged his shoulders. "I cannot speak to that, Admiral," he said. "The eastern command is administering Taiwan out of Nanjing.

They were not in my chain of command, and therefore I have no control over them."

Admiral Aikens had thought as much. He moved on to the next topic. "I was told you had secured the camps that had been holding the women who had been kidnapped from our country," he said pointedly.

The three men squirmed a bit in their chairs. They were obviously incredibly uncomfortable. Mr. Chan, the spy chief, spoke for the group. "Admiral, you have to understand, when this first started, most of us were unaware of what was going on. Once we learned, we were obviously appalled. It's one of the major reasons why we perpetrated this coup. We have liberated the camps where they were being held. We have also set free roughly eight thousand POWs that had been held in our territory. We will return them all to you—we just need to work out the logistics."

"That's fine," said Aikens. "Where are they being held right now, and what kind of condition are they in?"

"We have them here in Hong Kong," Mr. Lau replied. "We've put them up at a variety of hotels and local resorts. We have them under guard for their own safekeeping, but they are being attended to by medical personnel and fed. I think we could start to fly them to Australia if you'd like," he offered.

"I will need to talk with my headquarters about that. We'll need to make sure wherever they're sent, they're able to be taken care of first. But I'll hopefully have an answer for you shortly. Is it possible for me to see any of them now?"

Zeng and Mr. Lau whispered something to each other before Zeng turned to him. "If you can stay for a few more hours, then yes. I can drive you over to one of the locations nearby where they are being held."

"Yes, I can stay. We'll send a message back to our ship, letting them know we'll be here a little longer," Aikens replied, relieved that he'd be able to lay eyes on the captured Americans and confirm they were being appropriately tended to.

"Admiral, if we can—I want to talk about military operations," said Zeng. "I'm in a tough fight with forces loyal to President Chen. I would like to know if you may be able to lend some military assistance. I also need to know what you intend to do with General Han's force in North America. James here tells me General Han has made a request to end the war in your country and to be allowed to bring his army back to China." He had a hard look on his face as he laid his cards on the table.

Aikens let out a deep breath. "I understand your concern, General, about Han's force. I'm not sure what's being agreed to or what's happening with his army. I'm sure Secretary Kagel will be able to answer that question when she arrives here to speak with you. As to military assistance, I have been instructed that once the Secretary of State has spoken with you, military help is something that will be on the table. If we can, General, I would like to see the other Americans. Then I can return to my ship and report back to my command and we can get the ball rolling on the military and diplomatic fronts."

The meeting broke up as they headed out to the location where the Americans were being held. Later that evening, Admiral Aikens was back on his ship. He reported back to the Pentagon what had transpired and gave his assessment of General Zeng and the civilians in charge. It was agreed the Secretary of State would fly out to meet with them. If they could prop up this fledgling government long enough for them to get going, then it would be worth it. In the meantime, they still had to figure out what to do with General Han and his substantial force still in North America.

Chapter Seventeen
Regime Change

Beijing, China

General Ma felt uncomfortable meeting with General Wu away from his own command and soldiers he trusted. Wu had armed soldiers loyal to him surrounding the headquarters building and staged throughout the city. His soldiers had largely kept the city from falling into anarchy and chaos when the rioting and protests had started. It was unfortunate that his forces hadn't been able to put down the protests across much of the rest of the country.

Looking at Wu, Ma exclaimed, "It wasn't supposed to happen like this, Wu. How are we supposed to take charge of things with the country falling apart all around us? Now we have General Zeng leading a revolt in the south and General Han's forces trapped in North America. What are we supposed to do now?"

Wu sighed. "I don't know," he replied. "I want to deploy more forces south to deal with Zeng, but I don't know if General Luan might turn on us as well. I can't afford to have more divisions become trapped."

General Luan was the PLA commander for the Eastern sector. A large portion of his army was currently deployed on Taiwan. What forces he did have available were arrayed against General Wu's divisions in the south and trying to maintain order in the Shanghai area. They had been battling on and off for several weeks with both protesters and General Zeng's men. General Luan had requested additional reinforcements if Beijing wanted him to make any serious attempts on Zeng's territory.

"Are you questioning his loyalty?" Ma asked, concern in his voice.

"I don't know, Ma," Wu replied, shaking his head. "I thought General Zeng could be trusted. I was his mentor, for God's sake. If I deploy my reserve divisions down to help him and General Han's army groups return from North America, we won't be able to remove Chen. Han's army will be more than enough to put down Zeng and bring southern China back into the fold."

Ma shook his head in dismay. "Then we need to remove him now," he said. "We can't wait, Wu, or it'll be too late."

Taking a deep breath in, Wu held it for a moment before letting it out. He knew Ma was right. He just wasn't sure how they'd make it work.

If he moved against President Chen now, he'd also have to move against the MSS and at least two dozen other senior officials—not to mention a couple dozen other generals. Even if they were successful in executing the coup, there was no telling if General Luan and his army group would recognize his authority or if they'd try to break off and form their own fiefdom. China could end up breaking apart into many more small warring factions.

Finally, Wu nodded. "OK. We'll move forward with our plan. I'll need you to move your own forces into position. When we execute this, it'll need to be swift. Your Special Forces units will need to act quickly, or this entire thing will fall apart."

Ma smiled devilishly. "This will work, General Wu. Just make sure Peng is ready on his end."

****

President Chen sat there, dumbfounded by what he had just heard.

"There can be no doubt, Mr. President. They plan to make a move against you," Minister Geng Yun said somberly.

Looking at the military man who held the recorder, Chen asked, "When did you record this?"

General Gao Weiping promptly replied, "This morning."

"Is there any way this could be made up?" Chen followed up. He wanted to be absolutely certain before he acted on such news.

Lifting his chin, Gao said, "I am certain. We've been placing listening devices inside his headquarters for the past couple of weeks, always making sure we leave them a couple they could easily find and a few more they'd really have to work to locate."

"If his staff's been finding them, then how do you know this isn't a trap, to lure us into making a mistake?" Chen countered.

"Mr. President, we wanted General Wu to *know* he was being spied on," Gao insisted. "We allowed him to find some of the listening devices because we knew it would make him cautious. Once he believed he had found them all, he spoke more freely with his coconspirators. General Wu and General Ma are conspiring to assassinate you and assume control of China. You heard the recording. This is less than five hours old. If we move against them now, or at least in the next twenty-four hours, we'll be able to preempt them before they're able to do anything."

Turning away from his spy chief, President Chen looked out the windows of his office at the city and the skyscrapers off in the distance. *I just need to regain control of things here*, he thought. He didn't feel that all was lost. *My vision for a Greater China can still be realized...*

Changing topics, President Chen inquired, "What about General Han's forces in America? Can they continue to fight on, or is there a way to bring them home to assist us here?"

Blinking several times, Minister Geng blurted out, "General Han? We need to deal with General Wu and these vipers here at home first! Wu commands the Army. If he's not dealt with now, he could order the Army to seize power. He'll come for us all when he does."

There were a few seconds of silence. Finally, General Gao tried to answer the President's question. "General Han has asked to end hostilities in North America. He said he wants to take his army and return to China. If the Americans are unwilling to allow him to withdraw, then he will order his army to fight on to the last man."

With fire burning in his eyes, Chen demanded, "If the Americans won't allow him to withdraw, then I want Han's Army to systematically destroy every town and city as they continue a fighting retreat. They should kill every civilian they encounter. If the Americans will not allow our forces to leave, then we will leave a wave of devastation."

****

Ten hours later, General Luan was ushered into the President's office. The small cadre of officers he was told to bring with him for this meeting was left to wait outside.

When Luan entered the room, he got a feeling that this meeting wasn't about receiving an update on the pacification of Taiwan, or his attempts to regain control of southern China from General Zeng. He saw the Director of the Ministry of State Security along with the commander of the PLA's version of the American National Security Agency. Along the sides of the room were at least a dozen of Chen's bodyguards.

Walking toward the President of China, Luan came to attention and saluted. He stood ramrod straight as he waited for what would happen next. President Chen looked at him for a few seconds, sizing him up before he ordered him to sit.

Staring at him with those cold, dark eyes, Chen asked, "General Luan, how well do you know General Wu?"

Is this a trick question? he wondered.

"I've known General Wu for most of my military career. He's an exceptional military commander," replied Luan without hesitation. "The modernization of the PLA and our ability to fight beyond our borders have been largely due to his leadership and efforts."

General Luan instantly saw that this response didn't settle the President's demeanor—rather, it appeared to harden it. *Did I say something wrong?* he asked himself.

"What would you say if you found out General Wu was planning a coup against me?"

"I'm not sure I would believe that. General Wu has been a commensurate professional," Luan insisted. "His loyalty to you and China is without fault. It was General Zeng who has betrayed us. He's the man we need to worry about."

Could Wu be involved in something as well?

The President turned to the chief spy and nodded. The man produced a small device, turning it on. As it began playing an audio recording, he placed it on the desk in front of the President.

Suddenly, Luan's demeanor changed. *How could this be? How could Wu and Ma even talk like this?*

Luan immediately knew why he had been summoned to Beijing. He also understood why the head of his Special Forces had been summoned with him, along with most of their unit that wasn't heavily engaged or deployed in Taiwan. They were going to replace General Wu with him.

Chen smiled when he saw Luan's expression change. "General Luan, you are going to take over as head of the People's Liberation Army, effective immediately," he announced. "Your first job is to arrest General Wu and General Ma for treason. They will be handed over to Minister Geng. I want you to root out any further officers that appear to be disloyal to me and China. Install people you trust that will follow your orders and mine. When you have taken charge, I want you to draw up a military strategy to defeat General Zeng and his renegade force. You need to move swiftly and put down this growing rebellion within our country. The Americans are doing everything they can to divide our nation. We mustn't allow that to happen. Do you understand, General?"

Lifting his chin, Luan quickly replied, "Yes, Mr. President. I understand, and I will do my utmost to bring victory to our cause."

With nothing more to be said, Minister Geng got up with General Luan and the two of them left the President's office. For the next couple of hours, they spoke at length about how they were going to remove the two most powerful generals in China.

Chapter Eighteen
No Good Decision

Cheyenne Mountain
US Northern Command

General Tibbets felt sick to his stomach when he read the most recent demand from Beijing. The President had said he wanted everyone to take twenty-four hours and think about the demands and what they should do next. He wanted options. Right now, Tibbets didn't know what to tell him.

Looking at his watch, he saw he had nine hours left. Not getting anything done in his office in the mountain, Tibbets grabbed his cover and walked out of his office. He made his way through the corridors and eventually he was outside. He had his driver and escorts take him into town. He stopped at his house for twenty minutes, changing into some civilian clothes.

Now that he didn't look like the commanding general of US Forces in North America, he asked the driver to take him and his two bodyguards over to Burrowing Owl, not too far outside the base. He wanted a beer and some regular food, but more than that, he just wanted to be surrounded by regular civilians.

Traffic was light. There were not a lot of cars on the road and catching all the green lights on the way over made a world of difference.

When the driver pulled into the parking lot, Tibbets directed him to back into a parking space not far from the front entrance. That way, they could get out in a hurry if they needed to.

He turned to his guards. "I want to sit and eat alone," he told them. "You can keep an eye on me and the bar, but I want space."

They nodded but didn't look too pleased. One of them said something into the radio he was carrying. The trio then got out and made their way into the bar.

The place had several very comfortable-looking stools. Tibbets found an empty seat and asked the people on either side of it if it was free. They said it was. Once he got settled in, the bartender brought him a menu and asked what he wanted to drink.

Scanning the back of the bar for the beer list, he spotted one that looked good.

"I'll have a Pug Ryan Dunkel."

The barkeep smiled and went to work getting him his drink. Tibbets looked at the menu until he found something that was just his kind of grub—the Sloppy Shepherd's Pie. When the guy brought him his beer, he placed his order and then sat back in his chair and slowly drank his beer.

Taking the dark liquid in, he was reminded of the dark brews he was fond of when he had been stationed in Germany. Ever since he'd lived there, he'd found it hard to find a decent beer brewed in America. The Germans had a secret to their beer—due to their "purity laws," their beers had to be naturally fermented over time, not chemically expedited like so many mass-produced beers were in America. The only beers that came close to the German brews were the microbrews like this one.

After taking a couple of sips of his beer, Tibbets decided to strike up a conversation with the two men sitting next to him. "How are you guys doing today?" he asked.

They looked at him and smiled. "Well, we're on our third beer, so I guess you could say we're doing pretty good. How's about you?"

"Hungry. But damn if this beer isn't good. Have you tried the Pug Ryan before?"

Laughing, both men held up their own half-empty glasses. "That's what we're drinking," one of them said. "Yeah, it's pretty good. I'm George. This big loaf is Chet."

Tibbets extended his hand. "Nice to meet you guys. I'm Joe."

"Nice to meet you as well."

The three of them talked for a bit. Joe ordered them another round on him and one more for himself. When Tibbets's food arrived, he took a few minutes to eat some of it before he got to the real reason he had come to this bar.

"Chet, George, I have a question for you," he began. "I'm curious to know what you think of the war. What do you think the President should do with the Chinese now that we have them on the ropes?"

George looked at Tibbets with fire in his eyes. "We should kill every last one of them. That's what we should do to them."

Quickly chiming in, Chet said, "Come on, George. You know that isn't going to bring him back." Looking at Tibbets, he added, "George lost his son during that big battle south of here over the summer."

"A lot of people died in that battle," Tibbets said softly, somberly.

"I don't know what the President should do, Joe. All I know is millions of people have perished in this war. Our country is in ruins and this war just doesn't seem to end. I mean, what can we do? Invade China? God, I hope not. We'd lose for sure," Chet explained.

"I just want my son's death to mean something," George said angrily. "I heard the Chinese are having their own problems at home. Maybe we can do to them what they've done to us. Create their own internal civil war and let them kill each other. That's what they tried to do here." He finished his fourth beer and signaled the barkeep for a refill.

"What if the Chinese demanded that we let their army return to China or they'd systematically destroy our cities as they retreat and kill any and all civilians in the occupied zones?" asked Tibbets. "What do you think the President should do if *that* was his choice?" He wanted a sense of what the average person would think of this decision—he still wasn't sure what he should recommend to the President and why.

The two paused for a moment as they thought about his question. Chet answered first. "That's a tough one, Joe. I suppose if he was faced with that question, I'd tell him to let them leave. I mean, if I'm not mistaken, there are still millions of citizens trapped in the occupied zones. We've lost enough people. I'd hate for millions more to be killed because we wanted to keep fighting. It's not like we can't keep attacking them in China. I heard the Navy's newest superweapon is pounding the hell out of their coastal cities."

George answered next. "I'd let them retreat to China. But once their flotilla of ships was in the middle of the Pacific, I'd torpedo them all—kill every last one of them before they were able to make it back home."

Tibbets snorted at the suggestion, although he had to admit he liked that idea. He didn't think it'd work, though. If they did that, their word would never be trusted again. Then again, after the genocide the Chinese had committed on American soil, maybe it'd be payback.

Tibbets spent another hour eating and drinking with his two new friends. After glancing at his watch, he knew he needed to get going. He had enough time to head home and get a quick shower before changing into his uniform and going back to work.

****

Five hours later, the secured video teleconference connected with the White House Situation Room, the Pentagon's NMCC room and several outstations participating in the call.

For the next fifteen minutes, the generals and senior cabinet members talked about the Chinese proposal and what to do. The group was evenly split. The hawks in the room wanted to fight on—to wipe General Han's army out. They wanted to drop airborne soldiers near all the major urban areas in the occupied zones. The idea was to force the PLA formations to fight them rather than trying to destroy the cities or kill the people still living in the occupied zones. The problem with this strategy was that there were just too many urban centers to occupy them, even with airborne forces. Worse, once those units had been dropped in, they'd be on their own, having to rely only on the Air Force for support until the larger Army formations were able to break through.

The doves wanted an end to the fighting—at least the fighting in America. They were content with continuing to fight the Chinese in the Pacific and hitting their coastal cities and ports, but they were insistent on ending the combat and killing within the country. At this point, no one really knew how many people were still alive in the occupied zones. Granted, they had a lot of Special Forces units scattered inside the zone, but it was still hard to gauge with any certainty how many people were still alive.

In many cases, the smaller towns and communities hadn't seen many Chinese soldiers. For the most part, the PLA didn't pay them much attention unless they caused them problems. But few of the occupied zones had consistent utility services. The supply and logistical system inside the zone was nonexistent. With no resources, the power plants couldn't provide power. With no power, there wasn't running water or a sewage system to speak of. No food trucks delivered food to the local grocery stores, and CVS and Walgreen pharmacies didn't receive their deliveries of medicines.

Society had completely broken down in the occupied territories. It was one of the main reasons why a large faction of the President's advisors were advocating for some sort of peace or cease-fire. If letting the PLA Army escape capture or destruction meant they could get relief supplies into the occupied zones and save lives, they were for it.

Eventually, everyone stopped talking and turned to look at him. "General, you've been pretty silent during this conversation," said the President. "I suspect you have an alternate idea in mind?"

Looking at the camera, Tibbets nodded. "I do, Mr. President. The way I see it, we have a compelling case to be made for both opposing views. As the ground force commander, I recommend we destroy and eliminate General Han's force. If his force is allowed to return to China, it'll be used to put down the growing rebellion and insurgency we've spent so many months fomenting. That said, millions of our citizens may be killed if we pursue that path. My job is to kill the enemy, sir. Your job is to protect the American people. Therefore, I cannot in good conscience recommend a strategy that will sacrifice the lives of millions of Americans when there's an alternative that can save them."

"So you're saying we should let General Han's forces withdraw to China?" blurted out Robert Grey, looking surprised and hurt by the idea. Grey had been the most vocal about defeating Han's force on American soil.

"That's not what I'm saying, Mr. Grey," said Tibbets, shaking his head. He paused for a moment. "Mr. President, I have an idea, a proposal I'd like to make—but I'd like to make the request in person. Is it possible for us to reconvene this meeting in twenty-four hours?"

The group looked surprised. Several whispered amongst themselves, but no one voiced any audible opposition.

President Sachs looked at General Markus, who shrugged his shoulders and then nodded. Looking at his ground force commander, the President agreed. They'd reconvene in twenty-four hours, once Tibbets had arrived in D.C. and spoken with him privately.

****

Walking into the Oval Office, General Tibbets saw Robert Grey, along with General Markus and Secretary of Defense Mike Howell, sitting on the couches, cups of coffee in their hands. The President stood and extended his hand as he approached.

"General, it's good to see you in person again. We're eager to hear your proposal, though I'm not sure why we couldn't have gone over it on the call yesterday."

"Thank you for allowing me to meet with you in person. There are some things better discussed privately."

The President gestured for him to join them. He took his seat in the armchair between the two couches. A steward quickly brought Tibbets a fresh coffee and then left the room so that the five of them could discuss whatever it was Tibbets didn't feel should be discussed yesterday.

With all eyes looking at him, the general took a deep breath before he began. "Mr. Grey is right in that we cannot allow General Han's army to return to China. However, we also can't let his men go on a killing rampage across the occupied territories. We've lost too many people to this war to allow more to die needlessly."

"I take it you have an alternative," Grey prodded.

General Tibbets nodded. "I do. I recommend we allow his forces to leave, to effectively end the war in America. However—we force his Army to leave behind their equipment and remaining supplies. When Han's forces are gone, we take all the captured equipment and ship it to General Zeng's men. This will greatly bolster his forces and provide them with an enormous amount of equipment and munitions to continue their fight. I also recommend we provide his forces with substantial material support and Special Operations Forces assistance as they fight against Beijing."

"You know that won't be a popular decision," Robert Grey countered. "Half the country wants us to finish Han's force off and then carry the fight to China. The other half wants to end this war and allow General Zeng's forces to either fight and win or die trying on their own, without our help. You're proposing that we stay involved in China for what could be several more years."

"I like it, Mr. President," said General Markus, lending his support to the idea. "Zeng's forces have secured most of southern China faster than our analysts could have predicted. That'll change once Han's army returns home, but if they're going home with no equipment and a damaged industrial base needed to replace that equipment, it'll be hard for them to fight Zeng's forces—especially if we give him all of Han's abandoned equipment."

Thinking about this for a moment, the President finally nodded in approval. "OK, General. We'll go with your plan. But this part about us aiding General Zeng's force needs to stay hush-hush for a little while. We need General Han to agree to this deal. We're essentially getting him to surrender his forces in place, but instead of being interned, we're allowing them to return to China. Before I give the final OK, how are we going to make sure they leave? Walk me through the logistics."

"Well, as you said, he's essentially surrendering his forces in place and being allowed to depart. We'll have to work out some sort of arrangement with the Chinese commercial airlines. They'll need to be the ones to fly them out of the US."

Tibbets paused for a second as he brought up a map of California on his tablet.

"Right now, the Chinese still control the San Francisco Bay area. That gives them access to two large international airports. They can fly their forces we've trapped in Northern California out through there. In the south, they can use LAX and San Diego. They also have control of a number of our airbases down there. They can use them to fly planes into as well. In Texas, they still control San Antonio and the Air Force bases in the area. They also still have access to El Paso and the Mexican airports just across the border. We should coordinate exact times of the Chinese aircraft entering our airspace, giving them very tight approach and departure corridors, and use fighter escorts the entire way.

"I think the biggest challenge won't be the airports, it'll be getting their people all moved to these locations and then flown out. It's going to take a bit of time to relocate them all, but I'd like to put a deadline on the deal. I want them motivated to leave. Maybe we give them essentially two weeks to get out. If we catch them destroying any of their surrendered equipment, cities or killing any civilians in retribution, then we have the option of ending their withdrawal and interning their remaining forces. I think that'll keep them in check."

"That sounds like a good plan," said Secretary Howell. "What'll we do about the Russian private military contractors working with them, though? We can't allow them to flee back to China."

"I sure as hell won't agree to those bastards being allowed to leave," remarked the President with a nod. "Not after what they did to some of our cities."

"I agree," said General Tibbets. "I can see about incorporating that into the eventual surrender. Have General Han use his forces to capture and provide them to us. We can try them for war crimes to make an example of them. The Attorney General is setting up a war crimes tribunal in Bowling Green, Kentucky. We will obviously be trying the leaders of the Civil Defense Forces and some of the UN military commanders who participated in the atrocities. As we find individual soldiers or commanders that ordered some of these murders, we'll be adding them to the list as well."

Tibbets paused for a moment. "What do you want to do about Mexico?" he asked. "The Chinese still have a fair number of soldiers down there. I'll try to wrap them into the terms of surrender, but how do we want to handle the Mexican government since they were equally involved in all this?"

"That's a good question, Mr. President," Mike reiterated.

Turning to look at his Secretary of Defense, the President asked, "Thoughts on this, Mike? How should we handle them?"

"The American people aren't going to want to occupy them. That said, we're going to have to do something to shore up their government or install a new one. Personally, since we're still in a state of war with them and we'll have freed up a lot of our troops, I recommend we deal with the drug cartels once and for all. Let me send a brigade of soldiers down there to deal with them and unleash JSOC—unrestricted warfare against the narcos. We can wipe out their drug factories and take out the cartels in one fell swoop, a simultaneous blitz. With them gone, establishing a new government will be a lot easier."

Sachs blew some air out of his mouth as he thought about that one. He didn't want the US to get bogged down in a narco war, not after all that had happened. Then again, when would the US ever have another chance like this to take out the drug cartels? Probably never.

Looking at Mike, he replied, "OK. But I don't want this to turn into a long, drawn-out occupation or war. I want our guys in and out of there as quickly as possible. Go in there, wipe them out and hand it over to the Mexican government to maintain."

"Do you want prisoners for prosecution?" asked General Markus cautiously.

"No. We're still at war with Mexico," the President replied. "Use that as our pretext to wipe them out. No lawyers, no prisoners. Take out their drug factories and their distribution centers and eliminate the organization. This will be strictly a punitive campaign, from the couriers to the financiers—all of them gone. I want all money seized to be brought back to the US. We'll use it for reconstruction. Also, if we capture any major drug stashes, don't destroy them. Funnel all that crap back to China. Let them deal with a flood of drugs."

The Chinese had been sending hundreds of tons of fentanyl and other drugs into the US for years. It was time to return the favor.

The group talked for a bit longer about the details of the coming surrender. There was a lot to go over—especially how they were going to fan the flames of the growing civil war inside China.

****

The helicopter circled over the Buffalo Bill's Resort & Casino in Primm, Nevada, before eventually settling down in the parking lot. Dust, dirt and sand kicked up all over the place as the rotor wash blew everything around.

The pilot began the process of shutting down the engines while the occupants in the back stayed on for a few minutes, letting everything settle a bit.

Looking out the window of the V-280 Valor, General Tibbets saw a few dozen US and Chinese soldiers eyeballing each other. There were also a handful of Chinese and American infantry fighting vehicles and JLTVs in the parking lot.

"It looks like General Han and his entourage have already arrived," commented Secretary Kagel as she also looked out the window.

"That's good. We'll be able to get this meeting going quickly," Tibbets said.

The crew chief reached over and opened the side door now that the dust and dirt weren't whipping around the aircraft like they had been. Jumping out of the tiltrotor, the soldier offered his hand to the Secretary as she got out. Tibbets exited next along with two of his aides. Kagel had two of her aides with them as well.

A colonel walked up to Tibbets, saluting as he approached him. "General, Madam Secretary, we've secured a place for everyone to meet. General Han's group arrived about ten minutes ago. They're inside waiting."

Kagel and Tibbets nodded but didn't say anything. They followed the colonel as he led the way into the former casino resort. The building didn't look like it had been used in more than a year. It showed some signs of battle damage; there were some bullet holes on the ground level from an earlier engagement, but otherwise, it was still intact.

It felt strange walking into the casino. There was limited lighting, hastily put together by some engineers. The casino floor of the main room was dark, the slots all turned off. Heavy amounts of dust and dirt had settled on many of the tables, the floor, and the Western-themed decorations of the casino.

The American entourage continued to move through the building until they came to a restaurant that connected to the outside. Several tables had been set up just outside the building with a couple more inside. This way, they could use the natural light of the day for the moment and move inside and use the portable lights in the evening.

As the group got closer to the Chinese representatives, General Han stood. To everyone's surprise, Foreign Minister Jiang Yi had also flown in for this meeting.

The group greeted one another and then took their seats.

"Secretary Kagel, it's good to see you again," Minister Jiang said as he opened the meeting.

"Likewise, Minister Jiang," she responded, smiling warmly. "I am hopeful we can end this terrible war."

"Agreed. You've undoubtably talked over President Chen's proposal? To allow us to withdraw our forces from your country, back to ours."

"We have. There are some items that need to be discussed before we will agree to this request."

He nodded. "That's why I am here. President Chen has empowered me to negotiate on his behalf to bring this war to an end."

"Then let's get down to business, shall we?" General Tibbets announced.

General Han nodded. "I'd like to move forward with a cease-fire in place. My soldiers will stop their combat operations and will begin to move away from the current front lines. I'd like your forces to stop attacking mine and for your Air Force to cease their bombing missions, both on my forces here and on Mainland China."

Tibbets thought about that for a second, making Han and Jiang believe he was struggling with the idea. In reality, Secretary Kagel and he had already discussed all of this the day before. Their staffs had been working on this for a couple of days once the President had given them the go-order.

Finally, Tibbets responded. "OK. I'll order my Air Force to stop their attacks on your troops in the US and the Mainland. However, I want to make something abundantly clear—your forces are essentially surrendering in place. We're allowing you to withdraw to China as proposed, but this is not a victory for China. We'll allow you to move your men, but you're going to have to abandon your equipment. We want your soldiers out of the US *now*, not in two or three months once you've had a chance to move all your supplies out on transport ships."

"Unacceptable," General Han interjected. "China is *not* surrendering. My forces are merely withdrawing back to our territory."

Tibbets looked at the Chinese general as if he had two heads. "I'm sorry, General Han, but what alternate reality are you living in?" he asked condescendingly. "Your forces have been defeated. We've cut off your supply lines from China. We've surrounded your forces in Northern California and Texas. In a few more weeks, you'll be out of food, fuel, and ammunition."

"We are not surrendering."

"I'm perfectly happy to grind the rest of your force into ash if you want to keep fighting. I will rain fire from the sky, I will hunt and kill your men twenty-four hours a day, I will push your entire Army into the ocean, and I'll have our Navy chase you across the sea."

"And we'll destroy every city we currently occupy and kill everyone left in them," shot back General Han as if he'd be proud to do so.

Leaning forward, Tibbets angrily retorted, "Your men sure are good at killing unarmed civilians, aren't they? I suppose that makes them real warriors, shooting women and children."

"Enough! We're here to talk about ending this war, not continuing it," Minister Jiang said as he sought to calm General Han.

"China has become a pariah state on the world stage," General Tibbets said icily. "Everyone knows of the genocide your country has perpetrated on America and Taiwan. Your own country is crumbling from within. You're going to accept our terms of surrender or so help me God, I'm going to recommend to the President that we unleash biological weapons on Mainland China. If you want to kill off our civilians, then I'll make damn sure you don't even have a country to go home to!" He pushed his chair back and got up. Then he walked off—he needed to calm down.

Minister Jiang looked alarmed at the mention of biological weapons. Han, for his part, just looked indignant. He clearly wanted to keep fighting if this was going to be the arrangement.

"I'm sorry about that, Minister Jiang," said Secretary Kagel soothingly. "Perhaps it would be better if just you and I talk for the time being. We can bring the generals back later, once we've made some progress," she offered.

Jiang agreed. General Han left and headed back to one of his military vehicles. Tibbets did the same, leaving the two diplomats to discuss.

****

With just the two of them now, Kagel offered, "These are tough times our countries face, Jiang. It's up to us to put an end to the bloodshed. I understand the term 'surrender' is unacceptable. You need to save face."

"That's right," Jiang responded with a nod. "If America seeks to humiliate us, then we'll fight on. Even if it means we lose General Han's force and kill many millions more of your countrymen."

Her left eyebrow rose. She was surprised by how strong a stand he had taken. "Even if it means China breaks apart into many smaller countries?" she prodded.

Jiang shook his head in indignation. "That will not happen. We have a vast population and a very large military. The insurrection in the south will be put down soon enough. Now, let's talk about how we can end this war."

"Fine. I propose we call this an armistice: an end to hostilities. It avoids the term 'surrender,'" she offered.

"I think I can make that work," Jiang replied, nodding. "We need to talk logistics on how we're going to extricate our equipment."

"That's not possible, Jiang," Kagel insisted, shaking her head. "The President has said if this deal is going to happen, then China has exactly fourteen days to remove your forces from our country. There won't be time for you to organize any sort of sealift to move your military equipment back to China."

"What? You can't be serious about us abandoning all of our equipment," Jiang retorted. "You realize we're talking about one hundred and forty-two divisions. That's an incredible amount of equipment."

"It's an incredible amount of *people* to evacuate, Jiang," Secretary Kagel countered. "If you want to abandon your troops to use your time to move equipment, then I suppose that would be your choice. But there isn't time for you to organize a convoy from the Mainland to California or Mexico and move your equipment down to those ports. If this armistice is going to work, your forces need to leave our country as expeditiously as possible."

"What if we fall back into Mexico? We could use their ports," Jiang countered, almost pleading.

"I'm sorry, Jiang," she said, shaking her head. "That won't be possible. There's no way we're going to allow your forces to reorganize and marshal down in Mexico, or risk you bringing fresh supplies or reinforcements from the Mainland. This war needs to end, and it needs to end rapidly. That can only happen either with your forces surrendering and us interning them, or you withdrawing them as quickly as you can."

Jiang sat there for a moment, not saying anything. Kagel could tell he was calculating what to say next.

"If we agree to these terms, America will end its war with China?" he inquired. "You'll withdraw your forces from India and our western provinces? Your naval forces in the South China Sea will leave and you'll abandon Taiwan to us? I want America's assurances that if we agree to these terms, the war between our nations ends. It won't continue on through proxies."

Pausing as she thought about this, Kagel turned her head to look off in the distance. She could see a couple of American and Chinese soldiers talking with each other, sharing a cigarette break. Strange, considering on any other chance encounter they'd be trying to kill each other, but right there, right then, they were just young men talking and having a smoke.

This war needs to end, she thought. *Our people, our country, needs to heal, to rebuild...*

"The President will order our forces to withdraw from western China," Kagel confirmed. "As to Taiwan, there isn't anything we can really do about the situation at this point. So no, we won't get involved over that."

"The South China Sea—we need your forces gone," Jiang insisted. "No more sailing up and down the coast attacking our ports and military installations or industrial centers. No more blockade of our country or embargo."

He didn't even mention General Zeng, she realized. The Chinese must not have viewed him as a serious threat. *They believe getting Han's army back will make a difference, so they aren't worried...*

Secretary Kagel looked up at Jiang, then slowly nodded in agreement. "OK. We'll withdraw our naval forces from the area, and we'll lift our blockade. I can't say we'll be open to trading with China anytime soon, Jiang. But hopefully in time, when the wounds of this war have had time to heal, we'll be able to get back to that type of relationship."

He held a hand up to add something. "Madam Secretary, if I may. When the war has officially ended and our forces are out of your country, I do have one request. I know trade between our nations will be difficult, but I would be remiss if I didn't press you about this issue. China is facing a very serious food shortage, compounded further by your stealth bomber attacks. Would it be possible for China to purchase agricultural products?"

Kagel almost had to stifle a laugh at the suggestion. *Did he really just ask if we would sell them food?* she asked herself. After everything China had done to her nation, not they wanted America to sell them food so they wouldn't starve.

She opened her mouth to speak, then paused a second before adding, "I can ask the President about that, Minister Jiang. To be honest, I don't think he will agree to that. I understand China may be facing a food shortage, and that may have been compounded by our bombing campaigns, but China committed a yearlong genocide of our people. It is highly unlikely that our nation will sell any food products to China for many years to come."

Jiang nodded, then hung his head low for a moment. "OK. Then I think we have a deal," he conceded. "I would like to propose a continuation of the cease-fire between our nations for another five days until we can get the details of this armistice written up and approved by both sides. This will also give us the needed time to move our commercial airliners around to support the evacuation of our soldiers."

"All right, Minister Jiang. We can extend the cease-fire, but only for three days. These are simple terms we've agreed upon, and three days should be more than enough time for you to have your commercial airliners flown to the US to start the withdrawal of your forces. We want to put this war behind us. One more point that needs to be discussed, and this is a deal breaker for us. We want the private military contractors working with your forces handed over to us—especially the Wagner Group."

Jiang snorted. "Really? After we've agreed to everything else, you're now going to ask about the PMCs? You know we don't directly control them. How are we supposed to hand them over to you?"

"Have them rounded up and ready to be handed over by the time we sign this armistice," she insisted. Then she got up and signaled it was time for the military men to return to the discussion.

Minister Jiang and Secretary Kagel presented the proposals to the two commanding generals, who had no choice but to accept. The two men looked like they had sucked on a lemon, but the war was finally coming to close, and that was all that mattered.

****

"Well played, Madam Secretary," Tibbets said as the Valor lifted off the ground. The pilot turned the aircraft toward Nellis Air Force Base and picked up speed.

She smiled at the compliment. "You did a pretty good job yourself, General. Minister Jiang looked rather distraught when you mentioned the use of WMD. You really got General Han riled up."

Tibbets laughed. "All part of the good cop, bad cop routine. Ultimately it worked. What's going to be funny is what happens when all of this military equipment starts to show up in the hands of General Zeng. Losing all these divisions' worth of equipment will seriously hurt their ability to put down these insurrections."

"That's the goal, General. That's the goal."

The two talked a bit more on the way back. Once they landed, they'd head their separate ways as each of them went to work on getting their part of the agreement ready for signature.

After more than two years at war, the end was finally in sight. Now it would be time to mourn the dead and rebuild the country.

Chapter Nineteen
Texas Cleanup

Muleshoe, Texas

Sitting in the mess tent, Major Trey Regan looked at the black liquid in his cup, waiting for it to cool a bit more before he drank it down.

Is this war really over?

Suddenly, a large figure plopped down on a chair opposite him, his own plate of food and cup of coffee in hand. Looking up, Regan smiled when he saw it was Colonel Beasley.

"Morning, sir."

"Morning, Regan. Your men still holding up?"

His smile faded, replaced with a look of sadness. "They're still a bit shocked. But, yes, sir, they'll get through it."

Beasley nodded as he shoveled a forkful of eggs into his mouth. "They'll be looking to you now for leadership," he said between bites. "We're nearly done with this war, Regan. See them through to the finish line, OK?"

Regan lifted his coffee to his lips and drained the rest of the cup now that it had cooled a bit.

"Is it true all that black smoke we've been seeing the last few days is because the Chinese spiked the oil wells down south of us?" Regan asked since he had the guy in charge sitting in front of him.

Grimacing as he paused with a forkful midair, Beasley said, "It looks that way. The wind has been blowing it to the east, so we haven't been seeing much of it, but I suspect it'll be pretty bad the further south we get."

"I thought the Chinese weren't supposed to tear the place up on their way out the door?"

Captain Beasley shrugged. "It could have been some of the private military contractors working with them as well. I still haven't heard anything about whether the Chinese will be handing them over to us or if we'll just have to hunt them down ourselves."

Regan nodded before finishing off the last of his breakfast. "Any word yet on when we're rolling out?" he asked.

"I'm putting it out at the commanders' call in thirty minutes. But, yeah, we're pulling out of here tomorrow. Our brigade's been ordered to secure all the way down to Odessa. From there, we'll shift to Chihuahua, Mexico, some six hundred and fifteen kilometers to the south and hold there. I'll explain more at the meeting. Just make sure your battalion is ready."

A couple minutes later, the colonel got up and tossed his plate and cup in the trash before heading off to his command track to get ready for the briefing.

The day before the cease-fire with the Chinese had taken effect, their battalion commander, Lieutenant Colonel Short, the XO, and two other soldiers had been killed by an IED as the unit had moved into west Texas. They were the last guys in the battalion killed before the armistice. The battalion commander was a well-liked family man, a soldier's soldier, so his death on the eve of the end of the war had really felt like a kick to the groin.

Major Regan had been pulled from his S3 position and made the new battalion commander for the time being. He had already been a senior captain in the battalion prior to being pulled up to be the brigade S3. It felt good to be back with his original battalion, but he was sad about the circumstances that had led to it.

****

The following day, Regan was standing in the commander's hatch of his M1A2 Abrams battle tank as they headed south, down Texas County Road 214. He was riding with the lead company as they drove in a single-file column with alternating fields of fire. Each tank had their sector to watch as they moved steadily into the occupied zone.

They weren't expecting to run into trouble. This was the last day of the armistice. The Chinese were supposed to have left the country. Now it was time to move into the zone and see what was left. Some units, like his, would continue across the border into Mexico as the US looked to execute the next stage in the war: retribution against the Mexican government for having allowed the Chinese to stage out of their country and support the military operations against their former ally.

The further south they drove, the more smoke they saw on the horizon. The thick black smoke rose into the sky from hundreds of different fires that raged across the oilfields. It was an apocalyptic scene, driving through the plains of west Texas with so much death and destruction around them.

For the most part, they drove across nothing but flat empty spaces between towns surrounded by oil fires. The thick plumes of black smoke continued to blow to the east, obscuring their view at times of the road or a small city or town as they drove through it.

Aside from the fires and smoke, what the American tankers noticed the most was how empty the small towns and cities were as they rolled through them. In many cases, the entire town appeared to be empty, completely devoid of life. The lawns around people's homes hadn't been mowed in more than a year. Tall grass and weeds had sprung up along the sides of the roads, and had also created some cracks and potholes in the streets.

Many of the homes and buildings had broken windows; some had broken doors. All of them looked like no one had lived in them in a very long time. It was scary how empty and abandoned everything looked, almost like a set on the *Walking Dead* TV show from before the war.

Where have all the people gone? Regan asked himself.

The column of tanks moved steadily toward the town of Andrews. When they reached the outer city limits, the scout vehicle and tanks in front came to a halt. Regan got on the radio and asked what the holdup was. The scout vehicle said they'd encountered a small band of unarmed civilians trying to flag them down.

A few minutes after that initial call, the scout commander asked if Regan could come up there. The lieutenant said it was important for him to speak with the civilian who said he was in charge of the group. Regan ordered his driver to pull their tank out of the formation and move ahead toward the front of the column while the rest of his tankers and vehicles stayed put until he knew what was going on.

As he got closer to the scout vehicles and the lead tank, he saw what had to be forty or fifty civilians. Looking beyond the crowd, he saw another crowd streaming toward them from the city.

When his vehicle stopped near the scout vehicle, Regan finally had a chance to really see the people up close. What he saw broke his heart and angered him. The people looked so skinny. Their clothes were practically hanging off their bones. What nearly caused him to break down and cry right then and there was seeing some of the children with their bloated bellies, rags practically falling off them.

Once his tank had stopped, dozens of civilians circled around his vehicle. They held up hands, begging for food, begging for help. One woman was trying to hold her child up to him, begging him for clean water and food. The entire scene almost overwhelmed him.

Regan ordered the tank turned off and told his guys inside to grab whatever food they had and start passing it out to the civilians. He got on the radio next and called for any and all medics to come forward. He also wanted their supply section to move up and bring with them a water buffalo and food.

Regan called Colonel Beasley and told him what was going on. He explained the situation and said he'd ordered his unit to stop for the moment to help the civilians and see if they could provide him with any intelligence of enemy positions that might still be in the area. The colonel said he could spend an hour helping them but would need to get back on the move. They needed to be in Odessa by nightfall and it was already 1430 hours.

Jumping down from his tank, Regan walked through the crowd of emaciated people until he found a couple of men talking with one of his lieutenants. Walking up to them, he asked, "Are you the one in charge?"

The man looked at him with hollowed eye sockets and skin pulled taut against the bones of his skull. "I am. My name is Ray Thor. I used to be a city councilman before the war." The man stuck his hand out to shake Regan's.

Doing his best to maintain his composure and keep his emotions in check, Regan shook the man's hand. "I'm Major Trey Regan. I'm the battalion commander for this unit. If you don't mind, could we talk over here? I have some questions I'd like to ask you."

The man agreed and the two of them walked back toward Regan's headquarters track, which had pulled up at this point. His operations and intel chiefs were riding in the vehicle.

When they approached the vehicle, someone had gotten a quick brew of coffee going and handed Mr. Thor a cup. The man's eyes lit up when he saw the steaming hot java. He lifted it to his lips and savored the smell for a moment before drinking some.

Looking at Regan with tears in his eyes, he said, "Thank you, Major. I haven't had a cup of coffee in more than a year. But more than that, thank you for stopping. Thank you for helping the people of my town. I honestly didn't think any of us were going to survive this war."

Regan saw several of the officers and NCOs wiping away tears or turning to walk away. The sight of so much suffering, so much starvation, and the little kids—it was almost too much for any of them to bear.

"Mr. Thor, I know you all have been through a lot, and believe me, my men and I would love nothing more than to stay and help. Unfortunately, we have to get moving soon. More follow-on forces are going to come here, and they'll bring additional help with them."

Regan could see the look of panic in the man's face when he told him they'd have to leave soon. It was almost like they were abandoning them all over again.

Regan placed a hand on the man's shoulder—he couldn't feel an ounce of meat or fat anywhere, but he looked the man in the eyes. "We're going to leave you guys with most of our MREs and two of our water buffalos. That'll give you guys eleven hundred gallons of clean drinking water. You'll also have roughly three days' worth of food, though I wouldn't recommend eating two MREs a day just yet. You have to get yourselves acclimated to them, OK? That ought to stretch your food out to six days."

With tears running down his face, the man begged them not to leave them again. Regan had to turn away as he wiped away his own tears. He had more questions he needed to ask him, but it was so hard to hold it together.

"Mr. Thor, I promise you, more help is on the way. There are other units traveling toward your city behind us. Right now, my battalion is the lead tank unit for an entire division. I need to know—are there any additional Chinese or other hostile forces in the area? Any other threats I need to be worried about?"

The man looked confused at first, but then he started talking. "The Chinese left maybe ten days ago. We haven't seen or heard from them since then. Even when they were here, it was just a small unit. A much larger unit was further north of us near the front lines and then an even larger force down in Odessa.

"However, there's a militia force down in Odessa—those bastards are actually collaborators with the Chinese. They got extra rations, clean water, and medicine. They helped the Chinese identify the people who would cause trouble. At first, they rounded up the police, then they went after anyone who they knew to be a military veteran. Then they got ahold of a list of firearm background checks and helped the Chinese confiscate people's firearms. The traitors actually helped to disarm our own people, for God's sake."

The man shook as he recounted the story of what this militia unit had done, how they had participated in some of the atrocities that had been committed in the local area. He told them about several mass executions as well.

Looking at Regan, the man hissed, "When you get to Odessa, you need to kill those people. Something has to be done about what they did to us and everyone else in the occupied territories."

"Mr. Thor, I can assure you, a group like that will not be able to hide for very long," Regan insisted. "Once people see it's safe again, they'll turn them in. It's only a matter of time until that happens. Is there anything else that might endanger my men as we move south?"

The man shook his head, then finished drinking the cup of coffee before tearing into one of the MREs.

Turning to look for his S3, Regan ordered, "Pass the word to the rest of the unit: we're rolling out of here in twenty minutes. Make sure we leave a couple of water buffalos inside the town as we pass through along with half our MREs. We need to get moving down to Odessa. My money says we'll find the same situation down there as well."

****

Continuing down the road, Regan's scout vehicles reached the outer edge of the city when they encountered a roadblock of some sorts. Whoever was in charge of the town had placed a number of abandoned vehicles across the highway, forcing the column of vehicles to stop.

Sensing possible danger, Regan ordered one company of tanks to move around the left flank of the city while another company moved around to the right. He directed his infantry attachment to move forward with his lead tank unit and ordered their surveillance drones launched. They hadn't been using the drones up to this point because of the sheer volume of thick black smoke in the sky. They'd have been pretty useless with all the fires. Now that they had reached the outskirts of Odessa, they would be useful again.

Regan's driver pulled them out of their position near the rear of Alpha Company and moved them along the shoulder of the road near the scout vehicles and lead tank. When they had sidled up next to them,

Regan hopped out of his tank and walked over to the scout vehicle. He wanted to see what his drone operator was seeing.

The little scout drone had zipped ahead of them and moved over top of the roadblock. They saw a dozen or so civilians wearing some sort of camouflage clothing and armed with what looked like AR-15 style rifles.

"What do you make of them, sir?" asked the staff sergeant controlling the drone.

Regan furrowed his brow. "I'm not sure. They don't look like the emaciated folks we saw in Anderson. Is that body armor they're wearing? See if you can either zoom in a bit or go lower so we can get a better look."

The drone moved down in altitude a bit, settling in around five hundred feet. The men below appeared to also be wearing body armor with ballistic helmets—either stolen military gear or high-end civilian stuff. Then one of the men below aimed his rifle at the drone, and before the staff sergeant could move it, the drone's video cover blinked out.

"Damn it. They shot it down. Sorry about that, sir. I should have been paying better attention," the sergeant said, frustrated that he'd just lost one of their scout drones.

"No, that's OK, Sergeant. You helped us determine if these guys are friendly or not. Shooting down our drone isn't exactly a friendly gesture, especially considering they can see us. They know we're Americans."

Regan turned to the lieutenant in charge of his scout unit. "Lieutenant, we're going to put a couple of tank rounds into the roadblock," he announced. "I want your guys up on their crew-served weapons, ready to clear that position. We'll follow you guys in and link up at waypoint Delta."

The lieutenant nodded and relayed the orders to the guys in his vehicle and the other JLTV.

Regan climbed back up into the turret of his tank and plopped down into the commander's seat. After placing his helmet back on, he relayed what had happened with their drone to his other company commanders and his command track. He told them to proceed to waypoint Delta, which was the Odessa-Schlemeyer Field. Depending on the level of resistance they met, they'd then continue to waypoint Echo, which was the center of the city. Their job was to clear out any resistance so the rest of the division could continue to move deeper into Texas.

Depressing his talk button to address all units, Regan announced, "Dixie Six to all Dixie units. Our lead element has encountered a hostile roadblock leading into the city. I want all units to proceed into the city with extreme caution. I want all crew-served weapons manned and ready to deal with foot mobiles if we encounter them. Continue to push through any resistance you find and call it out as you encounter it. We need to clear this city. Dixie Six out.

"Staff Sergeant Schroder, I want you to stay on the gun. I'm going to be up top," Regan announced as he got their M2 .50-cal machine gun ready.

The lead tank for Alpha company turned his turret slightly as he readied the main gun to fire. Seconds later, the cannon belched flame and fire as the HEAT round covered the distance between them and the vehicles acting as a roadblock.

The roadblock exploded upon impact, sending chunks of the two cars and parts into the air. The JLTVs then advanced on the wreckage with the tanks moving in behind them.

When Regan's lead element got within a hundred meters of the roadblock, a handful of figures emerged, waving white flags or bedsheets in the air. The column stopped again as several of the vehicles began to spread out in a line formation. Some of the soldiers inside the JLTVs got out and called out to them, directing them to walk forward slowly. When they reached about fifty meters away, they had them take their vests and other gear off and lift their shirts up. They wanted to make sure these guys weren't hiding suicide vests or other weapons.

The dismounted infantrymen advanced forward until they reached the hostiles. They did a quick pat-down of them and then pulled out their zip ties. Once the prisoners were secured, the column continued on.

Regan ordered his tank to pull up next to the scout unit that had the prisoners. He wanted to speak with them and find out what the hell was going on in the city.

He jumped down from the tank and walked up to a group of five prisoners. Two of them appeared to have some minor wounds, which one of the medics was taking care of. As Regan got closer, though, he could quickly tell they were Americans. They had those stupid Velcro patches you could buy at a gun show taped to their body armor. They were also speaking fluent English with a Texas accent.

Regan approached the man who appeared to be the leader. "I'm Major Trey Regan, 2nd Battalion commander, 155th Armor Brigade Combat Team. Who are you guys and why did you shoot at us?"

A couple of the prisoners looked confused. The leader replied, "We didn't shoot at you. We didn't even know who you were. You just randomly attacked us."

Regan snorted at the deflection. "Really? So it wasn't your men that shot my scout drone down?" he pressed. "You guys pointed at it a couple of times before you shot it. You clearly saw our armored column stop half a mile from you guys, so you knew we were an American unit."

"We didn't know you guys were Americans. All we saw was a group of tanks approaching. The Chinese use drones all the time—so do the Russian mercenary groups."

Regan shook his head. "We're on a mission to link up with a militia unit operating out of Odessa. Do you know anything about them?"

Regan believed these might be the militiamen Mr. Thor from Anderson had warned them about. He needed to see if they would confirm it for him.

A couple of the militiamen looked at each other before the leader announced, "We're the only militia unit in Odessa."

Regan smiled at the admission. "Ah, well, then. I'm sorry about the misunderstanding. Sergeant—cut these men's ties and help them up."

As the sergeant began to cut their zip ties off, Regan asked, "What's your name?"

"I'm Jake. I'm not the leader, though. I'm just in charge of the checkpoint. Our leader's name is Jose. He's in town."

"OK, that's good to know. Can you tell me how many people are in your militia and what kind of weapons you guys are armed with? I have some extra weapons and ammo I brought for the Odessa militia unit to help us."

"Yeah. We've got about two hundred and twenty people," Jake explained, smiling at the offer. "Most everyone has an assault rifle, though. When the Chinese pulled out of the area a few weeks ago, they abandoned thousands of rounds of ammo, RPGs, and other weapons. I have no idea why they left, but when they did, we took charge of Ector County and the surrounding area. They even left a handful of fuel trucks and some of their armored vehicles. We're a fully equipped little army now."

The militiaman went on about how they had taken charge of things, restoring order now that the Chinese had left.

"Wow. That's pretty impressive, Jake—them leaving all that equipment like that. Hey, I have a question for you. Maybe you can help me with something."

"Sure thing, Major," Jake said with a nod. "What can the Odessa militia do for you?"

"When we drove through Anderson a few hours ago, most of the people there were starving. Come to think of it, nearly every person we've encountered in the occupied zone has been severally emaciated and starving, except you guys. Why is that?"

The smile on Jake's face disappeared. His right hand traveled down his left side, where he normally kept his pistol, only now it wasn't there.

"When we were in Anderson, the townspeople told us about a group of Americans who had collaborated with the Chinese. This group of Americans helped the Chinese identify 'troublemakers'—police officers, military veterans. They even helped the Chinese go door to door confiscating people's personal firearms. In exchange, they were given food, medicine, and a lot of authority in the area…"

The other prisoners' faces now showed a bit of fear. Regan's soldiers, who just moments ago had cut them loose and appeared to be somewhat friendly, had now moved their hands down to their rifles and backed up a bit, creating some space between them.

Jake fumbled for words. "I. Um…I don't know what you're talking about, Major. The Chinese were pretty brutal to everyone. Our little group banded together to scrounge for food and provide security. I suppose that's how we managed to survive."

Regan smirked at the response. "So all of these emaciated people were starved for no reason?" he pressed. "Your band of two hundred plus people somehow managed to find enough food to stay fat and healthy and they didn't? The Chinese just happened to let you guys keep your body armor and weapons?" Regan paused for a moment, crossing his arms across his chest and placing his hand near his Sig in the shoulder strap. "Is that what you're trying to tell me, Jake?"

The man didn't say anything as his mind searched for what to say next. One of the others, one of the guys their medic had been treating, blurted out, “I didn’t have a choice! If I didn’t do what they told me to do, my daughter wouldn’t get diabetic medicine. She’d die.”

Whipping his Sig out, Regan held it at his side but thumbed the safety off. His soldiers now moved their own rifles up in response, pointing them at the militiamen.

They immediately held their hands back up, begging not to be shot.

Pointing to the wounded man, Regan motioned for him to walk toward him. Jake tried to protest but Regan smacked him across the side of the face with the barrel of his Sig, shutting the man up.

“What’s your name?”

Looking terrified, the man answered, “I’m Adam. Please don’t kill me.”

Narrowing his eyes, Regan scrutinized the man. “What do you mean you didn’t have a choice? What did these guys make you do and how did you end up working for them?”

With a look of sheer terror, the man explained how, shortly after they had been occupied, the Chinese had cut off all medical supplies. The only exception was if you joined one of their “people’s militias.” If you worked for them, they’d give you and your family access to medicine, food, and clean water. Adam said he’d joined so he could get insulin for his diabetic daughter. He then went on to explain all the horrible things he’d had to do to keep his daughter alive. He cried through most of it, saying he didn’t deserve to live, but he wanted to give his daughter a chance at life.

Finally, Regan told them him he wouldn’t press charges against him. As to the others, he ordered them to be taken prisoner as enemy combatants. They’d be handed over to DHS and tried in one of the DHS prison camps.

As the rest of Regan’s battalion filtered into the city, they ran into more elements of this militia force. Some of them tried to play things off like Jake and his little group had; some opted to try and fight. Many others just gave up.

By the end of the day, Regan’s 2nd Battalion had secured the city. The following day they’d continue their push south, eventually arriving in Chihuahua, Mexico, four days later.

****

San Antonio, Texas

Lackland Air Force Base

Vice President Luke Powers couldn't believe the level of damage he saw across the city. As bad as the destruction was, seeing the tens of thousands of emaciated Americans was even harder to take. The civilians in the occupied zone had literally been left to starve by the Chinese.

FEMA and DHS were still trying to figure out how many people had died during the occupation of the city, but right now it was looking like more than half a million. It could even be as many as a million—there was no way to know. Many people had either died in their homes from starvation or died during the early days of the occupation when the supply of medicine in the area had run out. With no insulin or other daily life-saving medications, tens of thousands of people had died right away.

"Mr. Vice President? The generals are ready when you are," one of his advisors said, breaking his train of thought.

Powers turned to look at his advisor, then nodded and followed the man inside one of the buildings near the runway. When he entered the room, the two generals and a couple of colonels stood. He motioned for them to take a seat and begin.

"Were you able to see everything you needed to?" asked one of the generals, an Army commander.

"I was," said Vice President Powers with a nod. "Thank you, General, for arranging the security. I think I was able to see a lot more driving through the city than I would have by flying overhead. I know the President would like to see some of this firsthand, but I agree with you—the security situation isn't what it needs to be for us to bring him here just yet."

The Air Force general began, "Mr. Vice President, as you know, we're facing an unimaginable humanitarian crisis here in San Antonio. We have two Red Horse civil engineering squadrons arriving tomorrow and the day after. They'll help us get the power to the city turned back on. Once we have electricity, we'll be able to get the city's water system restored. FEMA is also bringing in emergency generators, which will help in some localized areas. We're also going to set up a couple of tent cities nearby for those who just need a safe, clean place to stay."

Luke just shook his head in disgust that things had gotten so bad. The entire city looked like a bombed-out third-world cesspool, not a once-great American city.

The Army general took over the rest of the briefing. "We've not seen any Chinese units since we took control of the area. We have found a few thousand PLA deserters, but they surrendered quickly. During their debriefs, they all said they didn't want to go back to China. They would rather take their chances as prisoners with us than return home."

Interrupting the general, one of the presidential advisors said, "What about the private military contractors? I hear you only received a small number of them from the final PLA units before they left."

Grimacing at the question, the general nodded. "I'm afraid that's true. They handed over about three hundred Russian PMCs. We believe there were around twelve hundred operating in Texas. I can't say if the rest of them fled across the border into Mexico, fled with the Chinese or simply faded into the population. With as starved as people are, the ones who appear to be well fed are sticking out like sore thumbs. We're quickly identifying them as collaborators or one of the PMCs that were working in Texas."

"What are you doing with the collaborators?"

"Per DoD guidance, we're handing them over to DHS to be charged as unlawful enemy combatants. Once DHS takes them, they're out of our hands. I believe the Air Force is flying them out on some Con Air flights, but I can't tell you where they're sending them," the Army commander explained.

He continued, "We're on track to start combat operations in Sinaloa, Mexico, in two weeks. General Tibbets is repositioning the 101st Air Assault Division and the Second Marine Division for that fight. Those'll be the main two divisions that will lead the fight against the cartels. The 1st Infantry Division is moving down to Mexico City while the 3rd Infantry Division moves into southern Mexico. He believes we should have our forces fully deployed across the country within the next couple of weeks. Then it'll be a matter of wiping out the cartel while the State Department works to establish a new government and judicial system."

This is going to result in years of nation building, thought the Vice President. He hoped the next administration would see it through to the end.

"What about JSOC? Are they ready to begin?" Powers asked.

"They are," said the general with a nod. "We're moving a couple of SEAL teams into the country along with most of 5th Group. They'll be responsible for a lot of the direct action operations and going after the leadership structure of the cartels."

"How are things shaking up out west in California?" Luke inquired. He was scheduled to fly out there tomorrow and tour a number of cities in the state.

The two generals shrugged their shoulders. They didn't appear to have much of an opinion; they must have been too busy trying to handle what was on their plates in Texas along with the Mexico campaign.

The rest of the day was spent talking with the soldiers and airmen on the base and meeting a number of survivor groups. The stories they told him of the occupation made him shudder. It was a miracle many of them had survived.

Chapter Twenty
China Strategy

February 2023
Hong Kong
Republic of Southern China

Walking off the plane, Haley Kagel took in a deep breath of fresh, salty air. After being cooped up in a plane for nearly twenty hours, it felt good to stand and walk.

The newly appointed CIA station chief approached her, along with Ambassador Larson, who had just arrived in country eight days ago. They greeted her and then led the way to a waiting limo that would take them to her hotel.

Once inside the posh vehicle, Ambassador Larson started the conversation. "Madam Secretary, there are several key action items General Zeng and Chief Executive Lau want to address with you," he said as he pulled a paper out of his folder and handed it to her.

She slipped her reading glasses on and scanned the documents, noting the key agenda items. She circled a couple of keywords, scribbling something next to them for later.

She looked up. "I think these are doable, but we're going to need some guarantees from them," Secretary Kagel asserted. "The President doesn't want a restart of hostilities between President Chen and the US. Our military assistance needs to be covert at best and preferably kept in the shadows."

The CIA man cleared his throat. "I hope I'm not speaking out of turn, Madam Secretary, but if you win the presidency, what will your position be with President Chen and General Zeng?"

She smiled at the question. "What is the military situation on the ground, Morgan?" she deflected. "How are things shaping up?"

Secretary Kagel hadn't formally announced that she was running for office, but everyone knew she would. She'd begun the process of putting together a campaign a couple of days after the war between the US and China had formally ended. She wanted to capitalize on her popularity and her part in ending the war, and President Sachs had made it clear that, as part of his effort to help heal and reunify the country, he would not seek reelection. Congress had announced a new election for November, and she intended to be the first woman to win the presidency.

The CIA station chief cleared his throat. "Things could definitely be better," he admitted. "General Luan is using the influx of soldiers from North America to bolster their forces still fighting in Taiwan and here in the south. It would appear that for the time being, they've reached a stalemate."

A couple minutes later, the vehicle pulled up to the Ritz-Carlton Hotel. The door to her vehicle was whisked open. A few seconds later, her head of security appeared and led her entourage up to the hotel. They took the elevator up to the 117th floor, which housed the illustrious Victoria Harbor suite, where she would be staying and working out of while she was in Hong Kong. The 3,930-square-foot suite boasted phenomenal views of the city, a separate sitting room, and a ten-person round table where they'd hold their discussions.

Upon entering the room, she smiled and nodded in satisfaction. Her advance team had everything arranged and set up just the way she liked it. She was going to have exactly three hours to lie down for a short nap before she'd need to get ready for her upcoming meeting—a meeting that would decide the fate of Asia.

****

It had only been two hours and twenty-eight minutes since her eyes had closed, but somehow, she sure did feel refreshed. Whipping the covers off, Haley Kagel made her way into the bathroom to take a quick shower. Once the jets of hot water had fully woken her up and breathed new life into her, she got dressed and put on her makeup in preparation for this important meeting.

When she had finished getting ready, Kagel opened the doors that led out of the master bedroom into the sitting room. She saw that her two other guests must have arrived while she was sleeping, and she nodded to herself in satisfaction. She wanted to go over the plan again before she agreed to pitch it to Mr. Lau and Zeng.

When she walked into the living room, the two men had been looking out the window, away from her. When her chief of staff stood, they turned around to greet her. She gasped. There stood Mr. Erik Jahn, in the flesh.

She looked at his extended hand with contempt. "I wasn't made aware that I would be meeting with you," she said icily. "Do you know how bad this could look for me? Even being in the same hotel at the same time as you could derail my future plans."

She shot her chief of staff a dirty look. *He and I will have words*, she thought angrily.

Erik withdrew his hand, not seeming the least bit offended. "I apologize for the deception, Madam Secretary. I can assure you no one saw me enter the hotel or this room. As a matter of fact, your NSA has gone to great lengths to create a digital footprint of me back in Virginia to cover my tracks."

The other man stepped forward. "I'm Lieutenant Colonel Seth Mitchell, ma'am. I'm his chaperone."

Secretary Kagel turned to look at the military man, who seemed a bit uncomfortable wearing a suit. He was good looking, solidly built with sharp eyes that probably didn't miss much. She promptly assessed him to probably be Special Forces. He also looked vaguely familiar, but she couldn't place him.

Pointing to the chairs, Kagel directed everyone to sit. She turned to her head of security. "Make sure no one disturbs us, and keep everyone else away from this room," she ordered. "Under *no* circumstances is anyone to enter this room with him out of his disguise." She pointed at Erik with disgust.

Kagel turned her attention back to the military man. "The President does know he's here meeting with me, right?" she pressed.

Nodding, Seth pulled a handwritten letter out of his breast pocket and handed it to her. As he did, she caught the briefest glimpse of the pistol he was wearing in a chest holster.

She accepted the note, although she wasn't quite sure what to make of it. She grabbed for her reading glasses and then opened the letter:

> *Haley,*
>
> *By now, you should have been introduced to Mr. Erik Jahn. Yes, I know he is one of the key individuals responsible for this war and all that has happened to our country. But you need to know that he is also one of the key individuals who has worked behind the scenes to help end it.*

Mr. Jahn is part of a secret organization, which he'll tell you more about shortly. Suffice it to say, we need his help to close this next chapter and start a new one. In a few short months, I will be leaving office. You will become the next President, and you'll have to put the world back together. I need you and Mr. Jahn to come to some sort of détente or agreement to make that happen.

If you need advice or have questions about Mr. Jahn or the organization he's a part of, please consult with Mr. Mitchell. He led the team that found and captured Mr. Jahn. He was also his interrogator and has questioned nearly every member of Mr. Jahn's organization that we've captured. I trust his judgment and the plans the CIA has put into place to manage Mr. Jahn and his organization.

When you become President, it will be incumbent upon you to enforce this plan and make sure all parties continue to abide by it. Bring Mr. Mitchell into your inner circle and use him as your go-between with Mr. Jahn. I have full faith and trust in your judgment and skills to work out a deal between the US, the Democratic Republic of Southern China, and the organization Mr. Jahn represents. When you have read this letter, please hand it back to Mr. Mitchell.

Signed,
Jonathan

Haley looked at the letter for a moment longer, trying to digest what she'd just read. She looked out the window, noticing the sun was still up but evening was quickly approaching.

"Would you like to read it one more time?" asked Seth as he eyed her.

"I think I would, if you don't mind."

Seth took the opportunity to get up and stretch his own legs. He stood in front of the window, looking out at the hustle and bustle of the majestic city.

As she reread the letter, it suddenly dawned on her why Mr. Jahn was here. If she remembered correctly, Peng An, who was the CEO of the China Investment Corporation, was supposedly part of this group. He had been purged, along with General Hu, the head of the PLA, and General Ma, the head of the PLA Strategic Rocket Service, about a month ago.

Haley handed the letter back to Seth. He walked over to the end table, grabbed the wastebasket, pulled a Zippo out of his pocket and lit the document on fire over the trash can. A moment later, the paper was burnt to a crisp. He crumpled the burnt remnants up so the note was completely destroyed.

"Thorough, aren't you?" she asked as he took a seat opposite her.

"Orders," he replied. He flashed her a mischievous smile and winked.

She snickered, then turned her attention to Mr. Jahn. "OK, Erik," she said. "I believe it's time for you to tell me about this society you're a member of and explain how we're going to put Humpty Dumpty back together."

For the next three hours, they talked about the origins of the Thule Society, how it had come about and why. Eventually, they came full circle to the present day and how the organization had been led astray by Secretary-General Johann Behr and others within the organization that felt the world was ready for a truly unified world government. Clearly, they had misjudged the situation. As a consequence, more than a hundred million people had died, and many prominent members of the organization had been hunted down and either imprisoned or killed.

Looking at her watch, Secretary Kagel became concerned that they were going to be late for their dinner with Mr. Lau and General Zeng. Seth noticed her looking at the time. "It's OK, Madam Secretary. The dinner for this evening was rescheduled for breakfast tomorrow," he assured. "The President said this was more important for you to know and understand before you meet with the Chinese. There's still a bit more at play that you need to be brought up to speed on."

She tilted her head to the side. "Really? I feel like a lot of this trip was prearranged well before I got here. Are there more surprises I should expect?"

Seth smiled. "A few, but we'll reveal them as Erik continues to peel back the onion for you."

"Well, then, let's continue, gentlemen," she said.

Erik nodded. "Since 1900, the only four people to become president of your country that were not directly picked by the Society were Teddy

Roosevelt, Harry Truman, John Kennedy, and Jonathan Sachs. All four of them stumbled into the presidency, and all four of them upturned the apple cart and the socioeconomic order the Society has sought to create."

Kagel crossed her arms. "How can an organization like the Society have so much power?" she pressed. "Perhaps you should tell me a bit more about its origins."

"I won't bore you with the European or Asian side of the organization," said Erik, waving his hand as if shooing away a fly. "Suffice it to say, it was the American side that really took the organization to the next level in the late 1800s and early 1900s. During the turn of the century, Andrew Carnegie was worth an estimated $372 billion in today's currency, and John D. Rockefeller was worth $409 billion. These men, along with John Pierpont Morgan Senior, believed in creating a safe and stable society that would allow corporations to thrive, but more importantly, their own families to generate enormous amounts of wealth.

"The challenge with creating a safe and stable society is it requires good order and discipline. That's hard to have if you truly believe in democracy. So these men, along with other influential leaders, sought to create a governing structure that would move to create peace and stability throughout the world. Some people call it the One World Order; others refer to it as the Trilateral Commission. Ultimately, the Society seeks to maintain stability throughout the world by inserting our members into various positions within the world's governments, businesses, and military structures. Potential leaders for each country are identified early on by various organizations within each country. Then we debate what would be the appropriate time at which each individual would best serve the organization's overarching goals—mainly ensuring economic stability that benefits our members."

Erik spent another hour explaining other aspects of the organization, including who some of their current members were and who had previously been a member.

For her part, Haley Kagel sat there on the couch, doing her best to digest everything she heard. It all sounded a bit spectacular; worse, it confirmed the truth of many of the conspiracy theories she had previously discounted. To think the world was controlled by secret organizations, cabals of industry and banks, infuriated her.

When Erik had finished speaking, Secretary Kagel looked at him for a moment, assessing him. "Why has the President asked you to speak with me?" she inquired. "Why disclose all of this to me here and now?"

Placing his coffee cup down on the table, Erik turned his body to face her. "The President came to the same conclusion that I hope you will."

Kagel's left eyebrow rose. "Really? And what conclusion is that?" she pressed, feeling that there must be an ultimatum coming.

"The President can continue to use the power of the state to hunt our members down. Lord knows, he's been very effective at it as of late. But ultimately, we'll survive his term in office. Mostly, President Sachs came to the conclusion that a truce could be called. A new set of rules, terms if you will, could be worked out between the Society and the United States—rules that will ensure something like this never happens again. These rules could benefit the average worker instead of treating them like tradable commodities. The President hopes that by telling you all this, you'll also agree to this new playing field, and together, we can work to help shape the aftermath of this terrible war."

With his piece said, Erik reached down to pick up his coffee and then sat back on the couch.

Secretary Kagel calculated her options for a moment. "I suppose by agreeing to work with you, you will help ensure I have a smooth election to the presidency?" she queried.

Tilting his head to the side, Erik didn't exactly say yes or no, but his facial expressions did confirm what she'd suspected. She realized that if she didn't agree to the new terms Sachs had negotiated, then the struggle between America and this secret cabal would continue.

Bastards, she thought.

She looked at Seth. "I would like to talk privately with Mr. Mitchell," she told Erik. "I'm going to leave you here to admire the view while Seth and I go for a short walk. I can't say for certain how long I'll be, but if you feel you must rest, you are welcome to catch a short nap on the couch here or have some food brought up."

She stood, and Seth nodded and followed her. The two of them didn't say anything as they walked out of the room and down the hall toward the elevator. Two of her security guards joined them as they got on the elevator.

They got out on the 102nd floor and walked to the Lounge and Bar, which was relatively empty. Kagel made a beeline toward one of the tables that faced a window looking out onto the city.

She turned to her security. "Please keep the other patrons away from us," she directed. They nodded and spread out nearby.

The maître d' approached. "What would you like to drink?" he asked.

Kagel smiled as she looked up at him. "I'll take an espresso martini and an order of oysters," she replied. Then she shot Seth a look to tell him he'd better order something so she wouldn't be eating or drinking alone.

Seth took his cue. "I'll take a double Scotch whiskey and your small sushi boat," he said.

With their orders taken, Haley studied Seth, sizing him up again. "The President says I should trust you—that you know more about this organization and these people than probably anyone who's not on the inside," she began. "So, what's your take on Mr. Jahn? Should I trust him?"

Seth paused for a moment, looking out the window. The sun was beginning to set, and the lights of the city below were softly flickering.

He turned back toward her and let out a deep breath. "I wouldn't trust him for a second, ma'am. However…we need him. He believes he has outmaneuvered us, that he has us over a barrel. And he's partially right. But I've also allowed him to believe he's outwitted us."

He paused for a moment and she weighed his words. "We can use him," Seth continued, "just as he's using us. But we have to keep him on a tight leash. Better yet, we need to infiltrate our own people into his organization and find a way to transform them from within."

"Is that even possible?" she asked. "It sounds like to me that this group is very selective about who they allow in."

Seth nodded. "They are. But no organization is immune to penetration. Our problem was we didn't know they existed. I mean, we had an idea that some organizations like this were around, but we didn't know who they were or the extent of their true power. That's changed, though. What Erik hasn't told you, and what wasn't in the letter, is that Task Force Avenger has been on a bit of a killing spree. We've eliminated more than four hundred of their known members and driven many more into hiding."

"Really?" she asked skeptically. "How did you find out about them?"

Seth's mouth turned up into a mischievous crooked grin. "Erik narked on them," he explained. "He traded them for his own freedom, if you can believe it. That's why I'm saying we can infiltrate their organization. If he was this weak, this susceptible to coercion, then there will be others in the organization that are as well."

"What if he's just playing us?" she countered. "Having us eliminate his competitors so he can take charge of the organization?"

"I thought about that as well, and I'm fairly certain that's exactly what he's done," Seth admitted. "But allowing him to take the organization over means we'll be dealing directly with the guy who can make the decisions going forward. But more importantly, it's allowed us to cull the herd, so to speak. It's also enabled us to identify more than five hundred data points that connect all of these people. I don't think Mr. Jahn knows that, but using those data points, we're now going to be able to identify others who work in his organization that he hasn't told us about. With this link diagram, we'll be able to apply pressure on them, and that'll be our opening to get inside."

Their drinks and food arrived, and they took a break from talking shop. Haley continued to ask Seth questions but turned to the topics of his background, what he'd done in the military, his family, educational background, and hobbies. She was steadily conducting her own vetting of him.

Soon, they had finished their dinner and a second round of drinks. "Seth, the President says I should keep you close going forward—that you'll be our main conduit into this organization," she said. "The more I learn about this group, the more I think he may be right. I want you to keep working an angle to get inside that organization. Find people we can use to infiltrate in, and let's build a network of informants from within."

She paused for a second. "What's your status with the military, and who do you technically work for?" she probed.

Seth breathed out deeply. "Technically, I'm still a lieutenant colonel in the Army, Special Forces to be precise. However, I've been loaned back to the Agency, so I guess I technically belong to them for the moment."

She nodded and mulled it over. "How hard would it be for you to get out of the military and leave the Agency?" she asked.

"Well, I'm still in the military, but for that, it's really just a matter of me putting in my retirement papers. As for getting out of the Agency, once I leave the military, unless I accept a permanent full-time position with them, I'm out." He leaned forward. "They'd obviously want to me to stay in, unless you had some other plans," he said, clearly pushing to see what her angle was.

Kagel looked around to make sure no one was nearby. "This is between you and me. Understand?"

He nodded.

"A few days after I get back from this trip, I'm going to officially resign and launch my bid to be President," she explained. "I've been working on establishing a campaign and prefilling all the necessary positions that'll be involved in that process. If you'd be willing, I'd like to bring you on board as one of my senior advisors and national security experts. You'll largely be kept in the shadows, but you'd be trotted out from time to time when needed. When I win this thing, I will either have you work as a special advisor or a key figure on my national security team. If we have to work with this organization going forward, then I'm going to want you close to me and involved in the administration. Would you be willing to do that for me…for your country?"

Seth reached for his half-empty glass of scotch and picked it up. He looked out the window for a second as he downed the liquid. "My wife is going to kill me, but I've devoted my life to the service of my country. She'll understand. You can count me in, Madam President."

Haley smiled. She liked the sound of that. *Madam President…*

"Excellent. Then let's go finish our discussion with Mr. Jahn and let him know we're in agreement. We have a lot to prepare for tomorrow. I know it may not have been on the agenda, but is it possible for you to accompany me to this meeting? We're going to be deciding the fate of Asia and since we're going to be working together, I'd like you to know what's being said in that room. The reconstruction of the country and the rebalance of power in Asia will most likely consume my first term."
****

Following Day

Secretary Kagel walked into the Central Government Complex Building across the harbor on Hong Kong Island, more ready than she felt she would have been yesterday had they met then. As she entered the grand entrance to the governing office for Hong Kong, she was greeted by Chief Executive Gordan Lau, Mr. James Chan, his head of security, and General Zeng Shaoshan, the de facto commander of all military forces for their fledgling country.

After exchanging their pleasantries, the Chinese leaders led them to a briefing room in the bowels of the building. Once everyone was present, a technician came in and did a quick sweep of the room for any electronic listening devices.

After everyone was sitting down, James Chan placed a small contraption on the center of the table between them and turned it on. "This device will create an electronic void in this room," he explained. "The Ministry of State Security is extremely tech savvy with their listening devices. This is the same mechanism I used when I would meet with President Chen. Even my former organization couldn't overhear when it is being used, so this will ensure we're able to talk freely."

Seth chuckled to himself. "These guys are even more paranoid about security than I am," he muttered quietly.

General Zeng didn't waste any time. "Madam Secretary, it's good to finally meet you in person. I hear you may be running for president shortly."

She didn't confirm or deny the rumor but flashed a smirk for a reply, letting them know it was true. "General, I read over the list of items you wanted to discuss during our meeting," she began. "I wanted to let you know that I spoke with President Sachs a few hours ago before coming here, and I believe a deal can be worked out on most of these items." She wanted it to be clear that she was there to talk business, not American politics.

Mr. Lau pushed into the conversation before the general could say anything. "Madam Secretary, the most urgent item on that list is food," he insisted. "We are running critically short on provisions to feed our people."

"And keep my troops fed," General Zeng confirmed. "I've already had to put them on half rations. Is there any way we can get some immediate relief?"

She smiled. "The President understands the need is dire and has agreed to send food aid. As we speak, there are five C-5 Galaxy cargo planes leaving the US to fly here directly. They are bringing six hundred and fifty thousand kilos of MREs, the packages that we use to feed our military when they're deployed. We're also working out an arrangement with Vietnam, Australia, and the Philippines to provide them with food stocks as well."

"What about American agricultural goods?" asked Mr. Lau nervously. "How soon until we can get piped back into a trading relationship with your farmers again?"

Secretary Kagel realized that while General Zeng was handling the military aspect of securing their country, Mr. Lau was trying to hold things together with the people. If food shortages got any worse than they already were, it could become even harder for them to hold their new nation together.

Kagel leaned forward. "We're working on that right now. I must be blunt, though. Right now, the only working ports we have that can handle any sort of grain or other agricultural shipments to China are the ones out of Washington State and Oregon. When General Han's forces left California, they destroyed many of the port facilities on their way out. The infrastructure across much of the southwestern part of our country is a complete disaster. President Sachs told me he'll do his best to get the supply lines going to Hong Kong, but you have to understand, our country is in ruins right now. It's going to take us decades to recover from the damage your country has inflicted on us."

Bristling a bit, General Zeng retorted, "Not all of us were in agreement with this war. That is why we have broken away and formed our own country. If there is one positive thing that has come from this war, Madam Secretary, it's the formation of the Democratic Republic of Southern China."

She sighed. "I agree, General. But not everyone in my country sees things the same way. We're still trying to get an idea of how many people died in the occupation, but the numbers have already surpassed twenty-five million."

"Excuse me, Madam Secretary. Did you say twenty-five million?" asked Mr. Lau, a genuine look of surprise on his face.

Kagel realized he probably had no idea what their army abroad had been doing. However, as she saw the facial expressions of Mr. Chen, the former MSS Director, she inferred that he had probably known exactly what had been going on.

"I suppose you've been kept in the dark about the atrocities that were committed by General Han's forces," she said, her voice betraying her own genuine sadness. "I'm not sure why or what led to this decision or policy, but inside the occupied zones, the PLA began a systematic purge of our people. At first, it was just the sick and elderly, but in time, they began to cull anyone who was too weak to work. Toward the end, they just started killing everyone they came across."

Zeng shook his head in disgust. "This was the more reason why we needed to separate from Beijing. I couldn't be a part of a country and military that was no better than the Nazis." He paused for a moment before staring daggers at Chen. "Do you want to tell her what the plans for America were, or should I?"

Squirming a bit in his seat, Chen reluctantly nodded. "Madam Secretary, my understanding is you've been briefed on the Thule Society, correct?"

Kagel nodded, surprised that Chen knew about them.

"I am a member as well," he admitted. "It was Erik Jahn who told me the Society needed to end this war. He said Chen had to go and it was time to restructure China. So, I started the ball rolling here." He glanced at Mr. Lau and General Zeng before continuing. "I briefed General Zeng and Mr. Lau on who and what the Society was and how it had shaped China and the world. I also told them of how Chen, Wu, and Ma had betrayed the Society and moved to an alternate plan. They agreed that something had to be done. Then we moved to restructure China into the vision the Society has always had for it: a true democratic free-market society."

Secretary Kagel shook her head. "You speak of restructuring China like the restructuring of a business deal or a merger."

Chen shrugged. "The Society revolves around money, economics, and political power. In a way, it is a business—just one without national borders or loyalties to one nation over another.

"Before I say anything further, I want to state plainly that I had no hand in the development of President Chen's alternate plans. He deceived the Society and used the organization to position himself and China to become the dominant world power—something that hadn't been agreed upon. "

"When the Society moved forward with its plan to remove President Sachs, President Chen had pledged to support it. What the Society didn't know was that President Chen had secretly developed an alternative plan to what Peng An, General Hu, and General Ma, who as you may know were also members of the Thule Society, had proposed. This is despite the fact that Peng, Hu and Ma were the highest-ranking members of the organization in Asia, higher than Chen.

"In exchange for being a part of this UN force, China was going to gain even more access to your country's tech sector and guaranteed long-term deals with your agriculture and petroleum industry. In theory, this would have met our long-term economic needs for decades—"

"I know about this already, Mr. Chen," Kagel interrupted. "Tell me something I don't know." Kagel was losing patience with the history lesson.

"President Chen, General Song, and General Han came up with an alternative plan—please indulge me for just a moment longer," Chen said hurriedly. "During World War II, the Nazis invaded Eastern Europe to advance their policy of Lebensraum and to acquire additional resources. President Chen wanted to implement the same policy in America, creating the People's Republic of North America. By capturing the states of Texas and Oklahoma, China would secure for it all of our energy needs. The capture of California, Mexico, and Central America would provide China with its agricultural and food needs.

"By eliminating the people within the occupied zones, he believed we'd be able to move in tens of millions of Chinese settlers, who'd face virtually no resistance from the local population. As to the kidnapping of your women—well, we face a demographic problem of having hordes of young men without any women available for them. That's why they developed the Q Program. They'd remove young, fertile women from the occupied zones and bring them back to China. Once here, they'd be placed in a reeducation camp where they'd undergo intensive language training and education on how to be a 'good Chinese wife' to the military men they'd be given to once the war was over. They were told that if they adhered to the training and became good wives, their husbands might be rewarded by being stationed in the People's Republic of North America and be allowed to resettle there. It was a horrible program, and I'm ashamed that my country created something like this," Mr. Chan concluded as he wiped away a tear.

Haley had to take a couple of deep breaths to keep herself from exploding in anger. She saw Seth was having a hard time keeping his cool as well. She had to remember that the three people sitting across from her hadn't been involved in this. They were trying to do the right thing by breaking away from the regime that had implemented these disastrous policies.

Kagel took a deep breath in and let it out slowly as she collected herself. "Thank you for the explanation, Mr. Chan. And thank you three for standing up to this. I know it's placed you all in great peril. I'll relay this to President Sachs."

She sighed. "I think it's going to be hard for my nation not to want to restart hostilities with the PRC, especially with Chen still in charge of it. We have an armistice in place, but that could easily end when more of this information becomes public."

The three men didn't say anything but seemed to resign themselves to what she'd just said.

"Putting that aside, I need to know from the three of you—can you defeat him?" Kagel probed. "Do you want to just maintain your own border or are you interested in reuniting all of China under your rule and guidance?" She needed to know what their endgame was. Their answers would greatly determine her own policy direction in her presidential campaign.

General Zeng nodded at the question and signaled to the others that he'd answer it for them. "I've thought about that very question, Madam Secretary. We've all thought about this," he elaborated as he nodded toward Chan and Lau. "I would love nothing more than reunite all of China under our banner, to liberate them from the chains of communism. But that is not going to be possible. General Han's returning force along with General Luan's army is too much for me to handle. As it is, I'm struggling to keep my forces equipped and supplied. Our industrial base is working on that problem right now, but until we get formal trade agreements in place and we're able to establish a functioning economy and banking system, there is only so much we can do."

Seth looked at Kagel with a look that said he desperately wanted to say something. Haley bit her lower lip, not knowing if she should let him speak. She didn't know him that well, but she had a feeling they'd be getting to know each other a lot more soon. After a moment of contemplation, she gave a slight nod for him to speak and held her breath.

Seth turned to look at Zeng. "General, I'm a military man myself, so I understand the challenge you're facing. What are you lacking more—money or equipment to defeat President Chen?"

General Zeng had barely seemed to notice Seth's presence until this moment, but he smiled at the question and studied this newcomer to the conversation as he answered. "We have enough money to fund our soldiers for at least four more months, but what I don't have is military equipment," Zeng explained. "When my forces along the border lose a tank or an infantry fighting vehicle, I don't have another one to replace it with. Our factories lack key resources to keep producing them organically, so until we can reestablish some foreign trade, I can't rely on our industrial base to meet our needs. Does that answer your question?"

Seth nodded. "What if we could provide you with sixty-three divisions' worth of PLA equipment?" he asked.

General Zeng practically lurched forward. "What? How?" he asked.

Seth turned to look at Secretary Kagel, who smiled and nodded slightly. "Go ahead," she whispered.

"When General Han surrendered, we only gave him two weeks to get his forces out of America. That meant he had to leave behind the vast majority of his military equipment. Now, I can't say that all sixty-three of these divisions were at full-equipment strength, but what I *can* say is we've been collecting and assembling the equipment at a handful of temporary depots. We could begin the process of shipping that equipment here, to support your forces. Would that make a difference?" Seth asked. He and Kagel had talked about the possibility of using the equipment as a bargaining chip the night before.

The three Chinese leaders briefly conferred with each other before turning to look at them. "Madam Secretary, if America provided us with this equipment and some additional logistical support, I am confident my army would be able to defeat General Han's forces," General Zeng announced. He grinned. "We'll finally be able to liberate the rest of China from communism."

Chapter Twenty-One
Sinaloa Campaign

April 2023
Arlington, Virginia
Pentagon
National Military Command Center

President Sachs looked nervously at General Markus and Mike Howell as General Tibbets finished providing them with the final brief before requesting to initiate Operation Blow. If all went according to plan, these would be the first of a series of missions that would decimate the drug cartels.

"You look like you have a concern, Mr. President," General Tibbets remarked. "Is there something else you have a question about?" He was clearly chomping at the bit to get this operation going.

President Sachs looked at Secretary Howell. "Can we please clear to the room and just have the key essential people?" he requested.

Nodding, Howell asked nearly everyone in the room to leave. He told the people on Tibbets's side of the line as well as those at the NSA, CIA, DHS, FBI, and State Department to do the same.

It took a couple of moments, but when everyone had shuffled out, only the cabinet members and a few key principals remained.

The President cleared his throat. "Our country has been at war now for longer than it should have been. It's time we wrap this thing up and bring an end to all hostilities. Our country needs to heal. It needs to rebuild and recover.

"All of that said, America, and for that matter, the rest of the world, have been battling the drug trade for decades with no real success. While we need to do better as a country to address the reasons why people have turned to hard drugs, right now, we're going to do something about the supply.

"While the country is still in a state of war, I want to leverage the war powers granted to me by the Constitution to finish this fight. In a handful of months, I will no longer be President. In the time I have left, I want to do what I can to leave whoever my successor is in a better position to handle and deal with this problem. Our nation is going to go through a lot of heartache and pain as we rebuild and look to put this war behind us, and I don't want our people to fall into the trap of drug addiction as a means of coping."

The President paused and surveyed the room. They were all listening intently. "I was reluctant at first to even consider this option," he continued. "But I think this is the right thing to do for our country and the world. We aren't going to end the drug trade. I'm not so naïve as to believe that. However, we *are* going to knock it back a few decades in capability. As we move forward in building a new nation and a new world, we're finally going to deal with a festering problem that couldn't have been addressed without the wartime powers granted to a president."

Sachs turned to look at Howell and then Tibbets. "I want this fight to be over quickly," he told them pointedly. "I don't care how dirty or how brutal it has to be. I want them hunted down and destroyed. I want their financial assets seized—any properties, vehicles, yachts, anything of value should be confiscated to be sold later. We're going to take everything we can away from them.

"When you find a plot of land being used to grow cocaine or marijuana, I want that land destroyed for future use. I'm not talking about burning it down. Salt the land so it can never be used to grow that product again. I want a scorched-earth approach, but more than that, I want this done so fast that we leave them little to no time to react."

He fixed Tibbets with a steely gaze. "I'm unleashing you, General," he affirmed. "I have prepared a full presidential pardon for you should it ever come to that, but I want you to understand my meaning. To paraphrase Sherman—leave them nothing but their eyes, so they may weep. Don't let me or the country down," the President concluded.

With that, he got up and left to head back to the White House. He'd let the Secretary of Defense and the generals handle how they wanted to carry out his vision.

****

Three Weeks Later
Indian Springs, Nevada
Creech Air Force Base

Captain Lacey Price just wanted to put the war behind her. She wanted out of the military and to return to the life she had before all of this. Deep down, though, she knew she'd never be able to go back to her old life—not after what she'd seen and done in this terrible war.

When the hostilities had broken out, she'd found herself transferred from training to be a logistics officer to becoming a UAV pilot. Her first assignment had been on a Reaper. While she'd been a damn good Reaper pilot, the killing had gotten to her. It was one mission after another, identifying a UN or CDF leader or officer and giving them a Hellfire for Christmas. She knew it was bringing the war one step closer to an end, but she couldn't sleep. Every time she closed her eyes, she would see the video game–like display of the target, her missile streaking in and plastering the person.

Finally, after a year, she'd told her commander she needed a transfer. At first, they weren't going to give her one. Then she'd threatened to go AWOL or kill herself if they kept her doing that job, and they'd relented. Of course, she'd gotten stuck with an hour of mandatory counseling every day, and her Air Force career was effectively over as soon as the war ended, but she didn't care. She could live with the job she was doing now.

Looking at the map display, Price saw she had reached the target zone. She set the autopilot on the RQ-4 Global Hawk as she relieved the previous one that had been on station. Her squadron had been flying figure-eight tracks over the city of Culiacán, Mexico, and the surrounding area nonstop for weeks now. In that timeframe, they'd been able to establish the daily activities of hundreds of cartel members. As each new member was discovered, they added that person to the list of individuals to track and backtrace. Using complex facial recognition pattern software and other AI algorithms, the intelligence community rapidly identified who was involved in the Sinaloa cartel, who they associated with, where they all lived, and where they were growing, producing, storing, and shipping their product through all the stages of their narcotics operation.

In addition to Captain Price's Global Hawk, a lone C-26 Metroliner flew in a similar racetrack pattern over the city, using its suite of electronic equipment to snatch up every email, text message, and phone call made by the inhabitants below. As the NSA connected a particular voice and phone, a link was then established and electronically followed to see who else that person and that device came into contact with. After weeks of collecting this mass of data, they'd identified the entire cartel, and target packages had been put together for future action.

Once the DoD and NSA had developed a solid picture of all who had been involved in the human trafficking and narcotics trade in Mexico, the web was expanded to include the rest of North America. If the individuals were operating in the US, then arrest warrants and folders were being put together to be actioned by DHS or the FBI. If they were outside the US, then lethal force mission profiles were being generated and assigned to the thousands of Special Operations Forces and regular Army units filtering into Mexico and Central America.

In the final stages of this terrible war in North America, the American President was going to use his remaining months in power to decimate the cartels and hopefully allow Mexico and the Central American countries a real chance of future success, one that wasn't dominated by their submission to these criminal gangs and their whims.

****

"This is Overwatch. We have eyes on the target," called out the UAV operator, letting the ground units know they were on station and ready to go.

Thirty seconds later, the ground units started calling in.

"Powder One, in position," Deuce said just above a whisper. His throat mic picked up the barely audible report and transmitted it to the UAVs high above them.

"Powder Two, in position."

"Powder Three, in position."

"Dust One, standing by." The noise of helicopter blades briefly rattled over their coms. Dust One was the AH-64 Apache attack helicopter on standby a few thousand feet above and behind them.

"Snow One, we're in position. Ready to take up orbit," the Air Force Special Operations pilot called in. The AC-130 gunship would provide the ground team with sustained fire support should they need it.

"Coke One, ready to begin." Coke was the call sign for the CIA part of the mission.

"All Chaos units are ready," announced the mission coordinator.

A few seconds of silence ensued before the radios crackled to life. "This is Chaos Actual. All units are a go. Execute, execute, execute!"

Once Brigadier General Lancaster had issued the final command, the pieces to the grand operation went into motion. The war against the cartels had officially started.

****

Culiacán, Mexico

The phone in the air conditioning repair shop in town started to ring. It rang twice before Pedro picked it up. The person on the other end told him that their A/C unit had stopped working, and they practically begged for him to send a repair person out immediately.

Pedro talked to the person on the other line and got some basic information. Once he knew where he was headed, he assured them that he'd be there shortly and he'd get the A/C working again.

A few minutes later, Pedro walked into the garage attached to the back of his repair shop to get his repair van loaded up with the most likely parts he'd need for the job. When he flicked the lights on, he nearly jumped out of his skin. Four heavily armed men stood before him.

He allowed himself to breathe when he saw a friend of his, Juan, step forward. "Pedro," Juan said in his lighthearted manner, "it's good to see you again, my friend. Please don't be alarmed. These are the associates I was telling you about—the ones you agreed to help when the time came."

Juan smiled his warm disarming smile as he placed two bricks of shrink-wrapped hundred-dollar bills on the worktable next to Pedro's toolbox.

Pedro eyed the money, almost forgetting about the heavily armed men standing nearby. He slowly nodded as he picked one of the bricks up. It weighed a lot. Turning to look at Juan, he almost asked how much was there.

Juan seemed to read his mind. "Each one of those bricks is one hundred thousand dollars, my friend. When we're done, Pedro, you'll get two more. All we need you to do is take us on this repair call you're about to head out on."

Suddenly Pedro panicked. "They'll kill me if I do this for you," he pleaded. "These people don't mess around. They kill you and they kill your entire family if you cross them."

One of the heavily armed men stepped forward. "No, they won't," he declared.

Pedro shook his head. "You say that, but these people have every judge paid off. They'll be back on the street in hours. And if they aren't, their people will put out a hit on me."

The armed soldier smiled. "No, they won't," he assured Pedro. "We aren't DEA. We aren't here to take prisoners. No one is going to harm you, Pedro. After tonight, there won't *be* a cartel."

Pedro was taken aback. Then he suddenly realized the armed men standing before him weren't Mexican police or even drug enforcement agents. They were US military, probably Special Forces if he had to guess.

Allowing a hesitant smile, Pedro agreed.

Not that I have a choice, he rationalized.

A few minutes later, the four heavily armed men piled into the back of his repair van and made themselves ready. Pedro climbed in and drove toward Rafael Gallardo's private estate, a few miles outside town. The owner was the head of the Sinaloa cartel.

As they drove toward the estate, a man who identified himself as Deuce told Pedro exactly what to say and do.

****

It had taken Jerry twelve hours to slither his way into position. His body and equipment were shrouded in the most advanced ghillie suit ever devised for the military. The suit could mask its user against IR and thermal detectors, but where the suit took things to the next level was its integration of millions of fiber-optic strands encasing its user. These strands appeared to be the same size and composition as the shredded burlap used to make standard ghillie suits; however, they essentially mimicked the visual background of their surroundings. When Jerry snaked his way next to a tree, half of his body would appear as if he was part of the tree while the other parts of his body would look like the foliage and underbrush nearby. In essence, DARPA had developed an invisibility cloak.

As Jerry got himself in position, he pulled out his experimental weapon and looked down at the device, admiring it.

He repeated the Spetsnaz Alpha Group sniper motto in his head: *While invisible, I seek...I destroy...*

Jerry turned the device on and did a quick systems check. When he felt satisfied that everything was in working order, he prepared his Remington MSR. Once he had the rifle situated next to him, Jerry reached down and grabbed the suppressor and attached it to the front of the barrel. Next, he attached his scope and made sure it was seated properly. Lastly, he grabbed the magazine containing seven .300 Winchester Magnum smart rounds and slapped it in place.

DARPA had really upgraded the world of ammunition. The smart rounds Jerry was using were the offspring of EXtreme ACcuracy Tasked Ordnance (EXACTO), and once the microprocessor in the round was synced to his Trackpoint III Advance Optic, the round would track to the target and kill it with 97.2 percent accuracy all on its own. Once his rifle was ready for action, Jerry set up his bipod and placed it down next to the futuristic-looking weapon.

Looking at his watch, Jerry saw he was a few minutes ahead of schedule. He pulled his tablet out of his patrol pack, turned it on and synced it with the UAV operating high above him. He saw that Powder One was about a kilometer away from the estate.

Time to get my part of this show going, he thought.

Reaching for the rifle, Jerry made sure it was turned on and then set his sights on the small scout drone that was circling above the estate. He peered through the scope until he saw the drone inside the targeting circle. He depressed the trigger. The little surveillance drone suddenly fell from the sky, its internal electronics fried from the burst of microwaves that had just hammered it.

With the lone surveillance drone down, Jerry reached for his sniper rifle next and got into position. He immediately sighted in on the roving patrol along the east side of the compound. There were three heavily armed guards and a German shepherd.

I need to take that dog out first, he realized.

Jerry knew the other sniper team would handle the patrol on the west side of the compound. Once those foot patrols had been dispatched and the assault team had breached the estate, the two sniper teams would begin looking for targets of opportunity.

Here comes the assault team now...

****

Deuce held his SCAR up, ready to engage the guard that approached the van if need be. A moment later, Pedro rolled his window down and began talking to the man in rapid Spanish. The guard looked tired, but also on edge. He lifted his radio to his mouth and said something Deuce couldn't make out, but a moment later, the steel gate to the estate opened up, and the guard waved Pedro through.

Smiling, Deuce clicked his radio twice, letting the other teams know they had made entry into the estate undetected. Looking at his three other team members in the van, Deuce saw they were ready. They seemed a bit antsy, like coiled vipers ready to be released when he gave the signal. In the next couple of minutes, they'd unleash a level of violence these guys had probably never seen before.

Circling above them was an AC-130 Gunship, a pair of Apache helicopters in the next valley over, and another twenty Delta operators waiting for the go order to assist them should they need it. The cartel was about to get hit so hard they would never know what had happened.

As the van traveled around a bend in the road, Deuce saw a couple of guards standing down by the edge of the driveway, waiting for the repair vehicle to arrive.

"Pedro, when you stop the vehicle and put it in park, exit the van and immediately drop to the ground," Deuce directed. "You'll need to stay down for at least sixty seconds before you try to run, or you will get caught in the crossfire."

Deuce could see that Pedro was sweating profusely, and he was glad the man didn't have to lead them into the house. Deuce doubted the mild-mannered A/C repairman could walk at this point with how scared he was.

The seconds ticked by tensely in slow motion. Finally, the van reached the center of the curved driveway, near the two guards. Pedro opened his door and immediately dropped to the ground, just as he'd been instructed.

In the flash of an eye, Deuce's right-hand man, Larry, had the side door to the van open and his suppressed P22 extended. In a fraction of a second, Larry placed two rapid shots into one man's head before moving to the other guard and doing the same. In less than two seconds, both guards had been eliminated without anyone hearing a shot fired.

Larry bolted out of the van, his pistol extended as he ran. Spider and Deuce were hot on his heels with their own rifles at the ready. The new guy on their team, Angel, had his own suppressed pistol out and was running alongside Larry. The two of them would fire first at any guards they encountered in hopes of maintaining their element of surprise. Once the first nonsuppressed shot was fired, it'd be a free-for-all as they moved to clear the structure.

Once Deuce saw that Larry and Angel had reached the front door of the estate, he broke radio silence to tell the units standing by to bring in the additional units.

Seconds after making the call, Deuce heard the snipers' muffled reports echoing as they started eliminating the foot patrols and the guards on the roofs and higher elevation of the multistory building.

Spider had just finished slapping the breaching charge on the centerline of the massive main entrance door when Deuce took up his position on the side of the wall. The four of them now had their SCARs in hand, ready for the gunfight that was about to ensue.

"Breaching!" Spider said just loud enough for them to hear. They all turned their heads away and briefly closed their eyes as the charge exploded, blowing the door apart down the centerline.

Deuce and Larry were the first through the doors, guns up and ready as they swept through the first room, a grand foyer. As they advanced down the hallway, they heard several men yelling something in rapid Spanish moments before an alarm blared.

Larry popped out from behind the side of the wall and fired several controlled bursts into the two guards that had been running toward them. The bullets slammed into their chests and knocked both men to the ground.

Deuce pulled the pin on a fragmentation grenade and chucked it down the hall into the next room. A couple of voices yelled frantically before a loud explosion rippled through the building.

Before anyone could react, Larry raced down the hall until he reached the next room. Once there, he opened fire on a handful of people who were still trying to recover from the grenade Deuce had just tossed into their midst.

Spider and Angel ran past Larry as he took a moment to reload his weapon, heading further into the house. Deuce saw a couple of rooms off the kitchen and pointed his weapon at them. He aimed at the walls on either side of the doorframes and fired a couple of bursts from his SCAR. Larry did the same thing before tossing a grenade into each room.

Deuce heard more shooting coming from further within the house, where Spider and Angel had run. Then he heard the thumping sound of helicopter blades, which meant the rest of their assault team was arriving. One team would rappel down onto the roof and work their way down while the other team would land near the A/C repair van and move into the house to help them clear it.

Five minutes later, the entire house had been cleared. A few minutes after that, the rest of the estate had been ridden of hostiles. No prisoners had been taken. This swift and deadly hit had been designed to neutralize and decapitate the leadership of the cartel. Not a single American or civilian had been injured in the assault.

As the Delta assaulters left the compound, the thermite and white phosphorus grenades they'd tossed throughout the estate's buildings made quick work as the flames reached up the night sky. As Deuce looked back, he heard the JSOC Commanding General's voice in his head: *Scorched earth.*

****

Culiacan, Mexico
Aeropuerto Internacional de Culiacán
JSOC Forward Headquarters

Glass crunched under his boots as Brigadier General "Paddy" Maine walked into the newly set up forward headquarters building.

"This way, General. He's inside the Ops room," a major called out to him as he pointed to the room where Lancaster was waiting for him.

As he walked down the hallway, Paddy could see the place had been fought over. There were bullet holes along the walls, and still a fair amount of broken glass. He noticed a couple of soldiers using some brooms to try to get at least most of the glass out of the way.

Outside, a ground crew crawled over a newly arrived C-17 Globemaster. The cargo plane was offloading pallets of ammo and other needed supplies to keep their operation going.

When the general approached a couple of heavily armed guards standing near a door, the two soldiers snapped to attention. One of them held the door open for Paddy so he could walk inside.

As soon as he entered the room, Paddy observed a lot of power and communication cables running in different directions. A handful of communication specialists were getting computers, monitors, radios, and other equipment set up.

"Ah. There you are, Paddy. I hope you don't mind me popping in like this," said Major General Lancaster as he walked over to his protégé to shake his hand.

Paddy smiled. "Not at all, General," he replied. "As you can see, we're still getting things set up." Paddy waved his hand around the mess that currently constituted his operations center. "What can I do for you, General?"

"Walk with me," Lancaster said. He led them to an empty room on the side of the ops center.

After checking to be certain no one was within earshot, Lancaster leaned in. "We're two days into this operation. How close are you to having our HVIs dealt with?" he pressed.

Paddy bristled at the question. "Are you telling me the folks in Washington are getting cold feet already?" he pressed. "I mean, we're deep in the weeds right now. We need to see this through."

Lancaster snickered and shook his head. "No. Nothing like that, my friend. The higher-ups want to get the boys rotated back home. There may be some additional operations coming down the pike. They'd like the Delta rested up."

"Really? What aren't you telling me? Because this is what we live for," Paddy responded, waving his arm around at the chaos. "We're probably the best unit for this type of operation, and you know it."

Lancaster looked around again, making sure no one was nearby. "It's hush-hush right now, but there's a likelihood we're going to be granted permission to go clean things up in Colombia and Bolivia. The Colombians have been watching what we're doing, and they've secretly reached out to the White House to find out if we could handle their problem for them as well. That's why they sent me out here. I need to find out how soon you could extricate your boys and get them ready for another operation."

Paddy lifted his head, and a smile spread across his face. "So, now that we're taking care of the bad guys here in Mexico, they want our help as well, huh?" He paused for a second as he blew out some air through pursed lips, mulling it all over. "I think the Rangers and our Tier 3 SOF can handle what's left here in Mexico and Central America—especially since they have four divisions of regular Army grunts to back them up.

But if you want us to go into Colombia and or Bolivia, we're going to need more than a squadron or two of our operators. Are we going to have more assets available to us?" he asked.

Lancaster nodded. "We will. DEVGRU will accompany you along with RCT 1 from the 1st Marine Division. They're being augmented with a Raider battalion to assist you guys."

Paddy shook his head in surprise. "The President really plans on going out with a bang, doesn't he? He does know this kind of operation isn't going to be over in a couple of days or weeks, right? We're talking about a few months to hunt these bastards down and fully eliminate them as a threat."

"Ours is not to question why, but to do or die," replied Lancaster, shrugging his shoulders.

Paddy laughed at the absurdity of the saying. "Yeah, I suppose. OK. You just point me where you want my boys to go and when you want us there, and we'll be there," he answered.

General Lancaster grinned. "Good. I'm glad we got that out of the way. So, you might as well stop putting this headquarters of yours together and get this stuff loaded back up," he said with a chuckle. "I want your logistics guys sent to Puerto Salgar, Colombia. The Air Force is already getting the place up and running for you. In the meantime, find a way to get your guys pulled from the line and swapped out with a Tier 3 unit. I need them ready in Colombia in three weeks. Get them as much R&R time as you can back home. I have a feeling the Colombia cartels are going to be a bit more ready for what's coming than the Mexican cartels were."

****

Cheyenne Mountain
US Northern Command

General Tibbets looked over the latest reports from Mexico. They were now five weeks into the occupation of the country and two weeks into their all-out war with the cartels. The casualties were starting to mount.

Three soldiers had been killed at a checkpoint in Guadalajara. Ten soldiers had perished in Culiacán, another eight in Mexico City. The cartels were in their final death throes at this point. As soon as the NSA identified a possible target, a team of Special Forces or a platoon of grunts was dispatched to investigate. They were swiftly forcing the remaining members underground.

Hearing a knock at the door, Tibbets looked up to see one of his aides walk in. He handed him the daily intelligence summary from El Salvador.

That place is becoming a bloody mess, he thought as he passed over the paper.

The 101st Air Assault Division had moved into the country eight days ago. The criminal gangs that had largely run the country were not going down without a fight. Tibbets knew he'd need to send some additional Special Forces units from Mexico down to help them out. The regular line units were a hammer, not a scalpel, and he needed more scalpels. Unfortunately, the Colombia operation was sucking them all up.

General Tibbets had wanted to finish the job in Mexico first before moving anywhere else. The President, on the other hand, wanted to finish all combat operations before the end of his term, and he was pushing his command hard to meet those objectives.

Just as he was getting his head wrapped around what to do in El Salvador and Colombia, Tibbets heard another knock at the door. Looking up, he saw a man in a suit and motioned for him to come in.

The general stood up and walked around his desk to shake his visitor's hand. "Lieutenant Colonel Seth Mitchell, right?" he confirmed.

The man's handshake was firm. He smiled. "I'm just Seth Mitchell now, sir."

Nodding, Tibbets directed them toward a couple of chairs in front of his desk. He hadn't officially met Seth before, but he recognized him from some of the interrogation videos. He knew he had been the point man going after this super-secret organization that had started this whole war. Now he was a special advisor to the former Secretary of State, who appeared all but assured the presidency.

"What can I do for you, Mr. Mitchell?" Tibbets inquired, unable to hide his confusion as to the purpose of this meeting.

Seth nodded. "Thank you for agreeing to meet with me last-minute like this," he began. "Sir, I need a frank assessment from you. How much of this mess down south of us is going to need to be cleaned up by the Secretary when she's sworn in?"

Direct and to the point. I like that...

"It depends on a few factors."

"OK. What are they?"

"We have two months until the election. I'm fairly confident I'll have the majority of the combat operations in Mexico and Central America taken care of by that point. We're going to need to maintain at least three divisions for occupation and security duty while Homeland and the State Department work with the host nations on taking things over," Tibbets explained candidly.

"What about Colombia?"

"That's a different ball game entirely. In Mexico and Central America, we caught the cartels by surprise. We were able to take most of them out in the first couple of days. That wasn't the case in Colombia. They knew we were coming, so they've gone to ground. We'll root them out, but I can't say we'll have things wrapped up by the time the election comes."

Tibbets saw Seth calculating something in his head. He then looked back at him with those piercing, sharp eyes. "If we need to intervene in China, how long would it take our ground forces to provide a limited level of support and assistance to General Zeng's forces?"

Tibbets had to think about that question for a moment. He wasn't immediately sure how to answer that one. Aside from maybe ten divisions, the rest of the Army was a wreck. All of his heavy divisions were deployed in Mexico and Central America. The remaining forces he had were seriously depleted of equipment. The ground force wasn't ready to fight a war beyond the shores of America—at least not yet.

Seth leaned in. "This is just a hypothetical question, General. The Secretary needs to know from the man in charge how bad a shape the force is in."

Tibbets nodded. He understood the question. He just wasn't sure how to answer it. Finally, he replied, "If we had to intervene in Asia, I'd advise that it largely be carried out by the Navy and the Air Force. The Navy has those new Arsenal ships, and the Air Force is starting to field the B-21s in some serious numbers. As to ground forces, we could probably support a limited role with our Tier 2 Special Operations Forces, but until we conclude operations in Mexico and Central America, we'd be very limited with conventional Army support."

Seth sat back in his chair and whispered something to himself as his eyes looked off at a corner of the room, probably doing some calculations. Then he turned his attention back to the general. "The draft has been paused now that the Chinese have been defeated here at home. How long would it take you to train and prepare a single Army group, should it be needed?"

Tibbets's left brow rose. "That's a lot of troops, Seth," he remarked. "I mean, we have the numbers for that kind of force right now, but they aren't nearly as trained as I'd have liked. We were rushing many of these new recruits through training so we could get them in the fight. If you're honestly asking, I'd like to have maybe three months to get them spun up and ready to go. The bigger challenge isn't the training or the troop numbers—we have to solve the chronic equipment shortages. I mean, aside from vehicles and other equipment, we're desperately short on ammunition for a force like that. Nearly all of the ammunition we've been producing is being sent down south to the units who are currently fighting."

The general paused for a moment. "If the Secretary is asking—I'm not saying it couldn't be done, but we need a lot more time to rebuild our war stocks and get this force fully outfitted with new equipment."

Seth bit his lower lip for a moment before he nodded. "That was my assessment as well, General. I can tell you that once Sachs has left, this war with China may not be fully over. Do what you can to get your force ready for what may come next. Finish the operations down south and stay ready."

With that, Seth got up, shook his hand, and left.

Tibbets let out a long sigh. Part of him was glad they might restart things with China. The other part of him said the military and the country was tired of war and needed a chance to catch its breath.

Chapter Twenty-Two
Homecoming

July 2023
Meridian, Mississippi

As he drove down the neighborhood road, Trey noticed all the houses flying American flags. He felt an immense sense of pride at the patriotic display. After the horrors he'd recently seen in Colorado, New Mexico, and Texas, he was just happy to see his hometown had remained untouched by the war. This quiet city hadn't been bombed or invaded. It hadn't been heavily fought over. One thing he did notice, though, was a number of Gold Stars in the corners of the windows of some of the homes. He knew those families felt the effects of the war, even if their community didn't.

"You saw a lot of action judging by the ribbons on your chest," said Trey's Uber driver as he caught his eye in the rearview mirror.

Trey turned away to look out the window again. "More than I care to think about," he said, his voice trailing off.

The Uber driver nodded. He didn't press the issue.

Traffic was still light. What constituted morning rush hour had already passed them by. Eventually, the driver turned down the street he had grown up on. He remembered play kickball and street hockey on this street during the summer.

I wonder what happened to some of my old friends, he pondered.

Soon, the vehicle pulled up to Trey's home. His first thought was that his dad had done a good job of keeping the yard looking nice. They had painted the house together and installed new windows during the spring of 2020, but that seemed like another lifetime now.

The Uber stopped in the driveway, and the driver popped the trunk, pulling out Trey's single duffel bag. Trey grabbed the patrol pack he had sitting next to him, and he had a moment of realization that the two bags essentially constituted all the worldly belongings he'd had since the start of the war.

As the driver pulled away, Trey gave his Uber driver a five-star rating and a generous tip. He knew economic times were tough, and he had more than enough money to at least help one hardworking individual out.

It felt strange walking up the steps to his childhood home. Trey was just about to ring the doorbell when his mother swung the front door open and squealed for joy. She yanked the screen door aside and threw her arms around him in a bear hug, tears streaming down her face.

As he entered the foyer, Trey's father joined their embrace, making no attempt to conceal his own tears. They were clearly ecstatic to see him and know that at long last, their son was safe.

When they'd finished a long hug, his father looked him over, sizing him up with obvious pride. They walked to the living room and sat down on the couches. "So, how long are you back?" asked his dad.

Trey smiled. He had to remind himself that this wasn't a short R&R trip; he was home. "I'm back for good, Dad," he said. "I mean, my guard unit has officially been demobilized. We're going back to one weekend a month and two weeks in the summer again."

His dad nodded, then there was an awkward pause before he asked, "What are your plans now that the Army is done with you?"

Trey let out a long sigh. "I was thinking I might go back to my job as a public defender," he finally replied. "Then again, I hear there are some real economic opportunities out in Texas and California right now."

His mother chimed in. "You just got home and now you're talking about picking up stakes and moving away from your family?" she asked, her voice choking up a bit. "Aren't those states pretty much destroyed?"

Trey nodded. "I know you'd like me to stay here, Mom, but I think I'd like to try my luck out west. Texas is in bad shape, but that also means there's a lot of opportunity. The reconstruction efforts out there are going to be huge. I was thinking I might take my money from the Army and go start my own law practice out there."

His dad had just returned from the kitchen, two beers in his hand. He handed one to Trey. "Well, whatever you decide to do, son, we'll support you," he said. "Obviously, I'd rather you stayed here in Meridian with your family, but I understand if you want to strike out on your own. Who knows, maybe your Mom and I will follow you out there if you think it's safe and there's some good opportunities for an old guy like me.

****

Solana Beach, California

First Sergeant Justin Mack looked at the pile of rubble and shook his head.

I sure hope I haven't bitten off more than I can chew, he thought.

Five days ago, First Sergeant Mack had become Justin Mack. Following the end of the Colombia campaign, his medical record had finally caught up with him. He'd been back at Pendleton helping to get their unit areas cleaned up when he'd gotten a call that the battalion commander had wanted to see him. When their unit had returned from Colombia, they had to go through medical in-processing, just like you did from any other deployment. It was during his medical checkup the doctors noticed his traumatic brain injury and then his medical report from Walter Reed recommending him for medical retirement.

When Mack showed up at the battalion commander's office, he was told he was being medically retired due to his brain injury he'd received when he had been shot in the head. Despite having served more than a year after that incident, the Marine Corps wasn't going to take any further chances on him. Not with the war now over.

With his departure from the Marines imminent, Mack took all the money he had saved up over the years and bought a tract of land in Solana Beach along the water. When he drove down to check out the area, he was both surprised and amazed by the level of destruction. Nearly every home in the area had been either destroyed or stripped bare of anything of value. Nearly all of the residents were listed as either killed or missing, which meant there was a lot of property with no owners. The federal government had stepped in at this point and bought the land back from the banks, making it available for purchase by any military veteran who wanted to buy it.

Mack used his VA loan to buy one of the plots of land to build his new house on, and a veteran's small business loan to finance the construction of a new oceanside bar and pool hall he was going to open. He smiled at the named he'd chosen. Coaches 2nd Corner, after a bar with a similar name of San Clemente Fame. Many a West Pac widow had found comfort in the arms of younger, more virile Marines there while their husbands were deployed. The two properties were just a few blocks away from each other. If he couldn't continue to serve in the military, then he'd make a place where fellow Jarheads could hang out and have fun together.

Once he parked his Jeep Wrangler, he pulled his six-pack out of the passenger seat and grabbed his rucksack. He walked toward the edge of the property near the cliff leading down to the water. He put the six-pack down and got his little tent set up for the evening. With that done, he leaned against his ruck, just looking at the water as he watched the sun set. He reached over for one of the beers and popped it open.

Lifting the bottle to his lips, he felt the liquid race down his throat and into his belly. He still wasn't used to drinking alcohol yet. He'd been in so much combat with little in the way of R&R, he just hadn't built his tolerance back up yet. It didn't take him long to finish the first one and reach for a second.

Looking at the sun as it got closer to the water, he reflected on everything that had happened to him these past couple of years. He suddenly felt a wave of emotions wash over him. He wasn't sure what was happening. He grabbed for a towel from his ruck and held it up against his face. For the next twenty minutes, he just bawled his eyes out. He sobbed and cried like he had never done before. The faces of all his friends he'd lost, all the men he'd killed, all the civilians he'd seen killed suddenly flashed in front of him when he closed his eyes.

It took him a little while to get all those emotions out of his system. When he had finished, he immediately felt better. He'd been holding all that in for so long. It wasn't until he was sitting here, alone and out of the Corps, that he'd felt he was in a safe position to just let it all go. When he'd finished crying, he reached for his third beer. He spent the rest of the night lying out there alone, finishing off the six-pack by himself as he thought about the future and what it might bring. For better or worse, he'd somehow survived this horrible war. He had two choices facing him. He could wallow in self-pity, or he could pick himself up by his bootstraps and make something of the rest of his life.

Lying there under the stars, listening the soothing sound of the waves crashing against the cliff below, he made the decision that no matter what happened next, he was going to live his life to the fullest. He'd build himself a new house on this very plot, find a beautiful woman to marry and build his bar and pool hall. Smiling, he thought way back to the little yellow footprints at MCRD San Diego a lifetime ago. Then, for the first time since the beginning of the war, he fell into a deep dream-free sleep.

Semper Gumby.

Chapter Twenty-Three
Rebuilding

White House
Cabinet Room

DHS Director Patty Hogan looked exhausted and emotional as she prepared to give the President the best post-occupation report her agency could provide. The data wasn't looking good. The magnitude of loss the country was enduring was only just now becoming known, and it was both shocking and horrifying.

"Mr. President, we're still months away from having a final tally, but suffice it to say, the loss of life going to be high. Prior to the war, the populations of California, Arizona, New Mexico, and Texas were roughly seventy-seven point five million people. These states were the most heavily fought-over territory of the war, and large portions of these states were also under Chinese occupation for an extended time before we were able to liberate them. To further compound the problem, the Chinese weren't exactly doing all they could to make sure our people were being fed and taken care of.

"A lot of people fled their homes ahead of the Chinese Army. But many more got trapped behind enemy lines during the first week of the war, when the lines were changing rapidly. So we have two problems right now. The first is that we have more than eighty million people from both the Southwest and the Midwest classifying themselves as refugees. These are the folks who left their homes ahead of the UN and Chinese armies and suddenly found themselves homeless.

"Now, the folks from the Midwest and Northeast began returning to their homes once the hostilities with the UN forces ended. Some of the cities and areas were more heavily fought over than others, so there's a lot of reconstruction going and not everyone is able to move back right away. Our bigger challenge is the refugees from the Southwest. Between the four states that were occupied by the Chinese, we have roughly thirty million people that need to be resettled. Most of them are currently living in FEMA camps we've set up in Kansas, Missouri, Iowa, and the southern states.

"As you know, many of the major cities in Texas, Arizona, and California were devastated. We can't allow the people to return to some of these cities until we can get basic utilities like electricity, water, and sewage going." Patty paused for a moment, her emotions kicking in as she prepared to deliver the worst part of the report they had compiled.

The President gently said, "It's OK, Patty. Take a moment if you need to. I know this is really tough. We appreciate all you and your department have been doing. This report is important. It's important that our people know the full truth about what led to this entire war, and the full consequences of it. This is now a part of our national history and identity, as much as our first Civil War and World War II."

Patty nodded slowly as she reached for a tissue to dab away a tear. Several of the other cabinet members seated at the table were likewise showing emotions as the full weight of everything was being laid bare for them all to see.

Taking a deep breath, she steeled herself for this next part of the report. "In the Northeast and the Upper Midwest, twenty-two thousand civilians were killed in the first couple months of fighting. It's estimated that another four or five thousand were killed as a result of politically motivated violence and retribution. Around thirty-four thousand people died from lack of medication and medical treatment. People who had been dependent on insulin, thyroid medications, or any other type of daily medication to keep themselves alive were the ones most directly affected by the war. Once the pharmacies ran out of medications, there weren't any further deliveries. Granted, the UN force did try to address this problem. The Germans, French and Dutch did a lot to fly in medications from Europe, which greatly reduced the number of people who died."

Pausing again, she looked down at the report before returning her gaze to the President. "The situation was not so good in the Southwest. Once the Chinese took control of an area, they implemented a sick, sadistic plan called the Q Program." Pausing, she asked, "Do you need me to elaborate on the Q program, or can I skip over that?"

Sachs looked at the other cabinet members before asking, "Does everyone know the full details of the Q program? Does anyone need Patty to elaborate before we continue?"

Secretary Tilly Brahm from the Department of Human and Health Services quickly interjected, "I believe I understand the full scope of the Q Program. Perhaps we should go over it again to just make sure everyone here understands it, and if there's a question, then we flesh it out before we make this report public. Once this thing goes live to the American people and the world, it's going to cause a lot of backlash and anger. It'd be best to make sure everything is clear and to the point. This way, no one can accuse us of trying to cover up or sugarcoat anything."

Sachs nodded in agreement. "Good call, Tilly. Patty, why don't you go ahead and bring us up to speed on the program as we know it? This is important not just for our people to know but also for the history books. This can never be allowed to happen again."

"As you wish, Mr. President," Patty replied before clearing her throat. "In the 1940s, the Germans looked to create a program called 'Lebensraum' or 'living space.' They wanted to expand the German empire for their people by systematically liquidating the existing population from the newly conquered territories or forcibly removing them. The Chinese, for their part, created something similar called the Q Program. From 1979 to roughly 2015, the government had a one-child policy in place. There were some exceptions to this rule, but in general, unless a family worked on a farm, they were only allowed one child. Due to cultural preference, many parents chose to abort any female babies. As a consequence, the country as a whole has a major demographic problem—huge swaths of the youngest generation of Chinese men have no hope of finding a woman to marry, which has created an enormous amount of political instability and angst within China.

"China also lacks good arable land for industrial farming to feed their growing population, which further adds to their sense of urgency to address these two growing problems. Based on a lot of the intelligence that has been collected throughout the war and what people within the Democratic Republic of Southern China have provided, it's clear that President Chen joined the UN peacekeeping mission with an ulterior motive, not just to remove President Sachs. When the UN launched their attack, Chen initially had their ground forces hold back. This was done intentionally, because Chen wanted us to smash the Russian and European armies, which would greatly reduce the military threat both powers posed to China for the foreseeable future.

"Chen's belief was that our forces would be too bloodied from our fight with the UN force to stop them from carving up our southwest border and the West Coast. Once the Chinese started to capture and occupy some of our states, they immediately began to implement their Q Program. Unlike the UN, the Chinese had no intention of maintaining the infrastructure needed to run the states—electricity, water treatment facilities, or the complicated pharmacy and food supply chain needed to facilitate the daily medication and dietary needs of people in the occupied zones. Their goal was to either force people into work gangs to facilitate their immediate needs or liquidate them. I'd rather not go into the details of how they did that, but it's in the report. This began their first major effort at depopulating the occupied zones. Next, they started addressing the demographic problem. Women between the ages of sixteen and thirty-five who fit certain criteria were rounded up and eventually sent back to China, where they would undergo months of reeducation and conditioning before they'd be awarded to young men in exchange for military service. In all, some three and a half million women were kidnapped and shipped back to China before the cease-fire was agreed to."

Audible grumbling and some not-so-subtle curses came from more than a few of the cabinet secretaries and their functionaries sitting behind them. This was one major part of the report that was sure to stir up a lot of anger.

"Fortunately for us, and these women, they were being held in reeducation camps that fell under the control of General Zeng. When he broke away from the central government in Beijing and formed his own country, he immediately ordered our prisoners moved to Hong Kong while arrangements were made for their safe return. We're currently working on getting these women reunited with their families and friends and providing them with whatever counseling they need. What they've experienced…isn't something I can even imagine," Patty said as she finished bringing them up to speed on her portion of the brief.

Shaking his head, Sachs replied, "Thank you, Patty, for going over this. I know it was tough." The President took a moment to look at everyone before he continued. "We need to collectively make sure this report is as factually accurate as possible. I don't want this thing sugarcoated. I want the American people to know exactly what happened and, more importantly, how this whole thing started. We cannot learn from this experience if we don't inform people why it happened. The nation needs to heal; we need to rebuild. This report will be a big part of that healing process—making sure everyone knows what the hell happened and how we're going to make sure it never happens again."

The meeting went on for a little while longer before it broke up. Each cabinet member would have a week to add in any further details to their portion of the report before it would be handed over to Congress and then the American people.

****

Walking into his private study, Sachs saw Rich was sitting in his usual chair waiting for him. At the end of each day, Rich would come in and get the fireplace going. A pot of fresh coffee was usually nearby, ready for the two of them. These informal talks were a way for the President and chief of staff to go over any outstanding issues from the day and make sure they had things ready for the following day.

Walking over to the side table with the pot of coffee on it, Sachs poured himself a cup. “How’s the election looking?”

“It’s looking like Secretary Kagel is going to win. I could be wrong, but that’s what all the polling and pundits seem to think.”

Nodding, Sachs walked around to the chair with his cup of coffee and sat down next to Rich. The two of them sat there not saying anything for a few minutes, listening to the wood crackling in the fireplace.

“How much money and assets have we been able to seize from the Beijing government?”

Rich flipped open his notepad, an item that never left his side no matter where he went. “Um, it looks like we seized around sixty billion dollars,” he remarked. “As to assets, that’s a lot higher—roughly four hundred and eighty billion. That’s companies’ land, buildings, and other tangible assets we were able to nationalize on them. We also canceled about eight hundred billion in treasury notes they weren’t able to liquidate before the war started.” Rich’s mouth curled up in a mischievous grin.

Sachs smiled too. “So between Norway, the other European countries, Russia, and China, we’ve been able to secure roughly three point one trillion dollars, correct?”

“Yes, Mr. President. It’s about that much.”

“Good. Then after the election tomorrow, I’d like to get a meeting set up with whoever wins as soon as possible. I want to let them know how much we’ve recovered and go over how some of this money should be spent.”

Reaching for his own coffee cup, Rich took a sip before asking, "You want to leave all that money to your successor?"

Shrugging his shoulders, Sachs said, "It depends on what the President-elect wants to do with it. I'd like to start some of their projects now so we can get them going. But I'd like whoever wins to be able to rebuild the country. That should be part of their legacy. Mine was keeping the country together and recovering as much compensation as I could. It'll be their legacy to rebuild and heal the nation."

Rich smiled and chuckled softly. "That's a noble gesture, Mr. President," he said. Then he leaned forward. "Have you given much thought as to what you'll do when you leave office?"

Not replying right away, Sachs looked at the fire, lost in thought for a moment. He hadn't really considered that yet. He had a lot he wanted to do, but he wasn't sure if it wouldn't be better for him to just fade away into the shadows and let his successor have their moment to shine. The country wasn't nearly as polarized as it had been, but it was still divided. It needed to be healed, and he didn't want to impede that process.

Finally, turning to look at his good friend who'd been with him from the beginning, he said, "I think I will largely focus on staying out of the public eye. I'd like to do what I could to help our military veterans, but aside from that, I think I'm just going to fade away."

Chapter Twenty-Four
A New Beginning

January 2024
Washington, D.C.
Capitol Building

The air was cold and crisp as the President-elect looked out at the throngs of people who had come out to see the swearing in of the forty-sixth President of the United States. They were bundled up, wearing gloves, scarfs, and hats, but they were there, ready to celebrate her victory and a new chapter in America.

Stepping up to the podium, President-elect Haley Kagel raised her right hand.

"Repeat after me," said the Chief Justice of the new Supreme Court as Kagel placed her left hand on the Bible he held out for her.

"I do solemnly swear that I will faithfully execute the office of President of the United States, and will, to the best of my ability, preserve, protect and defend the Constitution of the United States."

She slowly, steadily repeated the words she'd rehearsed a hundred times since she had officially won the election. Then, in the blink of an eye, it was over. The Chief Justice shook her hand, and so did the now former President, Jonathan Sachs.

I did it, she thought, in awe at her own accomplishment of becoming the first American female President.

She beamed with excitement before turning to face the podium to give her speech—the speech she'd be judged by. Taking a deep breath, she looked at the teleprompter, which showed the first few lines of her carefully written speech.

As she looked at the crowds of people before her, the sudden responsibility of the job hit her. It was now on her shoulders to guide, protect, and rebuild a ravaged nation. The buck would stop with her, as President Harry Truman had once said.

Taking a deep breath in, she held it for a second and then began.

"My fellow Americans, today marks the first day in a new chapter in America. Today the first woman was sworn in as President of these United States."

Raucous applause broke out amongst the throngs of people who stood before her. Holding her arms out briefly to calm them, she continued.

"The last four years were some of the toughest years our country has ever faced. In fact, we almost lost our Republic. But we didn't. We pulled ourselves together, and in time we put aside our petty differences and we came together as a nation to repel a foreign invader.

"President Lincoln once said, 'America will never be destroyed from the outside. If we falter and lose our freedoms, it will be because we destroyed ourselves.' That was never truer than it was during the lead-up to the 2020 election. In our individual and political parties' efforts to always be right, to never give ground, we nearly destroyed ourselves as a nation. We must come together as a people and be respectful that others have a different point of view and that different ideas don't necessarily make a person wrong or immoral.

"We as a people and country have so much in common with each other. We have just survived a nearly three-year civil war and invasion by more than two dozen countries. More than twenty million of our fellow citizens are no longer with us as a result. Tens of millions more are still without a home, and many of our cities and states lie in rubble."

She paused for a moment as she let her words sink in for both those listening to her here and those at home.

"I make this pledge to you as your new President—I will always strive to work with my political opponents and those of you who didn't vote for me. We are one people, one America, and it is time we begin a new chapter in our great experiment in democracy. While the wounds will take time to heal, I ask all of you to make an effort to get to know your neighbors, to hug your kids and family, and to do your best to be the kind of person you want to see in others around you."

Her speech went on for another twenty minutes as she outlined the major things she wanted to get accomplished during her first hundred days, but one thing was clear: she was going to focus the country on working together and building bridges between the divides.

****

Undisclosed Location

Erik Jahn sat with the remaining ruling council members of the Thule Society as they tried to figure out what they were going to do next. Hundreds of their members had been hunted down and killed, and many others had been outed and summarily thrown out of their positions of power in their home countries. As an organization, they were reeling from the continual body blows.

A council member from Jakarta spoke first. "We have lost a battle, ladies and gentlemen, not the war. Yes, many of our members have been jailed, and many others have been killed, but let us not forget the wealth and power we still have at our disposal. We can still win this war; we just need to let the dust settle."

Several council members nodded their heads in agreement.

The lone Russian at the table spoke next. "Sachs is gone. We achieved our goal. When the new American president is sworn into office, we can move forward with our plans for the United States. The devastation we've caused has given us an enormous opportunity to seize control of the recovery effort. We can still reshape their country. Not all is lost, my friends."

Erik Jahn saw more heads bob up and down. He shook his head in frustration.

They still don't get it, he thought. *We've lost!* Now it was all about trying to retain as much control as they could, not attempting to gain more.

Erik pushed his chair back and stood, causing everyone to stop what they were doing and look at him. He cleared his throat. "Ladies and gentlemen, it's time we get this meeting going. We have much that needs to be discussed.

"What I am going to say is hard, but it needs to be said. The Society needs to move forward, but under a new set of rules. Five years ago, when we set into motion the election events in America, we had no idea it would result in what transpired. Consequently, our Society has been exposed and many of our key members have been hunted down and killed. Our actions set into motion a series of tragedies even we couldn't control.

"The Society was also betrayed by President Chen and some of his closest advisors. Their disloyalty meant our well-laid plan to remove Jonathan Sachs was doomed to fail. That leads us to right here, right now. You all know I was taken into custody by the Norwegian government a while back. During my incarceration, I was handed over to the Americans and until three days ago, I was in American custody."

Several of the members at the table gasped in surprise. A few of them nervously looked around the room.

Erik held a hand up to try and calm their fears. "During my detainment, I was able to negotiate a deal to end the Americans' targeted assassinations of our members. A détente has been reached—"

"Traitor!" barked the council member from Jakarta. "How could you have betrayed us like this?"

"This war is *not* over!" roared the muscular Russian angrily as he stood up.

Suddenly, the burly man's head snapped back. A gory cloud of blood, brain matter, and bone ejected out the backside of his skull, and his body collapsed to the ground as a single gunshot echoed through the poorly lit room.

Several men yelled; a woman screamed. Then a lone figure emerged from the shadows, pointing a still smoking gun at the rest of them.

"Everyone, sit down and shut up!" Seth roared. He swept the room with his P230 Sig Sauer, as if signaling that each of them could be next unless they did exactly as instructed.

Erik Jahn announced, "I would like to introduce everyone to our newest council member, Seth Mitchell. To end the assassinations and restore order and peace to the alliance, a deal was struck."

"How dare you make a deal like this without consulting the council!" shouted the councilman from Jakarta. "You've brought a fox into the hen house. You expect us to all accept this unilateral deal you've struck with the Americans? You, Erik, do not speak for the entire Society. This isn't over."

"Farel, please calm down and think about what you are saying," Erik pleaded.

"No, Erik! It is you who have forgotten your place—"

Bang!

Another shot rang out as Farel's head whipped back. His body slumped in his seat and blood dripped onto the floor, pooling around his chair.

"Enough!" shouted Seth in a stern, commanding voice. "The time to talk is over. Erik has explained some new realities to you. I'm here to enforce them. If you cannot accept the new rules and guidelines the

Society will now have to operate under, then you are welcome to leave. Know this—if you leave, you leave penniless. If you stay, you will adhere to the new rules or you'll end up like Farel. Do I make myself clear?"

The remaining council members nodded their heads nervously.

Placing the Sig down on the table in front of him, Seth leaned forward, his hands on the table. He surveyed the faces of the men and women before him.

Erik cleared his throat again. "As I was saying, our newest member's name is Seth Mitchell," he continued. "The agreements of old are null and void, and a new agreement with President-Elect Kagel has been reached. Seth will be the American President's eyes and ears, and the point person for the Society."

Seth put his hand on Erik's shoulder. "I want to make something clear to you all," he interjected. "I am the man responsible for the death of more than four hundred of your members. It was my team that found them, hunted them down, and killed them. If the Society tries to pull another coup d'état like you just did, then the Society will cease to exist. Do I make myself clear?"

Erik and Seth looked at each person and made sure they each acknowledged the new order of things. Erik could tell many of them were not happy, but he didn't care.

"Good, now that everyone understands the situation, let's get down to business. We have a lot to discuss," Seth announced as he took a seat and opened a folder that seemed to have appeared out of nowhere.

Erik sat down too, prepared to listen to the list of demands and reparations President Kagel had told Seth to present to the group.

Epilogue

Following the election of a new American President, the Indian government successfully liberated the autonomous region of Tibet from the Beijing government. At this point, the two warring parties finally ended the war. For the first time since 1951, the people of Tibet were once again free. When the hostilities had finally ended, the newly appointed fifteenth Dalai Lama assumed control of Tibet. The Indian government pledged continued financial and economic support to the fledgling government until they could become self-sufficient.

When the central government in Beijing came to terms with India, President Chen officially ceded control of the Xinjiang Uygur Autonomous Region in western China. This territory now became Chinese Turkestan, as it had been prior to the communist takeover in the 1950s.

President Kagel's administration went to great lengths to support the Democratic Republic of Southern China. The United States, along with her allies in Asia and India, provided the new country with military and economic aid as they battled the PRC to maintain their independence. The allies, however, stopped short of offering direct military support. The Chinese civil war would have to be fought by the Chinese people.

President Chen, with the help of General Luan and General Song, remained in control of northern, eastern, and central China, to include the newly conquered province of Formosa or Taiwan. The PRC would battle General Zeng for control of southern China for another two years before an uneasy truce was finally agreed upon.

The first several years of the Kagel administration saw an economic boom not seen in America since the end of World War II. The country went on a spending spree, rebuilding its infrastructure and power grid after so much of it had been destroyed. The US also saw a massive increase in immigration from Europe and Central and South America. With tens of millions of open jobs, the number of work visa and immigration applications went through the roof.

Seth's work with the Thule Society brought in a substantial sum in war reparations to help with the reconstruction efforts in the United States. The financial assets allowed the country to rally around major improvements in infrastructure: nationwide high-speed rail lines were built, the power grid was upgraded to be more secure against attacks, and significant advancements were made in sustainable energy and food production. All together, these efforts not only improved the country but created many skilled jobs to help Americans recover from the war.

Character Fates

Lieutenant Colonel Seth Mitchell retired from the Army and went to work as a special advisor to President Haley Kagel. He continued to maintain a close relationship with Erik Jahn and was the primary go-between for the US government and the Thule Society. Following Kagel's rise to the presidency, the Society continued to be closely watched by US intelligence agencies.

****

President Jonathan Sachs spent the next several years working with various veteran organizations. After the death of former President Carter, Sachs took up the mantle of spearheading Habitat for Humanity as he sought to help struggling families who had lost everything during the war to recover.

****

General Joseph Tibbets was finally able to retire and enjoy a much less stressful and quieter life. He spent his first year of retirement working on his memoir detailing his thirty-eight years of service to the US Army and his role as the commander of US forces during the Second American Civil War and the invasion of America.

****

Staff Sergeant Silverman from the 82nd Airborne was awarded the Medal of Honor for his heroic actions during Operation Tropic Thunder. Once he recovered from his shrapnel wounds, he was medically retired. He went on to start a new business in Texas as he sought to build a new life for himself away from the Army.

****

Colonel Patrick "Paddy" Maine went on to become a brigadier general before retiring to become a scuba diving instructor in the Florida Keys.

****

Assistant Deputy Director Ashley Bonhauf would later go on to become the first female Director of the FBI. Her contribution in

uncovering the voter fraud scheme with the US postal workers was the key factor that unraveled the entire Thule Society plot to replace the American President with a person of their choosing.
****

Sergeant First Class Matt Higgins stayed in the Army after the war ended and would go on to become a command sergeant major. He married his girlfriend he met in Texas and the two of them went on to have four kids.
****

Leah Riesling was promoted to President Kagel's National Security Advisor. She would lead the administration's efforts to keep tabs on the Society and root out its members within the government and key industries.
****

Jacob Baine would later go on to become the governor of Washington State. His leadership and expertise during the reconstruction years helped the state to recover quickly and become a thriving economy on the West Coast. He became something of a folk hero when his part in the insurgency that helped to liberate the state became known.
****

Major Trey Regan continued to his career in the Army National Guard. He moved to Houston and set up his own legal practice as one of the new migrants from the south who wanted to help rebuild the great state of Texas. He'd eventually go on to marry a fellow attorney, and the two of them built a great legal practice in the city.
****

Tom Barringer was awarded the Presidential Medal of Freedom by President Sachs just prior to the end of his administration. Tom was also given some honors from US Army Special Forces for his militia's help in liberating Albuquerque and the rest of New Mexico from the Chinese.
****

General Zeng led the military forces of the Democratic Republic of Southern China in their fight against the PRC for two more years before a cease-fire and eventual peace agreement were reached. He stayed on as the head of the fledgling country's military for several more years.
****

Gordon Lau would go on to become the first democratically elected President of China. He led the new country as they transitioned from an autocratic communist dictatorship to a more open form of government. His new government would face many challenges and problems along the way, but with the people of Hong Kong lending a hand, the country continued to progress forward.
****

Lieutenant General Ryan Jackman was captured near the end of the war. He was eventually tried for treason and sedition for leading a militia force in arms to overthrow the federal government. He was given the death penalty and executed shortly after his sentencing.
****

Colonel Ethan Dawe from the Canada Force Two was captured and interned as a prisoner of war for the duration of the conflict and for a year afterwards. Eventually, he was repatriated to Canada and barred from ever reentering the United States.
****

Chief Warrant Officer Trent "Punisher" Lipton was awarded the Distinguished Service Cross for his actions during the Battle of New Mexico. He would later go on to become the most senior warrant officer in the Special Forces before retiring to a life of fishing and volunteering at his local community gun range.

****

Sample of our Newest Upcoming Series:
The Monroe Doctrine

****

Mid-Atlantic
50-Miles from Virginia

"I sure hope this works," declared the executive officer softly. "If not, we're dead."

Lieutenant Commander Fu Yuning softly whispered back, "It's going to work. For all intents and purposes, this is just a cargo ship on its way to the port. Just make sure that once we've fired off our missiles, you have someone paint the new name on the ship. It's imperative that we do our best to hide ourselves after this attack."

"Yes, captain. I'll personally see to it," the young officer replied.

Lieutenant Commander Fu Yuning felt nervous but filled with pride as his merchant raider neared their launch point. For the past two weeks, they'd been at sea, steadily heading towards their target, using the same international shipping route every other cargo vessel traveling from the Port of Thessaloniki to the Norfolk International Terminals would use. When the ship stopped in Malta, they conducted a crew change. That's where Fu's navy sailors swapped out with the typical merchant marines who operated the ship.

The original crew had no idea the bow of the ship had been retrofitted several months ago for this specific mission. As far as anyone else was concerned, this was a Greek-flagged cargo ship bringing goods from Europe to America.

Fu anxiously hoped that once they carried out this mission, it would have a real impact on the war. If they got really lucky, the Americans might even back down from their ultimatum.

I mean, who do they think they are to dictate what countries can operate in the Caribbean? he asked himself. It made him burn with ire to think that the United States had the audacity to run spy ships and planes along the coasts of China, but completely lost it when another nation did the same to them.

"Captain, we are nearly to the launch point. When should we begin to uncover the missile launchers?" asked the weapons officer, who sat at the fire control terminal. Unlike a typical cargo ship, this bridge was now outfitted with all sorts of computer stations and a specialized communication system with their DragonLink network up and running.

"Soon, Lieutenant," Fu responded. "We still have another hour until it is time to begin our attack. It's imperative that we not fire our missiles until the appointed time."

He turned to his communications officer. "Continue to monitor the DragonLink. You should receive two messages shortly. One message to begin uncovering the launchers, then a firing order. We don't act until then."

The communications officer nodded as he wiped some of the sweat from his forehead.

****

20 kilometers northwest of Beijing, China
Joint Battle Command Centre

President Jiang Jintao looked at the maps of North America and the Pacific. A string of red icons denoted the known locations of American warships, and some green icons showed the merchant raiders steadily moving towards their firing positions.

Foreign Minister Han Jinping leaned over and whispered, "It's not too late to stop this, Mr. President." The Foreign Minister had been opposed to the Project 10 proposal from the beginning. He had argued that they should stay the course, not try and provoke the Americans right now.

Jiang turned to his long-time friend and confidant. "Jin, we've been over this," he replied, calmly but emphatically. "Project 10 has war gamed this out. By striking first, we'll cripple the American military. It'll be years before they are able to rebuild and recover from this attack."

"Mr. President, our merchant raiders are nearly in position," announced Vice Admiral Yin Zhuo.

"We are ready to initiate the first phase of the attack, Mr. President," said Dr. Hu Zemin, the program director for Project 10.

President Jiang Jintao stood and turned to face his chief scientist and military advisors. "Today is a historic first," he declared. "This is the first time in history an artificial intelligence entity will be used as a first strike weapon against an adversary. Commence Operation Dragon Fire."

Zemin smiled as he walked over to the computer terminal and shooed away the operator. He sat down and then proceeded to type a few commands. Moments later, a prompt appeared, asking him to confirm he wanted to execute the plan. He turned around to President Jiang, who had walked up behind him.

"Your damn AI had better work, doctor," Jiang said with a nod. "Commence the attack."

Zemin clicked a button. In the blink of an eye, the execute command was uploaded to a ground base's laser communication system, which then shot the command code from the bowels of the JBCC to the DragonLink satellites high above.

Once the micro-satellites received the message, they'd transmit the kill code to a single cellular tower owned and operated by a company called American Tower. This particular cell tower had been specially modified with a Huawei router with an embedded malware code that would systematically infect a single industrial control unit in every cellular tower owned by American Tower. It would then spread to the rest of the cellular network across the United States in the span of minutes. Once the infection was complete, a final kill order would be issued and every cell tower in America would cease to function.

With the vast majority of the American communication grid down, the second wave of cyberattacks would begin with a targeted attack against the power grid supporting several key US military installations. When those grids went down, the merchant raiders would send their firing orders and the opening salvos of the new war would begin.

****

Colorado Springs
Peterson Air Force Base

"General, are you ready to head back to the mountain?" asked Colonel Conrad, who was often called Connie by his friends and fellow fliers.

General Anita Barrett yawned. She had opted to take the first nightshift watch so her deputy commander could spend another evening with his family before they moved the key personnel into the mountain fortress and buttoned it up. The guy still had little ones at home and her kids were all grown.

"Yeah, I'm ready. I found my go bag," she said. "You know, the SecDef thinks the Chinese may not back down so he wants us to start locking it all down in case things go south. Hopefully, once we start flying some fighters and bombers around Cuba, they'll take the hint that we aren't joking around and realize they need to leave."

"I think so," said Colonel Conrad with a nod. "When's the fleet going to start sortieing from their bases? I think once the Chinese see the Navy encircle the island, they'll really get the message. That's what caused the Soviets to backdown last time around when they tried to place missiles on Cuba."

General Barret reached for her coffee and took a long gulp. "Two days," she replied. "They're still taking on provisions and doing final maintenance checks. The Marines will start boarding their ships in about a week to head down to Florida."

Conrad blew some air out his lips forcefully. "I sure hope the Cubans and the Chinese realize we aren't messing around. I really don't want us in a shooting war with them, but if they think we're going to let them set up military bases ninety miles from our border, they have another thing coming."

"Right now, I think it's all posturing," Barrett countered. "In another day or two, some sort of agreement will be reached to allow everyone to save face and move on. The Chinese economy is in the toilet, just like the rest of the world. They aren't in a situation to wage a war, let alone a war with us."

"Come on, Connie," said General Barret as she grabbed her go-bag. "It's time to head out to the flight line and catch our ride back to the mountain. The crew here has things covered."

The two of them walked out of the command building to a waiting vehicle that would take them to a helicopter that was standing by to fly them over to Cheyenne Mountain. Barrett didn't like leaving the watch commander alone for more than an hour, but she had absolutely needed to come back to her office on Peterson to grab a few items before they sealed themselves into the mountain for however long this standoff would take.

Their helicopter had been in the air for a couple of minutes when she received a message from the pilots. Someone from the mountain was trying to reach her. She grabbed for one of the helmets and put it on.

"This is General Barrett," she said, loud enough to be heard over the noise of the helicopter.

"General Barrett, this is General Landers. We've just received a flash priority message from the NSA. They are saying there is a cyberattack underway against the nation's cellular network. Less than sixty seconds later, the NMCA issued an order for all military installations to go to THREATCON Delta. I have to seal the mountain. How far out are you?"

Holy crap, this can't be happening, she thought. She grabbed one of the pilot's shoulders and asked for an ETA.

"We're two minutes out."

"You need to get there in less than a minute. *Now!*" she bellowed.

The pilot dove them down to the deck, increasing speed on his way down. They were now racing all-out to reach the mountain.

"Landers, the pilot says we'll be there in a minute," Barret explained. "Please give me a few minutes to get inside before you seal the place up. I have no idea how long it could be before we're able to open back up."

"I'll give you exactly three minutes, General. Then I have to seal the mountain."

The call ended and Barrett felt a burning anger building inside her.

This had better not be the opening salvos of a war...

Moments later, the pilot yanked up hard on his controls, flaring the front of the helicopter as they bled off their speed. He'd skipped landing on the pad and settled down right in front of the entrance.

There was a vehicle waiting for them. Barrett and Conrad were out of the chopper and in the vehicle in seconds. The driver sped them away before they even had a chance to close their doors. They raced down the tunnel at an ungodly speed, especially considering how narrow the place was.

As they approached the blast doors at the end of the tunnel, General Barret could see they were already halfway closed and continuing to move together. People were rushing in, and the security forces airman standing next to the door was shouting and waving at anyone nearby to hurry them along.

The driver drove almost up to the doors before he slammed the brakes, which scared the hell out of everyone. General Barret and Colonel Conrad bailed out of the vehicle, running and almost stumbling their way to the blast door which was now almost completely shut. The two of them slid inside moments before it would have crushed their bodies.

A security forces captain greeted them. "Thank God you make it, General," he said. "Please come with me." The trio then ran through the corridors until they reached the command center.

When Barrett entered the command center, she saw Major General Landers on the yellow phone that was the hotline directly connecting him to the National Military Command Authority or NMCA, the command room in the bowels of the Pentagon. It was the same room that could order a full nuclear strike if ordered by the President.

As she walked up to the phone, Landers pulled the receiver down to his shoulder. "They're about to move us all over to a SVCT in a second, if you want to take your seat," he said, pointing to a table with a very wide computer screen and three chairs sitting in front of it. One seat was intended for the NORAD commander, one for the operations officer, and one for the watch commander.

General Barrett just taken her seat when the monitor came to life. Instantly, she saw feeds from the NSA, CIA, DHS, SOUTHCOM, SOCOM, the NMCA and the PEOC. There was also a video window that suddenly appeared from Air Force One. In that moment, she knew the Secret Service must be in the process of getting the President airborne. That meant it would be the VP down in the PEOC, unless it was someone from the Cabinet.

Moments later, the respective directors or their deputies appeared on the screens. There was a lot of chatter coming in from the various stations until someone from the NMCA muted everyone.

"This is General Pike. I'm the duty officer at the NMCA. I'm going to provide a very quick brief on what's going on. Once I've gotten everyone up to speed, the meeting will be handed over to the President and the Chairman of the Joint Chiefs."

Everyone from the various outstations all nodded.

"Twenty-eight minutes ago, we received a message from the NSA, alerting us to a concerted cyberattack on the nation's cellular network. It cannot be confirmed that this attack had originated out of China—

however, it has all the fingerprints of their hacker toolsets. At that point, we initiated Threat Condition Delta.

"Seven minutes ago, a second series of cyberattacks took place against our power grid. It wasn't an assault on the entire grid, but it impacted the power plants and transmission nodes that provide power to our military facilities in Hawaii, Alaska, Greenland, Virginia, Iowa, Florida and Texas. Please note, these weren't full statewide blackouts—these were very targeted attacks on the power grid to the military facilities in these states."

Suddenly, the missile launch warning alarm and lights started flashing around General Barrett. "Sorry to interrupt, General," she said hastily, "but we're receiving a missile launch warning from Pine Gap and our CONUS early warning systems!"

She turned away from the screen. "Where are those missile launches coming from?" she barked. "Do we know what kind of missiles they are?"

"Pine Gap is reporting missile launches in the Pacific, near Guam and Hawaii," called out one of the staff officers. "They're counting twenty-two, though the number continues to climb."

Another staff officer chimed in. "We're showing missile launches in the Gulf of Mexico. We have tracks heading towards Texas, Louisiana, and Florida."

General Barret sat back down and put her head in her hands. "They're going for our bomber bases," she said softly.

"*What?!*" screamed the President from Air Force One.

In that moment, Anita realized everyone on the conference call had been listening to what was going on in the command center. She turned to face the President. "Sir, I believe this is a preemptive attack to go after our bomber bases. The only viable military target we have in Louisiana is Barksdale Air Force Base, which is a B-52 base. I'll bet the missile tracks heading towards Texas will eventually start to track towards Dyess Air Force Base—that's a B-1 base."

The President shouted some obscenities at no one in particular. "What should we do next?" he demanded.

The National Security Advisor, the Chairman of the Joint Chiefs, and the Pentagon watch officer all began advising the President: they wanted him to alert those bases and see if they could get any of their bombers under shelter or in the air before those cruise missiles hit.

"General Barrett," the President finally said as he tried to regain control of the meeting over the shouts of advice being thrown at him. "I want you to move us from DEFCON 4 to DEFCON 2. Order our remaining bombers to get airborne with nuclear weapons and order our silos to begin spinning themselves up for possible launch orders. If any of those missiles that are about to impact us are nuclear, then I want us to be ready to respond in kind."

General Anita Barrett took a deep breath in and held it for a moment, almost not comprehending the orders she'd just been given by the President.

Please, God, don't make me have to be the one to initiate a nuclear strike against China, she thought. Then her training took over and she steeled her nerves. "Yes, Mr. President," she replied. "DEFCON 2."

****

****

Book Description for the First Novel in the Upcoming Military Sci-fi Series
Into the Stars

The stars are within mankind's reach...

...But what awaits in the void may end humanity...

Mars and the Moon have been colonized, piracy runs rampant in the asteroid belts, and a thriving society grows in the depths of space. Humanity prepares to embark upon its greatest journey—the colonization of Alpha Centauri.

Then everything changes...

A deep space reconnaissance probe discovers a new Earth-like planet twelve light-years from Earth's sun. The probe also finds something unusual, something…unnerving. A new mission is created, a space fleet is formed, and humanity embarks on unraveling the greatest mystery of all—the origins of life itself.

Can the factions of Earth remain united, or will old rivalries and animosities destroy the fragile peace in the face of this terrifying existential threat?

Will exploration prove to be a fatal mistake?

If you love new technologies, fast-paced action and gut-wrenching turns of fate, you'll love this first book in James Rosone's military sci-fi series, The Rise of the Republic.

Please visit Amazon to order your copy of this page-turner today.

From the Authors

Miranda and I hope you've enjoyed the Falling Empires Series. Sadly, all good things do come to an end. However, we have been cooking up two new series for your enjoyment. We already have a new military fiction series coming out called The Monroe Doctrine, which follows conflicts in the Western Hemisphere in a post-COVID-19 world. Visit Amazon to order your copy of *Volume I*. We will also be making our first venture into military sci-fi with our Rise of the Republic Series; the first book, *Into the Stars*, is also available on Amazon.

If you would like to stay up to date on new releases and receive emails about any special pricing deals we may make available, please sign up for our email distribution list. Simply go to https://www.frontlinepublishinginc.com/ and sign up.

If you enjoy audiobooks, we have a great selection that has been created for your listening pleasure. Our entire Red Storm series and our Falling Empire series have been recorded, and several books in our Rise of the Republic series and our Monroe Doctrine series are now available. Please see below for a complete listing.

As independent authors, reviews are very important to us and make a huge difference to other prospective readers. If you enjoyed this book, we humbly ask you to write up a positive review on Amazon and Goodreads. We sincerely appreciate each person that takes the time to write one.

We have really valued connecting with our readers via social media, especially on our Facebook page https://www.facebook.com/RosoneandWatson/. Sometimes we ask for help from our readers as we write future books—we love to draw upon all your different areas of expertise. We also have a group of beta readers who get to look at the books before they are officially published and help us fine-tune last-minute adjustments. If you would like to be a part of this team, please go to our author website, and send us a message through the "Contact" tab.

You may also enjoy some of our other works. A full list can be found below:

Nonfiction:

Iraq Memoir 2006–2007 Troop Surge
Interview with a Terrorist (audiobook available)

Fiction:

The Monroe Doctrine Series
Volume One (audiobook available)
Volume Two (audiobook available)
Volume Three (audiobook available)
Volume Four (audiobook still in production)
Volume Five (available for preorder)

Rise of the Republic Series
Into the Stars (audiobook available)
Into the Battle (audiobook available)
Into the War (audiobook available)
Into the Chaos (audiobook available)
Into the Fire (audiobook still in production)
Into the Calm (available for preorder)

Apollo's Arrows Series (co-authored with T.C. Manning)
Cherubim's Call (available for preorder)

Crisis in the Desert Series (co-authored with Matt Jackson)
Project 19 (audiobook available)
Desert Shield
Desert Storm

Falling Empires Series
Rigged (audiobook available)
Peacekeepers (audiobook available)
Invasion (audiobook available)
Vengeance (audiobook available)
Retribution (audiobook available)

Red Storm Series
Battlefield Ukraine (audiobook available)
Battlefield Korea (audiobook available)

Battlefield Taiwan (audiobook available)
Battlefield Pacific (audiobook available)
Battlefield Russia (audiobook available)
Battlefield China (audiobook available)

Michael Stone Series
Traitors Within (audiobook available)

World War III Series
Prelude to World War III: The Rise of the Islamic Republic and the Rebirth of America (audiobook available)
Operation Red Dragon and the Unthinkable (audiobook available)
Operation Red Dawn and the Siege of Europe (audiobook available)
Cyber Warfare and the New World Order (audiobook available)

Children's Books:
My Daddy has PTSD
My Mommy has PTSD

Abbreviation Key

AA	Anti-Aircraft
AFSOC	Air Force Special Operations Command
AKA	Also Known As
AO	Area of Operations
APC	Armored Personnel Carrier
AWACS	Airborne Early Warning and Control System
BDA	Battle Damage Assessment
BN	Battalion
BDE	Brigade
Brown Shoe	Slang for Aviators, particularly Naval Aviators
CAS	Close Air Support
CASEVAC	Evacuation of casualties by air
CCTV	Closed Circuit Television
CJSOTF	Combined Joint Special Operations Task Force
CNO	Chief of Naval Operations
CO	Commanding Officer
CPO	Chief Petty Officer
DARPA	Defense Advanced Research Projects Agency
DEVGRU	Development Group (SEAL Team Six)
DHS	Department of Homeland Security
DoD	Department of Defense
DZ	Drop Zone
EBR	Enhanced Battle Rifle
E & E	Emergency and Evacuation/ Escape and Evade
FAC	Forward Air Controller
Helo	Helicopter
HVAC	Heating, Ventilation, and Air Conditioning
HVI	High Value Individual
IFV	Infantry Fighting Vehicle
IR	Infrared
JDAM	Joint Direct Attack Munition
JLTV	Joint Light Tactical Vehicle
JSTAR	Joint System Threat Assessment Report
JSOC	Joint Special Operations Command
JTF	Joint Task Force
Klick	Kilometer

LAV Light Armored Vehicle
LT Lieutenant
LZ Landing Zone
MANPADS Man-Portable Air-Defense Systems
MASINT Measures and Signals Intelligence
MCRD Marine Corps Recruit Depot
MEDEVAC Medical Evacuation
MEU Marine Expeditionary Force
Merc'd To be killed by a professional mercenary not associated with a uniformed military
Mike Minute
MIT Massachusetts Institute of Technology
MRE Meals Ready-to-Eat
NAS Naval Air Station
NCO Noncommissioned Officer
Nine-line Nine step process for calling in help for an injured soldier/Marine
NVG Night Vision Goggles
ODA Operational Detachment Alpha (Special Forces)
OP Observation Post
PO Petty Officer
pos Position
PLA People's Liberation Army (Chinese Army)
PM Prime Minister
PMC Private Military Contractor
POW Prisoner of War
PRC People's Republic of China
QRF Quick Reaction Force
R&R Rest and Relaxation
R/C Remote Control
RCT Regimental Combat Team
RTO Radiotelephone Operator
S1 An Army/USMC term for an Admin officer
S2 An Army/USMC term for an Intelligence officer
S3 An Army/USMC term for an Operations officer
S4 An Army/USMC term for a Logistics officer
SAM Surface-to-Air Missile
SEAL Sea Air Land Naval Special Warfare

SecDef	Secretary of Defense
SF	Special Forces
SINCGARS	Single Channel Ground and Airborne Radio System
SITREP	Situation Report
Skipper	USMC/USN Slang for Captain
SM	Standard Missile
SMAW	Shoulder-Launched Multipurpose Assault Weapon
SOCOM	Special Operations Command
SOF	Special Operations Forces
TOW	Tube-Launched, Optically Tracked, Wire-Guided
USSOF	US Special Operations Forces
WMD	Weapons of Mass Destruction

Printed in Great Britain
by Amazon

79257824R00169